An Alternative History of Britain

An Alternative History of Britain

The Tudors

Timothy Venning

Pen & Sword
MILITARY

First published in Great Britain in 2014 by
Pen & Sword Military
an imprint of
Pen & Sword Books Ltd
47 Church Street
Barnsley
South Yorkshire
S70 2AS

ISBN 978-1-78346-272-8

A CIP catalogue record for this book is available from the British Library.

Typeset in 11pt Ehrhardt by
Mac Style, Bridlington, E. Yorkshire

Printed and bound in the UK by CPI Group (UK) Ltd, Croydon, CRO 4YY

Pen & Sword Books Ltd incorporates the imprints of Pen & Sword
Archaeology, Atlas, Aviation, Battleground, Discovery, Family History,
History, Maritime, Military, Naval, Politics, Railways, Select, Transport,
True Crime, and Fiction, Frontline Books, Leo Cooper, Praetorian Press,
Seaforth Publishing and Wharncliffe.

For a complete list of Pen & Sword titles please contact
PEN & SWORD BOOKS LIMITED
47 Church Street, Barnsley, South Yorkshire, S70 2AS, England
E-mail: enquiries@pen-and-sword.co.uk
Website: www.pen-and-sword.co.uk

Contents

Chapter One

What if the early Tudors had not had such dynastic bad luck?

Politics, biology, and chance from 1485 to 1547

Prince Arthur, 1502: the second loss of a potential 'King Arthur II'

A multitude of healthy, competing adult royal sons had its own political problems for a dynasty, as seen by the struggles among Edward III's sons and grandsons in the latter years of his reign and after his death. Edward IV's two brothers were a perennial problem once they were adult, one assisting his overthrow and both threatening the rights of his sons to succeed. Henry VII's relatively small family did not immediately present problems for the succession. He and Elizabeth of York had had three sons, of whom one (Edmund, born 1499) died as an infant – as had Edward IV's third son, George. But his eldest son, Arthur, died young at fifteen in April 1502, a few months after his marriage to Catherine of Aragon. The Prince of Wales was apparently delicate, and was less robust-looking than his surviving brother, Henry; it is uncertain if his health was the real reason for the delay in his marriage or in his being kept at court and not sent off to preside over the Council of the Marches at Ludlow as early as his predecessor Edward V had been.[1] Edward had left court at three; Arthur left at six; the next Prince(ss), Mary, left for Ludlow at eleven.

Arthur's sudden death – whether or not of the tubercular tendency that threatened generations of Tudors and accounted for both Henry VIII's sons in their teens – was unexpected and followed within months of his marriage, leaving the King with one son. (Even if the King's third son, Edmund, born in 1499, had lived he would have been too young to be of use for many years.) The obscure 'sweating sickness' that accounted for Arthur, involving a high temperature and kidney failure, may have been fatally exacerbated by a weak constitution and his decline took weeks;[2] straightforward epidemics' victims usually died quicker. It had possibly been spread from the town of Ludlow into the adjacent castle, and as such the King's decision to place Arthur's household there and not in a more isolated location may have made contagion easier. (His other main residence in the region was a hunting-lodge at Tickhill outside Bewdley by the Severn, which was possibly safer.) But a traveller from an infected location could put any household at risk; a prince's household would necessarily interact with local employees and travellers, and the heir would be expected to show himself to his people and attend public occasions. (Arthur's brother Henry VIII would keep moving from house to house to try to stay ahead of infection in other epidemics, e.g. that of 1528.) But for the Prince's demise, the putative 'Arthur II' – the second heir called Arthur to die young, the first having been Richard I's superseded and murdered nephew in 1203 – would have succeeded at the age of twenty-two in April 1509, with no legal question about his marriage to Catherine of Aragon. A less dominant personality than his younger brother, who even aged eight was impressing the visiting scholar Erasmus in the royal nursery,[3] he was likelier to have ruled in the more cautious mould of his father. This need not have led to avoidance of bold foreign policy-decisions such as the French war of 1512–13, where the vigorous Henry VIII was apparently restless to emulate Henry V in conquering France and led his troops in person, and his health might have permitted a French expedition on the cautious lines of his father's invasion of France in 1492. The circumstances of Franco-Spanish/Habsburg rivalry in the 1510s would have been the same for Arthur as for Henry. But Henry was to be well-known for handing the minutiae of political and administrative business over to his ministers in the first two decades of his reign, in which Thomas Wolsey proved to be his indispensable man of business. Henry was more conscientious than has been allowed for in myth, and Wolsey anticipated rather than pre-empted his decisions; his skill lay in relieving the King of tedious business without seeming to encroach on his prerogative. Henry VII's leading clerical adviser, Bishop Fox, was ageing by 1509, and Fox's protégé Wolsey might well have made himself indispensible to Arthur too. But Arthur would probably have spent less time and energy on physical sports, with there being no evidence that (health aside) he was at all interested in hunting or the tournament by the age of fifteen. A more sedentary and bookish ruler was more likely to have been involved in Council work in his twenties to a degree that Henry was not, with a lesser chance that quantities of business would be delegated to one minister. Certainly Arthur is unlikely to have been as shameless as Henry, already an idiosyncratic and ruthless personality, in sacrificing his father's ministers Empson and Dudley to the wrath of the 'higher-born' peers from whom they had been extorting money on Henry VII's behalf.

It is still possible that Arthur would have died young and Henry succeeded to the throne in his twenties, probably with a wife provided for him by the Habsburg/Spanish alliance of 1506–13 (perhaps one of Charles V's sisters). Arthur and Catherine might have had a son after 1502, when Catherine was seventeen; by the time she was married off to Henry in real life she was nearly twenty-four and had been harming her health with religious austerities as a widow,[4] living on reduced expenses while Henry VII and her father, Ferdinand, haggled over her dowry. Would years of satisfactory marriage to Arthur instead of widowhood cooped up at Durham House made her more fertile? Henry could then have been regent for an under-age nephew or niece, born in the 1500s, if Arthur died relatively young in c.1510–25. Alternatively, Henry VII (born in 1457) could have outlived Arthur and reached something like the age of his uncle Jasper Tudor, who died in his early sixties in 1495.[5]

Henry's decline in health does not seem to have been noticeable until 1508, except for one serious illness in 1503; however it seems that he was withdrawing more into his 'inner chambers' and access to him was controlled by men such as Empson and Dudley, which may imply that he was losing his confidence.[6] But if Henry had had a semi-adult and serious Arthur available for support, not the (five years) younger and joust-loving Prince Henry, could he have started to induct his heir into administration by the mid-late 1500s? Or would the emergence of the Prince have led to courtiers opposed to the 'low-born' favourites turning to him to try to influence the King?

The trend in international politics by 1509 was for the consolidation of the Tudor alliance with Ferdinand of Aragon (regent of Castile) and Emperor Maximilian against Louis XII of France, with the two rulers' joint heir Charles (Emperor Charles V) as destined husband of Henry VII's daughter, Mary; this was likely to have continued whether Henry VII or Arthur was king in the years after 1509. In that case, the marriage of Prince Henry to a Habsburg princess was the next logical dynastic move. Assuming Henry VIII and his Habsburg wife to have been less unlucky in childbirth than Catherine of Aragon, who would have stayed as Arthur's queen, and Catherine to have had no luck by Arthur either, Henry VIII might still have been king after Arthur c.1515–20 and had no difficulties over the lack of a male heir in the 1520s.

The rocky road to the marriage of Henry VIII and Catherine of Aragon: could it have been abandoned?

The marriage of Henry VIII to a wife six years his senior was ultimately the result of the political situation of England after 1485, where his father had been courting the alliance of her parents Ferdinand and Isabella. What were the alternative sources of a wife for his brother Arthur – and thus him – in the 1490s? No English alliance with their long-term foe France was secure, given the competition between the two mistrustful powers over the lost English domains in France and the surviving claim of the English sovereigns to the throne of France, which Henry V had successfully revived in 1415–22. Charles VIII's regency had backed Henry Tudor against Richard III in 1484–5, giving him sanctuary and troops when he had to flee from Brittany; but it was normal French policy to stir up trouble against a strong and militaristic English king who might invade. Louis XI had backed the refugee Queen Margaret of Anjou (a Frenchwoman, and Louis' cousin) against Edward IV in the 1460s, and Richard III was a threat to France as he had strongly opposed Edward's abandonment of the invasion of France when Louis bought him off at Picquigny in 1475.

Once Henry was king, he was as much of a threat to France as Edward and Richard had been and in 1488 the Anglo-French détente collapsed over Henry unsuccessfully endeavouring to save the independence of Brittany from a French invasion; in 1492 Henry invaded France like Edward had done. In any case, after peace was insecurely restored between the two countries the young French King (born 1470 and just married to the Breton heiress Anne) had no children and had no available sisters of the right age to marry Henry's sons. An Anglo-Habsburg alliance was also out of the question, as in the 1490s the new Emperor Maximilian was backing the claim of 'Perkin Warbeck' to the English throne – and the pretender was induced to name Maximilian as his heir in return. The new Emperor's stepmother-in-law, Margaret, Duchess of Burgundy, was Richard III's sister and thus supported both 'Simnel' and 'Warbeck'. In any case, England was seen as of marginal importance by the Empire and Maximilian was to betroth the only available princess of the 1490s, his daughter Margaret (born 1480), to Ferdinand and Isabella's son Juan. Closer to home, the end of the Anglo-Scottish confrontation of 1496 (when James IV invaded England on behalf of 'Warbeck') led to James' marriage in 1503 to Henry's eldest daughter, Margaret, but there were no princesses available to marry Princes Arthur or Henry in return. The Anglo-Spanish match was thus the only logical and prestigious alliance with a 'Great Power' available in the 1490s, and even so was long delayed – probably due to Catherine's parents' doubts over Henry's ability to survive as king, given the chronic instability in England, which showed no signs of subsiding. Catherine was only sent to England in 1501, and even then Henry had insecurities over the reason for her escort insisting on her remaining secluded from view during her journey across England – was she offputtingly ugly? – and insisted on being able to view her for himself in a confrontation with her courtiers at Dogmersfield Park, Hampshire.[7]

When Henry VIII finally married Catherine in his brother's place time was against the production of a large family, given that she was already nearly twenty-four and six years his senior. It was the delicate state of international relations, with Henry VII needing to keep up his prestigious alliance with Catherine's parents Ferdinand and Isabella, which meant that once Arthur was dead the idea was floated that the new Prince of Wales should marry his brother's widow rather than Henry sending her home. The possible legal excuse to invalidate the potential marriage to a brother's widow under canon law did not stand in the way of the new marriage-treaty for their union of June 1503 – possibly the lure of a second dowry encouraged the avaricious Henry VII to agree. Crucially, Catherine had no younger sisters nearer Prince Henry's age who could have married him – thus preserving the hard-won Anglo-Spanish alliance – and remained fertile for longer than Catherine did. This would have been a legally safer course, had it been available. But marrying the Prince to his brother's widow required complex legal manoeuvres, and the evidence of Catherine's lady-in-waiting Dona Elvira that her marriage to Arthur had not been consummated – thus making the first marriage legally questionable and the second easier – was not accepted.[8] This would also have meant that Catherine was not legally Princess of Wales and so saved Henry VII from paying her an appropriately large allowance. Nevertheless, despite accepting the legality of the Arthur–Catherine union he tried to save himself the money anyway at one point – out of miserliness or as a legal manoeuvre?

The form of legal application to the Pope for a dispensation for the Henry/Catherine union was that which accepted that a forbidden relationship already existed between them. The reason for Henry VII and the Spanish ambassador De Puebla, acting for Ferdinand and Isabella, taking this course instead of presenting evidence that Arthur and Catherine had never consummated the marriage is unclear. Catherine was to claim in 1527 that the marriage had never been consummated, as did her lady-in-waiting Dona Elvira, and they were the likeliest to know; and in 1533 Henry was supposed to have told imperial ambassador Chapuys that his wife had been a virgin. (He later claimed it had been a joke.[9]) The probability is that both parties knew that the marriage might have been consummated. But in 1505 – the point at which the 1503 treaty provided for Prince Henry, now fourteen, to marry Catherine – he was required to formally announce his opposition to marrying her. This was presumably part of his father's complex international diplomacy and a means of putting pressure on Ferdinand, and this and the resulting four-year delay in the marriage provided the Prince with a valid excuse to back out of the contract once he succeeded to the throne and could do as he wished.

In October 1505 Pope Julius granted legal backing to the Prince so he could restrain his 'wife' from excessive religious practices – probably obsessive fasting – that were potentially damaging to her health; this must have resulted from a formal request made by the Prince at his father's behest and implies that at this point they considered the union of Henry and Catherine as valid and worth preserving.[10] If they were not going to marry, why worry over her potential fertility? Even if the device of a formal appeal to the Pope – accepting that Catherine was the Prince's wife, as without that he and his father had no right to interfere with her behaviour – was necessary to secure the devout Catherine's submission, it shows that the King valued her (politically) as his son's potential queen and cared to save her health.

But the King and the latter's ministers meanwhile considered an alternative candidate for the Prince's hand, a Habsburg offer of either Maximilian's eldest grand-daughter Eleanor – which would require a delay as she was younger than Prince Henry – or a Bavarian princess. (Eleanor would thus have been a prime candidate to marry Henry in the later 1500s had Arthur survived.) Catherine remained isolated, short of money, and in ill-health at her 'dower' residence in London, Durham House, through 1503–9 and in 1507 the new Spanish ambassador Fuensalida reckoned her chances of marrying Henry minimal and sought to extricate her with as much of her dowry as he could prise back from Henry VII.[11] The King even arranged for his son to read out a formal renunciation of his desire for the marriage to chosen councillors on 27 June 1505, the eve of his fourteenth birthday when he would be eligible to marry her. This was done in private at Richmond Palace and witness (and probable organizer) Bishop Fox, a skilled canon lawyer, told the 1527–8 divorce proceedings that it had been done as the King was furious with Catherine's father for not paying the dowry.[12] It was not acted upon, but was obviously arranged so that the marriage could thenceforth be cancelled at short notice citing this document as evidence for the bridegroom being unwilling – and the latter could have used it himself to call off the marriage in 1509 if he had so desired.

The picture of an indifferent if not hostile Henry VII holding up the marriage indefinitely was strengthened by Catherine's own panicky letters to Ferdinand about her desperate situation, which have been cited as 'prima facie' evidence. By 1507 she was allegedly short of adequate clothing for her servants, forced to sell off her silver plate to pay them and keep up a semblance of dignity, and had not seen her betrothed for months, although they lived in the same royal household. The King treated her with polite lack of interest, though he was willing to wait patiently for Ferdinand to pay up.[13] She even wrote to her sister Juana to encourage her to stop vowing never to marry again and to marry Henry VII, hoping to win the King's goodwill that way.[14] (Her pleas were practically irrelevant, as even if the emotionally unbalanced Juana had changed her mind Ferdinand is highly unlikely to have let her do so.) By early 1509 Henry was even refusing to admit Catherine to his sickbed and her complaints about lack of money and royal indifference led her to think that she might have to give up and leave England after all[15] – but this situation may have been due to the new problem of the King's steepening physical decline.

Arguably, given Henry VII's cool attitude towards the marriage by 1505–7 and the rising eligibility of Princess Eleanor as she grew older the King's better health in 1505–9 and survival after April 1509 would have increased the chances of marrying off the Prince to the Habsburg alternative. Anger at Ferdinand's refusal to let him marry Juana, a solution on which he was keen in 1507,[16] could have pushed him into action. This would have been a viable diplomatic alternative to securing a Spanish alliance for a new war with France, and would have tied in with the December 1508 (abortive) betrothal of Henry VII's younger surviving daughter Mary Tudor to Maximilian's grandson and heir Charles.[17] (The latter was five years Mary's junior, and was in fact to marry into the Portuguese royal family as his Castilian forebears often had done.) Had this marriage been followed through Mary would have been Charles' Queen of Spain as of 1516 and Empress as of 1519, and Henry VIII would have been left with two sisters married out of the realm instead of one when he came to draw up his will in 1543. Mary's children by the Emperor, like Margaret Tudor's children by her Scots husbands, would not have been born in England and thus unquestionably eligible for the English throne. The Tudor succession-problems of the 1540s–1550s would have been even more complicated, unless Henry VII's youngest daughter, Catherine (born 1503) had survived infancy and been given an English husband. But would a son of Mary Tudor and Charles of Habsburg been a potential candidate to marry his first cousin, Henry VIII's daughter Mary, instead of her actual husband Philip (born 1527), the real-life son of Charles and his Portuguese wife Isabella? If Mary and Charles had two sons, the younger could marry the Princess without the danger (in 1554) of unifying England and Spain.

Fuensalida did not see any signs of pro-Spanish advice among the King's ministers as of 1507 and was apparently very surprised to be informed that Henry VIII would marry Catherine after all on the new sovereign's accession.[18] What had been going on in the new King's mind as he waited for his father to make his mind up in 1505–9 is unknowable, but perhaps he was genuinely attracted to Catherine as a 'princess in distress' awaiting rescue by him. It would have fitted in with the Arthurian romances that were in vogue at court. Alternatively, Catherine was the only princess available in England for a quick marriage – choosing someone else would have taken long negotiations and Henry was always impatient. Conceivably if Henry VII had lived for several more years he and Maximilian would have arranged the Henry VIII/Eleanor match instead for around 1510–11, and Catherine of Aragon been relegated to a footnote in history as the 'queen who never was' between Princesses of Wales Joan of Kent (widow of the 'Black Prince') and Augusta of Saxe-Gotha (widow of Prince Frederick Louis) leading to Diana Spencer. Eleanor was married off instead to Louis II of Hungary, whose death in battle against the Turks at Mohacs in 1526 extinguished his dynasty, and as a childless widow was then married to Francis I of France after the latter's reduction to a Habsburg vassal by his defeat at Pavia. We do not know if her lack of children was due to her or her husbands; the latter is more probable as Louis was a genetic oddity and Francis had probably contracted syphilis.

Henry and Catherine's marriage, 1509: the legal problems. An adequate enough excuse to call it off?
The long delay in Catherine's next marriage during Henry VII's lifetime did not seriously diminish the chances of producing offspring, as the Prince was much younger and a (more than titular) marriage was not feasible until he was around sixteen (June 1507). The initial arrangement for them to marry once Henry was fourteen in June 1505, if carried out and resulting in them setting up a joint household, was unlikely to have produced offspring soon. (The youngest age at which royal offspring had been conceived in recent centuries was fifteen for the future Henry IV, not then the direct heir, in 1382.) The royal couple eventually married in June 1509, amidst less than straightforward propaganda about it being a fulfilment of Henry VII's final wishes and/or his son's long romantic devotion to Catherine.[19] The enthusiastic and romantic new sovereign may well have believed himself to be in love with Catherine, though the close constraint on his freedom by his careful father until April 1509 would have reduced the chances of much unsupervised contact between them until Henry VIII became king and the attraction may only have developed strongly after that point. Even at this stage Henry was a ruthless young man who had no compunction about sacrificing his father's unpopular ministers Empson and Dudley (both of low social rank so without powerful noble dynastic allies) as scapegoats for the late King's financial policies in 1510. Had he found another match more attractive, he would have had an elastic conscience about his earlier promise

to marry Catherine and had the retraction of it in 1505 to excuse his action. It also seems that Archbishop William Warham, the supreme English Church authority on interpreting canon law bans on marrying a brother's widow, had doubts about the match.

There was also a potential legal excuse for cancelling any arrangement, as came out in the intensely detailed investigations after 1527; the papal bull of Julius II granting Henry and Catherine permission to marry referred to her marriage to Arthur 'probably' ('forsan') having been consummated. (Spanish sources claimed that the English court knew it had not been consummated at the time.) It thus granted permission for a second marriage to Henry's brother's widow on this basis – without any reference to the legal situation if the marriage had not been consummated. There was no reference either to the question of whether 'public honesty' about the circumstances of the first marriage had been observed, which if it had not could invalidate it. A 'watertight' bull would have had to grant a dispensation from this scenario too.[20] Either the English government, in requesting the papal dispensation, or the papal chancery – perhaps distracted in 1503 by having the third pope in a year – had not covered all the options. The legal experts in London must have noticed the omission when the bull belatedly arrived in 1505, and it could have been used as an excuse for arguing that it was legally safer for Henry to avoid a contentious and challengeable marriage.

In practical terms it kept up the Spanish alliance for a vigorous young king who was soon to need her father's support for an invasion of France in 1512. There was a shortage of alternative (and younger) princesses of allied states to marry instead in any case, except for Eleanor whose marriage would have taken longer than Catherine's to arrange and probably required tortuous diplomatic negotiations with the veteran politician Maximilian. As it was, Henry was able to marry Catherine quickly without a further round of diplomacy and get her pregnant within a year. The goodwill from a relieved Ferdinand would have been another consideration, as the restless King was probably already contemplating war with France for which he was to need Spanish help in an invasion. He was already insulting and threatening France within weeks of his coronation,[21] though the complexity of international diplomacy meant that at that moment in 1509 France and its usual Habsburg and Spanish enemies were all allies of the Pope against Venice in the League of Cambrai. Henry's ministers were apparently divided between partisans of France and of Spain, with the result of initial treaties with both, but as soon as was feasible Henry was at war with Louis XII with the evident intention of using Spain as a base to reconquer the duchy of Aquitaine. No doubt Henry now saw himself as the heir to Henry V, and he was still seeking lands to conquer in France when he besieged (and took) Boulogne in 1544.

In the event, the lack of Spanish help to the English expedition to north-east Spain in 1512 showed the limits of Ferdinand's goodwill; the army was stranded at Fuentarrabia without the promised horses, artillery, or military backing and morale collapsed. Ferdinand used the expedition as a cover to distract France while he took over the neighbouring part of Navarre, south of the Pyrenees, then abandoned Henry for a temporary peace with France. In retaliation, Henry concluded a swift peace with France and married his sister, Mary, off to Louis XII, thirty years her senior; if she had been married to Charles V as Henry VII had planned she would not have been available. The likelihood is that if Henry VII had lived longer the match would have been carried through, with him less likely to have been distracted into a quick war with France; Henry VII was more of a match for Maximilian and Ferdinand as of 1509–13 than was his naïve son. The result would have been that Mary was not widowed early – Louis XII died in 1514, aged fifty-three, and Charles lived until 1558 – and thus did not return to England and marry an English subject. Her children would have been Charles', born abroad, and they would have been at risk of being excluded from the succession as born overseas in the way that her sister Margaret's children were excluded by Henry in 1543. Her second marriage, to Charles Brandon, and the birth of her grand-daughter Lady Jane Grey (and thus the coup of 1553) resulted in the long term from Mary's marrying Louis not Charles V.

The lack of heirs from the marriage: and the potential of Henry's sisters to provide one

The period of Catherine's pregnancies from 1510 to 1518 should have been sufficient for several surviving children given the normal survival-rates in the royal nurseries in previous generations. Only two of Edward IV's seven daughters died young. The death of the infant Prince Henry in 1511 was followed by the survival of only one child, a girl – presenting the problem of her marriage to some foreign prince of equal status and the possible union of England with the latter's realm. Had Henry's younger brother, Prince Edmund, also survived infancy it is possible that Henry VIII would not have been determined to re-marry, as he would have had a male heir to fall back on or even to prefer to his daughter. Similarly, although his later will of 1546/7 shows that he intended to disregard the offspring of his sister Margaret (by James IV of Scotland) as born abroad[22] he could have had the alternative open to Richard III in 1484–5 – naming an English-born nephew.

Margaret had been married off to James IV in 1503, the linking of the 'Thistle and the Rose' ending the period of Anglo-Scottish tension arising from her husband's backing of 'Warbeck' in 1496. (James had even given the pretender a high-born Scottish wife, his cousin Lady Katherine Gordon, who 'Warbeck' left at St Michael's Mount as he invaded Cornwall and was duly collared by HenryVII.) The idea of the Scottish King marrying an English royal bride had originally been Edward IV's, with his younger daughter Cecily intended for James. One of James and Margaret's sons, the infant James V, survived his talented but reckless father who was killed at Flodden while invading England to assist his French allies in summer 1513. James V, foreign-born though genealogically the closest male heir after Henry's children, never seems to have been considered as a potential heir for the English throne. His succession to Henry would have carried out the Union of Crowns which the King sought in the 1540s. But Margaret was widowed aged thirty-four and was thus young enough to have more children; had she returned to England and acquired an English noble husband her heirs by a second marriage would have been eligible for the throne under the terms of Henry's will in 1543. As of autumn 1513 she was unable to leave Scotland easily as she was pregnant and also needed to back up the infant James V's regency regime in person. She married one of the leading Scots nobles involved in the regency Council, Archibald Douglas, the new Earl of Angus, in 1514, and their child (Margaret Douglas) was thus born in Scotland. But by 1517 Margaret and Douglas were at odds, and a divorce and third marriage (with children) was possible; as the late King's cousin, the French-backed Duke John of Albany, had taken over the regency she could have left Scotland more easily than in 1513–14. Had she not been pregnant then, she still had her child the new King to support and thus was unlikely to have left Scotland unless forced out by the distrustful Albany. But if she had not married Douglas her return home to marry an Englishman was feasible, and her real-life divorce from him gave a chance of this happening too. (She actually married another Scotsman, a dashing and younger guards-officer called Henry Stewart.) Was Margaret Douglas a feasible heir for EdwardVI in 1553 had she been Protestant not Catholic? Or could he have chosen another child of her mother (Margaret Tudor, Henry VIII's elder sister) had the latter had one younger than Margaret? This would have been by Margaret Tudor's second or third husbands. Notably, Henry had not put his sister and her offspring in the line of succession in 1543/4 – as they were born abroad?

An heir from Henry's other, younger sister Mary, was more feasible. Born in 1495, she had been due to marry Charles of Habsburg (born 1500) as per her father's plans of 1507–8 but Henry VIII had reversed this plan. Had he not been disappointed with the results of his alliance with Ferdinand of Aragon and Emperor Maximilian to attack France in 1512, her marriage to

Charles would have been more likely. In that eventuality, Charles' son –
Philip II of Spain in real life – would have had a chance of becoming King
of England by genealogical claim as well as conquest had Charles invaded
England after Henry had the Catherine of Aragon marriage annulled. This
boy could then have been married off to his cousin Princess Mary. Instead,
high politics intervened. Henry's rapprochement with France after
Ferdinand's failure to support his Aquitaine invasion in 1512 and the failure
of his own invasion of Flanders in 1513 led to his younger sister being
married to the much older King Louis XII of France (born 1462) in 1514.
No heir from this marriage was likely, and Louis died suddenly within
months; the 'Tudor Rose' then returned to England. She unexpectedly
married Henry's close companion Charles Brandon, Duke of Suffolk (about
ten years her senior), son of the Tudor standard-bearer cut down at
Bosworth by Richard. This pair had a son, Henry, born in 1516 (died 1534)
as well as two daughters, and the boy could have been married off to Princess
Mary had the King not had doubts over his sister's 'inferior' marriage and
insisted on a more 'suitable' royal marriage for his daughter. He had only
belatedly accepted the Princess' second marriage after initial fury.[23]

Had Henry's third sister, Catherine (born 1503), not died at birth she too
could have married a foreign prince – not due to succeed to a throne so
available to live in England – and produced a potential heir. The likelihood
is against the ever-cautious Henry VII allowing her a domestic match had he
still been alive at the time of her planned betrothal, even with a lack of
potential foreign suitors. Any English husband had to be of high social
standing – among fifteenth century precedents Edward IV's sisters, Anne
and Elizabeth, had married into the families of the dukedoms of Exeter and
Suffolk (Anne had contracted a 'lower-status' second marriage to a knight),
Edward's aunt Anne had married a semi-royal Bourchier, and John of
Gaunt's daughter Elizabeth had married the Duke of Exeter. Henry VII had
married off his wife's sisters, Edward IV's daughters, within the English
nobility – mostly to Lancastrian nobles (Cecily to Lord Welles, Elizabeth to
William Courtenay) but Anne to the son of the pardoned 'Ricardian'
(Howard) Earl of Surrey. He had needed foreign alliances for his new regime
at the time, c. 1485–95, but – unlike his son – probably preferred domestic
matches for the Princesses for reasons of security.

Tudor princesses married to nobles could produce heirs whose aristocratic
paternal relatives might back them in a succession-dispute. At a later period,
Elizabeth preferred not to marry off her potential heiress Mary Stuart to her
cousin Thomas Howard, Duke of Norfolk, in 1568–70 due to the security-
risk (though there was an additional religious factor as both were Catholics).
Henry VII in his later years showed substantial mistrust of the main noble

dynasties by seeking to bind their freedom of manoeuvre by extortionate royal fines and cognizances for good behaviour. Henry VIII was notably angry when his widowed sister Mary married an English aristocrat without his permission in 1515, though the culprit was his own close friend Charles Brandon, and seems to have thought the match beneath her rank. A potential aristocratic marriage for Catherine might well have had similar problems, and it should not be assumed that had more princesses been available to marry in the 1510s they would have been permitted to marry English nobles and produce heirs.

A chance for Henry VIII to have more siblings after 1503. Henry VII's second marriage? A note on the shortage of overseas candidates in the early sixteenth century

It was also conceivable that Henry VIII might have had half-brothers or sisters to rely on for the succession. His mother, Elizabeth of York, dying in childbirth in February 1503, left Henry VII a widower at the age of forty-six – younger than the age at which the widowed Edward I had re-married to a much younger French princess and had three more sons. The concentration of previously separate neighbouring European states in the hands of the Valois (Brittany and Anjou/Provence to add to France) and Habsburg (Burgundy and its Low Countries constituents, with Spain following in 1516) families reduced the number of suitable English diplomatic allies and hence royal brides available in the later fifteenth and early sixteenth centuries. The concept of a non-royal bride for a king had always been small, given the practical advantages from contracting a diplomatic alliance at the time of a royal heir or king's availability that entailed a marital link; but the limited evidence suggests that the two choices of a 'commoner', non-royal wife in the later medieval period were criticized. The marriage of Edward III's heir, the 'Black Prince', to his cousin Joan of Kent (of English royal blood) involved the question of how legal her two previous marriages had been, and if any offspring of the marriage could thus be declared illegitimate. The secret marriage of Edward IV and Elizabeth Woodville (of distant European royal blood) was criticized on account of her lowly rank, though with a political agenda to this opposition on account of the motives of those involved – principally her family's foe Richard Neville, Earl of Warwick, who had been seeking a foreign royal bride for the King and was left embarrassed. Henry VIII, always a law unto himself, resorted to seeking native-born English wives in the 1520s – though this was at a time when his lack of secure foreign alliances made it unlikely that he could acquire a foreign princess and neither Francis nor Charles V had daughters available. The personal attraction the King felt for Anne Boleyn in the mid-1520s coincided with a dearth of foreign candidates, alienation from Charles as the nephew of the wife Henry was about to reject, and the eclipse of Francis who was captured by Charles' army at Pavia in 1525.

Indeed, the repeated Unions of Crowns in the European royal marriage-market had indirect effects on English royal dynastic history. It made it less easy to find a suitable overseas royal bride and meant that a (frequent) English diplomatic rift with France or the Empire/Spain reduced the possibilities further. France being the most frequent English foe but now lacking as many Valois cadet lines as in the time of Charles VI and VII to provide brides, English royal marital diplomacy was more likely to centre on the Empire or Spain (who were dynastically united in 1519).Unlike in the fifteenth century with its multiplicity of states, Aragon and Castile were now united by the marriage of Ferdinand and Isabella; their daughter Juana's marriage to Maximilian of Habsburg's son Philip duly brought all Spain except Navarre (a minor power mostly occupied by Ferdinand in 1512) to Philip and Juana's son Charles. The Crown of Naples/Sicily was united with that of Aragon from 1506, despite French efforts, and the duchy of Milan (source of Edward III's son Lionel's second wife) was fought over by France and the Habsburgs and usually in the latter's hands. The Medici of Florence were only sporadically in power until 1527, had few females available, and were anyway regarded as ex-merchant 'parvenus', though Francis I of France secured Catherine de Medici for his son Henri in 1533. In the north, the united Crown of Denmark/Norway could provide a marital ally but Sweden, in successful revolt against it from 1523, was also governed by 'parvenus', the Vasa dynasty, with no princesses available anyway.

The early sixteenth century thus provided limited choice for England in seeking out a marital ally, and the situation continued to deteriorate. In effect, a husband for available princesses – in due course, Henry's probable heiress Mary (born 1516) – was limited to France or the Habsburg realms. The vast Habsburg 'conglomerate' of states duly encompassed Hungary and Bohemia as well under Charles' sole brother Ferdinand. Born in 1503, this prince was married to the Hungarian heiress so he had no need of a wife – and his sons were too young to be married to Mary. There was no younger Habsburg prince who could marry Mary, unlike the plethora of Habsburg males that had been available in the fourteenth and fifteenth centuries when their Central European realm had been divided into several dynasties centred in Austria and Tyrol. All this reduced the number of available princes and princesses for an English royal union, and once it was clear that Mary would have no younger brother it meant that Henry VIII could not marry her to a European prince without nationalistic fear of this leading to a union of Habsburg realms and England. The chances of a successful overseas marriage were also reduced by the speed in which alliances altered for European political reasons – England often did not stay allied to one rival for long enough to enable a marriage to be concluded. This was illustrated in the confusing diplomatic 'volte-face' concerning the marriage of Henry VIII's sister Mary in the 1500s – she was variously intended for a Habsburg or Valois bridegroom according to which neighbouring 'Power' Henry VII was currently allied with. Betrothed to Philip and Juana's son Charles, later Emperor Charles V (five years her junior) in Henry's lifetime and thus seemingly destined to be Empress of the Holy Roman Empire and Queen of Spain, she ended up married to the much-older Louis XII of France (thirty-three years her senior) due to the English diplomatic breach with her fiancé's grandfather Ferdinand in 1512. Henry VIII's daughter Mary was also to have several potential husbands in her father's shifting diplomatic alliances of 1516–27, as he moved between alliance with the Empire/Spain and France.

An earlier victim of a diplomatic breach between Henry VII's England and Ferdinand was the widower King's second marriage. In 1505, as Ferdinand's ally, he had expressed great interest in marrying the latter's niece Joan, widowed Queen of Naples, and had sent ambassadors to investigate her with detailed questions about her person and a request for a portrait.[24] This fell through after Ferdinand's rapprochement with Henry's current enemy Louis XII and marriage to a French lady (Germaine de Foix, of the royal house of Navarre) in 1506. A similar fate befell the alternative choice of bride as part of Henry's Habsburg alliance – Maximilian's widowed daughter Margaret of Savoy, regent of the Netherlands, who Henry instructed his ambassador Anthony Savage to investigate in 1505. The crucial questions for a satisfactory Tudor/Habsburg alliance were the extent of a dowry, the danger of Maximilian allying with France, and the nature of his hospitality to the refugee English Yorkist pretender Edmund de la Pole.[25] In the end Henry was able to persuade Maximilian's son Philip, driven ashore in Weymouth Bay by a storm in 1506 and offered hospitality at court but politically pressurized too, to surrender the pretender without a marital alliance. As an alternative to the Habsburg alliance, Louis XII offered Henry the hand of his niece Margaret of Angouleme in 1505 and promised Henry's ambassador as great a dowry as Ferdinand would give for Joan of Naples.[26] Nothing came of any of these rival proposals, but the marriage with Margaret of Savoy was still in discussion as late as 1507/8 when she turned Henry down. Had she not done so, the commercial difficulties over English trade in her Netherlands domains been sorted out, and the acquisitive Henry been satisfied over the dowry, the Tudor-Habsburg alliance of 1508 might have seen Henry marry Margaret as well as his daughter Mary being betrothed to Charles. The twenty-eight years' difference in age was regarded as immaterial in that era, as Mary's marriage to Louis XII soon showed. If a less sickly Henry had married Margaret in 1509 and lived for a few more years their offspring would have been in the same position to Henry VIII in the 1520s as Edward I's younger children, Edmund of Woodstock and Thomas of Brotherton, were to their half-brother Edward II in the 1320s. Their children would have been in prime position to succeed Elizabeth Tudor in 1603, unless they had already fallen victim to an epidemic or the snake-pit of Tudor court politics.

Chapter Two

Early Tudor dynastic bad luck

Henry VIII's annulment
Would an annulment have been easier in
a different European diplomatic context?

Section One. A possible husband for Princess Mary? Was it possible that Henry could have arranged for his daughter's succession properly before 1527/8, and so not felt impelled to re-marry?

Princess Mary, born in 1516, was soon seen to be the sole offspring of Henry VIII's marriage, with no more boys being born let alone surviving after 1511. The current view of a female's legal position meant that a queen regnant was still supposedly the inferior of her husband and duty-bound to accept his political direction. The husband had to be of royal rank, at least in England in the early sixteenth century – Mary Stuart in Scotland could marry an English nobleman of royal blood in 1565, Margaret Tudor's grandson Lord Darnley, but Robert Dudley was to be violently opposed by English nobles as too lowly in rank for Elizabeth I. The unpopularity of the 'upstart' Dudleys was an added complication, his father having been leader of a controversially reformist Protestant regime in 1549–53 and his grandfather had been executed in 1510 as a scapegoat for Henry VII's extortion. Nor would Elizabeth allow Dudley to marry Mary Stuart in the early 1560s, a solution that would have kept this potential threat tied to a trustable Protestant husband and so unlikely to press her claim to the English throne – though the possessive Queen was also no doubt unwilling to send her close companion Dudley away from her court to Scotland. As we shall see, Henry VIII was equally 'touchy' on the prospect of a royal marrying a partner of lower social status. But there were precedents for such a marriage as Edward IV had – controversially – married a 'commoner', Elizabeth Woodville (albeit one with a mother of ducal Luxembourg blood), his brothers, George and Richard, had married the daughters of their cousin Warwick 'the Kingmaker', and their sisters, Anne and Elizabeth, had married into the English nobility (the Duke of Exeter and the Earl of Suffolk). Further back, Edward III's heir Edward of Woodstock had married his semi-royal cousin, Countess Joan of Kent, who had already married two 'commoners', and Edward III's younger sons John and Thomas had married the heiresses of the noble lines of Lancaster and Hereford (both semi-royal).

Were the 'parvenu' Tudor dynasty more 'touchy' about keeping up their social status by marrying people of royal blood than were the later Plantagenets? The argument that marrying a princess off to a great noble gave the latter's family undue power, causing resentment among rivals, had not prevented such marriages occurring under the later Plantagenets. These kings were insecure and at risk of revolt as were Henry VII and VIII, at least once the first successful armed challenge had rocked Richard II's throne in 1387–8; and Henry IV and Edward IV were particularly at risk as usurpers. But the parallel is not exact, as the daughters of ruling kings tended to be married off (or at least betrothed) abroad, such as Henry IV's daughter Philippa (Denmark/Norway) and Edward IV's daughters Elizabeth (France) and Cecily (Scotland). The same occurred with Edward IV's sister Margaret (Burgundy). It was their female cousins, of lower rank, who usually married into the nobility – such as the two oldest of Edward IV's sisters, Anne (the Duke of Norfolk) and Elizabeth (the Earl of Suffolk), and Henry IV's semi-royal Beaufort kin. These women were not born princesses; at best they were kings' sisters. The semi-royal de la Pole line that threatened the early Tudors, i.e. John, Edmund, and Richard, were descended from the marriage of Edward IV's sister Elizabeth, as above, who did not have the rank of pincess as she was not a king's daughter. The number of potential 'White Rose' Yorkist challengers to Henry VII and VIII at large in England was due to Edward IV's brothers and sisters marrying into the upper nobility; Henry VII was an only child so he did not have siblings to provide 'reserve' heirs in that way. His line continuing would depend on his own children; if Edward IV's line failed (or were bastardized) his family could fall back on the heirs of his numerous brothers and sisters. Thus when his brother Richard III's son died in 1484 Richard fell back on his sister Elizabeth's eldest son, John de la Pole; Henry VII had no comparable 'reserve' heir for his sons.

The unexpected and dynastically dubious accession of Henry VII in 1485 made it more difficult for one of his or his son's children to marry into the surviving semi-royal English dynasties, e.g. the Dukes of Buckingham, as such people's loyalty to the new regime was suspect. No late medieval

Plantagenet had had to face the prospect of his daughter succeeding, as all had had sons – and when Edward I was without a surviving son at times in the 1270s he had a brother (Edmund of Lancaster) to fall back on. Given the tradition that a king's daughter usually married someone of royal rank, if Henry VIII was anxious about his daughter and heiress marrying a foreign prince or king whose own interests would be pursued at England's expense then a semi-royal English noble was a logical if 'demeaning' alternative. But the isolated and (justifiably?) paranoid attitudes of Henry VII and Henry VIII to their great magnates meant that this would necessitate a degree of trust in the bridegroom's family, which was implausible for both these men.

The 'fall-back' candidate for the throne in the 1530s: Henry Fitzroy. Would his survival have altered the crisis of early 1547 and saved the Howards?

Henry VIII's grant of the family title (raised to a dukedom) of Richmond, his father's original earldom, and extensive estates to his bastard by Elizabeth Blount, Henry Fitzroy (born in 1519), shows that he toyed with the idea of making him his heir. Legitimation by the sovereign and/or Parliament was perfectly legal, as carried out in 1396 for the offspring out of wedlock of John of Gaunt and Catherine Swynford. More recently, Edward IV's children had been bastardized in 1483 and re-legitimated in 1485. It was, however, more normal for the offspring of a long-standing union, with John and Catherine (lovers since c. 1370) having married once his wife Constance was dead; Edward IV had never sought to legitimate his son by Elizabeth Lucy, Arthur Plantagenet (the Lord Lisle of the valuable 'Lisle Letters', a primary source for contemporary history) and there had never been any question of Henry II or Edward I or III legitimating their illegitimate sons.[1] The last bastard to ascend the English throne – in a much more legally flexible age – had been William 'the Conqueror', who in any case owed his position to conquest and had not been the legitimated bastard of an English but of a Norman ruler. The mistress of Henry VIII and mother of Henry Fitzroy, Elizabeth Blount, may well not have been his first extra-marital affair but was never given any prominence at court and was married off to a complaisant courtier in the usual fashion.

Henry Fitzroy was married into the powerful and royally descended Howard family, and thus could count on the support of his father-in-law, Thomas Howard, Duke of Norfolk from 1524, Henry's Lord Treasurer, and the leading conservative noble at court. Equally important, he had military experience and a large 'affinity' if it came to a showdown with rivals over the succession. The principal landed dynast in East Anglia and a shrewd political operator, this master of court politics had experienced the vicissitudes of favour in his youth when his grandfather John Howard, first Duke, had been Richard III's favourite but after his death at Bosworth the family estates had been seized. Norfolk's father, Thomas, had been imprisoned in the Tower when his son was twelve, been attainted, and eventually won over Henry VII to grant a pardon; but he had to wait for Henry VII's reign to have his dukedom restored after leading the royal army to victory over James IV at Flodden. Norfolk had served Henry VIII as loyally as his father had done, being a successful Lord Deputy of Ireland in the early 1520s, and had married as his first wife Edward IV's daughter Anne; following her death his second marriage was notoriously turbulent and ended with separation as he set up his mistress in his wife's place. His discarded wife was to accuse him and his minions of using violence against her, though this may have been exaggerated to embarrass him.

From the fall of Wolsey in 1529 (in which he participated) Norfolk was one of the King's closest counsellors, and a study of his career from 1529 to 1547 shows him to be a ruthless and cunning manipulator who was quite capable of outmanoeuvring his rivals to have his son-in-law made the King's heir. He was suspected of pandering three successive nieces (Mary and Anne Boleyn and Catherine Howard) to the King for his political advancement, and had the skill to save himself from the consequences of Anne's disgrace in 1536 and subsequently succeed in alienating Henry from his pro-Protestant rival Thomas Cromwell in 1540.[2] Had Henry Fitzroy not inconveniently died in the summer of 1536 Norfolk had the skill and resources to promote his chances in the succession, at least while the King lacked a son in 1536–7. Late in 1546 the King's decline in health when Prince Edward was only nine would have seen him backing Fitzroy's right as nearest adult male heir to head the inevitable regency council, assuming that the King distrusted the Duke himself for that role. In real life, the most serious political charge made against Norfolk and his son Surrey at their arrest in December 1546 was to be that Surrey had bragged that his father had the natural right to be regent. Given Surrey's conceit about his noble blood (the Howards were direct descendants of Edward I's youngest son, Thomas of Brotherton, in the female line via the Mowbrays), his rationale for this boast was presumably Norfolk's ancestry rather than his credentials as leader of the arch-conservatives at court or as Lord Treasurer. His personal feud with the leading court religious reformist, the future regent Edward Seymour (Duke of Somerset), was another reason for the Howards to act vigorously to counter the threat of a Seymour-led regency – and Fitzroy would have been a useful weapon.[3] Had Fitzroy still been alive, and thus Surrey's brother-in-law, Surrey could have backed him instead of Norfolk as regent. This is to assume that Surrey's elevated concern for noble ancestry did not mean he looked on Fitzroy's bastardy as ruling him out as regent. But the need to preserve the Howards from the likely danger of a Seymour regency would have argued for Norfolk and Surrey to use the best available means to work on Henry VIII to provide an alternative to Seymour as regent. The affection that Henry VII had shown his bastard son makes it unlikely that the ailing King would have been as suspicious of and alienated from him as he was to be of the Howards in his final months.

The King had indulged his illegitimate son throughout his life and might have listened to a request for him to head the regency council. This would have fitted in with the precedent headship of regency councils by royal paternal uncles Duke John of Lancaster (1377), Duke Humphrey of Gloucester (1422), and Duke Richard of Gloucester (1483) – though all had been legitimate sons of kings. The Howards would have been lobbying for this, as a means of excluding Prince Edward's maternal uncle Edward Seymour, Earl of Hertford – Surrey's rival as leading young military commander of the realm (and successor as governor of the vital Boulogne garrison), his reported rival in love for Anne Stanhope, and already identifiable as sympathetic with religious reform. The bad blood between Surrey and Hertford was apparent by 1546, and had manifested itself in a physical assault during a game of tennis (as two decades later Surrey's son was to come to blows on the tennis-court with his enemy, the Earl of Leicester).[4] But the influence that Norfolk had had at Council – and his personal attendance – had dropped sharply since the fiasco of Henry's turning on Catherine Howard in autumn 1541, when he is supposed to have berated the Duke for presenting him with the latter's niece as an unchaste wife. Still technically Lord Treasurer, Norfolk had seen his leadership of military matters, evident as late as the Scots war of 1542, eclipsed by the King's younger – and less religiously conservative – advisers Hertford (Duke of Somerset from 1547) and Lord Lisle (John Dudley, Earl of Warwick from 1547). The King himself was still staunchly conservative in religious matters as much as Norfolk, as seen by the 'heresy-hunts' of 1543–6, and Hertford/Somerset's radical religious reforms could only commence once Henry was dead. But it was the Lord Chancellor Thomas Wriothesley and Bishop Stephen Gardiner of Winchester, not the marginalized Norfolk, who took the lead in attempting to have Archbishop Cranmer and then Queen Catherine Parr arrested for heresy (as later recounted by John Foxe).[5] Evidently the conservatives at court felt that Henry would trust their advice more, and the King had noticeably diminished his willingness to ally with 'heretic' Lutherans in Germany after the fall of their ally Cromwell in 1540. But had Norfolk had the advantage of his son-in-law as a candidate to head the regency council as of late 1546, would the mistrustful Henry reinstate the Duke in favour by naming him as a member in the face of the fierce opposition of Hertford to it? Like Gardiner (excluded from the regency council when the King was still capable of making such decisions), Norfolk could have been seen as a threat to its smooth running by his feuds with its intended leadership.

In real life the arrogance and 'treasonable' boasting of Norfolk's outspoken heir Henry Howard, the talented but boorish 'Poet Earl' of Surrey, brought about the family's ruin as the King entered his final decline. As the main lay promoter of the conservative Catholic 'status quo' in 1540–6 Norfolk was the main obstacle to the religious reformers, and their lay leader Hertford – who as Prince Edward 's uncle was the alternative regent – secured his downfall through Surrey's behaviour alienating the paranoid King. Surrey had already been in trouble for loutish behaviour on occasion, most notably for a drunken rampage around London in 1543,[6] so his potentially damaging behaviour did not follow on from the Howards' political eclipse; it would have been likely to occur even had his close friend Fitzroy been alive. The minor if significant episode of Surrey daring to use royal heraldic arms (of Edward the Confessor) without permission, thus showing his arrogant pretensions and implicit political claims during a regency as royal kin, was played up to disgrace him. In fact, it would seem from the latest analysis that the precise nature of his heraldic 'crime' was played up by the Council's heraldic expert, Thomas Wriothesley, to damn him.[7] Wriothesley, son of a royal herald, was religiously conservative and so a natural ally for the Howards, but was also a former protégé of their foe Thomas Cromwell and was probably despised by them as 'low-born'. Surrey's arrogant and disrespectful behaviour towards the law over years as a court hothead could easily have led to charges over some other episode had this not been used; he was languishing unemployed in England brooding over his supersession at Boulogne by Hertford and some outbreak of lawlessness was possible.

Surrey made indiscreet boasts about his father's right to be regent and ridiculed the idea that the King should appoint a mixed body of councillors to carry out the role in an apparent argument with his ex-friend George Blagge, a former Privy Council crony, in late summer 1546. This was technically denying the King's right to do as he wished and so was treasonous – and his hot words and threats to Blagge led to the latter, a religious liberal, recounting (or exaggerating?) the incident to Seymour faction enquirers.[8] The latter were clearly looking out for evidence to implicate Surrey or his father and enrage the King – as the Howards should have realized. Surrey and his father were also supposed to have called privately on the King to pressurize him about the regency, or so the imperial ambassador (and Hertford?) heard.[9] Surrey was supposed to have hopes of using another

Howard lady as sexual bait to ensnare the King, as revealed to (and possibly exaggerated by) the inquisitors who sought out incriminating information from Howard friends and servants after the arrests.[10] This was logical 'realpolitik' but needed to be done more discreetly. The people who were willing to be helpful in destroying the Earl included his own sister, Fitzroy's widow the Duchess of Richmond, who was furious at Surrey and Norfolk for their miserliness towards her as a widow and dependant.[11] Had Fitzroy been alive this situation would not have occurred, but there was enough other evidence such as the gossip of Howard servants and the heraldic arms on the canopy over Surrey's bed at his house in the City. His denunciations of low-born ministers as 'foul churls' who had usurped the rightful place of the aristocracy were not calculated to win him friends.[12] The point here is that the methods to be expected from court rivals in digging up discreditable stories and poisoning the King's mind were well known within the court elite, and wise people – i.e. not the Howards – took precautions and did not say or do anything risky. (Surrey had decided not to have his late brother-in-law Richmond included in a heraldic portrait he was having painted so as not to offend the King;[13] so why did he not take more care about his bed?) Tudor state investigations of politically targeted suspects, like the similar twentieth century Soviet-era 'show trials', rarely failed to secure enough evidence for a conviction; the accused were expected to confess at their trials not argue and were denied advance knowledge of the charges. It was also important that the Seymour ally Sir Anthony Denny, a senior Gentleman of the King's Bedchamber and 'insider', had now acquired a stencil of the King's official signature to sign documents for him if he was ill[14] – so if Henry were sick was a forged death-warrant for a Seymour foe possible?

More important than the precise nature of Surrey's 'treason' was the desertion of his family's cause by the conservative Wriothesley, who had been endeavouring to destroy Queen Catherine Parr and Archbishop Cranmer earlier in 1546 and had no usual reason to back Hertford. Was he trying to strike a political 'deal' with Hertford, soon to be expected to become regent when Henry VIII died, by abandoning the Howards? Would he have done so if Fitzroy had been available as an alternative, conservative regent? And would Fitzroy have been able to demand access to the King (presumably from Hertford and Denny) to plead for his friend Surrey? Would Henry have been prepared to indulge his son over this issue? He had been indulgent to some senior figures accused of treason or heresy recently, such as Catherine Parr, so could have spared the Howards but taken their lands. In the event, the usual 'show trial' followed with Hertford leading the attack, Surrey was beheaded on 13 January 1547, and only the King's death saved Norfolk from following his son to the execution-block – by hours.[15]

If Fitzroy had still been alive, the King's indulged son, and an alternative candidate for regent Hertford would have had an obstacle in destroying the Howards and securing power in January 1547. At the least Fitzroy – probably with military experience in France in 1544–7 to rival Hertford's – could have interceded for his 'in-laws'. This would not necessarily have succeeded, as by 1546 the King was withdrawing favour from or terrorizing even those closest to him. He was capable of toying with the idea of arresting his queen at Wriothesley's and Gardiner's behest; the Foxe account of Catherine Parr's narrow escape from heresy-charges shows that Henry refrained from reassuring her that he was going to pardon her for her presumptuous religious advice longer than strictly necessary. As with the threat to Archbishop Cranmer earlier, the sadist in him enjoying her discomfiture there has a distinct similarity with the behaviour of the declining Stalin. He was thus capable of ignoring his son's appeal for the Howards and still appointing Hertford to head the regency council instead, though Fitzroy's blood rank would probably have secured a post for himself on the Council. The men who should have expected a place from their rank but who the King declared he would exclude when he reviewed the royal will(s) on 26 December 1546, primarily Gardiner, were objects of his current disapproval on various matters. Henry said that Gardiner was too strong-willed and implicitly that he was a danger to the stability of the regency council,[16] which would have been primarily on religious grounds; a Fitzroy at odds with Hertford over the fall of the Howards would also have been a threat but leaving him out would have been more difficult on account of his royal blood. Even had he been included, he could have been isolated and sidelined once the old King was dead – as happened to Wriothesley – and put in the Tower as a potential 'Richard III'.

Fitzroy's attitude to religious reform and the Seymour faction's plans for further 'Reformation' is impossible to predict, although he showed no great interest in scholarship as a boy unlike Henry VIII (as seen by Erasmus) or his half-brother Edward VI and sister Elizabeth. In the role of councillor he is likely to have endeavoured to save his wife's family from his father or, if ignored and under suspicion as a potential threat to Edward, rallied to the conservative faction in the regency council in 1547–9. Had he not been put in the Tower and had his estates confiscated, he would then have played a part in bringing Hertford (now Duke of Somerset) down in revenge for Surrey's execution. In the event of a militarily experienced Fitzroy being available to help defeat the peasant rebels in summer 1549, and then lead troops against Somerset that autumn, he is more likely than John Dudley to have emerged as leader of the Council after Somerset's fall and he would have been a powerful ally for conservatives opposed to further religious reform. Dudley might still have bought him off with lands and a military role in Scotland or Ireland, but is likely to have proceeded with more caution in religious reform unless Fitzroy was personally persuaded of its good. Fitzroy is certainly more likely to have backed his half-sister Mary than the 'usurping' Jane Grey in 1553, and could even have been considered as heir by Edward VI if he was suitably well-inclined to Protestantism.

The shortage of candidates to marry Mary: could Henry VIII have found a 'safe' consort for her as queen in the 1510s–1520s? In this case, would there have been any need for ending his first marriage?

It was unfortunate that the concentration of leading European states in the hands of the Habsburg dynasty, and the small number of available male members of that family, meant that the status-conscious Henry could not resort to the solution for his daughter Mary that was available to Mary herself in 1554 and to her half-sister Elizabeth in the 1560s and 1570s. At this date, prolonging the royal line by marrying off the Queen Regnant was seen almost universally as desirable. In both cases, a domestic or a foreign contender for the Crown Matrimonial was possible – though Elizabeth, unlike Mary, considered some men who were not rulers so their marriage to the English Queen would not bring about a 'union' between their countries. Mary, to the alarm of many of her subjects, was determined in 1554 to marry her cousin Charles V's heir Philip, governor of the Netherlands and soon (1556) to take over the rule of Spain;[17] Elizabeth considered junior Habsburg archdukes and French Valois dukes who might or might not inherit a throne. She also supposedly considered Philip at the start of her reign; but this was probably just a 'show' to keep him as an ally during her confrontation with France in 1559–60. In the case of Henry's finding a husband for Mary, one solution was to choose someone who would not inherit a throne so that the marriage would not lead to dangers of England being politically or diplomatically tied to its new consort's state. But Henry did not consider this. There was one major problem, in that neither of his main international 'partners' and rivals – his contemporaries, Francis I of France (three years younger) and Emperor Charles V (nine years younger) – had available unmarried younger brothers or younger sons in the 1510s. But he probably also considered such a match socially beneath his daughter; he was initially angry at his younger sister's secret match with his friend and political 'trusty' Charles Brandon, who was only a knight until Henry ennobled him.[18]

A domestic candidate was one alternative, and would not tie the kingdom to a foreign alliance that might prove unwise. But the attitude that Henry took to his much-loved sister (the original 'Mary Rose' after whom the warship was named) daring to marry a commoner and his distrust of great nobles like the semi-royal Duke of Buckingham imply that this was unlikely. In both cases of Henry's daughters' matches the domestic solution was avoided too, although serious and politically powerful suitors emerged for both new queens in 1553 and 1558 – in Mary's case the much younger Edward Courtenay, son of one of her father's victims and a descendant of Edward IV's younger daughter, Elizabeth. Fourteen years his intended fiancée's junior and a political novice due to a boyhood spent in the Tower of London, he was backed by her powerful Lord Chancellor and Bishop of Winchester, Stephen Gardiner (former leader of the conservative 'Anglo-Catholics' at Henry's court) in 1553–4 but was not chosen.[19] Marrying him would have avoided the danger of a too-powerful husband who was already a senior figure in English politics overshadowing his wife and his triumphant faction abusing their power. In Elizabeth's case from 1558 the candidates included another younger and politically inexperienced noble relative at the head of a great family, her cousin Thomas Howard, Earl of Norfolk; the older conservative noble Henry Fitzalan, Earl of Arundel (who seems to have rated his chances as high); and her own personal favourite and confidant, her 'Eyes', the much-resented and controversial Robert Dudley, Earl of Leicester.[20] The problem of a politically powerful 'home' candidate being chosen and alienating all his detractors from the Queen was especially acute with Dudley, who met vitriolic abuse for his presumption in daring to set his cap at his sovereign. The political risk of alienating his enemies was probably the decisive factor in Elizabeth's failure to marry him quite apart from the unfortunate scandal of his ailing wife, Amy Robsart, conveniently falling downstairs and breaking her neck at the height of the speculation about the Dudley match in summer 1560.[21] The same threat of faction facing a new 'consort' who was of English blood and had a family to advance would have warned Henry off marrying Mary to a native Englishman, irrespective of his desire to find her a 'high-status' royal husband. It was only sixty years since the marriage of Edward IV to a subject had led to the contentious emergence of her large and reputedly avaricious Woodville family as being perceived as too dominant at court – and within five years of the marriage Edward's cousin Warwick 'the Kingmaker' had resorted to armed revolt to try to destroy them. Civil war was to be avoided at all costs, and marrying off Mary into the most noble magnate dynasties of semi-royal blood – e.g. the Staffords (Dukes of Buckingham) or Howards (Dukes of Norfolk) – was problematic in arousing their rivals. The likelier choice – had Henry not considered this too 'low-status' – would have been the Howards, given that his father and grandmother had married off one of his aunts to the later (1524) Duke of

Norfolk, Henry's minister. The socially lower-status but genealogically more royal Poles, descendants of the King's great-uncle Duke George of Clarence, were blighted from 1527 by Lady Margaret Pole's backing for Catherine of Aragon.

The alternative was a foreign match within a royal family – to a prince of equal social status to his wife. This need not be a reigning sovereign who had to put his own kingdom first and thus might jeopardize English interests. (The argument also applied to a sovereign's heir.) But, as mentioned, there were no Habsburg or Valois princes available at first in Mary's infancy: and Francis and Charles did not have their first sons until 1519 and 1527 respectively. The situation for Henry VIII's choice of son-in-law in the 1520s was not hopeless even when it seemed that he would have to betroth Mary to a foreign partner's heir. But there was another major problem – keeping a marriage-treaty in being long enough for it to be implemented, given the young ages of the principals. The many fluctuations of Anglo-French-imperial relations meant that keeping an alliance in being long enough to enable a marital agreement to be carried out was problematic. A diplomatic 'spat' would usually lead to a change of alliance, meaning the cancellation of any extant marital plans. Similarly, a definitive choice of France or the Empire as a marital partner necessitated coming down from the fence on the side of one of those rivals, alienating the other. This was no more palatable to Henry in the 1520s than it was to be for Elizabeth, considering a husband from the same two rival 'power-blocs', in the 1560s and 1570s. Marrying Mary to the Dauphin would be unwise and unnecessary, leading to a union of the two realms. Francis I of France had younger sons, only a few years Mary's junior, to whom she could have been married in the Anglo-French rapprochement seen at the 'Field of the Cloth of Gold'. One of them, Henri (born 1519), eventually succeeded Francis so if Mary had married him she would have been Queen of France not England in the 1550s. In real life Henri and his wife, Catherine de Medici, had a large but mostly sickly family, most of them ultra-Catholics, and their sons Francis II, Charles IX, and Henri III ruled to 1589; but if Henri had married Mary he would have had half-Tudor heirs (if they had children). But the Anglo-French entente of 1520 did not last long, so the 'window of opportunity' for this marriage was short and by the time of the next Anglo-French entente in 1532 Mary had been bastardized by her father. The only serious negotiations for Mary's hand were thus with the Habsburg Empire where Charles V, nine years Henry's junior, was sovereign and his brother Ferdinand was heir to him and to Hungary (and ruler of the latter from 1526).[22]

Could either the Empire or France tolerate Henry marrying his heiress to the other's representative and so enable the marriage to go ahead without major diplomatic risk?
The likeliest fiancé for Mary at the time when she was still regarded as legitimate and Henry's probable heir was Emperor Charles V. This candidate would thus be her most probable husband, given that Henry was opposed to royal marriages within the English nobility. He was Henry's ally before and after the brief Anglo–French rapprochement of 1518–20, and even at the height of the 'entente' between Henry and Francis the relationship between those two men was uneasy and unlikely to last. Nearly equal in age and similar in temperament, ruthless, arrogant, and extravagant, they were observed to 'hate each other cordially' at the spectacular Anglo–French summit near Calais, the 'Field of the Cloth of Gold', in 1520. At the time Henry did all he could to match Francis' performance at the meeting, obsessively determined to match or better him at everything, and he no doubt resented being thrown by him at a 'friendly' wrestling-bout.[23] Their cordiality was unlikely to last long and produce an Anglo–French marriage unless there were overwhelming political reasons for it. Henry's personal relationship with Charles, six years younger and different in temperament, was easier quite apart from the commercial reasons for English alliance with the owner of the Netherlands (Charles) and the King's repeated assertion of his ancestral claims to France (as late as 1544). Nor did Henry let the Anglo–French entente affect his good relations with Charles and imply an Anglo-imperial breach; he was as keen as Charles was to maintain that alliance and made time to meet the new Emperor in Dover just before he sailed to Calais for the Anglo–French meeting. (A tripartite 'summit' of all three was suggested; Charles was less keen on it than Henry or Wolsey.) The relationship with France soured; by 1524 Charles and Henry were planning to divide France between them and their candidate to replace Francis as king (the Duc de Bourbon). Occupying a part of his ancestral dominions in France and matching his forebear Henry V was much more to the young – and the old – Henry's glory-seeking taste than peace, and his natural military target was always the traditional enemy of England.

Had the possibility of Francis successfully challenging Charles for the latter's election as emperor in June 1519 occurred, the strategic imbalance in Europe would have impelled Henry even more strongly against France. For once the Habsburg grip on the imperial office (established in 1452) was in danger, and apparently two of the seven electors – the Archbishop of Mainz and the Elector Palatine – and possibly a third (the Archbishop of Trier) were in Francis' favour. Charles, despite being his predecessor Maximilian's grandson, was an 'external' not a German ruler (King of Spain) and so at a disadvantage; and Henry bizarrely even contemplated being elected emperor himself, which Maximilian had once suggested. Henry had no obvious backers at the election 'Diet' in June 1519, unlike Francis, and his envoy Richard Pace was not given huge bribes to win over sceptics – though Pope Leo X was opposed to the accretion of Habsburg power and preferred a non-Habsburg candidate. But if Francis had prevailed with papal backing, Europe was likely to have been plunged into even more intense Habsburg–Valois conflict and Henry to have taken the Habsburg side against his usual, French, rival.

There was also the possibility that all three rulers might have been reconciled – temporarily – into a tripartite alliance in which Francis would tolerate Mary marrying a Habsburg or Charles tolerate Mary marrying a Valois. In a general peace, an English (marital?) alliance with one power would not automatically cause war with the other – as it either threatened to do or did in the fierce Valois/Habsburg struggle of the 1550s and 1560s. Originally, in the Anglo–French rapprochement of 1518 the idea of Mary marrying the Dauphin was proposed – thus implying an Anglo-French Union of Crowns.[24] This was unlikely to work in practice, given the strong anti-French feeling noted among the English nobility at the time of the 'Field of Cloth of Gold' summit in 1520.[25] Pope Leo X proposed a general peace for the purpose of a Crusade to recover Constantinople in 1518 and sent letters to the European sovereigns, followed by legates (the first appearance of Wolsey's nemesis Cardinal Campeggio in England). This was upstaged and sabotaged by Wolsey's own plan for a 'general peace', without the Crusade as its centrepiece and with himself as the organizer and centre of diplomacy (and no doubt praise).[26] The idea of such a peace – with a diplomatic mechanism of a permanent council of 'Powers' – had been mooted before, in Italy and Bohemia in the mid-fifteenth century, and was urged by prestigious and well-connected humanist scholars. It had never had 'mainstream' support from one or more 'Great Powers'; and England now provided it, with an idealistic if mercurial young king in search of a glorious reputation that might be satisfied by peace as well as by conventional inter-European war. Wolsey now saw himself as the arbiter of Europe,[27] and used his considerable energy and talents for that purpose in the crucial years of 1518–20. No doubt it was partly intended as self-aggrandisement; but his commitment provided a chance for it to succeed until such time as Henry, Francis, or Charles found it to their better interest to revert to the usual diplomatic chicanery and military confrontation.

The Anglo-French treaty of autumn 1518, whereby England returned Tournai to France and Mary was betrothed to the Dauphin, duly included unprecedented proposals for the signatories to pledge themselves to

European peace and take action against breaches of that. More 'powers', including Charles (then King of Spain, and Emperor from 1519), the Pope, and Venice, later signed up – and in theory they were all prepared and legally bound to intervene against an aggressor, thus deterring breaches of the pact. But legal agreements were one thing, and goodwill another; though England could play a crucial role for inducing Charles and Francis to deal together peacefully as each rival sought English support to make war on the other. English refusal to co-operate with a reversion to war might give its proposer pause, provided that Henry and Wolsey stood firm. Would they be too anxious to secure a firm ally (in the form of the 'Power' proposing to break the treaty) to be high-minded and insist that they would refuse to make war? The only chance the 'general peace' had was for Henry, Charles, and Francis to be prepared to deal with each other on terms of peace if not trust, for which a tripartite meeting would be crucial. This was suggested in 1519 but never 'pushed' with vigour, and it did not take place; in the crucial royal movements of April to June 1520 the chance was passed up. Charles, en route back to Spain after his imperial election, was pressing for a meeting with Henry before the latter sailed from Kent to Calais to meet Francis; he could have stayed on in Kent and accompanied Henry to the 'Field of the Cloth of Gold'. Possibly he feared being overshadowed by the other two monarchs' unwelcome amity, and preferred to deal with them individually.

Instead he visited Henry on his own, and sailed on to Spain while Henry proceeded on schedule to Calais; by spring 1521 Charles was pressing Henry to break with France and Wolsey's resultant mission to Flanders had the contradictory diplomatic aims of reassuring Francis about English commitment to peace while simultaneously negotiating with Charles for a military alliance.[28] The Cardinal has been seen as a hypocrite for doing so, but it is more probable that he was in an impossible position, trying to satisfy Henry, Charles, and Francis at the same time and lose the favour of none of them; Charles (backed by Pope Leo) was now intent on war and could not be won back to the terms of general alliance. England thus had to choose an ally or lose its chance of influence over at least one 'Power', and Henry and Wolsey duly chose the Emperor as their ally. The fault for undermining the terms of the 'Treaty of London' in 1518 lay with Charles rather than Wolsey. The latter had indeed suggested the obvious best means of securing a more long-lasting peace in the form of a permanently sitting 'council' of 'Powers' in 1520–1 – an embryonic 'League of Nations', based on 'humanist' literary and fifteenth-century Italian political suggestions.[29] (Beyond that lay the precedent of the sitting councils of allies in Ancient Greece, e.g. the Amphictyonic League.) But this was mere words without commitment to it by a significant number of European powers, and the latter was lacking. Had

Charles not been so intent on resuming the conflict with Francis in 1521 Wolsey might have had a 'breathing-space' to explore the idea further and send out emissaries. The Habsburg-Valois/Bourbon conflict resumed, to last into the eighteenth century.

Ultimately Wolsey lacked the authority to require England's European neighbours to co-operate with his plans, even when Henry was unequivocally backing him. That moral 'high ground' lay with the traditional arbiter of Christendom, the Pope; and ironically Wolsey's 1518 plan had sidelined the current papal initiative about general peace for a Crusade and so diminished its impact. Francis, soon to be a Turkish ally, was hardly likely to take part in a Crusade for the recovery of Constantinople – though Charles, as lord of Sicily and from 1519 Austria, had strategic reasons to do so. Even without a Crusade following, the papacy's continued initiatives for a truce in Europe were the strongest contemporary efforts for a Habsburg-Valois peace, which could in turn have led to Henry betrothing his heiress to a neighbouring prince from a 'Great Power' without that ally's rival immediately turning on England. The incumbent Sultan of 1512–20, Selim, concentrated on securing the Levant and after destroying the Safavid Persian army at Chaldiran in 1514 overran Egypt in 1517. His son Sulaiman was, however, more interested in a European empire as heir of Caesars and the lord of 'New Rome', and resumed the aggression of Mehmed 'the Conqueror'. His successful attack on Belgrade in 1521 reversed the halt in Ottoman conquests that Hungary had secured there in 1456, opening Hungary – and ultimately Charles' new dominions – to invasion and alarming both Pope and Emperor. But the Church's renewed efforts to restore Christian unity for action against the Ottoman Turks, never secured enough mutual trust to succeed even after the fall of Rhodes in 1522 and the conquest of Hungary in 1526. (The west of the latter was taken over by Charles' brother Ferdinand, giving the Emperor a direct stake in its survival.) The main obstacle to a papal-sponsored general truce and Anglo-imperial-French alliance against Sulaiman 'the Magnificent' was Francis. The latter was more willing to use the Turks as a weapon against Charles – who had destroyed his army, captured him, and forced a humiliating treaty out of him in 1525 – than to put Christian unity first.

In 1521 Henry, faced with a choice of allies, chose Charles over Francis and duly began to make plans to dismember France. This now meant that his heiress Mary would have a Habsburg husband if the alliance held. But crucially, Charles only had one son (Philip, born in 1527) so the latter's marriage to Mary brought the probability of a union between England and Spain (and/or the Netherlands). This occurred on Charles' abdication in 1555/6, but was an active issue as soon as it became apparent that Charles would not have more sons. His brother Ferdinand's eldest son, future Emperor Maximilian, was only born in 1527, and the latter's younger brothers were even less viable for the marriage. A younger son of Charles and his Portuguese wife would have been a less risky choice as husband for Mary, though much her junior. Had Philip not been the only son this would have been a less risky option, but by the time that such a child would have been born in the late 1520s Henry and Charles were at odds over the King's divorce from Catherine of Aragon.

Section Two. The annulment – how could it have been different? Would a different situation in Europe – or a different pope – in the 1520s have made Henry's search for an annulment easier?

(i) The importance of the Italian context as of 1527
The King's doubts about the legality of his marriage to Catherine developed conveniently at a time when he was seeking a way to find a male heir, and his ruthlessness and elastic conscience were as apparent in this period as later. Sir Thomas More claimed cynically that for all Henry's professions of friendship towards him the King would cut his head off if it could win him a castle in France.[30] Thus even if Henry had not fallen in love with his ex-mistress Mary Boleyn's sister Anne around 1525 – and the latter had not held out for marriage – an attempt to divorce Catherine was possible. Also, in precise legal terms it was crucial that Henry's brother Arthur and Catherine had lived together for some months as man and wife in 1501–2 at Ludlow, so that Henry could claim and provide household witnesses to show that the marriage had been consummated. If the Prince and Princess had continued to live in separate households as Henry VII's court, as was considered at the time on account of Arthur's youth (and health?), proving consummation would have been more implausible and the difficulty might have given the King pause to reconsider. Conversely, the longer that Arthur and Catherine had lived together the greater the chances of consummation – if Arthur had lived to c. 1506 not 1502 and died aged aged around twenty Henry's argument for consummation would have been stronger. Catherine would have been on weaker grounds had she held out for the argument that the marriage had not been consummated. Achieving a divorce without fatally offending Charles V was a major obstacle, with Henry's strained relations with Charles' rival Francis from 1521 making it difficult for Henry to form a fixed alliance with France in which context imperial enmity would not matter.

Francis' catastrophic rout and capture by Charles' army at Pavia in 1525 gave the Emperor unprecedented power in Europe, meaning that until the

French King was released, restored his nation's fortunes, and felt emboldened to break with the Empire Henry could not count on a worthwhile French alliance if he offended Charles. The course of events in Italy, arising from the long Franco–Habsburg dispute over control of the Duchy of Milan, thus played a major role in the divorce. Had Francis won at Pavia and secured French control of Milan, the crises of the Turkish invasion of Hungary in 1526 and the peasant revolt in Munster should have put Charles in a weak enough military position for Henry to calculate that the Emperor could not afford to break with England. Thus Henry could have proceeded with the divorce without a major risk of imperial intervention and a papal veto. Had Francis won at Pavia, he would have been the major military power in Northern Italy and Charles unable to use his army to intimidate the Pope. The Emperor's weakness would have enabled Pope Clement to risk offending him by granting a divorce to Henry, and it is possible that a victorious Francis (who was to receive Henry and Anne Boleyn without query in 1532) would have backed Henry's demand for an annulment. Anne had been educated at the French court as lady-in-waiting to Henry's sister Queen Mary in 1514, was more pro-French than Catherine so a useful ally, and may have already known Francis.

(ii) The imperialist army's sack of Rome: not necessarily fatal to the annulment?

The unpaid and loot-hungry imperial army sacked Rome at the crucial moment for the divorce-case in 1527 and reduced the Pope to a virtual hostage. This itself followed Pope Clement's miscalculation of playing a leading role in a new, premature anti-imperial alliance with France and Venice (Cognac, 1526) to reverse the disaster of Pavia without having the military means to defeat Charles. Had he waited longer before defying the Emperor and stayed neutral, the retaliatory attack on the papal states in 1527 was unlikely to have happened – though his agreeing to Henry's divorce would logically have infuriated Charles anyway. Besieged in the Castel St Angelo at the height of the sack and then forced to surrender and live under house-arrest for months, Clement was badly shaken and his natural timidity was even more dominant thereafter. Even after his escape from ravaged Rome to the relative safety of Viterbo, which freed him from immediate military pressure, in practical terms he had to govern an occupied papal state at the mercy of Charles' troops. He could not now rely on Francis to help expel the imperial armies, though after Charles had secured his delayed coronation by Clement in 1530 the latter had more freedom of manoeuvre.

This poor situation curtailed the ability of the Pope (born a Medici and thus used to thinking in terms of Florence's priorities) to act to Charles' detriment; the power of the Empire in Italy from 1525–30 was such that papal acquiescence with Henry's divorce could not be taken for granted. Italian power-politics not the needs of England would determine the papal attitude; the adherence of Charles to the annulment was seemingly necessary to produce a favourable resolution. But it may not have been essential; soon after the sack of Rome Wolsey came up with one solution of getting the Pope to declare that he was unable to act freely and thus delegated his legal powers to a nominee – himself. Wolsey's emissaries, led by the papal legate Gambara and mostly Italians (thus able to move about Rome without suspicion), were to slip into the Castel St Angelo and get Clement to sign a document giving Wolsey such powers, without telling him that it was for the purpose of the divorce and could enrage Charles.[31] The Cardinal could thus rule on annulment without having to secure papal agreement. However, Henry vetoed the plan, in favour of his own emissary William Knight making a direct approach to Clement. Nearly murdered en route in war-torn central Italy, Knight reached Rome shortly before the Pope fled to Orvieto and put Henry's request to him. Might the Pope be so angry at Charles' troops' onslaught that he preferred to defy him, supported by Henry, rather than seek imperial permission? Having given a promising reply when first sounded out by Knight, Clement recovered his nerve after his move to Viterbo and insisted that Henry's request went before his legal expert, Cardinal Pucci, who ruled it legally inadmissible; all that Clement would do was to give Henry permission to remarry if his first marriage was judged illegal, not rule that it was so.[32] But might Clement have panicked and given Henry what he requested without Pucci's imprimatur if he was still under pressure in Rome at the time?

The frustrated Wolsey managed to persuade Henry to send the Cardinal's intended mission, now to Viterbo not Rome, in December 1527. His representative, Gregory Casale, was told to secure a papal decree handing over resolution of the case to a legatine court set up in England, under a cardinal sent from Rome (not Wolsey himself, so to make it seem less 'fixed') with a papal legal ruling on the case. The divorce was to rest on the canon law faults in the bull of Pope Julius II, which had granted Henry and Catherine permission to marry, not on the more easily challengeable Old Testament injunction (Leviticus) about marrying a brother's widow, and the legate was to be ordered solely to prove that the bull was invalid and if so to grant the annulment. There was no need to argue about the validity of the Levitical injunction or whether Arthur and Catherine had consummated their marriage in 1502; and once the legate ruled there was to be no right of appeal to Rome.[33] Thus Catherine could not appeal to a papal court and rely on Charles to pressurize the Pope to deny the divorce, as was to occur in

1529. A second mission was sent early in spring 1528, led by Wolsey's secretary Stephen Gardiner (later Bishop of Winchester and principal Anglo-Catholic leader until 1555) and the royal almoner Edward Fox. They were to seek a commission for a legatine court, which this time included Wolsey, with either an Italian legate (preferably one of the two Italian cardinals holding English bishoprics, Campeggio and Ghinucci) or his fellow-Archbishop, Warham; and they were to warn that if this was not granted there was a threat to English legal obedience to Rome.[34] Evidently the latter, drastic resolution to the crisis was already being mooted in London, presumably by the Cardinal's court foes and even by the exasperated King. Norfolk was said to have explicitly linked the supposed English political decline to its domination by churchmen.

Gardiner's embassy did its best to bully Clement into acquiescence at Orvieto, with its leader boldly stating what form of words would be suitable to Henry and pressing for a written statement on that basis. If the Pope would not grant his legate(s) the right to make a final judgement, could he at least promise to ratify whatever judgement they came to? The latter would be reached in London, not Italy, and so be out of reach of imperial interference; Clement could then argue to Charles that he could not stop the divorce as his hands were legally tied. But Clement would not give a lead and subjected the terminology to the veto of his Chancery, producing a document that did not go as far as Gardiner required and even then worrying that the Emperor would punish him for it. The legates' decision was to be immune from a legal appeal to Rome; but it could still be invalidated on the grounds of impartiality, i.e. undue pressure, Clement had not ruled that the bull of Julius II was legally invalid (which would make the legates' task much simpler), and he would only verbally promise to confirm the legates' decision.[35] Henry's relief on Fox's return with the document in April 1528 evaporated once he and his legal experts had read the 'small print'. A further request was now sent back to Gardiner in Orvieto to secure more in the form of a secret papal commission to Wolsey for him to grant an unchallengeable annulment – with a patently dubious promise that this was only for improving the Cardinal's personal confidence and would not be revealed to anyone.[36]

It seems that the embassy did secure documents that granted what Henry required, with a written papal promise not to revoke the legates' decision, but that the choice of the ageing and timid Campeggio to act with Wolsey virtually nullified its effectiveness. In the meantime, the long delay before he set out added to Henry's impatience and suspicion of papal goodwill – and of Wolsey's ability to secure what he had promised. Henry is supposed to have told the Cardinal's ambassadors that if the papal mission did not bring the legal guarantees he required they need not return, and Wolsey's frantic warnings to Campeggio on his arrival of official English ill-will to the papacy if the annulment was not finalized are unlikely to have been bluff.[37] Delayed by illness and the slow pace of travel for a man of his infirmities, Campeggio did not arrive in England until late 1528 and then resorted (no doubt on papal instructions) to trying to persuade Catherine to enter a convent. This would provide impeachable proof to Charles that she did not wish her marriage to be saved, and prevent an embarrassing court case, which could get out of hand or cause imperial revenge. But Catherine refused both the two cardinals' entreaties and Henry's threats,[38] and the court case had to go ahead.

To make matters worse, the vital legal document that Gardiner and Fox had forced Clement to issue to prevent Catherine appealing to Rome proved a 'dud'. This was the definitive papal document that allowed Campeggio and Wolsey to issue a final verdict in London without right of appeal, i.e. Clement's own 'final' statement (as fount of the law) of the canon law on Julius' bull, which they were merely to confirm satisfied the facts of Catherine's case. Campeggio had it in his possession and Henry required to see it to confirm its existence, but it subsequently disappeared; apparently Campeggio destroyed it at his master's request as Clement had had second thoughts about it enraging Charles.[39] Nor did the requested papal 'pollicitation', a legal statement confirming that Clement would never reverse or invalidate his commission to the legates to reach a final decision, prove as watertight as hoped when it belatedly reached England. Meanwhile the imperial armies were having major successes against the Italian partisans of Henry and Francis, reinforcing Clement's unwillingness to offend Charles. He ordered Campeggio to hold up starting the trial, let alone coming to a verdict, while assuring Charles that any decision to grant annulment in London would be revoked in Rome later.[40] With the Pope equivocal and seeking to satisfy Charles as more of an immediate threat to him than the distant Henry, only a bolder unilateral approach by Campeggio would have secured Henry what he required – and even then Clement could disavow his legate's decision later. Even public production of the papal warrant to the legates allowing their decision to be final could come under a subsequent challenge. Catherine was also emboldened to hold out by Campeggio's failure to back Henry's intimidating line towards her, and luckily for her the validity of Julius' bull granting dispensation for the marriage could now be challenged due to the appearance in Spain of Julius' subsequent 'brief' on the matter of her and Arthur's consummation of their marriage.[41] This new discovery added weight to her case, by arguing that Pope Clement had not been in full possession of the facts when he had issued his instructions to the legates and needed to make a second ruling to take account of the 'brief'. (The latter had avoided some of the obvious legal flaws in the canon law arguments made in the bull, and so stood on firmer grounds.) It has also been suggested that Henry would have stood on far firmer legal ground if he had avoided concentrating on the issue of the consummation of his brother's marriage in 1502 and gone after the issue of the flaws in the bull of Pope Julius – particularly its failure to refer to the matter of 'public honesty' over the circumstances of consummation. The bull had avoided granting absolution for Catherine to marry Henry on this issue of 'honesty' as well as over consummation; it could thus be legally challenged. Wolsey apparently realized this, and checked up with the aged ministerial survivor from 1503, Bishop Fox of Winchester, about it;[42] but Henry did not take the matter up. Did Wolsey never tell him, or did he ignore the Cardinal's suggestion in favour of his own theological expertise?

The King's 'party' seem to have been wrong-footed by the unexpected appearance of the 'brief', and were certainly outwitted by the concerted efforts of Catherine's English supporters (led by Bishop Fisher) and the royal/imperial administration in her homeland. A copy of the 'brief' was sent from Spain to Catherine to help her case, and she showed it to Campeggio; it added to the existing pressure on him from Clement to delay any decision. Catherine was forced by her husband to send a letter to Spain requesting the delivery of the original document to London for the court-case, but the messenger chosen (Thomas Abel) turned out to be a strong partisan of the Queen and warned Charles not to send it in case Henry had it destroyed.[43] The Emperor might not have done as Catherine requested in any case, suspecting that Henry had bullied her into the request to her own detriment, so the choice of Abel as messenger was perhaps not decisive; but this confirmed his caution.

The original 'brief', a stronger argument for a fully watertight past papal ruling in favour of the King's current marriage, survived to embarrass Henry's case. In reply, Henry sent a new embassy to Rome to search the papal archives for evidence that could be manipulated into showing that the 'brief' was a forgery or to pressurize Clement into granting another, more decisive document giving his legates final powers to revoke the marriage without right of appeal. Bizarrely, they were also to suggest the possibility that Henry could be given a dispensation to legally marry Anne without divorcing Catherine, on the grounds of Old Testament figures having had two wives at once – a clear sign of desperation.[44] A secret letter from Catherine was smuggled out of England to Rome requesting that the case be revoked from London to the Curia, making her views unquestionably clear,[45] and with imperial pressure on him mounting Clement ignored Henry's offers to restore his influence in Italy and assist him to preside at an imperial-French peace conference. Despite Henry's emissaries having called in on Francis en route to Rome to win his support for this, and two of the four staying on there, Henry was in no position to enforce his proposals to help Clement. The military facts in Italy gave Charles the sole power to compel papal obedience unless the always hesitant Clement took the uncharacteristically bold step of relocating to Avignon. Clement duly decided that spring of 1529 to come to terms with the Emperor,[46] which meant refusing the divorce or at least (if he wished to avoid a breach with Henry) postponing a decision by adjourning the trial. Henry's new embassy, recognizing the implication of firm refusals in the Curia to come to a decision, gave up and requested their recall, and the King had to proceed with the trial in London without obtaining any further papal rulings that could counter Catherine's expected moves. Campeggio, rather than giving way to royal pressure to rule in Henry's favour, had written already to Rome asking for the case to be returned to the Curia, as had both Catherine and Charles' envoys in Rome.

On 18 June the trial opened at Blackfriars; on 5 July Catherine's request for adjournment to Rome arrived at the Curia; on 15 July Clement ruled in her favour. It was bold but futile for Henry's ambassadors to try to hold up a papal order for revocation being sent to England by denying that the case had opened,[47] in defiance of the facts. The scene was set for the great 'show-piece' at Blackfriars of the Queen's appeal to Rome and Campeggio's decision in her favour, with the resultant humiliation and political ruin of Wolsey.

Given the military situation in Italy after the summer of 1527, the failure of Clement to stand up to the Emperor – either by defiance or by flight to France – was crucial. Henry's tempting offers to help the Pope arrange a imperial-French truce and peace conference were not backed by any military ability to enforce it, and Francis was at best lukewarm in his support. The unwavering hostility of Charles to the divorce, backed by the clear and repeated expression of Catherine's own wishes (with Henry unable to intercept her letters and cut her off from her foreign support), was vital. The adherence of Charles to the King's plans would only have been likely either if he needed Henry's political and military support or if Catherine had made it clear that she would give way. The former would have been possible had Francis, not Charles, won at Pavia and occupied Milan in 1525 – thus cutting off Charles' land-route between his other Italian domains (particularly Naples) and Austria and the Netherlands.

(iii) Another pope than Clement, a more favourable reaction to Henry's plans?

But what if Clement had not been pope as of the mid-1520s? His predecessor-but-one, his cousin Leo X (Giulio de'Medici, son of Lorenzo 'il Magnifico'), had died in 1521 aged only fifty – though his weight and health problems meant that he was unlikely to have reached old age. Leo had a personal debt of gratitude to Henry for 'writing' the 'Defence of the Seven Sacraments' against Luther and had granted him the title of 'Defender of the Faith'; would he have granted him a divorce more easily? Or would he have been at Charles' mercy by 1527–8 like Clement was? The complexities of papal elections were notorious and the choice of candidate was usually down to current 'voting strengths' among the cardinals, quite apart from intimidation or bribery; the main political groupings of voters in the 1520s could broadly be described as pro-French and pro-imperial. The circumstances of Italian politics were now such that they could interfere militarily in Rome if displeased by papal policy, unlike in Clement's uncle Lorenzo de Medici's time. Both countries had been interfering in Italian politics since the first French invasion of 1494 (aimed at securing the Valois claim to Milan), with the Empire having the advantage of an ancient claim on suzerainty dating back to Otto 'the Great' in the 960s and in practical terms centred on the control of Naples and Sicily. The 'Kingdom of Two Sicilies', the papacy's southern neighbour, had been in Aragonese – thence Spanish – hands since 1442, but had been ruled by Ferdinand's relatives until he secured direct control in 1506; France failed to evict them on several occasions from 1494 onwards. Thereafter it formed the centre of Spanish/Habsburg control of Italy until 1713. A military threat to the papacy since the days when Robert Guiscard created the mainland kingdom in the 1050s, its diversion to Spanish and thence Habsburg hands in 1442 eventually re-created the medieval spectre of imperial power in Italy from which Charles was able to dominate Clement's decision-making over Henry's divorce.

As of 1527 Charles and his army were the dominant factors in papal politics, and without this phenomenon a more independent papacy would have been able to decide on the divorce free from such political pressure. The papacy of the mid- and late fifteenth century had been a far more independent and confident political actor, and a practical and worldly pope such as Alexander VI (Rodrigo Borgia), who died in 1503, would have had no hesitation in meeting Henry's requirements for political reasons. But the last militarily powerful and vigorous pope had been Julius II in 1504–13 – a man who had unfortunately devoted his considerable energies to ruining Venice not uniting central-Northern Italy against France and the Empire. The papacy of Clement's day was not the military power of Alexander's or Julius' pontificates. The age and diverse origins of successive popes made it more difficult than in a lay monarchy for political 'continuity' long term, with one strong pope handing on his position and military resources to his equally determined successor. Thus even if Julius had not wasted his substantial resources and goodwill on his feud with Venice it is possible, if not probable, that his and Alexander VI's military power and relative political autonomy would have been diminished by 1527. The papacy could never match either the Empire or France in military might, and was likely to have been chary of infuriating Charles V by supporting Henry against Catherine unless Francis of France, as an English ally, was currently in the military ascendant in Italy as of 1527. The disaster at Pavia in 1525 ended this possibility.

English influence at the Curia was minimal, with only one English cardinal usually in office at any one time, and was dependent on the goodwill of more locally powerful and rich players; even Wolsey had little influence at Rome. (His predecessor as cardinal and as Archbishop of York, Christopher Bainbridge, was supposed to have been poisoned.) The main chance for Henry VIII of a favourable papal hearing would have been if Wolsey had managed to have himself elected pope, as Charles first proposed in 1520 and Henry took up enthusiastically.[48] Wolsey was lukewarm about it, but was willing to put his name forward if the King and the Emperor both supported him – which they promised to do. On the death of Pope Leo X in 1521 the Emperor went back on his word and secured the election of his Dutch tutor as Adrian VI instead, but the latter's death led to a second attempt on the Holy See in 1523 with Wolsey instructing his Rome diplomats to produce royal letters of support if he stood a chance of defeating the Medici candidate (Leo's cousin, the son of Lorenzo 'Il Magnifico's murdered co-ruler).[49] The latter was elected as Clement VII, but if Charles had been willing to order his partisans in the Consistory to back Wolsey the latter could have been elected despite his lack of personal backing in Italy. Wolsey was less easy for Charles to influence than his own tutor, so he was a less satisfactory choice, but Adrian could have turned the chance of the papacy down. Wolsey would thus have been pope in 1527–9 and so able to support his patron's request for a divorce. Henry would have had no need for a breach with Rome to secure legal independence for the English Church courts, and if Wolsey had been pope Catherine is unlikely to have considered it worth risking appealing to him to ban the divorce. The papal legate appointed to hear the case, Cardinal Campeggio, would have been instructed to do what the King desired. The great dramatic scene of Catherine appealing to Rome at the hearing into her marriage at Blackfriars would have been unlikely, and as a result Wolsey would not have been humiliated by failing to secure the King's wishes. This disaster made it easier for his detractors, the Dukes of Norfolk and Suffolk, to work on Henry to dismiss him.

Had Charles put military pressure on Wolsey as his army did on Pope Clement in 1527, the English pope – with stronger ties outside Italy than Clement – was capable of fleeing Italy to France like other threatened popes had done and rallying France and England to his cause. Popes threatened by local powers in Italy had been fleeing to France to seek aid since the eighth century, so it was a normal option and the papacy owned the local mini–state of Avignon (with a large, fortified palace to appeal to the sybaritic Wolsey). The papacy had been resident at Avignon from 1309 to 1377 and the French Crown had sponsored a rival line of popes there for another forty years, and as the papacy still owned Avignon Wolsey could have retreated there safe from imperial pressure. Henry would then have appeared as the papal champion, a role he evidently found congenial in the 1520s as shown by his literary attack on Luther, not as the Pope's enemy. He would have had no political reason to break with Rome or to encourage German Lutherans, unless Wolsey's death had led to Charles securing a compliant pope who objected to Henry's divorce in retrospect. The latter would have meant that Henry's marriage to Anne Boleyn was invalidated at Charles' behest once he had a compliant pope, but Henry – and his daughter Elizabeth in due course – would have been in a stronger position if the marriage had been legal at the time it was carried out. In real life Wolsey died at the age of around fifty-seven, late in 1530, probably partly due to the shock of his arrest for treason and the chances of final disgrace. The marshy Roman climate or the upheavals of fleeing Rome for France could have carried him off early in a similar way – but hardly before he had granted Henry his divorce. Had the majority of cardinals fled Rome with him, the option would have remained of them electing a new pro-English pope who would grant the divorce – and for this to occur Henry would have had to rely on France putting appropriate pressure on them.

In the meantime, the removal of the Cardinal from England would have lessened the real-life conflict between him and the Dukes of Norfolk and Suffolk, which hastened his downfall in 1529. Wolsey's ambitious protégé Thomas Cromwell would have been an obvious choice to act as the English Pope's principal 'conduit' to Henry. Cromwell would thus have made himself as indispensable in real life, but with Henry and the papacy as allies not been able to take charge of a legislative programme against papal powers unless Charles V had used a subsequent pope to question Henry's new marriage. The need to cut England off from papal authority would then have followed the invalidation of Henry's second marriage. Some degree of 'inquisition' into the monasteries was, however, possible, leading to the closure of smaller and/or 'corrupt' institutions, given the King's need for money in the continuing European rivalry with Charles and Francis in the 1530s.

(iv) Wolsey's example of worldly aggrandisement: unfortunate timing for him and for the Church's reputation?

Henry's own wish was for his wife to meekly stand aside and retire into private life, given her religious interests possibly to a convent.[50] There was a recent European precedent, in France, when Louis XII's first wife, Jeanne, retired to a convent to enable the King to marry his predecessor Charles VIII's widow Anne of Brittany and so retain French control of her patrimony. If Catherine herself had not opposed the divorce and contested all the 'evidence' of the full nature of her marriage to Arthur, Henry would have been able to present her agreement to Charles as a *fait accompli* and allege that she had accepted all his legal arguments. This seems to have been what Henry expected, with his devout wife prepared to accept defeat gracefully and retire to a nunnery. The Emperor would have been unlikely to issue more than a protest at the dishonour to his aunt if she had written to him announcing her decision to obey Henry, and the papal legates' court of 1529 in London would have been a formality. Henry would have been remarried to Anne Boleyn c. 1530 with the acceptance of all Church and legal authorities, with no more problems than for other sovereigns on the Continent who had divorced (usually on the grounds of consanguinity), and there would have been no major question of Elizabeth's legitimacy to dog her career. By the time of her birth (7 September 1533) her parents' marriage would have received international recognition, from the Church if not from an angry Charles – unless the latter chose to summon anti-papal cardinals to his dominions, have the Pope declared deposed, and set up a rival pope, a drastic move with no recent precedent. Had Elizabeth's parents been legally married by Catholic law in 1533, Henri II of France would have had no excuse to recognize Mary Stuart instead of her as the new Queen of England in 1558.

That is not to say that the restless and acquisitive Henry would have remained content with the Chancellorship of Wolsey for many more years, and Norfolk and his allies would have been undermining the Chancellor. The latter had already had to surrender his new, sumptuously semi-royal residence at Hampton Court to the King in 1525 to satisfy his master's desires, and reduce the number of sees that he held in plurality. The barbed comments of poet John Skelton about the showy Cardinal overshadowing the King's glory in 'Why come ye not to Court?'[51] evidently represented a widespread public feeling, and the Cardinal's surrender of Hampton Court was an indication of his unease at potential royal jealousy. Even without a divorce, the Cardinal was likely at some point to meet the fate that the equally irritated Louis XIV meted out to his over-rich chief minister Fouquet in 1661, with a swift and comprehensive seizure of the favourite's resources showing who was really master and reassuring the royal ego. Norfolk and Suffolk would have remained Wolsey's constant critics. Quite apart from the apparent snobbery of Norfolk's resentment of the 'butcher's cur' from Ipswich presuming to govern political life, Wolsey was more at risk than other powerful archbishops (and cardinals) who had held the chancellorship and been a King's senior minister such as Henry VII's adviser John Morton. All had possessed large estates and households like great secular peers on account of their office; the Reformation-era archbishops of Canterbury had a vast mansion the size of Hampton Court at their disposal at Knole (later owned by the Sackville-Wests) and those of York had a similar large palace at Bishopthorpe. The pre-eminent wealth and pomp of the archbishops reflected their secular as well as lay importance, and some archbishops and bishops (mostly diplomats) had been given a cardinal's hat since 1440, e.g. Archbishops John Kemp (d. 1454), John Morton (d. 1500) and Bishop Henry Beaufort (d. 1447). Beaufort, the great-uncle of Henry VI, had built a large mansion at Bishop's Waltham, Hampshire, had striven for power during Henry's regency with his nephew Duke Humphrey of Gloucester, and had been prominent on the international 'stage' as a diplomat and left a fortune to the King. But none of Wolsey's predecessors had lived with quite his degree of pomp – though there was an element of snobbery in the resentment of his ostentation by great nobles, which ignored the fact that many archbishops had been of humble birth.

No objections had been raised to Archbishops Rotherham of York and Morton of Canterbury serving Edward IV and Henry VII long-term as chancellors. Morton was as much of a 'political' cleric as ex-diplomat Wolsey, and was the closest of the episcopate to the new dynasty in 1483. He had originally been a Lancastrian partisan loyal to Henry VI and Margaret of Anjou, had worked for Edward IV following the final Yorkist victory in 1471, and had been arrested for 'plotting' by Richard III in June 1483, encouraged his gaoler the Duke of Buckingham to revolt against Richard, and had then fled to Brittany to join Henry Tudor. He then replaced the Yorkist John Alcock (the new Queen's brother Edward V's ex-tutor) as chancellor in 1487, and was regarded in popular myth as the originator of Henry's harsh 'heads I win, tails you lose' tax-schemes ('Morton's Fork'). The real culprit was another 'political' ecclesiastic and Tudor henchman, Bishop Fox of Winchester. The combination of State administration and a senior ecclesiastical role was the norm, not the exception, before 1530 – with the vital learned training provided by the two English universities a normal religious, not lay education. Indeed Wolsey's replacement More was the first chancellor who had not taken ecclesiastical orders for centuries, although the literacy and knowledge of Latin needed for such a role was more widespread among – now better-educated – secular personnel by the early sixteenth century so the Church monopoly was bound to be broken. That Henry chose to do this in 1529 did not reflect anti-clericalism as much as a desire to appoint someone that he could trust, with More arguably being seen as a 'King's man' who would obey orders in the same manner as Henry II chose Thomas Becket as chancellor/archbishop. Both were catastrophic mistakes and fatal to the recipient of the honour. The concept of a senior churchman putting his conscience above his duty to the lay power was an anomaly in the early sixteenth century; most of the bishops meekly accepted the 'Break with Rome' and only the notably austere, zealous Bishop Fisher refused to accept it as legal. There was far greater politicization, or courage, shown in 1558 when almost the entire episcopal bench refused to crown 'bastard' Elizabeth I as queen.

But had the growth of lay literacy, stimulated and symbolized by the invention of printing, accelerated previously restricted and containable anti-clerical feeling? Thus, did Wolsey's ambition, worldliness and amassment of lands and offices meet more criticism than had previous ecclesiastical excesses and make his position easier to undermine? There had been criticism of churchmen's unseemly worldliness for centuries, with 'low-level' satire of such men provided by both Chaucer and Langland in the late fourteenth century. Contemporary resentment of 'proud prelates' who lived like secular peers had fed into the recruitment of support for the Lollards, though this 'proto-Protestant' movement was much more minimal and marginalized by 1500 than in 1400. Such feelings against worldly clerics still re-surfaced from time to time due to specific abuses, such as the furore in London over an unjust gaoling and judicial killing linked to Bishop Fitzjames in 1514.[52] Discontent was undoubtedly stimulated by greater lay literacy and awareness of Biblical precepts about desirable Christian conduct – but was this only the concern of a small cultural elite such as Erasmus by the 1520s?

The evidence is unclear, but the growth of literacy, the ownership and use of books (often on Christian life), and interest in religious ideals among well-off laymen was greater in the early sixteenth century than previously and printing was spreading it faster than before. Until now, however, desire for reform had centred on discontented individuals living a more holy life themselves and setting a good example – within, not in defiance of, the established Church. The structure of the Church and habits of its personnel were not challenged. Such lay piety involved Sir Thomas More, famous for wearing a hairshirt and writing both biting social satire and polemics against heretics, and in her later life Henry VII's ultra-pious mother, Lady Margaret Beaufort, who lived a life like a nun in her widowhood after 1504.[53] There was also a greater degree of international exchange of ideas among the cultural elite, and hence suggestions for the improvement of Christianity by 'well-connected' writers – such as Erasmus himself, and in England More – could spread faster and further. These two were loyal if questioning Catholics, but the same intellectual process could aid those who proceeded beyond the legally allowable limits within current Church law. By the same reckoning, religio-political developments in Europe had a greater effect within England than they would have done earlier, aided by written propaganda that could be smuggled past the authorities, giving the intellectual as well as political developments in the early 1520s greater resonance. The writings of theological innovators, primarily but not only Luther, were known to be present in England in the early 1520s, and there was considerable alarm at the radical 'republic' set up by rebellious, theologically influenced peasants in Munster in 1524–5 as the ultimate outcome of Lutheranism. Doctrinal innovation could be seen as leading to anarchy and the overthrow of the social order sanctioned in the Bible if the 'lower orders' were allowed to take the lead; the proper leadership of reform lay with princes not presumptuous self-promoted theologians and populists. But until he found 'reformist' ideas useful Henry VIII had shown no interest in innovative religiosity; indeed he was to blame for allowing his protégé Wolsey to amass religious sees in the early-mid 1510s in defiance of canon law banning pluralism.

Prominent and vocal critics of clerical abuses within the framework of a 'loyal opposition' within the political elite or within the Church, such as More, were not a direct threat to papal power over the Church in England or the maintenance of the existing clerical order. Current orders of monks and clerics in lesser orders had indeed regularly been condemned for abandoning their forerunners' and founders' idealism in the medieval period, often by fellow-clerics who then went on to found their own 'reformist' orders to recapture the old zeal. This had been the tone of monastic reformers such as St Bernard of Clairvaux (d. 1153), virtual founder of the Cistercian Order, who had condemned the slothful, worldly life of the Benedictine Order and set up his new monasteries out in the 'wilderness' to keep his monks far from temptation and require hard labour of them. (This had duly created the great monastic houses in the remote Yorkshire dales, such as Fountains, Jervaulx, and Rievaulx, which provided invaluable social aid and employment and were to be Henry's most visible social and architectural victims in 1538–40.) Such regular 'renewal' of the Christian life was still visible in the early sixteenth century Church. Within England Bishop Fisher, ironically a leading victim of the Reformation, came within this tradition of zeal for reform of the monastic orders and a personal commitment to living the life of the Apostles. The most significant 1530s Continental equivalent of this was Ignatius Loyola. This tradition of 'renewal' in the Church to reassert spiritual vigour over sloth and greed was a part of medieval Christianity, though so far it had normally been within the acceptable bounds of setting up new Orders rather than defying papal authority. English kings had indeed taken a lead on occasion by founding new and even closing down (a few) (foreign-owned) monasteries, as Henry V, patron of the Observantines, had done.[54] But in the crucial dispute over the King's marriage in the late 1520s the only zealous contemporary monastic 'reformers' in England, in the Carthusian Order, strongly backed Queen Catherine and papal rights and so were seen as a political threat by Henry. Rather than serving as the vanguard for a reformed and pruned monasticism, they faced arrest and execution for defying the King and provided notable 'martyrs' in 1534–5. Did the round-up of 'impudent' monks who defied their King and put the international Church first in this crisis fatally alienate Henry from the monastic order as such, causing him to fall prey to insinuations that its members were all secret or potential traitors – or would their wealth have made them victims anyway?

(v) Reformist notions of the 'godly prince', personal ambition, and the annulment coincide for Henry VIII. What if all three had not coincided in the late 1520s?
If the Pope would not act, the logical substitute was the 'godly magistrate', the secular power – in national terms, the prince or king – acting for the good of his subjects (lay and clerical) out of his Christian duty. Henry VIII seems to have seen himself in this light, which pandered to his vanity as well as stimulating his Christian 'activist' idealism; and in his revealing first interview with the new imperial ambassador, Eustace Chapuys, on 28 October 1529 he said that Luther would not have taken drastic action against the Pope had the latter shown that he could reform the Church; as the papacy had shown itself unwilling it was up to him to act.[55] The question of papal authority over the matter of the divorce became linked to the more general question of royal as opposed to papal authority in the Church of England in the period 1527–3, at least in Henry's mind. The 'imperial' (as opposed to merely royal) authority that he claimed within England, a terminology in occasional use by him for over a decade, was now to be a legal

justification for rejecting papal authority over English kings, which he endeavoured to prove was a legal innovation absent from the early Church. Accordingly the King's envoys to Rome in autumn 1530 were told to search the papal archives to find proof of this, and to specify – with past papal bulls cited in support – that the imperial rank gave its holder the requisite legal autonomy. The theological arguments for reform led by the secular authorities was put by William Tyndale in his 'Obedience of a Christian Man', which the pro-reformist Anne Boleyn obligingly provided for Henry VIII. He said appreciatively that it was 'a book for all kings to read'.[56]

The close linkage of his theoretical royal rights as head of the Church of England, and his Christian duty to use this for reforming the Church of its abuses, to the personal issue of his divorce thus became inextricably connected for Henry. But the question must arise of whether he would have been pressing for this sort of legal autonomy without the impetus of his divorce. Would there have been a legal break with Rome – which did not mean a theological abandonment of Catholicism – without the divorce? The evidence suggests that Henry had an enhanced view of the office of 'King of England' and its legal rights, which included those over the Church, well before 1529.[57] Arguably, the traditional literary story of his early exemplar King Arthur as an 'emperor' – one who had militarily defied the authorities in Rome, albeit a secular ruler, Lucius Hiberius – added to this concept in his mind. Ironically, he had briefly sought out the office of Holy Roman Emperor itself in 1519. The orders to his ambassadors in Rome in 1530 to seek legal documentary proof of his autonomist rights preceded the 'Break with Rome' by three years, at a time when the issue of a quick divorce had not been made urgent by Anne Boleyn's pregnancy.

Given Henry's high concept of his office (and personal arrogance) and his determination to have his way in everything, it is quite conceivable that some other legal dispute with Rome's authority would have given him the urge to prove his point and show the Pope who was legally master in England. Incapable of backing down, he would then have proceeded to a legal break with papal authority sooner than submit or negotiate a 'face-saving' compromise for both sides. The existence of the economic wealth of the monasteries – required by their statutes to be loyal to the Pope – would put them in the 'firing-line' of a choice of masters, and provide a bold and 'reformist' minister with a source of wealth that he could offer to the King. It was a coincidence, but a lucky one for Henry, that Thomas Cromwell's recent role as an efficient administrative subordinate of Wolsey and his willingness to offer his services to Henry in 1529 provided the King with a ruthless and skilled political operator who had a similar vision to his of royal authority and a concept of how to bring it about by remodelling the entire

Church and secular government. Despite subsequent cynicism by his many detractors and later analysts, there is no reason to doubt that Cromwell had as sincere a vision of his future for a Christian state as More did and was more than the low-born, greedy, scheming adventurer that many thought him.[58] The concept of the King's supreme legal authority within his 'empire' aided Henry to do what he wished over marriage and seize the wealth of the monasteries, but it had contemporary 'reformist' ideological overtones to which Cromwell was attuned. Without him in a position of power, the 'Break with Rome' would have been less ideologically driven, might well have lacked the enthusiastic iconoclasm of the attack on 'abuses' of 1538–9, and would have lacked the (theological as well as diplomatic) flirtation with Lutheranism of the mid-late 1530s.

Henry boasted an interest in theology, but as far as his personal beliefs are guessable they seem to have been theologically conventional and conservative. He was 'reformist' in that he abandoned 'superstitious' ceremonies like 'creeping to the Cross' and worshipping saints, though his assault on the cult of St Thomas Becket would have owed much to the latter's 'treason' to Henry II. His zealous stripping of the rich and ornate shrines of the nations' saints in 1538–40 had an iconoclastic tinge in its actions and its explanatory propaganda, and was certainly carried out by enthusiastic and ruthless operatives, some of whom may have had puritanical 'reformist' motives. It was seen as 'purifying' religion – but it also served to acquire vast riches for the King at a time of threatened foreign invasion and a costly expansion of the Royal Navy. (Some monastic buildings were indeed to be demolished and used for building coastal fortresses, e.g. in Hampshire and Sussex.)

Was the idealistic tinge to the destruction a 'side-issue' to its practical usefulness n Henry's mind, if not Cromwell's? Even before Cromwell fell from power in 1540 Henry reverted to Catholic orthodoxy in matters of theology, as seen by the Act of Six Articles – the 'whip with six strings'.[59] Reformist bishops Latimer and Shaxton were dismissed and the 'Reformers' on the Continent were duly dismayed, Melanchthon in particular writing off the Henry of 1540–7[60] – though it is clear that very few people were prosecuted under the new legislation. Almost all of those rounded up in the diocese of London by the persecutory Bishop Bonner in the first flush of enthusiasm after Cromwell's fall were soon released, and a general pardon was issued. The radical theological allies of Cromwell's who suffered (led by Barnes) were all accused of being Anabaptists, i.e. extremists linked to the 1524–5 Munster radicals, not Lutherans.[61] This was a useful term of abuse, implying socially destructive anarchism as well as a specific heresy – much like Communism in the 1950s. Cranmer certainly thought Henry still favourable to reform throughout this period, and the King seems to have been less keen on unthinking orthodoxy than sometimes thought. Possibly too much has been made of the few 'high-profile' cases made much of by John Foxe in his subsequent martyrology, in which Henry assumed the role of a less applaudable Catholic predecessor of the heroic reformer Edward VI – Manasseh to his Josiah.[62] But he was notably obsessive about the danger of 'sacramentarians' who denied that the bread and wine used in the Mass became the body and blood of Christ, showing his Catholic orthodoxy on this crucial issue.

The rising level of expectations of the clergy and angry disappointment with the corruption of secular clerics and monks were a different matter from the endemic 'low-level' cynicism about clerical worldliness and grasping, lazy monks in Late Medieval England. This criticism had been widespread in the later fourteenth century and can be seen in Chaucer's *Canterbury Tales*. It had been one aspect of John Wycliffe's dramatic proposals for clerical reform – and the latter had involved threats of unilateral, nationalistic action if the Church in Rome did not reform itself. The 'Lollards' had been marginalized and were kept under firm control by Church action, backed by the machinery of State legislative and punitive powers, from the time of Archbishop Arundel in the 1400s; they were numerically small and powerless as of the early sixteenth century although the Lutheran outbreak in Germany and the spread of printing gave anti-clerical agitation new Europe-based impetus. There were at most only a few Lutherans in London in the 1520s; the danger to the Church would be if the State and Church authorities abandoned disciplinary control of agitation, which they did as Cromwell sought intellectual allies against the papacy in the early 1530s. The role of Cromwell as 'Vicar-General' and effective controller of censorship and 'police action' was vital, and with both Charles V and Francis of France hostile he was prepared to seek out European allies among the Emperor's Lutheran critics in the mid-1530s. Anti-imperial North German Lutheran states' ambassadors were invited to England, and English diplomatic requirements became entangled with the advantages of stirring up anti-clerical opinion in England to justify the draconian State action against its religious opponents. There was a relaxation of State supervision and banning of importing 'heretical' works under Cromwell; his targets were the 'seditious' deniers of the royal supremacy over the Church.

But the events of 1539–40 were to show that once the diplomatic usefulness of the North German princes was reduced and Henry was reconciled with Charles V, the King was prepared to abandon this potentially theologically suspect alliance. The crucial blow here was the lack of empathy

– indeed the open repulsion – that Henry felt towards the human symbol of this alliance, Anne of Cleves (sister of one of the leading Protestant princes in the lower Rhineland, Duke William of Julich-Cleves). For once, Thomas Cromwell gambled on a project without adequate assessment of the risks – in this case, checking the personal appearance of the new queen-to-be and ensuring that the King would find her suitable. The traditional story has it that Henry fell in love with an over-flattering portrait of Anne done for him by the painter Hans Holbein; and it appears that Anne's brother would not let the inspecting English ambassadors see Anne close to in strong light, for reasons of modesty.[63] As a result, Henry had a shock when he impulsively waylaid Anne en route to meet him in Kent by bursting into her chambers at Rochester in disguise – a variant on the 'courtly disguise' games he had used to play with Catherine of Aragon. The future queen was understandably bewildered and unable to respond graciously or coherently, and Henry found out what she actually looked like – though her sallow complexion, marked skin, and ungainliness would have been added to by her lack of fashionable clothes or manners. Unlike his first two wives, she was a 'provincial' from a minor court unused to Renaissance cultural accomplishments. Henry VII had insisted on checking Catherine of Aragon's appearance before she married his elder son in 1501 and found his fears to be groundless; in January 1540 Henry VIII was not expecting to find someone so plain and awkward and was appalled and furious. Nor did he cover it up, announcing 'I like her not' on the spot.[64] He tried to cancel the wedding, was persuaded to go through with it for diplomatic reasons, and when he still found Anne repulsive he found someone else to blame for the fiasco – Cromwell. Indeed, for once his minister seems to have been stumped for a solution, even when he was warned that he could be the scapegoat.[65] The marriage collapsed and the architect of it was executed, weeks after being elevated to an earldom (which shows that Henry still had confidence in him after the wedding). But had Anne been more attractive, would the Rhineland alliance and Cromwell have survived and Henry not turned against Lutheranism so dramatically in his theological settlement and executions of 1540–1? The fact that Norfolk and other conservatives could alarm the King with 'evidence' of Cromwell's protection of reformist thinkers with suspect theology suggests that Cromwell's lack of religious orthodoxy was more crucial than the Cleves marriage. His support for 'subversives' could imply a threat to royal control of religious life. But Cromwell was making financial arrangements for his household's livelihoods should he be arrested weeks before his fall, so he was aware of the risk. Henry could also change his mind after making initial arrangements for an arrest for 'heresy', as he showed towards his final wife in 1546. But Catherine

Parr was able to grovel to him in person – Cromwell, already in the Tower, could only do so by letter.

As with the falls of Anne Boleyn in 1536 and Catherine Howard in 1541, Henry shied away from a personal confrontation with his victim on 10 June 1540. Cromwell was hustled by arriving guards out of a Council meeting that Henry had not attended and could not defend himself to the King. The decisive charge seems to have been encouragement of heresy, with Cromwell's pro-Protestant foreign policy in Germany not cited in the list of accusations or swiftly abandoned. The notion of a drastic reversal of foreign policy with his fall has been exaggerated, as rapprochement with the Catholic emperor Charles was already underway without any sign of Cromwell resisting this; nor was Cleves abandoned. For that matter, the allegedly fierce Catholic 'reaction' at home only involved the execution of three 'heretics', with hundreds who were questioned later released. But Cromwell allowed himself to be 'smeared' by incautious approval for doctrinal innovation, and it was 1543 before Henry would again consider the latter (and then only in the liturgy). Apparently within months of his execution Henry was complaining that he had been tricked into ridding himself of his most loyal and competent minister.[66] But even if he had survived 1540, would Cromwell have been brought down for 'heresy' by Bishop Gardiner's next 'purge' in 1546?

Chapter Three

What if Henry VIII had been killed in the near-fatal tiltyard accident of January 1536?

The potential situation as of late January 1536

What if Henry had been killed in the tiltyard accident at Greenwich in January 1536 that preceded Anne Boleyn's miscarriage? Arguably, this accident precipitated the collapse of his second marriage in that the miscarriage – possibly due to the Queen's shock – removed her best chance of giving birth to a male heir and fulfilling her political purpose for Henry. He had already met his next wife, Jane Seymour, on a visit to her father's Wiltshire estate in autumn 1535, and occasional marital spats with Anne were becoming more frequent. His main potential European ally Charles V remained implacably opposed to recognizing Anne as queen or her heirs as rightful successors to Henry, so any child of that marriage ran the risk of imperial intervention on behalf of the disinherited Princess Mary. But would Henry's probable fascination with Jane have turned into a desire to remove Anne had she given him a son?

What if the King had been killed? He was only stunned in real life, but the weight of a horse falling on top of him added to his armour might well have killed him at a most inconvenient time for his regime. This made the danger to the regime worse than the King's two previous accidents, which had both preceded the separation from Catherine of Aragon. His clash with Suffolk in the tiltyard in 1524, when he accidentally left his visor open before galloping at his opponent and splinters went into his helmet narrowly missing his eyes, nearly gave him the real-life fate of Henri II of France in 1559 (who was fatally pierced by a splinter in the brain). In 1525 he stumbled while vaulting a ditch near Hitchin with a pole and fell head-first into a ditch, where the mud nearly suffocated him. In either of these cases, Mary would have succeeded unopposed (aged eight or nine); there was no available male kinsman to act as regent and Catherine, already governing for the King in his absence abroad in 1513, would have been the likeliest regent. The other potential threat of Henry dying early was in May 1538, when his already chronic leg-problem led to a blood-clot, which appears to have migrated to his brain as he was speechless for several days. Had he died then Edward VI would have succeeded aged seven months, with the need for a long regency as with the eight-month-old Henry VI in 1422 but no male kinsman as regent. The King's marriage to Jane Seymour, Edward's mother, followed Catherine's death so it was legitimate from the Catholic standpoint, unlike the marriage to Anne Boleyn in her predecessor's lifetime; Edward could not be called a bastard. In this case, there was no sign of any careful preparation for a regency with a will and regency Council 'in place' as the King lapsed into unconsciousness. A political struggle or uneasy compromise between Thomas Cromwell, the Duke of Norfolk, and Edward Seymour would have been likely, with precedent favouring Seymour as the baby king's guardian as his closest kin.

The principal actors, late January 1536
Indications are in 1536 that one party of nobles favoured proclaiming Mary as Queen,[1] partly from her being adult and partly out of conservative sentiment. The late Queen Catherine's backers, the male kinsfolk of her faithful ladies-in-waiting, and the conservative magnate and Yorkist descendant Lord Montague (son of Mary's ex-governess, Lady Margaret Pole), would have formed the nucleus of this group. Despite the loss of men such as Lord Dacre in 1536 and the Percy brothers in 1537 to execution they might have prevailed in a civil war, with Charles V sending imperial troops from the Netherlands; the destruction of conservative personnel and resources in the North after the 'Pilgrimage of Grace' need not have proved fatal to them. But if the crisis had occurred in January 1536, the rebellion would not yet have happened and so these centres of conservative sentiment would have been intact. Men such as the future rebel Lord Dacre could have been counted on to back any move to place Mary on the throne, if a prominent peer made an open declaration for this.

In the situation of January 1536, Henry would also have had a baby as his heir. The only 'legitimate' offspring he had by Parliamentary statute was his current wife Anne Boleyn's two-year-old daughter, Elizabeth, though his illegitimate son Henry Fitzroy was seventeen. (Fitzroy died of tuberculosis later that year, but his condition was not widely known at this time.) Anne Boleyn and her uncle the Duke of Norfolk – as the popular Fitzroy's father-in-law and potential backer, aware of his physical condition so not able to back his claim – would have proclaimed Elizabeth queen, with Anne as regent. (Arguably, if Fitzroy had not been in physical decline at this time Norfolk would probably have supported him as a near-adult claimant and far less contentious than the offspring of Henry's dubious marriage to a woman widely regarded by public opinion as a whore.) Fitzroy was too young and inexperienced to be regent even had he been in good health, which is not certain for this date.

What then? Probably Norfolk and Anne secure the person of Henry's disinherited elder daughter Mary (aged nineteen) to prevent a conservative revolt on her behalf by the partisans of Catherine of Aragon and opponents of the break with Rome. Again, it was lucky that the discarded but popular Catherine had died a few weeks before; if Henry had been killed in her lifetime her past decades as queen, her public support, and the number of noble courtier families whose members had served her meant that there would have been wide support for reinstating her and Mary and every chance of a rebellion or a coup. She was isolated at outlying manors in the Fens (Buckden, then Kimbolton) but not that far from London. Crucially, Catherine's remaining small group of female attendants and past Household loyalists could serve as a link to their menfolk in organizing her rescue. Nobles alienated from Cromwell – regarded as a low-born 'parvenu' – would have been likely to march on Catherine's residence (probably at this date at Buckden or Kimbolton) and proclaim her as regent for her daughter pending the latter's rescue. There were inevitable accusations that Catherine, aged fifty, had been poisoned by Anne Boleyn to resolve her as a threat to Elizabeth's succession, and Henry tastelessly refused to go into mourning (Catherine was at least his sister-in-law if not wife).

Thomas Cromwell, the King's Secretary and 'Vicar-General', as chief minister and organizer of the religious upheavals of the past few years, could have thrown his weight behind the pro-'Reform' Anne Boleyn in order to keep the recent reforms safe despite their poor personal relations. A coup on Mary's behalf would have inevitably ruined him for his attitude to the Princess' mother, with the nucleus of conservative nobles attached to Catherine's and Mary's cause hostile to Cromwell for his attacks on the monasteries. Anne was as committed to the importance of an English Bible and 'humanist' reform of the Church as Cromwell, was a patron of English and Continental writers of reformist tracts, and had links with moderate French reformers from the 1510s (dating back to her time as a lady-in-waiting to Henry's sister Mary, Queen of France in 1514–15). She believed in useful 'good works' as practical Christianity rather than being a devotee of traditional cults and ritual, unlike the religious approach of her predecessor as queen, and was interested in the written Christian word. A backer of the new Archbishop Thomas Cranmer for his approach to Church reform, she had a circle of reformist university-educated younger clerics, among them her own chaplains, including Hugh Latimer, Nicholas Shaxton, and Matthew Parker. However, her interests lay in the 'Erasmian' tradition of regeneration within the Catholic Church rather than with the Lutherans, despite the subsequent posthumous eulogy of her s a Protestant pioneer by Foxe. (See the analysis of the nature of Anne's reformist sympathies in Eric Ives' biography.) She was not as convinced of the need to abolish all the monasteries as Cromwell – she appeared to have been arguing against their complete secularisation in 1535–6.[2]

The even more cautious Duke of Norfolk, Anne's uncle and initial patron in the mid-1520s and now the government's leading general, was critical of Wolsey's power and wanted a reduction of Church influence in the 1520s, but was a traditional Catholic, totally opposed to Lutheranism and new ideas about the Bible, and reform in general. He supported the breach with Rome, was able to square his conscience with receiving confiscated monastic land from the King, but disapproved of Cromwell's increasing tolerance of and links with Lutherans. (He was supposed to have deplored the effects of the Erasmian 'New Learning'.) The other mainstay of the government was Henry's former brother-in-law and long-time social companion, Charles Brandon, Duke of Suffolk, widower of Henry's sister Queen Mary of France and allied with Norfolk in bringing Wolsey down in 1529–30. Suffolk's late wife Mary was a supporter of Catherine of Aragon – as were a number of the King's 'inner circle' of Gentlemen of the Privy Chamber, led by Sir Nicholas Carew, and senior aristocrats with less influence at court such as the Marquis of Exeter and Lord Montague. The latter two – the son of Edward IV's daughter Katherine and the grandson of the Duke of Clarence – also dangerously had claims to the throne. They could act on their own behalf or on Mary's in 1536, and in real life Henry had them executed for alleged plotting in 1538/9 (followed by Montague's mother, Clarence's daughter the Countess of Salisbury, in 1541). Norfolk and Suffolk had a joint interest in keeping them from staging a revolt on Mary's behalf, and would have had to secure their persons quickly if Henry had been killed.

Potential developments – the regency
The breach with Rome was now complete, and the adult male population had been forced to take an oath to the Royal Supremacy and accept the bastardization of Mary in Elizabeth's favour in 1534–5. The most prominent opponents, Sir Thomas More and Bishop John Fisher, had been thrown in the Tower, pressurized to abandon their opposition, and finally executed, and equally bloody examples had been made of a number of vocal monastic critics (most notably Richard Reynolds and his Carthusian colleagues). The victims were widely regarded as martyrs and Anne Boleyn blamed for their

deaths, the executions adding to the unpopularity of Henry's divorce. The accounts that Cromwell's intelligencers collected of treasonable criticism of the King's actions show that this extended across all social classes, though it was most vocal among the ordinary citizenry; 'Nan Bullen' was derided as a whore and accused in some circles of being a witch. There had even been an outburst of millenarian prophecies connected to the recent crisis, with Anne regarded as the principal agent of evil forces who were bringing about national disaster; Cromwell had had to make examples of the most vocal, such as the 'Nun of Kent' Elizabeth Barton in 1533. If anything untoward had happened to Henry it would have been seen as proof that the 'prophets' had been divinely inspired and God was punishing the adulterous King for destroying his wife and the Church.

Anne was certainly the most unpopular queen for centuries with her marriage widely regarded as illegal, which would not have been a propitious circumstance for her to assume the leadership of a regency government for a daughter whose right to the throne was disputed. 'Lady' Mary, held under guard at assorted isolated royal country residences north of London since 1529 and stripped of her royal rank and attendants at the divorce, had been reduced from her role as heiress, Princess of Wales, and titular head of the 'Council of the Marches' at Ludlow – in succession to the last two Princes, Henry's elder brother Arthur and uncle Edward V – to a royal bastard in a few years. She had even been forced to join her supplanting half-sister's household and subjected to threats from both Henry and Anne – although the 'humiliating' requirement to serve her half-sister was normal procedure for a royal bastard. Leaving Mary at large with her own household would have run the risk that her pro-Catherine servants or their allies would abduct her, to lead a rebellion or to flee to Charles V abroad. The permanently defiant Catherine of Aragon had died earlier in January 1536, with Henry and Anne distastefully celebrating the event, so no clique of conservative nobles could attempt to rescue her and reinstate her as queen – something that would have been widely supported. Conversely, however, Catherine's death meant that Henry could now rid himself of Anne to assuage public opinion or Catherine's nephew Charles V – without having to take Catherine back. He had apparently already been attracted by Jane Seymour on a visit to her family home in Wiltshire in late summer 1535, though it is unclear if she was under serious consideration as his next wife at this stage. The position of Charles V in being able to intimidate England over his relatives' treatment had strengthened with his sister's marriage to Francis of France, Anne's principal foreign supporter at the start of her marriage in 1533. Cromwell allegedly hinted to Charles' ambassador Chapuys at this time that Anglo-imperial reconciliation could entail Mary's restoration to the succession (presumably after Elizabeth),[3] but his attitude to religious reform and the hatred for him felt by pro-Marian nobles such as Montague and Exeter make it very unlikely that he would have risked backing Mary as an adult sovereign in Elizabeth's place in 1536. That would have won him Charles' support via Chapuys, but put his own position at risk as a governing clique of conservative 'Marian' nobles would have been likely to execute him as a scapegoat to appease the public in pro-monastic areas such as the North.

The likely attitudes of the great nobles, the potential rebels in the North, and Charles V

At Elizabeth's accession conservative magnates such as Exeter and Montague would have had every reason to resist the new regime and strike quickly against the unpopular Anne and Cromwell. The majority of the country seemingly regarded Mary as the legitimate heir, from the amount of criticism of the change in succession that Cromwell's agents noted. A plot could be expected to kidnap the Princess and acclaim her as queen. Much would depend on the efficiency of Cromwell's intelligencers to abort this, and the detailed evidence that exists of his agents' exhaustive investigation of every murmur of opposition to the King and Anne in the 1530s shows how extensive his network was. It would have been essential to bring Mary to London under guard, which could be done quickly as she was in a household (Elizabeth's) full of Anne's nominees not her own allies who might resist. It would be wise to pre-emptively arrest Exeter and Montague, potential claimants to the throne on their own behalf (as the sons of Henry VIII's aunt Catherine Plantagenet and of the Duke of Clarence's daughter Margaret Pole), and possibly other conservative peers.

Without aristocratic leadership for a revolt and with Mary herself under guard it is unlikely that a serious rising would have broken out, however much the accession of Elizabeth was resented. At most a minor outbreak might be expected well away from London, led by conservative peers loyal to Mary's cause. Fortunately measures had been taken since 1485 to reduce the numbers of retainers available to a potentially rebellious peer with the bans on 'livery and maintenance' – even if Henry VII may have been as keen to extract large fines from law-breakers as to end the law-breaking. Great nobles could still call on armed tenants, particularly on the Northern border with Scotland where there was supposed to be 'no king but a Percy'. The most powerful of the senior landed peers in England, the Duke of Buckingham, son of the rebel against Richard III and a royal descendant, had been executed in 1521 and his huge estates and armed affinity broken up. The most crucial figure in the more militarized North, the current Earl of Northumberland (Henry Percy), also 'Warden-General ' of the Marches and

so in command of the troops there, was Anne's former fiancé and would not
have resisted her regency. The junior Wardens of the Marches would obey
royal orders as long as Percy did so. Due to Percy's ill-health (he died later
in 1536) the effective military leader was his deputy, Lord Warden Henry
Clifford, head of the senior landed dynasty of Cumberland and
Westmorland. Luckily for the London regime at this juncture, he was a
pragmatic royal servant and an unpopular landlord who steered clear of the
'Pilgrimage' later in 1536; his conservative predecessor Lord Dacre had been
deposed and tried by Cromwell's orders for alleged treason in 1534. The
religious leader of the North, Archbishop Rowland Lee of York, was
antagonistic to Lutherans but not a noted religious conservative, appointed
as a safe and moderately reformist successor to Wolsey in 1531 with
Cromwell's support and unlikely to lead a revolt.

Any conservative rising against the new order would depend on the
initiative of local nobles or possibly gentry, and it is clear from the apparently
spontaneous rising in Mary's favour in 1553 that an unwelcome and 'illegal'
coup in London could not depend on the inevitable acquiescence of all the
leaders of local society. Elizabeth as queen in 1536 would have seemed as
unnatural as Jane Grey was in 1553. Later in real-life 1536 ordinary
Northern farmers and peasants, led by a small group of determined gentry
under Robert Aske, were to rally against the religious reforms without
waiting for leadership from the upper classes. This sort of action could not
be ruled out if it was suddenly announced that the King was dead by
violence – which the superstitious would have seen as Divine vengeance –
and Anne Boleyn's 'bastard' on the throne in the place of Mary. But the
catalyst in the 'Pilgrimage of Grace' that autumn was to be the bill for the
dissolution of the lesser monasteries, with the rumour that the larger ones
were next. The great Cistercian monasteries of Yorkshire had been the centre
of economic and social life for centuries and invoked fierce loyalty, and the
threat to their existence seemed to presage economic ruin quite apart from
being an 'impious' and 'heretical' innovation no doubt inspired by Lutheran
foreigners and the greedy court clique led by Cromwell. Accordingly, armed
resistance was quickly organized with the help of some of the abbots and
their local rural employees whose careers were under threat. It was carefully
presented as not being a rebellion against the lawful authority of the King,
but a 'loyal' protest to warn him about the designs of his wicked and
covetous ministers.

At this point, February 1536, the bill to dissolve all religious houses worth
less than £200 p.a. was only just going before Parliament. But Cromwell's
religious commissioners, led in the North by the notorious Richard Layton
and Robert Legh, had been touring the country since late 1535 assessing the

value of all the monastic houses and their contents so the populace was aware of what was underway. The rude comments that Layton and Legh made to Cromwell about the superstition and insolence of the Northern rural populace would also have reflected their personal contacts with the latter, which helped to build up resentment of the planned closures ahead of the outbreak of the 'Pilgrimage'. Rising taxes and the rumoured debasement of the currency were fuelling general discontent, and the exclusion of Mary from the throne could have sparked off the same sort of indignant local protests that generated the 'Pilgrimage' seven to eight months later – had the weather not dampened people's spirits. The threat to the monasteries and the recent royal killing of the Carthusian 'martyrs' and More and Fisher provided religious impetus for a movement, and if it had been centred on Yorkshire the likeliest member of the minor nobility to lead it was Thomas, Lord Darcy, a military veteran and commander of Pontefract Castle. Apparently the conservative Darcy, a man of punctilious honour unhappy at the royal divorce and infuriated at Mary's bastardization, had approached Emperor Charles' ambassador Eustace Chapuys in 1534 about kidnapping her from Greenwich and starting a rebellion on her behalf, and promised local aid for an invasion. As superintendent of the King's castles in Yorkshire in 1536 he was the only senior official to join the rebels, albeit under pressure, abused Cromwell roundly at his trial as author of the nation's woes, and was duly executed. Aged sixty-nine and in poor health, he would not have been a particularly dynamic rebel commander but his past record and current role suggests that he would have joined in if not initiated any Northern attempt to put Mary on the throne. But these men, as with the pilgrims later in the year, would have lacked experienced troops, weapons, or widespread noble support. Unlike Mary's rebels in 1553, they would not have had their candidate present to lead them in person. Their chances would have improved if the revolt had coincided with a rising in the south of England that kept the government occupied there, but that would have been unlikely unless Montague or Exeter had escaped attempts to arrest them. Given that Henry's accident occurred in mid-winter, it would have been risky for Charles V to send warships across the Channel from the Netherlands to assist the rebels in seizing a port in January or February.

The only outside assistance for a revolt would have come from Charles V, who could have sent a fleet from the Netherlands or Spain to assist a rising organized by his ambassador Eustace Chapuys (a strong partisan of Catherine and Mary since 1527) had he had a few weeks' notice. This intervention was more likely in April or May, and by that time the most senior dissident nobles would have been safely lodged in the Tower unless they had evaded capture. The best hope they had for success would have been if Chapuys had been able to have Mary 'rescued' from Elizabeth's household north of London and carried off to a safe place to act as focus for a revolt possibly by boat from Essex to the Continent. This would have necessitated quick action before Anne and Norfolk sent royal guards from London to seize her, and the suddenness of Henry's death would have meant that pro-Marian noblemen with the retainers and horses to use (e.g. Montague or Exeter) would have had to be in or near London at the time. Luckily for Anne, in April/May 1536 Charles was to be distracted by a dynastic dispute with Francis I of France over the duchy of Milan and was threatened with war against France. The new government would probably have survived its crisis of legitimacy provided that Cromwell could act fast and secure Mary and other leading opponents. If the rising had occurred in the North, Norfolk would have had to deal with it with whatever troops could be spared like he did that autumn – though if he had had to temporize any peace conference with the rebel leadership would have led to awkward demands that Norfolk proclaim Mary queen before they would disband.

It is even possible that, wary of Anne's poor public standing, the Dukes of Norfolk and Suffolk would have insisted that one of them take the lead in the regency Council, and announced that Mary was now regarded as heir after Elizabeth – reassuring conservatives who would think Elizabeth's early death probable. Suffolk had a dynastic claim as Henry's sister's widower, and his daughters Frances and Margaret were logically the next heirs to the throne after Henry's children. Norfolk, Anne's uncle and head of a large family, appears to have played a greater role in politics from the 1510s to 1547 and been more skilled at court intrigue, as well as having pronounced conservative Catholic views. He was also Henry's main military commander, and would have been vital in suppressing any riots against Elizabeth's accession or attempt by minor gentry not rounded up by Cromwell to proclaim Mary as queen. Norfolk's actions in the 1540s show him to be deeply opposed to Cromwell's pro–Lutheran stance and any idea of doctrinal reform in England, but he was a regime loyalist first even with Cromwell in the ascendant and he led Henry's troops against the 'Pilgrimage of Grace' (with whose aims he clearly had some sympathy) in 1536. He would have remained loyal to his niece's regime after Henry's death rather than backed Mary provided that the majority of the Council supported this course. (He was to abandon two successive nieces and queens in 1536 and 1541 when the King turned on them, but with Henry dead he would have had more freedom to support his own family.) As a pragmatist, he would also have had need of Cromwell's network of agents to prevent a rising by conservative magnates on Mary's behalf and so been unlikely to move against Cromwell at once. It is improbable that he would have preferred to work with his aristocratic rivals, Montague or Exeter, for Mary as queen rather than pass up the chance of his great-niece Elizabeth being the new sovereign with a long regency that he could lead. His commitment to Anne personally is less certain; he seems to have expected his female kinsfolk to act as his obedient agents and was accused of placing three attractive young nieces in succession in front of Henry as sexual bait. His estranged wife was to accuse him of having her assaulted, though she was possibly unreliable as a witness.

Cromwell and the monasteries

Would Cromwell have pressed on with the dissolution of the lesser monasteries, in order to provide land and loot for the gentry to win them over to the cause of reform and undermine the likeliest backers of Mary's accession, alarmed abbots? (The Carthusians had been the most vocal defiers of the 1534–5 legal measures, and in 1535 the Pope had excommunicated Henry.) Given that Anne herself does not seem to have been a firm supporter of dissolving the monasteries, the Queen and Norfolk would have had the combined 'weight' to argue that any dissolutions would increase popular anger and might cause dangerous rioting from the abbots' local allies.

Appeasing the monastic tenants and employees in isolated Northern rural areas, where the great Cistercian houses were the principal landlords and a source of social aid, would have reduced the chances of a serious revolt in Mary's name there. Anne seems to have preferred transferring the buildings and assets of any closed monasteries to charitable uses, probably as schools and hospitals, and a programme of this sort could have been commenced cautiously. The immediate abandonment of the bill for the wholesale closure of lesser monasteries would have reassured opinion, particularly in the North, though the sacking of Cromwell as 'Vicar-General' and the execution of a few of his senior commissioners as Lutherans would have done more. The pursuit of some 'necessary' reform by the closure of a few small houses with only a few occupants, or places where fairly serious allegations of indiscipline could be raised legitimately, was a different matter to Cromwell's wholesale plan for stigmatizing all the lesser monasteries as dens of laziness and corruption and using his commissioners to manufacture evidence of this. There had been occasional closures of smaller or poorly governed monasteries before, and one substantial 'rationalization' of the 'alien priories' by Henry V, and this sort of reform had precedents.

A limited number of closures could have been instituted among smaller institutions in 1536–7 following the first commission's visits, providing some lands to be distributed to loyal gentry and nobles, without raising alarm by a massive programme or exacerbating rumours that the larger monasteries would have been next. If no more closures had followed, alarm would have lessened in due course. Given the cynical and methodical approach of Cromwell to the realities of power, it would seem likely that some prize 'plums' of monastic estates would have been provided for important families who he was hoping to win over to his cause – such as the Howards (whose power was concentrated in Norfolk) and the Brandons, the dynasties of the Dukes of Norfolk and Suffolk. In real life, the theologically conservative Duke of Norfolk and the other 1540s 'Anglo-Catholic' leader marginalized by Protector Somerset, Cromwell's lieutenant Thomas Wriothesley, might have cavilled at 'Lutheran heretic' theology but never objected to receiving and keeping confiscated abbeys for themselves. Their large appetites may suggest that the sacrifice of some larger abbeys to these courtiers would have been a likely move for a 'second stage' of closures in due course – but not necessarily a total closure of all the monasteries. Was it the 'Pilgrimage of Grace' that led to that drastic solution, with the King now convinced that too many abbots were plotting his downfall? Did the rumours of a total closure that were around in the North of England in 1536 reflect the reality of what was planned even then, or just exaggerated boasts by those Cromwellian commissioners most hostile to the monasteries as an institution? Possibly if the King had died suddenly after his accident in January 1536 the resulting regency would have been too cautious to go ahead with more closures, whether it was Anne, Cromwell, or Norfolk in the 'driving seat' of policy-making.

Given Cromwell's immense unpopularity only his usefulness as the government's effective chief of intelligence – vital to prevent a conservative plot to rescue Mary – would have saved him from immediate sacrifice in 1536. Like Oliver Cromwell's arrested chief of intelligence, John Thurloe, in 1660, he would have had to use his possession of embarrassing information about his enemies and his usefulness as the 'spymaster' to secure his immediate safety. But his Lutheran connections were anathema to Norfolk and a number of other senior figures, he was disliked by the nobility at large as an 'arriviste', and he was the focus of popular resentment at the changes to centuries of religious practice. He was also the leading actor in the victimization of More and Fisher, and if the King had died in a tilting-accident in January 1536 this would have seemed to the superstitious to be Divine vengeance for killing such holy men. Handing over Thomas Cromwell for an ostentatious public execution would have been an obvious way for the new government to gain some popularity, and once the immediate threats of revolt and invasion were over Cromwell's position would have been under serious threat. As the 'King's man', taken on from Wolsey's entourage with no important family or noble patron to back him up, Cromwell would have been in a difficult position and had to rely on Anne for protection.

The regency's policies

Anne's attitude to Cromwell's ideas for a German Lutheran alliance to counter Emperor Charles are unknown, and his proposed attacks on 'superstition' in public worship by destroying the Church's leading shrines may have been less offensive to her than to court and local gentry conservatives. This part of his religious programme might have survived easier than the closure of the major monasteries, provided that it did not cause immediate riots as royal commissioners started despoiling shrines. The government would have needed the silver and gold ornaments involved to melt down for coin, particularly if more troops had to be raised and paid to deter Emperor Charles from invading. Anne is unlikely to have been able to save Cromwell from his aristocratic enemies once the need of his services for security was over.

If the regency had still gone ahead with the complete abolition of the lesser monasteries in 1536–7, rumours would have started about the likely fate of the greater institutions. An attack on 'superstitious' shrines would have had a similar effect in warning the conservative peasantry and minor gentry that their traditional religion was under threat, even if Cromwell had been executed and any Lutherans invited to London by Cromwell expelled. (The 1536 rebels were to demand the return of religious festivals as well as of monasteries.) But Norfolk and Anne are likely to have been more flexible than the stubborn Henry in pulling back at the first signs of any rising in the North – if they could not suppress the latter at once, anyway. Even if there had not been a rising in Mary's name at Elizabeth's accession, the religious rising could have been linked by conservative gentry like Darcy to Mary's cause as the legitimate queen in place of the daughter of the 'whore' Anne Boleyn. By the autumn of 1536 Northumberland, supreme commander on the Borders, was dying and Lord Clifford would have had to bring in the Border troops and loyalists' tenants to fight the rebels in association with an advance by Norfolk from London. But if the majority of the nobility had rallied to the Crown and been bought off with promises by Norfolk or by Cromwell's execution, he should have been able to muster enough support to put down the revolt.

What if Cromwell and Anne between them had kept enough of the religious reform programme to lead to spontaneous – or organized – protests that spiralled into a revolt? Would a serious 'Pilgrimage of Grace', linked to Mary's cause and with the threat of Charles V sending troops to join in, have been defeated by Norfolk militarily? He did not have enough troops to do it in real life and had to make concessions to persuade the pilgrims to disperse, then attacking once their leadership was isolated. If he had been fighting on behalf of a dubiously legitimate infant queen the cause of an older 'legitimate' half-sister could have attracted more support from the gentry and nobles. Aske could have been joined by more peers, even if Exeter and Montague had been executed in spring 1536 with the government's action preventing a rising then. The worst danger would have come if Exeter and/or Montague had been able to flee abroad in time to escape arrest, as they were natural allies for Charles V and would have been able to inform him of the state of aristocratic opinion and the chances of more nobles deserting the isolated regency government in case of an invasion. They were less likely to have been recognized as rightful monarchs, given that the prior claim belonged to Mary; both were older than her and married, but Exeter's son Edward, born c. 1530 (a real-life potential husband for Mary in 1553), could have been proposed as Mary's husband if the Emperor invaded on her behalf to rally the conservative nobility to her cause.

Having bought off ultra-Catholic lords such as the Percies (leaders of a 1537 rising in real life) and Dacre with a promise to stop the dissolution of the monasteries, and thus prevented a civil war on Mary's behalf, Norfolk could have insisted that the regency carried out his promises – and thrown Cromwell into the Tower. The execution of the unpopular 'upstart' Cromwell would have satisfied a large sector of the opposition to Henry's reforms. Would Anne not have been able to save Cromwell in the face of her need to halt rebellion?

Doctrinal reforms would have halted at the position they were at in 1535 – the breach with Rome would have stayed in place, with religious reform stuck at 'English Catholicism' purged of some of the worst abuses. Possibly the attack on some greater shrines, to strip them of treasure that the government could use, would have proceeded in the late 1530s or early 1540s within the aegis of 'Erasmian' internal Catholic reform under Anne's organization. Practically, seizing the shrines' treasures would have gained finance for the government. Anne would have been assisted in her endeavours for a more 'practical' and philanthropic form of Church organization by Cranmer and her younger acolytes, with government propaganda emphasizing the Queen's devotion to good works and the poor (a mainstay of the posthumous appreciation of her role by Foxe). The buildings and other resources of confiscated monasteries would have been ostentatiously used for schools and hospitals, no doubt plastered with the Queen's name as their patron as with the later real-life 'Edward VI Grammar Schools'. Unlike in real life, there would have been no large-scale sale of monastic property to the landed gentry and nobility – and probably far less architectural destruction and pillaging of those places that were closed.

Anne and Norfolk would have been uneasy co-operators, but had too much common interest in the safety of their family and the regency to fall out. Anne would have had to put her enthusiasms for reform 'on hold' apart from attacks on those abuses that could be carried out without sparking off another rebellion. In due course, with the regime stable and a probable alliance with Francis I's France where she had been educated and which had no family link to Princess Mary, further measures could have been taken cautiously. Any intrigues by abbots in favour of Mary or links to Charles V via his meddling diplomats would have been an excuse to execute them and close their monasteries as centres of 'abuses', but a wholesale closure of all monasteries would have been unlikely in case of another rising. Mary's convenient poisoning as a rival to Elizabeth would have been risky – it is unclear if there were any real-life attempts to poison her on Anne's behalf – and the Emperor's interest in her fate meant that once he was at liberty to invade England by c. 1538 she would have been a valuable counter or hostage. Any new treaty with Charles would have entailed negotiations concerning her status and safety, and it might have been found prudent (as considered in real-life discussions in 1536) to return her royal status and a place in the succession. The latter would have been popular and have reassured public opinion, and conservative peers could have consoled themselves as to the chances of Elizabeth not surviving to adulthood.

Marrying Mary off to a minor Continental prince, in alliance with either France or the Empire depending on which rival was England's current ally, would remove her from the country but risk her and her husband invading England in case of a subsequent break in diplomatic relations. The Dauphin was already married to Catherine de Medici and no other French princes were available except one brother who died young; an Italian prince might have sufficed to remove Mary from the nearer part of the Continent. It is possible that the Emperor would have demanded her as the bride of his eldest son, Philip – born in 1527, and eleven years her junior – as his price for abandoning an invasion, despite the difference in ages. She would then be the heir to England along with her husband, giving the alarmed Francis I of France every reason to ensure that Elizabeth stayed on the throne and had children.

The English government would not have the amount of stonework from the dissolved monasteries for new coastal fortresses that it did in reality. The new line of southern coastal defences built in 1538–9 found the stone from local monasteries invaluable, e.g. that of Beaulieu and Titchfield for the chain of forts around the Solent and Portsmouth and that of Battle for Camber Castle. But some new programme of coastal fortification would have been necessary in the insecure circumstances of the late 1530s, and the loot from sacked shrines could hire troops. Unable to attack the leading monasteries for fear of a revolt or as a result of a 'climb down' when initial closures caused riots, the government would have needed an alternative source of funds for militarization and land to buy support. They might thus have been in a weaker position to resist invasion than Henry was in 1538–9. However, in real life the ominous reconciliation of Charles and Francis did not lead to invasion, and even if Charles had refused English approaches and insisted on Mary being made queen as his terms for peace he need not have attacked. A cautious ruler with many domestic and foreign problems, he would have been unwilling to commit large forces to an expedition with the Turks (in Hungary and Tunisia), Francis, and the Lutherans all possible threats once he had sent his main fleet to the English Channel or even removed himself to Brussels or Antwerp to supervise an invasion. Anne's government would have had need of German Lutheran alliances as Henry did in real life, and the priority of national security made Norfolk's conservatives accept such talks and/or a more tolerant attitude to foreign 'heretics' visiting or proselytizing in London in 1538–40. Also, the advantages of inertia would be on the English side, though they would have been tied to alliance with France and might even have had to return Calais if Francis I insisted on it.

Once the new government had survived securely for a decade or so, would Anne have outmanoeuvred her uncle – possibly with her brother Lord Rochford as her chief adviser, or ambitious pro-reform young nobles like the Seymour brothers and John Dudley? Rochford was close to his sister, and in 1536 was to be accused of resorting to desperate measures – even incest, an unlikely charge – to back up her cause by getting her pregnant. His wife Jane (Morley) was also active in court politics, and in real life she was to be accused of betraying both him and later Catherine Howard to Henry VIII. (There is a possibility that her bad reputation was exaggerated later.) The Queen would have been the main dispenser of court patronage, even with an absence of a male monarch and so no Privy Chamber gentlemanships to bind the younger nobles and aspirant gentry personally to the sovereign.

The real-life leading conservative at court in the 1540s, Norfolk played a major role in bringing down Cromwell and his Lutheran alliance, used his niece Catherine Howard to renew a Howard family link to Henry and then abandoned her to save his career, and allied to clerics such as Stephen Gardiner against Church reform. Any attempt by the blunt and unscrupulous Norfolk to domineer at the Privy Council would have led to factions coalescing against him, and Anne was capable of lending them assistance in which role she could have ended up supporting a more liberal approach to religious conformity.

Anne would have been equally tempestuous with her uncle, as in reality in early 1536, as with the King – though dependent on his support during the years of military threat to England. If she had seemed to be resisting his advice he was capable of plotting to have her arrested and packed off to a nunnery, which would have been popular in the country. In due course a power-struggle between them would have been probable, with potential rivals of the Howards rallying to the Queen. Her personal clique would have included her brother, her father (if he was still alive), and her close retainers – the men disgraced or killed by Henry as her 'lovers' in real-life 1536, such as Norris. The Seymour brothers, Edward in particular a useful military commander, may have had to be forgiven for encouraging the King to favour their sister in 1535–6, and John Dudley and William Parr were other important younger court figures who could be expected to oppose the Howard dominance. Given Norfolk's abrasive character, there could even have been a split in the large Howard family.

Due to Norfolk's religious views he would have been opposed by Cranmer, who would have had to be preserved from conservative wrath in 1536–7 but as the cleric who had married Henry and Anne and legitimated Elizabeth would have had a strong stake in the regime. Cranmer was cautious on acting for reform under the conservative Henry but proceeded more openly once the firmly Catholic King was no longer an obstacle in 1547, so he could have been equally constrained while Norfolk was the leading player in the regency but gained confidence to tackle 'abuses' and patronize reforming clerics once Anne could move against her uncle. Anne's own religious protégés, e.g. Hooper and Shaxton, did not progress beyond Catholicism until the mid-1540s in real life; they could have been equally open to 'reformist' influence once Norfolk's veto had been removed. The abolition of the remaining monasteries and then the assault on the chantries could have proceeded in the later 1540s, a major flood of land and other property serving to gain wealth for the Crown and assets to be sold off to gain support, though from her earlier attitude Anne could be expected to make better philanthropic use of this than Henry or Somerset did.

The 'caveat' to this is that Anne had been brought up in the 'Erasmian' tradition of reform within Catholicism in the 1510s and 1520s, and even when her ultra-conservative uncle lost influence could have proceeded cautiously. There were sound practical reasons for seizing monastic and/or chantry properties, but in doctrinal terms the reformers might have had to rest content with promotion of an English Bible and lax enforcement (or repeal?) of the laws against 'heretical' books. Anne had shown no interest in replacing the Mass in the 1530s, and the doctrinal position of real-life 1540–7 thus been that of her regency government – though probably without Henry's occasional assaults on heresy. The most conservative bishops, particularly Gardiner, were not her natural allies.

Once Norfolk had been outmanoeuvred and retired Rochford, Dudley, and possibly the Seymours would have been in the ascendant. Norfolk's eldest son, Surrey, as the leading young military commander of the regime (assisting France at war with Charles in the mid-1540s?), would have been as arrogant and contentious as in real life and inclined to boast about his importance, so his forcible removal is possible. Surrey could have been accused of claiming a right to the throne if the sovereign died, as his heraldic pretensions infuriated Henry in real-life 1546, and once Anne had lost her need of Norfolk the pretensions of the Duke's son could have provided a useful catalyst for cutting the family's influence. The socially and religiously radical policies of Edward Seymour as Lord Protector in 1547–9 would not have taken place, as he was no more than one of a number of younger nobles with a 'stake' in the regime.

The adult reign of Elizabeth I: changes from reality
Anne would have been in charge of the regime until the precocious Elizabeth was at least eighteen, as even Henry VIII had needed his grandmother Margaret Beaufort in 1509 until his eighteenth birthday. Thereafter, from September 1551, Elizabeth would have been effective ruler but still dependent on her mother and Cranmer on policy-matters. Her probable tutors would have included the rising Cambridge scholar John Cheke, in real life selected for her brother by Henry, as well as Roger Ascham. As Anne's former chaplain, Matthew Parker would have been in a good position to succeed Cranmer as Archbishop (c. 1555/60?) instead of having to wait out Mary's reign as in real life. It is possible that the real-life theological advances away from the Mass of the late 1540s would have occurred in the early years of Elizabeth's adult reign, with her more open to new ideas than Anne.

Would either Seymour or Dudley have emerged as chief minister in the 1550s, given their commitment to 'reform' Protestantism, and carried out reforms in line with the rest of the Edwardian programme? And Dudley's protégé William Cecil emerged as the secretary and senior bureaucrat? Presumably the effective men of business who served successive Tudor regimes of varied religious hue, such as Paget and Paulet/Winchester, would have been on the Council, along with the ruthless time-server Lord Rich – and the conservative Wriothesley, a useful assistant to Norfolk in the 1540s, would have been eclipsed once he had fallen and religious reform had resumed. In real life Dudley was a more effective politician, and a more conciliatory head of the Council of State in 1549–53, than Seymour was and the latter's pretensions and miscalculations led to his overthrow. Seymour's importance was also substantially boosted during 1537–47 as he was the oldest uncle of the next king and so, even when Jane Seymour died, a likely 'power-broker' in his nephew's reign. He would have lacked this advantage under Anne Boleyn's regency, and had to rely on his military expertise and his support for ecclesiastical reform to increase his influence. He would have been a likely recipient of Anne's patronage as a commander more open to her influence and control than her uncle, probably ending up as the principal general of the regime by the late 1540s – though the French alliance would have meant that Henry's real-life war for Boulogne in 1544 was less probable than an anti-Habsburg war in the Netherlands.

Would Dudley have sought to encourage the friendship of his third son Robert and the Queen, in order to make his son consort and secure his power at court? The older sons, John (who died in the Tower following his father's execution in real life) and Ambrose, would probably have been married off for dynastic advancement as in real life but Robert, nearer to Elizabeth in age and possibly well known to her even by 1553, might have been promoted by Dudley as a suitable consort if it seemed that foreign princes were baulking at marrying a queen of dubious legitimacy. Elizabeth would have needed to marry someone to keep the Tudor dynasty in power, and if there had been trouble over her foreign prospects Anne might then have hesitated at the idea of a husband from her own Howard kinsfolk on account of rival families' jealousy. The logical Howard choice was Anne's uncle Norfolk's grandson and eventual heir Thomas, fourth Duke of Norfolk (born 1536), whose father, the Earl of Surrey, would not in this scenario have been executed for treason in 1547 but still been a prominent courtier and poet into the 1550s.

Elizabeth would not have had the trauma of her mother's execution and her father's sporadic disfavour or the episodes of the Thomas Seymour affair in 1548 and the stay in the Tower in 1554. It is legitimate to speculate that her extreme mistrust of potential rivals in her time as queen owed much to her early experiences, when she had been closely questioned by the Council about her part in Seymour's politically dangerous flirtation with her in 1548 and had nearly been executed for her suspicious attitude to the February 1554 Wyatt revolt. Without these episodes she might well have been a more equable personality, though still acutely aware from an early age of the ebb and flow of intrigue at court as its nominally presiding queen. Even as queen from the age of two, she would not have been able to marry whom she liked – Robert Dudley included. The question is whether Anne would have been in favour of or been able to attract a foreign prince, presumably a younger son of a major dynasty who had little chance of succeeding to his family's crown and so uniting England with his country, as the consort. No French prince was near Elizabeth's age, with Henri II's eldest son born in 1544 and second son born in 1551.

A Lutheran son of Gustavus I from Sweden was possible as the 'parvenu' Vasa dynasty had no reason to avoid an alliance with a queen of dubious legitimacy. Prince Eric, nearest Elizabeth in age, was heir; his younger brother John was a likelier choice. Had either match been considered, the princes would have proved as much of a problem as Lord Darnley was to be to Mary Stuart given their mental instability; John had a violent temper but Eric was to turn into a paranoid homicidal eccentric who was deposed in 1568. Alternatively, what about a Saxon prince? Anne might have preferred a Swede or a minor North German Lutheran prince as consort to a Dudley, whether or not the latter were unpopular and intrigued against by court rivals, due to the fear of the Dudley family usurping too much power. The execution of John Dudley's 'parvenu' father Edmund in 1510 was cited against them in real life, his successful operation of Henry VII's ingenious fiscal schemes for mulcting the nobility of money having won the family enemies among court families. The Duke of Norfolk's arrogant son Surrey would have included Dudley among the targets of his complaints against jumped-up 'parvenus' who needed to be dealt with, and if Surrey had not been executed (as in real life in 1547) he would duly have been Duke of Norfolk from his father's death in 1554 and asserting his rights at his cousin Elizabeth's court. Without the marriage of Jane Seymour to Henry VIII, her brothers Edward (Duke of Somerset in real life) and Thomas would have been without that crucial bonus to their political rise in the 1540s and the more politically skilled Dudley could have outmatched them.

Elizabeth and either Robert Dudley or a German/Swedish prince could have been married in the early 1550s – and had children to continue the Tudor dynasty. The Queen's regime might have been at risk of Charles V aiding Mary in a Franco–Spanish/imperial war in the 1550s, assuming that Mary was available at the time and out of England and that Anne's French alliance had dragged England into the war, but the peace of 1559 would have ended that threat.

Scotland
The death of James V of Scotland would have left the Northern kingdom under a week-old girl as in real life. But there would be no male English heir to marry to Mary Stuart, and so no possibility of a Union of Crowns unless instead of Mary an older brother had survived to succeed. There would thus be no 'Rough Wooing'. Henri II of France would have been Anne's ally against the Empire in succession to his father Francis I from 1547, so not at war with England over Scotland in the later 1540s. But the French leadership were still capable of pursuing its own plans for a Union of Crowns with Scotland by marrying Mary Stuart to the Dauphin.

If the English regime had backed a 'Reformation' in Scotland against the regency of Marie de Guise in the 1550s it would have caused Anglo-French tension, or added to existing tension over the engagement of Mary to Francis II. Anne might have put forward a male Howard relative to marry Mary Stuart, perhaps Mary's real-life potential husband Thomas Howard, 4th Duke of Norfolk, born in 1536 and so six years Mary's senior. Henri, not wanting England to swallow up Scotland and disapproving of the reforms being forced on Scottish Catholics, might then have encouraged Marie de Guise to arrange Mary Stuart's marriage to his son and heir Francis to counter English power, with the bonus that if Elizabeth died childless Mary could be made Queen of England as a French client. The English government could not abandon the French alliance in retaliation for this double-dealing, as the Empire was linked to Anne's late enemy Catherine of Aragon and could back Mary Tudor or (if she had married abroad) her children in a war. The death of Francis II in 1560 and Mary Stuart's return to Scotland would have been a relief for England; and as in real life Elizabeth would have been encouraged to marry Mary safely to an English client.

Elizabeth would have been England's longest-serving sovereign in this scenario, ruling from January 1536 to March 1603 – sixty-seven years.

Chapter Four

Other possibilities to be considered for Henry VIII's reign – three queens survive for longer, or a different queen in 1538/40

(i) What if Anne Boleyn had given Henry a son or more daughters?

The timing of the pregnancy and marriage, 1532–3. Inconvenient?

Henry VIII had gambled that Anne would give him a son where Catherine had failed, and had appropriate hopes that their first child would be a boy. A rash astrologer predicted that the child expected at the time of their marriage would be a son,[1] no doubt hoping for due reward and prestige if he was proved right. Taking no chances about arguments concerning the baby's legitimacy, Henry arranged for his marriage to Anne (?January 1533) and her coronation to be speeded up, probably carrying the former out as soon as he heard she was pregnant. The blocked papal annulment that would legitimize the marriage could not be hurried up, so instead he arranged for English constitutional law to take precedent over Roman canon law. It was now the King and his clergy within the realm who decided such matters, not Rome, and a patriotic and obedient Parliament duly carried all the necessary legislation into effect. Thus once the Archbishop of Canterbury, now his ally Thomas Cranmer who as a Cambridge theologian had backed the rights of English over Roman canon law, ruled in Henry's favour the King's first marriage could be counted as dissolved. It would have been more questionable if the elderly Archbishop Warham, who backed Catherine, had not conveniently died in 1532 but had had to be dismissed; the last Archbishops to be removed had been Thomas Fitzalan (Arundel) and Roger Waldby, for political reasons as the opponents of the current kings, in 1397–9.[2] Warham had been holding up the annulment within England in 1531–2,and could have been expected to keep up his opposition; and there was strong Council opposition to proceeding with the marriage to Anne, led by the Duke of Suffolk (married to Henry's sister Mary, with their son and two daughters available as alternative heirs to the throne). Conservative peers such as Lord Dacre (future leader of the Pilgrimage of Grace in 1536) made threats in the Lords, though these were less likely than court pressure to influence Henry.

There was another reason for delay in 1532–3, which Anne's pregnancy ended. There was a chance that Henry's foreign ally Francis I might yet prevail on the Pope to grant the annulment at that point; this seems to have caused Henry to delay the legal procedure within England where the Parliamentary actions of autumn 1531 had cleared the way to proceed. Instead of a smooth, continuing legal procedure to put the power of annulment in Henry's hands and then a grand marriage to Anne once the legal mechanism was in place, Henry had to rush it through and marry in secret once Anne became pregnant. The situation had not been straightforward for her before the pregnancy expedited matters, as in spring 1532 her father, Thomas Boleyn, Earl of Wiltshire, and her uncle Norfolk were said to have been opposed to a quick marriage.[3]

Indeed, in July 1532 there was a brief panic over a story (leaked to Catherine's partisans) that Anne's previous admirer, Henry Percy, Earl of Northumberland,[4] had been secretly but legally contracted to marry her – as with Edward IV and Eleanor Butler's arrangement, this could be regarded as invalidating any subsequent marriage to another party. Fortunately for Henry, this scion of the once-formidable clan of Northern warlords was a timid and submissive character who obediently swore to Henry's investigators that there had been no such contract. (He later attended Anne's trial and voted to condemn her as the King wished, allegedly at the cost of a fatal breakdown afterwards.) Had he held out that Anne had been his legally contracted fiancée, had Warham been alive to back him in 1532–3, and had Suffolk and Princess Mary had more court support the Boleyn marriage would have been in serious trouble – at least until Anne became pregnant. Ominously, she and Henry had already been quarrelling in 1531 over her determined attitude to the obstructive Princess Mary, Henry's fifteen-year-old daughter, who refused to accept her bastardization. Henry, always touchy of his dignity, complained that Catherine had never dared to shout at him like Anne did.[5] He was still, however, in love with Anne, and prepared to acknowledge her future role as his queen in the decorative scheme for Whitehall Palace (as extended after its confiscation from Wolsey) in 1531–2; all these problems were unlikely to have halted his second marriage.

Anne becoming pregnant in late November/December 1532 was the clinching factor. Had she not been pregnant in early 1533, Henry could have proceeded with less haste then and had the marriage carried out formally by Cranmer as Archbishop of Canterbury once his papal recognition had arrived in late March. The fact that his marriage was not in public – it was probably carried out in Whitehall Palace c. 25 January – would lead to rumours that it had not taken place at all and even the ever-vigilant foreign ambassadors did not hear of it for some weeks. Indeed, Henry himself originally preferred to carry it out publicly in the presence of his ally Francis in Calais during the 'summit' that he, Anne, and the French King held there in October 1532 – thus binding Francis to support it in the face of probable papal and imperial fury. The clever move of tying the French King to being complicit would have improved Henry's international position and reduced the risk of the Pope retaliating as now Clement could hardly condemn Henry for defying him without punishing his ally too, quite apart from keeping the ceremony public and undeniable but avoiding the likely riots against the 'whore Nan Bullen' if it was carried out in England. The papacy needed France, a valuable political force in Italy even after it finally lost control of Milan at the battle of Pavia in 1525, as an ally against the Empire more than it needed Henry. Thus in 1533 the papal–French alliance was to be cemented by the marriage of the Pope's niece Catherine de Medici to Francis' son the Dauphin, at Marseilles.

The formal Parliamentary legalisation of the ban on Church court appeals (such as Catherine's) to Rome and the arrival of papal recognition of Cranmer as Archbishop both took place late in March 1533, and court rumours reaching the imperial ambassador Chapuys and others spoke of Henry marrying Anne later that spring.[6] There was no confirmation for weeks that the marriage had already taken place. Indeed, once the news did emerge there was confusion over who had been the celebrant – possibly Rowland Lee, Bishop of Lichfield, or an Augustinian friar called George Brown as Chapuys heard – and who had attended. It was supposed to have taken place in a chamber over the Holbein Gate, not a consecrated chapel, and Catherine's partisans plausibly claimed that the conscientious priest had asked if Henry had received papal approval[7] and the King gave an evasive or lying answer. To Catholic partisans for decades to come, the marriage was a fraud and Elizabeth a bastard – which was to be an important political weapon against her during Mary I's reign and into the 1570s. A public marriage at Calais, reluctantly recognized by the impeachable orthodox French King, or in a chapel/cathedral in England and performed by Cranmer as Archbishop, would have been less easy to attack. Elizabeth's detractors would have had to fall back on the argument that the legal breach with Rome was illegal and the King of England and his clerical appointees had no right to be supreme in canon law matters – and the less scrupulous Catholics would have had to rely on the possible implications for her legitimacy of her mother's alleged adultery (revealed in 1536).

Elizabeth – and other potential heirs by Anne Boleyn. The possibilities of different outcomes to events in September 1533 – April 1536
The birth of Elizabeth at Greenwich on 7 September 1533 was an embarrassment for the King, though he put a brave face on it, paraded the baby, and claimed that he was satisfied that with God's help sons would follow.[8] To Henry's opponents, the birth of another daughter after all his efforts showed that God had punished him for his unjust and illegal treatment of Catherine.[9] If Elizabeth had been a boy as her parents hoped, the arguments for accepting the *fait accompli* of Henry's second marriage and the security implied by a male heir would have been overwhelming for most domestic and foreign critics. Henry's daughter Mary would have found it hard to hold out against recognizing the claims of her half-brother as heir at the time, even if she still maintained that he was a bastard, due to the circumstances of his birth and would have had reduced support from the English nobility and from Emperor Charles out of 'realpolitik'. It was easier to deny the claims of a new female heir in 1533–6, particularly as she was an infant and her succession ahead of a near-adult rival would mean a long regency under Boleyn control.

Had Elizabeth been a boy, her position in the line of succession would have remained strong – indeed invulnerable – even if Anne Boleyn was subsequently disgraced or died; she rather than any son of a subsequent royal marriage would have been the heir to 1547 and then king, though with a legal taint over her legitimacy such as that which from now on affected Mary. That legal question mark did not prevent Mary being regarded as Edward's heiress in 1547–53 and greeted with widespread public support by nobles, gentry, and populace (Protestants included) in defying the usurpation of Jane Grey in July 1553; the legal question about the legitimacy of Henry and Anne's marriage would have been of even more minor import for the new king after 1547. Mary never challenged Edward VI as her legitimate sovereign, even when he put pressure on her to renounce her religion. Her deference to her brother – the natural way of things for a sixteenth century female – would have been similar to a son of Anne's, except possibly as a last resort if he and his ministers threatened her religious worship and the Emperor offered her backing against a regime that was closely linked to his French foes. At most her Boleyn half-brother would have been in a weaker position to command her loyalty *in extremis* on legal grounds, Mary having recognized Henry's marriage to Jane Seymour (which took place when both Catherine and Anne were dead) but not his marriage to Anne so Catholic casuists could argue that a 'heretic' Boleyn half-brother was a bastard. Moreover, if Elizabeth had been a boy he would have been aged thirteen and four months when Henry died, older than Richard II in

1377 and Edward V in 1483 and slightly younger than Edward III in 1327. Any regency and/or 'Protectorate' would have been of shorter duration than that for Edward VI in real life, Edward being aged nine and three months; Elizabeth was thirteen and four months old in January 1547, older than Edward V had been (twelve) but younger than Edward III (fourteen). The capacity of the new King's councillors to determine political and religious policy without royal interference would have been shorter. Nor would it have been Jane Seymour's 'reformist' brother Hertford/Somerset who was head of the regency Council; this role would have been earmarked for the new king's kin, either his maternal uncle George Boleyn, Lord Rochford (if not executed as in real life) or his great-uncle Norfolk.

There were several other occasions when Anne Boleyn became pregnant and could have provided Henry with a son. In any of these cases, the resulting prince would have been ahead of both Mary and Elizabeth in the line of succession and occupied the position which Edward VI did in real life. Anne was pregnant again by February 1534, when Chapuys heard, and miscarried in July.[10] The rumours about her possible estrangement from Henry in the next year or so seem to have been exaggerated court gossip, played up by her foes and relayed to an ever-hopeful Chapuys;[11] even if the King was occasionally disgruntled with her temper and assertiveness he needed a male heir and repudiating her would only imply Catherine was his legal wife.[12] The rumours of Henry having a new mistress or fancy in autumn 1535 may or may not refer to his interest in his next wife, Jane Seymour, whose family home at Wolf Hall (Wiltshire) he had recently visited, but other reports suggest that he and Anne were still compatible; Chapuys only heard of the association of Jane with Henry in early February 1536 (and claimed it had been going on for three months, on uncertain evidence). Anne was safe while Catherine was still alive, though this is not adequate proof that she decided to poison her rival to safeguard her position as her detractors were to claim.[13] Given the dates, it is highly unlikely that she poisoned Catherine to save herself from being repudiated in favour of Jane; and Catherine's devoted ladies-in-waiting were doubtless vigilant. Catherine was aged fifty in 1535 (her mother Isabella had died at that age) and had been living in straightened circumstances with a reduced household since 1531; any personal blame for Catherine's declining health can be placed on Henry who had sent her to live in remote manor houses in the unhealthy Fenland. The remoteness of the area made it more difficult for partisans to rescue Catherine from there, as well as its marshes' noxious airs hopefully removing her as a problem. Catherine died on 7 January 1536, and Henry's public celebration of it unnecessarily infuriated Charles' ambassador Chapuys – the man who would advise him if an invasion was feasible – as well as adding to the public discontent. Catherine was now a 'martyr' and Mary received extra support from the public, as seen by the popular reactions reported to Thomas Cromwell.[14] Could this tip the balance to invasion – and would it have done but for the international situation?

Anne was pregnant again late in 1535, at a time when the renewed imperial-French clash over Milan (whose duke died in November) led to a military distraction for Charles V from any possible invasion of England. The Pope's excommunication of Henry for executing Bishop Fisher of Rochester was thus not the legal prelude to invasion by Charles on Mary's behalf; and Francis, who invaded Milan in January, needed Henry as an ally rather than being able to join the imperial-papal alliance. In the next major English/imperial crisis of 1539, Charles and Francis were not at odds and temporarily allied against England under papal auspices; had this occurred in early 1536 the public anger over Catherine's and Mary's treatment would have added inducements for them (or Charles, with Francis standing aside) to invade.

But on 24 January 1536 Henry had a serious accident in the tilting-yard at Greenwich, was knocked off his horse, and was unconscious for several hours, and on 29 January Anne miscarried. The child was a boy, as her detractors gleefully reported; and Henry's immediate reaction was reported as being superstitious fear that God was punishing him for his sinful second marriage.[15] Anne was more resilient and was sure of conceiving again, and seems to have mishandled her first encounter with Henry after the miscarriage as it ended with harsh words about his fidelity to her. The story that she blamed the King for upsetting her by paying recent attention to other women (Jane Seymour?) may have been exaggerated, and the version that Chapuys reported on 10 February[16] owed much to wishful thinking – Anne and Henry had long had a stormy relationship without it affecting their determination to conceive another child or their underlying closeness. Nor is it certain that the accident caused the miscarriage, though it was said that Norfolk's report of it to his niece caused her serious alarm and so may have been a contributory factor. But this episode seems to have been a turning point, at least as seen in retrospect when the royal marriage did break down late in April. It was exploited by the partisans of Catherine and Mary, who were now safe from the logical argument that repudiating Anne made her predecessor the rightful queen again – now that Catherine was dead Henry could even proclaim Mary, aged twenty so old enough to reign in an emergency, his heiress instead of the two-year-old Elizabeth without having to restore his ex-wife too.

An alliance seems to have followed between the conservative partisans of Mary and the Seymour family, with Jane's brother Edward Seymour (the future Duke of Somerset and Protector, and not yet identifiable as a religious radical) usefully a Gentleman of the Privy Chamber as of March 1536. Jane was the object of love letters and gifts from the smitten King, and was encouraged to hold out for marriage as the price of submission to his advances as Anne had done effectively in the mid-1520s. The Marquis of Exeter, conservative son of Henry's aunt Princess Catherine Plantagenet, Lord Montague (son of Mary's ex-governess Lady Margaret Pole) and Sir Nicholas Carew aided the plot at court and set up a link via Chapuys to Charles V,[17] and Anne was outmanoeuvred. Exeter and Montague both had a claim to the throne, which was to make them the next victims of the paranoid King in 1538; presumably they regarded themselves as 'old' nobility opposing the 'upstart' Boleyns. The King's mistrust and jealousy of her alleged admirers and resulting explosion of rage at the May Day tournament followed, with Anne possibly over-acting (manically?) in her flirtatious behaviour to put a brave face on her fears. If she had hoped to tease Henry into feeling jealous this was a fatal miscalculation. Once he had given the 'go-ahead' for a legal investigation the Queen's enemies were able to manufacture the evidence that they needed to ruin her.

Flirtation, injudicious dramatic flourishes of devotion from the 'courtly knights' in her entourage to their lady, and the King's brooding conviction that he was living in sin and being punished for it (again) were turned into a lethal cocktail. It was aided by Cromwell's torturers getting to work on her musician Mark Smeaton to investigate and exaggerate probably innocent but potentially 'improper' exchanges between him and the Queen overheard at court at the end of April. More serious was an exchange between the Queen and her more well-born courtier admirer Henry Norris, who was supposed to have delayed his marriage out of hopeless love for his employer. Anne is supposed to have made a teasing and foolish joke (if not worse) to him at Greenwich on 30 April that if 'aught come but good to the King you would look to have me', which was bound to be reported by her enemies and would have the worst possible interpretation put on it. 'Imagining the King's death' was a form of treason, and Anne and Norris were foolish as well as tasteless. Henry was duly furious and there was a violent argument between them; over twenty years later a Scottish visitor to Elizabeth's court who had been at Greenwich then and had no axe to grind testified to the Queen that he had seen Anne hold up Elizabeth at the window to the departing Henry in a last attempt at an appeal to him.[18]

Henry duly postponed his intended trip to Calais. This may have been more important than the dubiously accurate accounts of Henry storming off from the May Day tournament after a knightly admirer was allowed to wipe the sweat off his face with Anne's handkerchief; in any case the King went into seclusion, immune to appeals from the most highly placed Boleyn partisans. Anne's brother Lord Rochford, still at large on 1–2 May, was prevented from seeing Henry by Cromwell and arrested next day; most allies, led by Anne's father and Sir Francis Bryan,[19] made haste to abandon her (at least once the cause was hopeless). Henry in a rage was always difficult to reason with, and in a deferential court and age few people would have dared to do so even if they had the opportunity – which Cromwell denied them. Only Rochford might have dared, and he was speedily neutralized with Cromwell including him in the indictment against his sister and securing damning evidence that he had been discussing Henry's sexual inadequacies with Anne (which was guaranteed to enrage the King). The confessions of Rochford's wife to his alleged indiscretions have long been taken as damning to her reputation, and possibly due to spite rather than stupidity or fear – though an attempt has been made to rehabilitate her.[20] Possibly Cromwell blackmailed her so that she could save her own life by sending her husband and sister-in-law to the block.

The charge that Anne had committed incest with Rochford, with the intention of getting herself pregnant again so she could pass off the baby as the King's, was almost certainly an ingenious but twisted invention of Cromwell's to rouse up opinion at their carefully vetted trials. If Anne could be condemned for incest she could be executed whether the rest of the accusations of adultery were proved or not. Moreover, it is quite possible that Henry and Cromwell feared that she would falsely claim to be pregnant at her trial, in order to hold up her condemnation and give the King time to have second thoughts. Holding the trial in secret within the Tower would diminish the impact of such a claim, but news of it could still leak out. Thus, alleging that any child Anne was carrying was her brother's would warn her off making such a claim. If she tried to claim she was pregnant, the King could deny that the baby was his and her admission would therefore be 'proof' of incest.

A mixture of threats and blandishments produced the evidence that Cromwell and the conservatives needed from the accused aristocratic figures who had paid extravagant court to Anne, and the advantages that the interrogators had in working on their targets in the Tower meant that however innocent all such relationships had been someone was bound to 'confess' to what the government wanted them to say in the hope of clemency. In Tudor times as in Soviet-era Eastern Europe, once the State had decided on its course of action and determined the result any judicial investigation and trial was a foregone conclusion. Once Henry had been isolated from appeals by Anne's supporters she was doomed. But the importance of the King's outburst of anger at and physical abandonment of her on 30 April–1 May cannot be denied, and it is probable that Cromwell made the most of this unexpected quarrel to hastily round up suspects and build up a dossier of the most incriminating evidence (or inventions) possible rather than putting a long-planned scheme into effect on schedule. Without this chance the alienation of King and Queen could have built up for months more before causing a fatal clash, though Anne's character was such that she was likelier to confront him than play for time if she felt her influence slipping away. Once Catherine of Aragon was dead and the King was infatuated with Jane Seymour her position was under threat, at least in the long term. Indeed, now Henry could name his own heir at will – without having to be married to the heir's mother – he could even have kept a son by Anne as heir and removed the baby's mother in case of a serious quarrel or another infatuation.

Princes Mary's legitimization and other factors – could Anne have survived as queen after her loss of the baby in January 1536 had the Seymours not intervened? Or Mary been legitimized without removing Anne?

Ironically, the international crisis meant that Charles as well as Francis needed Henry's goodwill and was as a result temporarily less hostile to the Boleyn marriage and the Boleyn faction – as Anne's brother Lord Rochford endeavoured to exploit it with an approach to Chapuys.[21] In March 1536 Charles even made an offer to the English ambassador in Rome to back the Boleyn marriage provided that Henry re-legitimated Princess Mary ahead of Elizabeth[22] – the possibility that Henry would divorce Anne ironically now meant that the King could marry a French princess instead so Charles had reasons to block a divorce for the moment. This meant that as of March–April 1536 Charles was not definitely committed to aiding the plot to remove Anne, and had Henry gone along with re-legitimating Mary he could have backed away from it. The legitimacy of Mary was more important to Charles than removing Anne – and when Catherine was dead it was easier for Henry to grant this demand of his.

Anne had done her best to humiliate and intimidate Mary throughout 1533–6 and would have opposed this blow to her own daughter Elizabeth's rights, though arguably her insistence that Mary serve in Elizabeth's household – the norm for a royal bastard, e.g. Edward IV's daughter Grace[23] – was as much a security-measure as humiliation. (The ex-princess could less easily be kidnapped by her partisans there.) But would she have dared to risk her marriage on this issue if Henry ignored her demands to keep Mary illegitimate? Nor could Anne rely on Francis as a counter to Chapuys and the conservatives in influencing Henry; thanks to the Milan war he needed

Henry's aid in spring 1536 too much to risk annoying him. Anne was in a weak position to prevent Henry doing exactly what he liked about the succession, and his accident in January had clearly made him aware of his insecure position and potential Divine disfavour as seen by his comments to his intimates at the time. But it appears from Henry's subsequent insistence that Mary had to acknowledge her illegitimacy before he would rehabilitate her that in 1536 he was determined to teach his elder daughter a lesson. Presumably now Catherine was dead he transferred his anger at her defiance in 1527–36 to their daughter.

If the King had not been flirting with Jane and so been approachable to her court partisans, the plan to remove Anne could yet have failed. The re-legitimization of Mary would have satisfied one of the main demands of her backers, in and outside England. The initiative on that issue lay with the King, though events later in 1536 were to show that he still insisted that Mary accept that her parents' marriage was illegal as the prelude to any restoration to court even when Anne was dead. This was technically only placing the ex-princess in the same category as all Henry's other subjects, in accepting the primacy of English law (which had bastardized her) over Rome. Mary was to give in and accept her bastardy, but only reluctantly and no doubt at immense psychological cost – and her obstinacy over submission to her father would have similarly soured any attempt from him to offer her re-legitimization (on his, not Rome's, authority) as the reward for submission over his right to annul her parents' marriage.

The long-term future of Anne and her children

The loss of Henry and Anne's child in January 1536 was thus not fatal to their marriage; nor was the death of Catherine of Aragon; nor was the international situation. Indeed, temporarily imperial hostility was reduced over Charles fearing that Henry would marry a French candidate next – provided that the King re-legitimated Mary. But the King's new ability to nominate heirs at will gave him a wider range of options, and meant that he was less tied to Anne as his wife; even if they had a son he could safely remove her. Given the tempestuous nature of their relationship and his growing ruthlessness, his need of foreign allies (as in real-life 1538–9) could have impelled him to seek a 'respectable', legal foreign wife as part of a renewed alliance with either Charles or Francis then. In real life his next wife Jane Seymour had died; but he had the legal power to rid himself of Anne at will and the diplomatic imperative could have made it seem attractive. All the evidence suggests that though Jane was the catalyst for the collapse of his marriage he was capable of finding others – another woman at court, or another valuable foreign princess – whenever he wished. His frequent complaints at Anne's temper and lack of respect for her sovereign make it evident that he could weary of her attractions, and decide in favour of a more acquiescent wife. Their sexual attraction was not going to be overwhelming indefinitely and Anne's anger at Jane's alleged role in spring 1536 shows that she was not capable of putting up with a rival as royal mistress.

Her indiscretions and flashes of temper were likely to be reported by her rivals and worked upon with the King, and possibly her support for the Lutheran cause in Germany in the 1530s was another useful weapon if and when the King turned against them and Cromwell (as he was to do in 1540). Within the limits of 1530s religious politics she was probably less adventurous in 'reformist' experimentation than her subsequent admirers proclaimed – much was written in hindsight when she could be portrayed as the forerunner of her Protestant daughter.[24] Those of her protégés who were earnest reformers in the 1540s and 1550s were not necessarily known as such at the time. But she was undeniably interested in religion and active in religious thought and patronage as her successor Jane Seymour was not and Henry preferred the latter. He is reliably supposed to have told Jane not to meddle when she spoke up for the conservative victims of his post-rebellion punishments in 1537, and by 1546 he was capable of toying with the idea of arresting Catherine Parr for her reformist religious activities. She had to grovel and assure him that she had only sought to aid his studies and learn from his superior wisdom, which Anne would have found impossible to admit. It is hard to think of an ailing, ageing, anti-reformist Henry in 1545–6 tolerating Anne's outspokenness.

Whether or not Anne survived as queen, any son of hers would have been king in 1547 and any daughter born subsequently to Elizabeth would have been the latter's next heir. It is improbable that a half-Boleyn heir as king in 1547 would have had Jane Seymour's brother Somerset as regent, even if he had still emerged as a major player at court in 1537–47 and his sister Jane been queen after a dead or divorced Anne. His great advantage in court politics in the 1540s was as maternal uncle to the next king, and he had the right as nearest adult male kin to be regent – though Henry only made him head of the Council and his role as full legal regent from January 1547 was a result of a secret legal coup.[25] If Anne's brother Lord Rochford had survived until 1547 he would have been in a similar legal position, and had the greatest right to be regent as Anne's son's uncle – and he would have succeeded his father Sir Thomas Boleyn as earl of Wiltshire in 1539 so been a senior peer. His involvement in court politics in the early-mid 1530s was as thorough and effective as Seymour's was to be in the 1540s, and he had similarly 'reformist' religious views. Both the London merchant Richard Hilles and Chapuys testified to Rochford's interest in religious reform, and on the scaffold in May 1536 he spoke of his interest in reading and interpreting the Bible.[26]

This self-declared 'mighty reader and great debater of the word of God' (Bentley 1831: 263) would have been as determined in backing reform as Seymour was to be, and similar religious experiments could have been expected of him as Lord Protector or head of the regency council – with the 'caveat' that his outspokenness and rash character could have brought him down at Henry's and Gardiner's hands after the fall of his ally Cromwell in 1540. At least according to his wife's alleged confessions to Cromwell, he was indiscreet about the King and thus capable of being ruined once stories about that leaked out to his enemies. Had Rochford survived this conservative backlash, he was less likely than Seymour to have been at odds with the Howards in 1546 and sought their ruin, given their dynastic links – though his uncle Norfolk and cousin Surrey would have deplored his religious leanings. The Howards would have had a stronger claim to the regency for Henry's son in January 1547 as Norfolk was the boy's great-uncle, making Surrey even more outspoken on the regency being theirs by 'right'. Conversely, their potential threat to their court rivals would have presented strong reasons for the latter to influence a paranoid King against them, and rivalry for control of the next King (aged thirteen in 1546 if born to Anne in 1533, ten if born in 1536) have alienated the Howards from the younger Boleyns. Religion could have provided the decisive issue, not kinship, in Rochford joining Seymour and John Dudley (and the Boleyn ally Archbishop Cranmer) in seeking to ruin the Howards before Henry VIII died. The Boleyns and the cause of reformed religion could then expect to prosper under the new King, provided that he did not inherit the Tudor ill-health and die young. If he did die Boleyn backing would be likely for Elizabeth (or a full sister of hers) against Mary as the next sovereign.

(ii) What if Jane Seymour had not died in childbirth in 1537 but provided Henry with more children?

Any daughter would have had the advantage of having a 'legitimate' status in 1553, unlike Elizabeth and Mary with their illegalized parental unions. Mary's opponents could claim that her mother's marriage to Henry VIII had been invalidated by Parliament and the newly independent Church; Elizabeth's could claim that Henry had married her mother while his previous wife was still alive. No such taint lay over the wedding of Henry and Jane Seymour. A daughter as well as a second son of Henry and Jane would have been the likeliest candidate to be chosen to succeed Edward VI in 1553 even if they had been only around ten to twelve. In that case, a revolt against their accession was unlikely as Henry's third marriage was generally regarded as legal unlike his second. John Dudley would have been able to continue as head of the government in his new capacity as leader of the regency Council for her, rather than leading the attempt to exclude the next Tudor heiress (Mary, a Catholic) as in real life. He might even have aspired to marrying Edward's full sister to one of his sons to continue the Dudley family's domination of court life for decades. By 1553 most of them were married, but Guildford or the youngest (Henry) were possibilities. This outcome would not have been just a symptom of insatiable Dudley greed for power, as in their detractors' legend of their behaviour; it would have protected him in his retirement from prosecution for the death of Somerset in 1552.

The alternative choice of a consort would have been one of the younger sons of Henri II of France, a vital ally against Emperor Charles V and Mary Tudor – but the King's second son, Charles, was born in 1551 so he would have been about a decade younger than the new English queen. No more than a nominal betrothal could have been arranged, and the long delay before the children could have offspring would have militated against the match being carried out. England and France were likely to be quarrelling again before either child reached maturity, most obviously over the determination of Henri II to marry his ward Queen Mary Stuart of Scotland off to his heir Francis (King Francis II from July 1559). This union of Scotland and France was a politico-military threat to England, and the real-life English expedient of assisting a Protestant Scots noble revolt in 1560 to curtail the powers of the Scots Catholic Queen's Crown was an obvious reply to it. But an English rapprochement with the Empire instead was unlikely given Charles V's support for Mary Tudor, particularly if that rival to a Seymour queen had fled to the Continent in the 1550s.

Mary Tudor would have stood less chance against a daughter of Jane Seymour, who Henry had not married until Catherine of Aragon was dead, than against the unexpected choice of Jane Grey to succeed Edward. She is unlikely to have challenged her at all unless desperate – or to have received the popular support that Mary did against 'usurper' Jane in real life. If the second child of Jane Seymour had been a son – presumably to be called Henry – he would have been unlikely to be challenged at all. He would have been brought up Protestant, and both Edward VI and Dudley/Northumberland would have accepted his succession. Assuming him to have been born around 1539 to 1541, his succession would have needed a full return to Council control of State business for several years from 1553 but the antagonisms that Somerset had made as 'Lord Protector' make it no likelier that Northumberland would have assumed that title now than in October 1549. Northumberland would have been head of the Council to the mid- to late 1550s, having to postpone the apparent partial withdrawal from business that some have detected in early 1553, assuming that his health held out. His elder sons were too young to succeed him to political power, being still in their twenties, and the chances of his competent protégé William Cecil, already secretary, as chief minister from the late 1550s would have been substantial. A male half-Seymour king could also be expected to rehabilitate his first cousin, Somerset's eldest son Edward, born in 1539 so a close contemporary, to assorted titles and lands taken from the Duke in 1549–52.

Edward Seymour's marriage to Jane Grey's sister Catherine could have been looked on more favourably than Elizabeth did in real life, when they both ended in the Tower. He would have been a close blood relative of the new sovereign. The young King Henry IX, or the new queen, could thus have restored their first cousin Edward Seymour to favour and a semi-royal bride after the retirement of the Seymour clan's foe Northumberland. But Catherine Grey's elder sister Jane and her 'heirs male' by Guildford Dudley, Northumberland's son, would have had had priority in the line of succession. Mary Tudor would still have been under threat as a defiant attender of illegal Catholic masses after 1553, and if Northumberland had kept up the pressure on her to conform her secret departure for the Continent was a possibility. As she would not have been the next heir to Edward, she would have had less reason to stay on in England once her religion came under threat – and once she was safe in Flanders Charles V would have been able to marry her off to Philip as a useful diplomatic pawn in any war with England.

What if England had had a new queen, daughter of Henry VIII and Jane Seymour, after July 1553 and Northumberland had not dared to marry her to a younger son of his? In due course the same problems about marriage would have affected the new queen as did Elizabeth in reality, but she would have had the advantage of being some years younger had she been born in 1539–40 and hence able to have children for longer. A Habsburg marriage was possible for the 1560s, had England and France ended up clashing over French influence over Mary Stuart in Scotland from 1561 or the French religious wars led to England backing the Huguenots against the court and the Guises. France had been England's close ally as of the 1550s, with Northumberland in real life seeking a French expedition to rescue the cause of Lady Jane Grey from Mary Tudor in 1553. If Edward VI had been succeeded by a full brother or sister in July 1553, the regime would have continued in alliance with France and it is possible that Edward's betrothed, Henri II's daughter Elizabeth, would have been transferred to a male successor. (Thus she would not have been available to marry Philip of Spain in 1559/60 as in real life.) Henri would then have had no political reason to break with the English regime and proclaim his daughter-in-law Mary Stuart as rightful queen – except in the unlikely event of an English diplomatic alliance with the Habsburgs against him. But, as in real life, he would have been killed in a tournament-accident in July 1559, his son Francis II died young, and the latter's widow, Mary Stuart, thus returned as a widow to Scotland when her mother and regent Marie de Guise died. The prospect of Scotland subject to French – and militant Catholic Guise – influence in the 1560s would have strained peaceful relations with England. The outbreak of the French religious civil wars from 1562 would also have led to calls for England to intervene to assist the Huguenots, whether it had an aggressive young king 'Henry IX' (born around 1539–41 so of the right age to fight in a campaign) or not. It is indeed possible that 'Henry IX', like Edward I of England in 1286, would have decided that marrying the Scottish queen into the English royal family would permanently end the threat of a Franco–Scots alliance against his country. If Henry was married already – to Elizabeth of France, Francis II's sister? – Mary Stuart could have been offered a senior English noble.

Prince John of Sweden, second son of King Gustavus, was a serious possibility to marry any daughter of Henry VIII and Jane Seymour who succeeded Edward VI as queen. His elder brother Eric – closer to the new English queen in age – was the heir and a 'Union of Crowns' was undesirable quite apart from his mental instability. He succeeded their father Gustavus Vasa in 1560, and was deposed for reasons of semi-violent manic behaviour in 1568 in John's favour. If John had been put on the Swedish throne in the deposed Eric's place before a Tudor match was finalized, there was another prince available in the form of his brother Charles. In real life John was married off to the Polish royal heiress Catherine and their son Sigismund duly succeeded to Poland in 1587, adding Sweden on John's death in 1592 but losing it later due to his Catholicism. Charles then succeeded to Sweden. Marrying either John or Charles to the English queen would thus have had repercussions for north-eastern European politics for decades to come.

Jane Seymour was noted for her quiet and unobtrusive demeanour, unlike Anne Boleyn. What little evidence there is about her opinions suggests that she seems to have favoured the retention of some monasteries and argued in their favour with her husband at the time of the Pilgrimage of Grace.[27] But Henry became annoyed at her presumption, and unlike Anne she preferred to be discreet and retain her husband's favour. Jane as queen after 1537 would not have had the political role that Anne did in her reign, and would not have had the nerve to intervene. Thus the execution of Cromwell and the Catholic religious predominance of the 1540s would not have been prevented by Jane being queen. Her elder brother Edward Seymour was to emerge as the leader of ecclesiastical reform in 1547, but his sympathies at the earlier period are unknown so his resistance to the Howards and Bishop Gardiner in 1540–3 with his sister's help cannot be taken for granted. Henry VIII did not like his wives to indulge in giving him religious advice, and when Catherine Parr did so in 1546 he arranged a sadistic charade of pretending to have her arrested for heresy to frighten her into wifely obedience.[28] His declining temper and rising paranoia were likely to have been exercised on any wife, as on any minister; by 1546 even Cranmer was not safe from his moodiness and desire to humiliate his intimates.

Cromwell would not have been able to use Henry's next marriage as the bait for a German Lutheran alliance in 1539, or been humiliated by the failure of the match with Anne of Cleves. His political relationship with Jane is unknown. If Jane had still been alive Norfolk would not have been able to use his niece Catherine Howard to his benefit and marry her off to the King in July 1540, or have to extricate himself from her subsequent disgrace. It is, however, still probable that Henry would have dispensed with Cromwell's services at some point, particularly if he needed to reassure the Emperor about his attitude towards Cromwell's Continental Lutheran allies.

Jane's importance in 1547–9

Jane's political importance would have been more crucial in 1547, when if she was still alive she rather than her brother would have been a possible head of the Council under Henry's will. (Margaret Beaufort had been regent briefly in 1509, and Catherine of Aragon served as regent in Henry's own absences abroad in the 1510s.) Henry may still have kept his queen away from his bedside in his final weeks and so out of the vicious Council and court struggles, as he rather surprisingly did to his final queen, Catherine Parr. The King may have disregarded Jane's claims to be regent – or assessed her administrative ability and political skills as inadequate – and chosen the nearest male relative, her brother Edward Seymour, as Edward IV chose the heir's uncle rather than mother in 1483. An adult male was necessary as war-leader, and England and France (and Scotland) likely to be in conflict soon. But as Queen-Mother Jane would have been an invaluable personal support to her son, as in real life his stepmother Catherine Parr soon left court and married her old admirer Thomas Seymour despite the wishes of the latter's brother the Protector. The absence of a Queen-Mother from the court during 1547–8 made the new King more dependent on Somerset, who he seems to have come to resent for not giving him sufficient deference or making the pretence of consulting him. It is quite possible that it was this distance between a sidelined and resentful Edward VI and his uncle that gave the latter's brother Thomas Seymour his chance to attempt to secure the King's acquiescence for a plot.

The mutual hostility of the Seymour brothers was an important crisis, which undermined the Lord Protectorship in 1547–8 as Thomas secretly married Catherine Parr and seemed to be planning to remove his brother. If Jane had been alive and queen in 1537–47 Thomas would have had no obstacle to marrying Catherine Parr, his apparent intended fiancé, back in 1543 (which the King's interest in her prevented in real life). His marriage to her would thus not have caused an inter-Seymour crisis soon after Henry's death, though if Catherine had died in childbirth he would have been at liberty to flirt with and allegedly plot to marry Princess Elizabeth. It was this that precipitated the younger Seymour's arrest and execution, so if ambition had still led the widowed Thomas to make a play for the Princess his sister Queen Jane may have been unable to prevent the crisis and Thomas' execution.

Jane's importance in and after 1549. Would she have saved her brothers from execution?
If the Council had been united in their opposition to Edward Seymour in 1549 he would still have been forced to resign as Protector. The Queen's existence would have posed a problem to John Dudley, Earl of Warwick (and soon to be Duke of Northumberland), emerging as leader of the new government, as he could hardly banish her from court without arousing the King's wrath. He would have had to proceed much more cautiously in his manoeuvres against his rival who would have been able to use Jane as his conduit to the King. Jane would have had to be reconciled to her brother's loss of power, but might still have lent him her support in regaining his position in 1551. Even if it is arguable that it was Seymour not Dudley who initiated the plot that ended with Seymour's arrest and execution, which Dudley had genuinely sought to avoid,[29] Jane's presence at court would have made the execution of her brother in January 1552 more unlikely. Finally, if Edward VI had died in July 1553 leaving no full brother or sister to succeed, Jane's attitude to the proposed exclusion of Mary from the throne would have been crucial. Jane had sought to reconcile Henry and Mary in 1536, and her support for the claim of Jane Grey (her namesake?) cannot be regarded as certain. If she had been in London and backing Mary's claims on 6–9 July the wavering councillors might have been less inclined to follow Northumberland and Jane Grey's father, Suffolk, in staging a coup. Jane Seymour would have been an invaluable support to Mary as queen, probably advising clemency to the rebels of 1553 and 1554 as she did to Henry concerning the rebels of 1536, and would have been a political

counterweight to the influence of Bishop Gardiner and later Cardinal Reginald Pole

(iii) What if Henry had not been warned about Catherine Howard's affairs with Culpeper and Dereham in October–November 1541 and had her tried and executed?

The second of Henry's wives to be arrested, tried, and executed for alleged adultery, Catherine was many years his junior – around twenty at her marriage to his forty-nine. She had been promoted as his new queen after Anne of Cleves by the ever-ambitious Norfolk, now (summer–autumn 1540) at an unprecedented prominence at court following the destruction of his rival Thomas Cromwell. Henry seems to have been in love with her in stark contrast to his attitude to Anne, although with hindsight it is evident that the attraction on her part was more to the status of queenship than to her overweight and semi-invalid husband as a person. Apparently the lax supervision of the young Howard females at a family mansion near Horsham and at Lambeth before her marriage was mooted as having been the opportunity for this bold and uninhibited young woman to indulge in a sexual relationship with an admirer, Francis Dereham, and possibly her music teacher Henry Mannox. It was reliably reported that unchaperoned young men had been climbing into the bedchamber of Catherine and her roommates at Horsham before her marriage;[30] what they did there was less certain but her court enemies could make the most of the possibilities. Once she was married and becoming bored with Henry she risked resuming the Dereham affair, having him invited to join her household, and also became involved with a junior gentleman of the Privy Chamber, Thomas Culpeper, and others. The dangerous secret assignations became bolder as it appeared that the King and his minions had noticed nothing, and led to furtive meetings during the King's progress to York in early autumn 1541. The 'go-between' who helped the Queen admit her admirers to her rooms was none other than George Boleyn's widow, Lady Rochford, back at court after her pardon in 1536. Her subsequent confessions and execution for her part in betraying the King's honour did her reputation no good, but if she had refused to assist her mistress she would have risked a ruinous dismissal from court by the sulking Queen.

When rumours of Catherine's behaviour with her courtiers leaked out the Council were at first reluctant to investigate and then nervous about telling Henry, given his devotion to her and his emotional instability. They feared being blamed for exposing the Queen and ruining his happiness, and in the end only Archbishop Cranmer dared to intervene by slipping him a note at prayers at Hampton Court. Catherine's uncle Norfolk, having had to deny the possible allegation that he had deliberately pandered an unchaste girl to the

King for the sake of his ambition, found it prudent to retire from court and his influence went into decline as that of Edward Seymour and John Dudley rose. Catherine was removed from Hampton Court to Syon House to be investigated for adultery – there was a legend that she was able to escape her guards at Hampton and attempt to reach the King at prayers to plead her case, before being caught and dragged away screaming, and the location for her capture was duly supposed to be haunted by her ghost. This now appears unlikely, as Henry left the Palace as soon as he heard of the allegations and deliberately steered clear of a confrontation.[31] As with Anne Boleyn, the King avoided a personal 'showdown' with his errant wife – thus enabling his courtiers to ensure that the latter could never make a personal appeal to him.

Catherine avoided immediate despatch to the Tower, which suggests that Henry waited until his investigators had acquired convincing evidence. A united 'front' by the accused men and by Lady Rochford, refusing to implicate the Queen, was unlikely; as in any authoritarian State 'show trial', individuals were eager to save themselves by implicating others. There was no chance for them to concoct viable alibis. The stories about Horsham were enough to have the Queen divorced as unchaste. But Catherine might have evaded the death sentence and the block if it had been proved that she had made (private but still legal by canon law) arrangements with Dereham for their betrothal. Such a compact was legally as valid as a marriage, as was seen by the similar instance of the unverifiable private compact alleged to have taken place between Edward IV and (?) Eleanor Butler before he married Elizabeth Woodville. But Catherine denied this 'face-saving' possibility, which would have made her a bigamist but not an adulteress, insisting to Henry's investigators that she was legally queen, and Henry did not press for this solution, which would have saved her life.

The accounts imply that he was initially furious to the point of threatening to stab his wife before lapsing into depression, and he was determined on vengeance.[32] But was there another reason for Henry desiring to execute his wife? There had been rumours surrounding the similar arrest, trial, and execution of her cousin Anne Boleyn in spring 1536, concerning Anne being – or hoping to become – pregnant by another man and to pass off her child as the King's.[33] The new queen's principal abettor in her adultery was indeed Anne's sister-in-law Lady Rochford, who Henry also had executed for the scandal. Whether Lady Rochford was foolish or malevolent remains under question, as the worst allegations against her may not have been contemporary but eighteenth century guesswork.[34] But what if the affairs between Catherine and Dereham/Culpeper had not been detected in autumn 1541, and Catherine had later become pregnant?

The Queen could have announced a pregnancy in 1542 or 1543 and Henry been delighted at this proof of his fertility, with no inkling of her behaviour if she had shown more discretion. Indeed, the child could have been his – but until the discovery of DNA there was no certain way of proving parentage. (This presumably lies behind the statute of Edward III declaring it treason for a man not her husband to have relations with the Princess of Wales, which was hopefully being cited against Princess Diana's lovers in the 1990s.) But if the child had been a boy it could have taken precedence over Mary and Elizabeth as the child of an undoubtedly legitimate marriage and thus been Edward VI's heir in 1553.

Catherine (born 1520?) might have survived that long and been available as the potential regent or, if judged too young and incompetent, a senior figure at court with the queen's usual powers of patronage. As a Howard, she would not have been sympathetic to the efforts of Edward Seymour to arrange the disgrace of her uncle and patron Norfolk and her cousin Surrey in January 1547, out of family solidarity even if she personally disliked them. She would have been expected to intercede with the King on their behalf, though Henry sent his real-life wife Catherine Parr away from court in his final weeks and Seymour could have induced him to do so to Catherine Howard too. Given her mercurial temperament and lack of political skills, the demands of an obese and bad-tempered husband in his final year or so could easily have led to them living apart for much of the time. In 1541 he was still able to ride to York on his great Northern expedition; after the 1544 expedition to France his mobility decreased sharply though he still moved from one residence to another until December 1546. The famous statement that Henry relied on a 'device' to move up and down stairs by 1546 probably refers to a sedan-chair not a contraption with pulleys,[35] but his decline in 1545–6 cannot be denied and the Queen was unlikely to have evolved into a patient nurse as her successor did in real life. She does not seem to have possessed the equable temperament and emollient skills of Catherine Parr, who had had two much older husbands before Henry, so Seymour could have found it easier to induce the King to live apart from her. Her being queen in January 1547 need not have halted the Howards' disgrace, particularly as by this point Seymour's ally Sir Anthony Denny (Chief Gentleman of the Bedchamber) not only controlled access to the King but had a 'rubber stamp' of his signature. Once Henry had become confused and unlikely to recover, as in mid-January 1547, his signature on execution warrants could always be forged by Denny – we do not know if Henry was actually responsible for deciding on Surrey's execution in real life given how soon afterwards he died (eight days). Catherine Howard's position with regards the 1547–9 Protectorate would have been difficult, and like

Catherine Parr she might have decided as a vigorous young widow (twenty-seven in 1547?) to marry some ambitious nobleman who could ensure her comfort and position. Or would she have scandalized the court and been arrested for trying to marry her alleged ex-fiancé Francis Dereham, far beneath her social station?

If Catherine had had a daughter she would have seemed a legitimate heir to Edward VI in 1553, and if raised as a Protestant the girl would have been considered as his heir instead of Jane Grey. But the situation of a child of Henry and Catherine in 1553 raises the prospect that some court rival could have heard old stories about Catherine and her lovers having affairs at the court in 1541 behind the King's back, with the implication that the child was not Henry's. Thus the coup of 6–9 July 1553 could have been on behalf of Catherine's child, and the arguments used against the 'usurpation' by Mary's partisans centred on the boy or girl being a bastard.

The Duke of Norfolk, still in the Tower from 1547, would have been in an interesting position as the child's great-uncle and a noted conservative whose Norfolk county lands were the potential centre of Mary's revolt. His support for his niece and her child would have been invaluable to Northumberland, assuming that the Duke was acting to carry out Edward's wishes on the succession, and Norfolk could use his family and household to clamp down on Marian partisans' stories about Catherine's immoral life before her marriage. Thus an informal agreement between Norfolk and Northumberland – centred no doubt on Norfolk's complete rehabilitation – would have assisted the Edwardian leadership in securing the succession of the child claimed to be Henry's and Catherine's instead of Mary Tudor.

From what little is known of her Catherine was not interested in religion and took no sides in the current religious disputes of the 1540s, unlike her successor Catherine Parr, so if she had survived as queen until Henry died she is unlikely to have been one of the Howards involved in politics like her cousin Anne Boleyn. Her safety and material well-being would have been more important to her than taking a part in the political and religious intrigues of the 1540s, and she is most likely to have hurried into a new marriage as soon as she could once she was widowed. If this had managed to avoid scandal and she had maintained a position of honour at court, feted as the King's stepmother and parent of the possible successor, she is unlikely to have bothered herself with government if her child succeeded in 1553. Northumberland would have been able to control the government and continue his policies. If Mary's supporters had succeeded in spreading the stories of alleged or genuine witnesses as to her conduct as queen with her lovers twelve years before and enough people had believed that there were doubts over the child's father, the succession would have seemed as illegal as Jane's and Northumberland's cause would have collapsed. Catherine would have been wise to flee the country before she faced trial as an adulteress or her supporters fought on hopelessly in a civil war.

The exposure of her conduct in 1541 thus may have caused Henry VIII great shock and suffering at the time, and her execution seemed harsh. But what if she had been divorced and subsequently turned out to be pregnant? Despite royal denials, some ambitious nobles opposed to the current sovereign could subsequently have declared the child to be Henry's and started a rebellion on its behalf. Given the dubious legitimacy of both Mary Tudor and Elizabeth, a child of one of Henry's fully lawful marriages had some advantages. Henry's action may have saved England from at least one of its many bloody Tudor rebellions.

(iv) What if Henry had married a different queen after Jane Seymour's death? Marie of Guise as Queen of England – no Mary Queen of Scots?

Henry started his search for his fourth queen within days of the death of Jane, at the request of his Council rather than on his own initiative according to Thomas Cromwell.[36] Ambassadors were sent to the two rival Western European sovereigns, Emperor Charles V and Francis I of France, to search for suitable candidates and the marriage was linked to a diplomatic alliance with the successful lady's sponsor based on their agreeing to include Henry in any treaty with their rival and assisting him in preventing a papally led Church Council. Pope Paul was already seeking Henry's overthrow as a heretic in retaliation for the withdrawal of recognition of papal rights in England and sending Henry's exiled cousin Reginald Pole to encourage Charles and Francis to end their diplomatic rift and unite to depose Henry. An imperial/French rapprochement was feared as the precursor of invasion, hence Henry's concern to ally closely with one of the two great powers and cement it with a marriage. While negotiations were ongoing in 1538–9, a vast programme of defensive work was put in place along the south coast from Pendennis Castle (Falmouth) to Sandgate in Kent, with a system of new 'blockhouse' mini–castles unprecedented in scale since the Late Roman 'Saxon Shore' fortresses. This provided a new impetus to closing down the larger monasteries, as their stone was used to build nearby castles (e.g. Titchfield and Netley in Hampshire for the Isle of Wight system, Beaulieu Abbey for Hurst Castle, and Battle Abbey for Camber in East Sussex).

The French candidates – and the possibility of marrying off Mary Tudor to a French prince
Henry's first choice of ally was Francis of France, and his first potential wife was the widowed Marie de Guise, a member of the cadet Valois line of Anjou (related to Margaret of Anjou) in the female line and the House of Lorraine

in the male line. In her mid-twenties, she was his preference over the alternative French candidate (Francis' daughter) as mature and Peter Meawtas was sent to interview her in December 1537, followed by Hans Holbein to do a portrait. But before a second embassy in February she chose Henry's recently widowed nephew James V of Scotland instead, thus becoming the mother of Mary Queen of Scots and grandmother of James I of England.[37] James was a close ally of France and likely to have chosen a wife from their royal family, but had he not lost his first wife (Francis' daughter Madeleine) in 1537 Marie might well have chosen Henry instead as Meawtas was confident she would do. Once she was out of the running her younger sisters Louise and Renee were considered instead during spring–summer 1538, and Francis proposed that Henry's elder daughter, Mary Tudor (then twenty-two) should marry his younger son Charles (then sixteen). Had this come about, Mary would have been out of England at least until Charles died in 1545, married to a Catholic at a Catholic court. Even had she returned to her father when widowed it might have been with a half-French child as a potential heir. If Mary had already had a child, born c. 1540–2, she would have been in a stronger position to refuse to marry in 1553 as she did not need to provide an heir. But would Charles V still have wanted to marry his son to her in 1553 if she had become an ally of the 'right-wing' Catholic religious faction at Francis I's French court during her French marriage?

If Mary had been in this position in 1553, her French connection and half-French child would have given Henri II pause for thought before backing Lady Jane Grey and Northumberland. The child would also have had precedence over Elizabeth in the succession in 1558, whether or not Mary had decided to marry again in the meantime. But the chances of a child born in France in the early 1540s as the new monarch of England might then have been pitched against Elizabeth and her partisans in a civil war, with the disadvantage of foreign birth weighing against the younger claimant. Would Henry VIII have excluded a half-French, foreign-born child of Mary's from the succession in his will of 1543–4? He was then at war with France, and in the parallel case of his elder sister Margaret's children he excluded them (as born abroad) in favour of his younger sister Mary's native-born children. Later Francis' cousins, Anne of Lorraine and the Duchess of Vendome, were also suggested to marry Henry and Henry proposed that the rival candidates should all come to Calais so that he could interview them in person and make his choice. That was a sensible precaution given that Holbein's portraits might be too flattering and a candidate chosen without inspection turn out to be objectionable – as the real-life debacle over the 'Flanders mare' Anne of Cleves in 1540 showed. But Francis was unwilling to grant this concession, and his representatives protested at Henry's unchivalrous idea.

The imperial candidate: Duchess Christina of Milan

The alternative imperial candidate, offered by Charles after Henry had raised the idea, was the widowed Duchess of Milan, Christina (aged sixteen) the niece of Charles and daughter of the deposed King Christian II of Denmark. She had recently arrived in Brussels, and in January 1538 Henry asked his ambassador at Charles' court (Sir Thomas Wyatt the poet) to ask Charles about her. Holbein was sent to do a portrait, and Henry suggested that if the marriage went ahead his daughter Mary should marry the brother of Charles' cousin and ally the King of Portugal. Christina insisted on guarantees for her safety if her marriage to Henry went ahead but failed, not unreasonably in view of his homicidal reputation, and there was a problem over the bride's consanguinity to Catherine of Aragon (meaning that Charles would need a papal dispensation at a time when the Pope was trying to depose Henry), but Henry was enthusiastic about success late that spring. In the event, Charles met Francis for a peace-summit at Nice in June and in January 1539 came to an agreement that neither should make a treaty with England without including the other.[38]

A joint war with England, as urged by the Pope, was rumoured to be in the offing and in spring 1539 Henry toured the south coast and reviewed his troops; the leading 'White Rose' suspected plotters (related to the House of York) were executed, including Reginald Pole's elder brother. The war never materialized, but Henry turned to Charles' North German Protestant foes as potential allies and began talks with their leader, the Elector of Saxony. Cromwell was more sympathetic to their Lutheranism than Henry, who never entirely broke with Charles and was soon to show his determined theological conservatism by reasserting the traditional Catholic doctrine for England in the Act of Six Articles. But the planned alliance with Saxony led to the conclusion of a German Protestant marriage treaty with the Elector's brother, the Duke of Cleves, and the fiasco of the brief marriage to Anne of Cleves in January 1540. (A Cleves marriage was also suggested for Mary, who if it had gone ahead would probably have been out of England and unavailable for the throne in 1553.[39])

Henry and Anne of Cleves lived together for six weeks or so at the most and the King was clearly unpleasantly surprised at her appearance, though ironically they seem to have been on better terms once they were divorced. But if he had married either a French candidate or Duchess Christina (the latter less likely unless Charles had coerced the Pope into granting a dispensation) the marriage is likely to have lasted longer than that of Henry and Anne. Marie de Guise lived until 1560 and proved a more than competent – and Catholic – regent of Scotland for her daughter in 1548–60. It is possible that Henry would have had another child, as was considered possible from the Cleves marriage in 1540 at a court where no medical secret such as obvious royal impotence would have lasted for long. Had the child been a boy, he would have been ahead of Mary and Elizabeth in the line of succession as arranged by Henry's will – the male heir(s) came first, followed by females in line of age. Thus a 'Prince Henry' born to Henry VIII and a Guise girl or Christina around 1540 would have been able to succeed Edward VI in July 1553 at the age of around thirteen, probably with John Dudley as regent given that the boy would have no available kin on his mother's side in England. (Foreign kin were unacceptable to councillors as political actors in England.)

A Guise bride – Guise influence in England, France, and Scotland?
If one of the Guise sisters had been chosen as Henry's bride, the Anglo-French alliance of the early 1550s would have meant that the accession of a half-French prince with maternal kin in the Guise dynasty would present no problem to this diplomatic alliance as the half-Spanish Mary's accession did. England and France would have remained allies under 'Henry IX', with his mother Marie of Guise as a conduit of Guise and Catholic influence at the English court. If another Guise sister had been chosen as James V's wife (Marie being unavailable) then that woman, 'Henry IX's aunt, would probably now be regent of Scotland. This should have helped Anglo-Scottish relations improve from 1553, and presented a possibility that Mary Queen of Scots (born December 1542, so probably a little younger than Henry) would be sought as the King's bride for an Anglo-Scottish union after her first husband died in 1560. The Guise family were voracious in their ambition, as their domestic foes in France found, and marrying Mary off to the half-Guise King of England would have bolstered their power. It would also have saved Mary Stuart's Scottish regime from the real-life political threat that it faced in 1560, when the new government of Elizabeth Tudor in England backed the 'Lords of the Congregation' in overthrowing Marie de Guise's regency. Marie died and her daughter Mary returned to a land where power lay in the hands of a coalition of great nobles led by her half-brother the Earl of Moray, James V's illegitimate son, and religious power with fanatical Presbyterian preachers led by John Knox. Whether or not Mary was married to England's half-Guise King under her relatives' auspices, their political relationship would have been easier than that of Mary and Elizabeth.

Mary might have been able to rely on her English cousin for restoration after her deposition in 1567, or at least for sanctuary without fears that she sought his crown. (Not being Anne Boleyn's child, his parentage would have been legitimate by Catholic canon law. Therefore Mary Stuart would not have claimed to be rightful Queen of England.) In these circumstances, it would be unlikely that England would have a Protestant regime bent on extending the Reformation to Scotland in 1560; more likely the Guises would have led a 'Catholic restoration' in England from 1553 as Mary Tudor did in real life.

It should also be noted that the Guise family were consistently rigidly Catholic in their religion, with Mary Stuart's uncles (Marie's brothers) the Duke and Cardinal of Guise leading the Catholic forces in the French civil war of the early 1560s. This might have posed a problem to the firmly Protestant John Dudley, a close French ally, but the sponsor of further religious reform in 1549–53, if the Queen Dowager was Catholic and seeking to restore her son, the new king, to a more conservative faith than Edward VI had backed. The Protestant nature of Edward's education only seems to have become pronounced after 1547, when the prime movers in hiring tutors and exerting influence (principally Somerset and then Dudley) were free from Henry VIII's conservative control. They would have been keen to see that any younger half-brother of Edward also had a Protestant education, but the boy's accession could then have provided the opportunity for his Guise mother and conservative councillors to use the French alliance to promote a move back toward Catholicism. Wriothesley being dead (1550) and Norfolk nearly eighty (he died in 1554), the senior lay conservatives would have been led by the Earls of Arundel – the conservative choice to marry Elizabeth in the early 1560s – and Sussex. Dudley/Northumberland had interestingly allied himself to conservative peers, led by Wriothesley and Arundel, in 1549–50 in mutual distrust of Somerset and only abandoned them when his position in power became more secure.[40] Thus he was capable of renewing this link under a new young king in 1553–4, perhaps by releasing Norfolk from the Tower and returning his lands. As he would not have been disgraced by a failed coup in 1553, he would still have been heading the regency Council for the new king and so been able to block any move to restore religious conservatism by pro-Catholic peers – or giving confiscated bishoprics back to men like Gardiner. The religious settlement of 1552 could have stayed in place, led by Cranmer as Archbishop, however much Dudley needed French support; or the conservative councillors and the new king's mother, Marie de Guise, could have replaced Northumberland in control of the government. Is it likely that a new king, born around 1540–2 and educated as a Protestant at least from Somerset's seizure of power in 1547, would have been willing to return to Catholicism once he had the choice as an adult?

Chapter Five

What if Edward VI had not died at fifteen in 1553, and the 'Edwardian Reformation' was not halted by Mary I?

Contrary to the old myth of Edward as a sickly child whose early death was inevitable, his health appears to have given no major cause for concern until his final illness. Henry VIII's extreme precautions to keep infection away from his household were a matter of prudence arising from a desire to preserve the heir he had taken so long to acquire, rather than of Edward being particularly prone to illness. The question of hereditary problems is valid, considering that Henry VIII's father, elder brother, and eldest son all died of some tubercular complaint – but Henry and his two daughters were all free of it. Edward certainly seemed a normal child to the acute observers at the Henrician court, foreign ambassadors in particular, who would have been quick to note any weakness. Apart from a 'quartan ague' in 1541 and an attack of measles in 1552, he suffered no major illness and in his early teens was taking part in the normal chivalric pursuits of an upper-class boy of his age. There were no signs until his prolonged ill-health in spring 1553 that his reign would not last for decades to come, and no concern about an early succession-crisis.

Edward's precocious interest in politics and administration, wisely indulged by the Duke of Northumberland after 1550, led to him taking an active part in Council discussions by the age of fifteen in 1552 and having details of the current currency crisis explained to him. In addition to his famous *Journal*, a diary kept since extreme youth, which is as revealing for what it leaves out as for its contents, Edward drew up notes on potential future policies. (Some commentators have detected a certain Tudor callousness reminiscent of his father, as in the brief comment on his uncle Somerset's execution.) He took an interest in 'reformed' religion with an unusual degree of zeal, listening avidly to long sermons and playing up to the image that reformers presented of him as their inspirational patron, the

'Young Josiah' who was expected to lead the nation against idolatry like his seventh century BC Jewish exemplar. Some writers like the *Journal*'s editor W.K. Jordan have declared hopefully that the lack of interest in sermons showed in that work indicates evangelical over-confidence about Edward's religious zeal. But in fact a separate royal notebook on his favourite sermons existed in the Royal Library in the 1620s when Bishop Montague saw it, though it has since disappeared.[1]

Edward shared a voracious capacity for classical and Biblical learning with his half-sister Elizabeth and his cousin Jane Grey. At a nearly similar age, his father (king at seventeen and ten months) – equally interested in learning as a boy according to nursery-visitor Erasmus[2] – had shown no interest in administration and had preferred sports, martial pursuits, and entertainments, though he was also an accomplished musician and Edward was not too 'puritanical' to enjoy watching or taking part in displays. Henry's interest in theology appears to have developed later than Edward's, and it is dubious how much of his learned 'Defence of the Seven Sacraments' against Luther (which won him the title of 'Defender of the Fiath' from Pope Leo X) was his own work. The themes developed for Edwardian pageantry, presumably chosen to reflect the boy's known interests, were chivalrous and martial as well as religious. Edward's interests and obsession with minute detail were more reminiscent of his grandfather Henry VII, and his personal piety and thirst for learning recall his great-grandmother Lady Margaret Beaufort.

The first long royal 'progress' that Edward made, during the summer of 1552, may have weakened his constitution further after the measles, but his loss of energy and the cough he developed the following winter gave no initial cause for major concern. His prolonged if not yet serious problems led to a consultation with a distinguished Italian doctor, Girolamo Cardano, early in 1553; he later claimed to have realized that Edward was dying but could not risk his ministers' anger by making an unfavourable prognosis. Mary and Elizabeth were summoned to see him, and the unusual deference and politeness shown by assorted councillors and courtiers would indicate that they were considering the possibility that Mary would soon be queen. Notably Northumberland showed no signs of having an alternative successor planned. Unable to shake his ill health off, by March the King was confined to Whitehall and unable to travel the short distance to Westminster to open Parliament. Observers were concerned at the ominous reports of his decline that spring, but serious planning for the succession came remarkably late, in June. The personal nature of kingly rule was such that the paralysis in government occasioned by a major royal illness inhibited action unless some senior minister took a lead. Even if Edward himself was unwilling to face the truth and his doctors were scared to warn him, the supposedly calculating Northumberland – possibly distracted by his own poor health – seems to have been taken by surprise and had no long-term plans drawn up when the crisis reached a peak in June. Indeed, the latest interpretation of events suggests that the infamous 'King's Device' to divert the succession to Lady Jane Grey was Edward's idea rather than Northumberland's.[3] If the *sine qua non* was a Protestant sovereign able to defend the religious reforms of 1547–53, it would have been more logical to back Elizabeth who was older than Jane and was named next to Mary in Henry VIII's will. Edward could not have doubted her religious loyalties, so presumably he or his advisers – Northumberland, a foe of Elizabeth's executed *inamorata* Thomas Seymour? – believed that the question mark over the legitimacy of her parents' marriage would undermine her acceptability abroad.

All of this indicates that the King's early death was not a serious consideration until the spring of 1553, and was not faced up to until late in his final illness. Even the alleged arch-Machiavellian 'power-broker' Northumberland was not preparing for the possibility months ahead of the King's death, though this may have been due to over-optimism by a man 'in denial' about the situation. But what if the King hailed by reformers had gone on to reign for decades? What if he had not succumbed, and gone on to reign as long as was expected? Edward had showed remarkably early talent for government, and was on the verge of achieving genuine power when he died. (W. K. Jordan, whose two-volume study of Edward's reign is the most thorough to date, is particularly praiseworthy about his potential as a ruler of uncommon ability.[4]) Northumberland had already initiated him into Council business, showing more of an ability to accommodate his wishes than the often overbearing Somerset had done as Lord Protector to 1549, and within the next couple of years the King could be expected to take on more day-to-day matters and initiate policies. He had already shown a desire to be a 'godly' ruler concerned for his subjects' well-being, with direction by legal measures if necessary, and his appetite for routine paperwork indicated that he was more likely to follow Henry VII rather than Henry VIII in his attitude to government. Unlike his father, there would be no ubiquitous 'Cardinal Wolsey' minister to take the burden of Council routine off his shoulders. If he had survived to adulthood, he should have proved an effective and conscientious king – and a determined 'evangelical' Protestant, as indicated by his personal papers and religious interests. The court would have continued to take the tone it had had in the early 1550s, with regular sermons and ideological zeal for the 'godly' cause (including in court iconography), which with the King now an active adult would develop in a militaristic manner. As has been noticed by historians, even in 1550–1

Edward showed distinct radical Protestant tendencies in his own handwritten drafts for the proposed revision of the statutes of the Order of the Garter. He was totally opposed to continuing an association with St George, worship of the saints being a 'papist' relic. He also showed early antagonism to the use of the name of Mass rather than Communion and any notion of the 'real presence' (instead of a mere 'remembrance') of Christ in the blood and wine, showing himself closer to Calvin than Luther in Reformation terms. At the age of eleven in spring–summer 1549, his treatise in French on the papal supremacy written as a present for Somerset roundly attacked papal leadership of Protestant persecution and criticized his father's executions of Protestants in the wake of the conservative Six Articles of 1539. The work was probably suggested by his French tutor Jean Belmain and heavily influenced by John Ponet's translation of Bernardino Ochino's attack on the papal claims for primacy, but showed individual touches and passionate identification with the 'martyrs'.[5]

The religious radicalism of the 1552 Prayer-Book was thus personally congenial to his views, not forced on him by Northumberland, and further moves in this direction would have followed his majority. His personal attitude towards Catholics may be seen in his uncompromising attitude towards his sister Mary's continued defiance of laws banning celebrating the Mass in the crisis of early 1551, though this had the added element of his sister's open and personal defiance at their interview. It was once assumed that Edward was a puppet in the hands of radical councillors, led by Northumberland, who meant to break the Princess' defiance, but in fact he warned Mary not to expect continuance of the previous forbearance towards her as only now did he take part in decision-making. When Emperor Charles V threatened war if Mary was not allowed to continue hearing Mass it appears that Secretary William Cecil informed the English ambassador Morrison that Edward was resisting the Council's desire to give way and threatened to burst into tears in his anger.[6] The Council had to resort to the leading radical bishops to persuade Edward, and even then he quoted the Old Testament about God's wrath on backsliders in ancient Israel. He clearly thought that both saving her soul and doing her duty to her king should impel Mary to give way, and could be expected to think similarly about the multitude of his Catholic subjects as an adult unless restrained or diverted. Would he have been as determined to execute Catholics for their own good as Mary was to be towards Protestants?

The idea of English support for international Protestantism that the (surviving) younger Dudleys and their supporters promoted under a doubtful and parsimonious Elizabeth in the 1560s and 1570s would have had unequivocal royal support – from a male ruler able to fight in person. The mixture of Arthurian chivalry and Protestant zeal seen in the works and actions of Sir Philip Sidney would have been likely to appeal to Edward. (Philip Sidney, born in 1554 as the son of Edward's older friend Henry Sidney and the godson of the new King-Consort Philip of Spain, would probably have been named 'Edward' Sidney.) Thus a more enthusiastic attitude than Elizabeth's could be expected towards giving sanctuary to the Dutch 'Sea Beggar' pirate rebels against Spanish Catholicism from 1568, and military aid to the Dutch revolt in due course. The idea of revolt against an anointed sovereign was distasteful to Elizabeth, but as Edward had already put – Protestant – conscience above obedience he could be expected to take a different view of 'godly' revolt. The Old Testament 's militant Kings of Israel were favourites of Edwardian sermonizers and authors, and once he was adult could provide inspiration for war on the ungodly in the manner of David, Soloman, and later rulers. It was leniency, not massacre, that brought Divine retribution (as seen with Saul's punishment for sparing the Amelikites). Edward, like Oliver Cromwell, showed every sign of taking his Old Testament seriously and being steeped in its language and precedents.

It should be mentioned in passing that the ascendancy of Northumberland over the government after autumn 1549 was not inevitable, and was due to a large extent o the mistakes and arrogance of Edward's uncles, the Duke of Somerset and Sir Thomas Seymour. Had either still been alive in 1553 events could have taken a different course.

French Protestants and the King's marriage
The Huguenot nobles' revolts against Catholic dominance in France in the early 1560s would have been the probable first occasion for such practical international action. France had been England's close ally in 1549–53, and if the intended alliance agreed in 1551 had been followed through Edward would have been married to King Henri II's daughter Elizabeth, born in 1545 (in real life married to Philip II instead after the Franco–Spanish rapprochement in 1559). The timing of the Franco–Spanish war in the 1550s, which proceeded independently of events in England and was primarily driven by Continental factors, would have made it probable that Henri would have been in need of English assistance in the mid-1550s and so forced to carry out the planned marriage to an impatient adult Edward. In the early 1550s Northumberland's England had been the junior partner, weakened by a costly war in Scotland from 1547 and a currency crisis in 1552, but despite the poor harvest and plague of 1558 (which in real life undermined Mary's reputation further) France would now be weaker as Henri was killed in a tournament accident in 1559. Lacking an adult ruler and with Francis II a sickly boy who soon died, the French court would have

been divided among rival factions as in real life and Huguenot nobles such as Coligny and Anthony of Bourbon would have been seeking Edward's aid in case of war with the Catholic Guises.

The combined power of Spain and the Empire, a threat to England under Charles' rule, would have been divided up in 1556–8. Philip would have been ruling Spain and the Netherlands, and even if Mary Tudor had escaped to the Continent in 1550–3 (or at a later date as she was ordered to choose between celebrating Mass and the Tower) she would presumably have died in 1558 or within a few years. Lacking more than one child due to Mary's infertility, Philip would have married one of Henri II's daughters (not Elizabeth had she married Edward), as part of the Habsburg-French peace of 1559. But the marriage of Elizabeth and Edward would not have affected the Spanish succession; Philip's heir was his son by his first marriage, the psychologically unbalanced Don Carlos, until he died in 1568 and he was succeeded in 1598 by his son by a subsequent wife, his niece Mary of Austria.

Like Mary but unlike Elizabeth, an adult King Edward would have encouraged militant piety at court. The clerics in favour would have been the providers of appropriately zealous sermons, again in contrast to the men who Elizabeth favoured, with the use of the 'Preaching Place' pulpit in the Pebble Court at Whitehall Palace (east of the extant Banqueting House) continuing as it had from 1547 as the main site for expositions on useful texts in front of a zealous king. Scholarly debates over theology with the sovereign would have been as important to the latter as they were to James I, and probably the monarch would also be regarded as impressively learned by some impressed foreign visitors and pedantic by others. An adult king would mean a proper privy chamber of aspirant young nobles (in real life denied to court until 1603); but unlike James' court, there would be no endemic drunkenness and unseemly behaviour given the strict Biblical morality that Edward was already showing by 1553. Edward was likely to have insisted on order and seemliness as the equally self-disciplined Charles I did after 1625 in real life.

More foreign Protestants would have followed those already coming to England as refugees or evangelizers before 1553, e.g. Ochino, Bucer, and Peter Martyr, and they would have been encouraging royal support for their communities at home at a time of inter-faith tension. The easy Channel crossing would have made England under its 'godly' ruler attractive for persecuted Huguenots once they lost out at the French court and the regency for Charles IX proved to be firmly Catholic from c. 1561. Huguenot nobles such as Coligny would have been keen to come to Edward's court as tension increased at home, taking part in tournaments and encouraging armed support for their co-religionists. There would have been more extravagant display and entertainment at Edward's court on the scale of that organized for the French diplomatic visit of 1551, which the King clearly enjoyed – with the King taking part in tournaments in person if it was not too dangerous. (In real life he started to take a limited role in 1552, showing no signs of constraint due to poor health.) Grandiose display was more common than is sometimes allowed for Edward's reign, as the King indulged the active young nobles around him (primarily the five Dudley brothers) in their love of display and competitiveness. They would have been among his closest companions, with the prospect of court offices and titles when the King was older – a return to the atmosphere of Henry VIII's boisterous companions in the 1510s was less certain given Edward's greater interest in religion and the strict behaviour of his clerical exemplars.

One major question is whom Edward would have married. Following the close alliance that Northumberland had arranged with France, would the initial talks of 1551 have borne fruit?[7] At the time Henri II had charge of the person of the candidate intended for Edward by his father – Mary Stuart, Queen of Scots, a refugee in France from the English attacks on her homeland since 1548. Henri, having sent troops to Scotland then to aid the national fight against Somerset's invasion and partial occupation, intended her as the bride of his eldest son, Francis, but in 1551 they were still too young to marry (eight and seven respectively). Somerset's attempts in 1547–8 to carry out Henry's plan for a Union of Crowns between England and Scotland had been thwarted by his troops' failure to secure all the Lowlands and/or Mary, the pro-English party among the Scots nobles that Henry had built up in 1542–3 having proved inadequate. Hidden away north of Glasgow, Mary had duly sailed for France to be brought up with Henri's children while French troops helped to wear down Somerset's occupation-army. (The final English positions in south-eastern Scotland had been abandoned in 1549.) Northumberland had resorted to resuming the plan for union by agreement with Henri, but the latter obviously preferred Mary for his own son and a union of Scotland with France, and would not abandon that even for his current close ally England. He needed English aid against the Emperor Charles V, the hereditary Valois enemy whose Habsburg dominions outnumbered and surrounded his own France, and the fervently Protestant English regime was not likely to prefer alliance with the ultra-Catholic Emperor to alliance with France. But Henri was not in enough need of England's goodwill to sacrifice his Scots marital link by handing over Mary Stuart, and one of his own daughters was a more likely candidate to be offered to Edward in the mid-1550s. Mary Stuart would thus have married Henri's eldest son Francis in 1558 as in reality. If Edward had secured

Henri's daughter Elizabeth and the marriage been carried out by 1559, she would not have been available to marry to Philip of Spain but might easily have fallen victim to childbirth or an epidemic. Her siblings were noticeably unhealthy, one brother dying as King of France at sixteen and a second at twenty-three; in real life she died at twenty-three in Spain. There was no guarantee that this match would have produced an heir for Edward VI; the combination of Tudor and later Valois ill-heath would have made it unlikely.

The latest outbreak of Habsburg-Valois warfare in 1557–9 was the most probable occasion of a marriage to cement the Anglo-French alliance; Edward's father had first married at just eighteen. But whereas Mary Stuart (born December 1542) was five years' Edward's junior, Henri's eldest daughter, Elizabeth, was eight years younger and his next daughter, Claude, ten years younger. If one of them had been chosen as Queen of England c. 1557 there would therefore be a long wait for children. Offering a non-royal noble girl of more appropriate age, presumably from a closely allied ducal house (as Marie de Guise had been offered to James V of Scotland), might be interpreted as an insult after the initial offer of the King's eldest daughter; in any case the English might have insisted that the bride convert to Protestantism. That would have held up a marriage under the devout Catherine de Medici as regent from 1559/60, though Henri had evidently not let the English State religion's similarity to French heretics' beliefs get in the way of 'realpolitik' in the 1551 alliance. A German Protestant princess of nearer Edward's own age was an alternative if the French talks stalled, in a continuation of Thomas Cromwell's German alliance plans of the late 1530s (c.f. Henry VIII and Anne of Cleves).

If the alliance had settled on a French royal bride, probably Elizabeth, her age would probably have meant no marriage until around 1560 (when she was fifteen) and no children for a year or two after that. In the interim, any sign of ill-health on Edward's part would have renewed anxiety about the succession and if he had insisted on emulating his father with personal participation in the war in Flanders he could well have been campaigning on the Continent in 1555–7. Lacking a wife to act as regent in his absence as Henry had arranged, he could not have used Mary Tudor as she was closely related to and religiously sympathetic to Charles V. Elizabeth had been kept away from court ever since her rumoured entanglement with Thomas Seymour's plot against Somerset had led to interrogation and disgrace in 1548, but was a possibility as a 'safe' and loyal Protestant had the King insisted on using a member of the scarce royal kin as regent. Alternatively, Northumberland could have taken the role with his poor health excusing his absence from campaign.

It would seem that the marriage of Jane Grey, Edward's cousin and eventual choice as his heir (though he had first settled on a hypothetical son of hers), and Northumberland's son Guildford in May 1553 was not arranged specifically to gain them the Crown as used to be assumed.[8] Edward's physical state in May/June 1553 means that it cannot be taken as certain that Jane – or her son – would have been his choice as heir in the 1550s or 1560s if he had been in good health but childless. But if he had ended up marrying Elizabeth of France a child was unlikely until the early 1560s, and some Protestant would need to be considered as heir in case Edward died (particularly on campaign). Jane and Guildford may well have had a son by this point (1555/7), and the choice would have lain between this boy and the much older Elizabeth whose accession would not mean another long regency.

Edward marries Mary Stuart?
But what if the English army invading Scotland in 1547/8 had been aided by some local Protestant lords into carrying out Henry VIII's plans to force the marriage of Edward and Queen Mary Stuart? Somerset's endeavour to force the issue was a repeat of Henry's failure – using him, then Earl of Hertford, as his general – in the 'Rough Wooing' of 1544. It only led to the Scots rallying against Henry's plans. But the useful capture of a number of leading Scots nobles at Solway Moss in 1542 had enabled Henry to bully or flatter them into acting as his agents, aided by dislike of the French orientation of Marie de Guise's regency, and some had converted to Protestantism, which gave them an ideological link to post-1547 England. John Knox and other preachers had been welcomed in Edwardian England. What if some bribed Scots Protestant lord kidnapped Mary to prevent her being taken off to France, and handed her over to the English for removal to London? (Kidnapping young Scots monarchs for political purposes was common under the Stuart dynasty, and from 1406 the young James I had been kept prisoner at the English court.) Alternatively, their physical possession of the Queen could have broken resistance, enabling them to install her as figurehead of a pro-English regime in Edinburgh. Presumably led by the Douglases and/or Lennoxes, this government would then have refused French military aid and imposed a Reformation on Scotland to politically neuter the Church and Catholic lords – the English policy for Scotland of 1560 imposed by Somerset in 1548? This would have meant that the English government did not have the real-life cost of occupying positions in Southern Scotland like Haddington in 1547–9, reducing the financial problems for Somerset. The French would not have been able to send armed support to the Scots government, as they did in real-life 1548, though as

they would still have been fighting England over Boulogne (occupied by England in 1544) in 1547 they could have endeavoured to start a revolt among Catholic nobles alienated from the pro-English regency. The Hamiltons, Catholic and the next heirs to Scotland after Mary, would have been their natural Lowland allies, with the Huntlys in Buchan within equally easy reach of French shipping.

How would Mary Stuart, brought up as a Protestant either in London or as the pawn of a faction of English-backed Protestant nobles (Henry VIII's allies of 1543?), fared as Edward VI's wife? Their temperaments were very different, with Edward's written words and public gravity showing him to be calm and methodical like Henry VII. Mary's later misjudgements of the 1560s were as much political as personal and she cannot be safely dismissed as a thoughtless, passionate girl romantically unsuited as a wife to the workaholic 'Young Josiah'. She gave a very favourable impression as Queen of France in 1559–60, and her isolation and traumatic reign in Scotland increased her misjudgements of men, not least her last two husbands and assorted eager plotters. She had no natural allies to trust in Scotland, a place alien to her under the control of rough noble faction-leaders who must have seemed a shock after polished French courtiers, in 1561, and faced the unbending suspicion of Knox and his clerics. Even when she married her young and equally untried second husband Darnley he turned out to be a feckless, immature, and spiteful drunk who collaborated with the murder of her Italian secretary Rizzio in front of her eyes, no doubt out of jealousy of his influence. It is possible that Darnley hoped his wife would have a fatal miscarriage from the shock of seeing Rizzio killed and believed the child to be Rizzio's, although Mary managed to win him round to backing her in escaping from his aristocratic allies after the killing. Her subsequent misjudgements of men and politics have to be seen in the light of her turbulent experiences in 1565–6, lacking anyone to trust, though comparable traumas did not make Elizabeth so prone to disastrous mistakes. The issue of her culpability in Darnley's murder and her 'abduction' by Bothwell are largely irrelevant to considering how she would have turned out as Edward VI's queen, English politics being less (openly) violent.

As Queen of England Mary would not have had the responsibility of ultimate political leadership, and it is unlikely that a careful and rigidly Protestant king like Edward (detail-obsessed even at fifteen as seen in his papers) would have allowed her many – if any – English Catholic ladies-in-waiting. As with Charles I's French Catholic wife Henrietta Maria in 1625, her own non-English Catholic entourage could be guaranteed by treaty – but sent home later by her husband. She would, however, have had ladies-in-waiting from 'safe', pro-English Scots dynasties that had backed the

Reformation. She did not enter into politics at the French court, where she resided until the age of eighteen, though she was young and overshadowed by the Guises and her mother-in-law; she may have asserted herself more at Edward's court with help from Catholic nobles who sought to use her as a conduit to the King for religious relief. Probably the atmosphere at the English court, more restrained and less full of open feuding than that in Edinburgh in the 1560s, and her reduced role as queen consort not regnant would have made her less vulnerable to mistakes. But she and Edward would have been a disparate pair, particularly if she had not been raised as a Protestant, and her opinions of the puritanical John Knox may indicate her potential bafflement at an adult Edward's similar theological zeal. This marriage would have carried out the Anglo-Scottish 'Union' a generation earlier than in reality, with Edward and Mary's marriage formally uniting the kingdoms – around 1556, once they were old enough (Edward eighteen, Mary fifteen?). In the long run, it is not impossible that mutual incompatibility could have led to a spectacular breakdown in their relationship with religion the main issue; anti-English lords in Scotland and the Catholic Guises were likely in this case to have encouraged her to return home and defy Edward. Edward, by all the early signs as cold-blooded as his father and grandfather, was capable of enforcing her continued residence in England lest she seek to reverse the 'godly' Reformation back in Scotland as a sovereign queen.

Mary Tudor – abroad or marginalized?

As for Mary Tudor – what if she had fled East Anglia by boat to the Netherlands rather than give up her Catholic worship as demanded by her brother, which nearly happened in 1550? Charles V had sent ships to lie off Harwich ready to collect her, but she chose not to leave. It is arguable that her main reason for staying was her role as Edward's next heir by her father's will, which meant that staying could yet bring about her succession and a chance to do God's work for her co-religionists. Would she have left England if Jane Seymour had had a second child and this person was Edward's heiress as of 1550, not Mary?

Given Edward's self-righteous hectoring of his sister for her obduracy in defying the law on her visits to court, his tolerance could not be expected to last indefinitely. In 1551 the Council had arrested her senior household officials, and if Edward's health had not declined another crisis could have broken out in a year or two. Edward's personal obduracy towards her at their interview of early 1551 shows that he had no intention of giving up pressure on her to conform, though on this occasion Charles V's threats saved her. In addition, the King's adulthood would decrease the chances that he might die young and Mary come to the throne, meaning that the Council treated her less warily, and if he had married Mary Stuart he could have had an heir around 1557/8, which removed her further from the throne. Once the English joined in the Valois–Habsburg war (1555/6?) Mary Tudor would have seemed to be the potential ally of an enemy potentate, particularly if resident in or near rebellious East Anglia within reach of Flanders. Mary never used her unhappiness at Edward's religious policies to plot against him, respecting her father's choice of heir, but her enemies would have been eager to accuse her of treachery and demand that the King lodge her in security (particularly if he left England to join Henri II on campaign). Faced with arrest and/or intimidation by her brother in the same manner as her father had treated her twenty years earlier, she could have decided to flee England after all – and then been married off to Philip of Spain by his father Charles V as a counter to the Anglo–French alliance?

Elizabeth Tudor. Would she have been able to marry Robert Dudley?
What of Elizabeth Tudor – would she have been married off by Edward to a Protestant prince as a political ally, despite the doubts over the legal legitimacy of Henry VIII and Anne Boleyn's marriage making some Continental sovereigns reject her? (Erik XIV of Sweden, her real-life suitor in the 1560s, is one possibility.) Or would the quibbles over her legitimacy have enabled her to wait until Amy Robsart fell down the stairs at Cumnor Place in 1560, and then marry Robert Dudley? By that point his father John Dudley, Duke of Northumberland, would presumably have retired as chief minister (in his late fifties), and Robert and his older brothers John (d. 1554 in real life, but after a Tower incarceration that would not have happened if Edward VI had been alive) and Ambrose would have continued the Dudley influence at court as mainstays of the regime. Their influence would have been as controversial as in real life, with John as Duke of Northumberland, Ambrose as Earl of Warwick or a new creation, and Robert among the King's close young courtiers. The Dudleys would have suffered no loss of estates in the period 1553–8, and have faced the enmity of the younger Seymours (for Somerset's execution) and the Howards (for Surrey's execution and the late Duke of Norfolk's disgrace). If Robert had tried to secure Elizabeth's hand (as no Continental ally of Edward's would have her?), the criticism of their family's pretensions would have been vicious. Success would depend on the King's decision as to whether the marriage was suitable. As in real life, it would have seemed that the Dudleys were aiming at the throne – particularly if Edward and Elizabeth of France or Mary Stuart had not yet had an heir. In a similar situation in 1515 Henry VIII's sister Mary (unlike Elizabeth, undeniably legitimate) had secretly married Henry's boon

companion Charles Brandon to force the King's hands, and they had faced his wrath and temporary disgrace but ultimately been accepted. Edward gave no signs of his father's violent temper as a teenager, but might still have found a secret marriage an affront to his dignity – with ever-helpful courtiers ready to point out that Elizabeth had been questioned for suspicious flirting with Thomas Seymour in 1548.

In the early 1550s Robert Dudley's brother-in-law Sir Henry Sidney was particularly close to the young King, along with the young Irish nobleman Barnaby Fitzpatrick (heir of the lordship of Ossory), and they would have been particularly important at the Edwardian court. Sidney would have been a favourite for preferment, as under Elizabeth, and the Irish Midlands connections of Fitzpatrick could have led to the zealous young King using him as the local leader of a Protestant 'plantation' in the area (as in real life Philip and Mary settled in Laios and Offaly). Sidney could have been Lord Deputy of Ireland in the 1560s, as in real life, but with a longer-term appointment and firmer royal support for large-scale Anglicization of native Catholic territories. Edward was more likely than Elizabeth to have made major efforts to 'plant' loyal and godly Englishmen in Ireland as early as the 1560s, once the Franco-Spanish war had ended and he could send troops to clear out local nobles who refused to convert to Protestantism. As with Elizabeth, native resentment would duly have been encouraged by the Tudor sovereign's international foes and rebellions been financed from Spain.

Government and foreign policy in the 1560s and 1570s

Northumberland was already showing a weariness with power by 1553, and as long as his position was safe from post-resignation reprisals from victorious enemies he would have had little need to stay indefinitely. More likely he would have retired in the mid- to late 1550s once his protégé had established a sure footing as an adult ruler. His younger sons Ambrose and Robert were friends of the King and as active young warriors could play a leading role in an English expeditionary force aiding France in Flanders c.1557. (In real life, they had to prove their loyalty to Mary by fighting in the war for the Empire/Spain, and their brother Henry was killed at the battle of St Quentin.) If the eldest Dudley son, John, survived he would have succeeded his father as duke in due course, with earldoms for the others and a prominent role at court for Guildford had his wife or son been heir until Edward had a son.

It is quite possible that Edward would have rehabilitated his cousin Edward Seymour, Lord Hertford, Somerset's son, with some of the late Duke's lands – or even that Hertford may have married Catherine Grey with Edward's blessing rather than Elizabeth's wrath. The other main victim of the 1549–51 power-struggles, Edward's other uncle Thomas Seymour, had left no male heir to rehabilitate (though possibly a daughter by Edward's stepmother Catherine Parr?). As in the real-life 1560s after Mary's death, other stalwarts of the regime would have included Catherine Parr's brother the Marquis of Northampton and the aristocratic 'survivors', the Earls of Pembroke (pro-reform) and Arundel (pro-Catholic conservative). Paget and Paulet/Winchester, and the naval commander Lord Clinton, would have been serving Edward as they did both Mary and Elizabeth, loyal to whoever was in power. Unlike in real life, Jane Grey's father, the Marquis of Dorset (descendant of Edward IV's queen, Elizabeth Woodville, by her first husband), would have continued to be one of the senior nobles at court and would in due course have passed his lands and titles to the Grey sisters. Jane would have inherited her boorish parents' country house, Bradgate Manor in Northamptonshire, and probably been Marchioness or Countess of Dorset. Among Northumberland's own clientage who owed their rise exclusively to his favour, Thomas Palmer and John Gates would have been controversial figures on account of their role in Somerset's entrapment (or, if he was guilty of plotting, exposure) and other dubious activities on their master's behalf. In real life Mary Tudor executed them in 1553 for opposing her accession. It is possible that once Northumberland was dead or in retirement their enemies, led by the Seymours, would have closed in and Edward – needing to blame someone for his uncle's death apart from himself and Northumberland? – would have been tempted to abandon them or at least require their retirement. They could then have played the sacrificial role that Northumberland's father Edmund Dudley did in real life for Henry VIII in 1509–10.

The next chief minister would probably have been Northumberland's protégé William Cecil, already 'Secretary' in 1553, with his rise to power uninterrupted by Mary's reign. (The Lord Chancellor of 1553, Bishop Nicholas Goodrich, and Lord Treasurer Paulet/Winchester were much older and less likely to hold great influence.) Ubiquitous as Elizabeth's man of business in the 1560s, Cecil would have been equally invaluable to Edward with his passion for paperwork and was in a position to forge as close a relationship with his master as Thomas Cromwell did with Henry VIII. As far as can be assessed both also had similar views on the need to support international Protestantism, with Edward probably less wary about spending money on overseas ventures than Elizabeth due to a desire to win a reputation as a European warrior-statesman like his father. (The iconography of Edwardian pageants in the King's adolescence suggested such a future role for him, appropriate for a male sovereign.) The number of Protestant European refugees or visitors who had sought patronage in

Edwardian England would have continued to rise, with the King's possible participation in an anti-Habsburg war in the 1550s an obvious stimulus to his role as a militant Protestant champion. Men of European renown and 'radical' scholarship such as Bucer would provide the Protestant stimulus to the Church of England that in reality fell to English-born returned exiles after 1559, though Edward – like Elizabeth – may have looked askance at Calvin on account of his views on monarchy. Calvin and John Knox would have excluded Edward from their fulminations about inadequate rulers on account of his being a 'godly magistrate' and an example to his peers, but it is likely that whether or not the English were able to bring about a reformation in Scotland in the 1550s the turbulent Knox would have made too many enemies to stay long in England. (He had already clashed with Cranmer, the King's revered godfather, before Edward's death.) Sending him back to Edinburgh to use his energies in cleaning up the 'liberated' Scottish Church from Popery would have been advantageous to all concerned.

Cranmer, already over seventy in 1553, would have been able to live out his final years in comparative peace as archbishop, and probably would have died before 1560. Jewel and other Anglican thinkers would not have been radicalized by exile, but the same sort of influence would have been provided by foreign-born Protestants resident in England through the 1550s and as the French government began to crack down on Huguenot congregations in the early 1560s there would have been an influx of émigrés – both seeking aid against the French government and, as zealots inclined to a Presbyterian form of worship, encouraging that extension of reform in the English Church. The London 'overseas church' congregations would have been the obvious centre for Huguenot propaganda and debate, with a stimulus to the 'radical' wing of the Church that would have served to encourage younger English theologians and prevent any abandonment of the 1552 'status quo' after the deaths of Northumberland and Cranmer.

Matthew Parker would have been the main contender to succeed Cranmer as Archbishop of Canterbury, as his protégé, having probably received some minor bishopric in the 1550s, with the more senior and outstanding Nicholas Hooper probably too controversial for his criticisms of aristocratic 'un-Christian' greed and neglect of the poor. His defiance of the 'moderate' Church position of continuing to use the clerical garments prescribed by the previous, Catholic era also isolated him – even from Cranmer – and made him unlikely to be chosen except by a royal 'fiat' in defiance of majority episcopal opinion. Hugh Ridley, aged around sixty in 1560, would have had a chance to be made archbishop of Canterbury had Cranmer died by then but would subsequently have been seen as too old. He was a staunch upholder of the traditional vestments unlike Hooper, and his appointment would have led to a preservation of the 'status quo' as in fact re-emerged after 1559.

Elizabeth firmly backed the traditionalist clerics and required the use of the established finery instead of the plain black 'Geneva gown' used by the Calvinists; indeed clergy who defied this rule were deprived of office. Edward is likely to have been more open-minded, or even to have been persuaded of his duty to banish the 'popish' survival of traditional vestments by theological argument by visiting Calvinist preachers. Calvin did not achieve serious influence over English radicals until the mid-1550s, so in reality he had no chance to send preachers to Edwardian England and his followers had to turn to the exiles settled in Switzerland around 1555. Had there still been a Protestant king in England at this stage, the latter would have been open to persuasion – but at risk of deciding that Calvin's attitude towards crowned sovereigns was not respectful enough of their authority.

The Anglican Church would have been more 'radical' than in Elizabeth's 1560s, with the 1552 Prayer-Book as its mainstay and Hooper and Ridley still alive and in office probably into the 1560s. But without exile in the mid-1550s in Switzerland to radicalize a number of leading figures, further inclination towards Calvinism would have had to come via foreign visitors. The zealous, autocratic Edward VI would not have faced the criticisms of his lukewarm attitude towards radicals, preaching, and vestiarian reform that Elizabeth did, but would have been likely to be cautious about 'devolved' religion that was not under strict episcopal control such as the 'prophesyings'. Edward could have ended up as suspicious of local Church congregations acting outside episcopal control as Elizabeth was, and sought to impose a series of strict disciplinarians as bishops with rigorous enforcement of canon law. But, given the atmosphere in which he had been brought up at court in the early 1550s, he would not have taken such a conservative standpoint about issues such as the wearing of surplices and clerical marriage; his Church would have been able to comprehend more radicals than Elizabeth's did, with men such as Edmund Grindal less likely to meet trouble unless they had been too tolerant about breaches of royal instructions and/or canon law.

Edward is likely to have been eager to convert his remaining Catholic subjects to the paths of righteousness and thus to have made an effort to provide more active Protestant proselytizers among the clergy in areas such as Catholic Lancashire and the North-East, perhaps led by zealot bishops, and the halt to radical initiatives in Catholic areas after 1549 – politically necessary then – would probably have been reversed once the adult King had the time and energy to consider such matters. The 'young Josiah' flattered by zealot preachers would have considered it his duty to deal with obstructive Catholics as much as Mary did concerning Protestants, and any moves by Catholic peers in the North on Mary Tudor's behalf during the Habsburg-Valois war would have brought back memories of the locals' disloyalty to their King in the mid-1530s. His father's son, Edward would not have tolerated the 'laissez faire' policy that Elizabeth found wise in the North in the 1560s longer than necessary. Once England was at peace, possibly after the resolution of the first round of French civil wars in the mid-1560s, the North would have received more royal attention – perhaps with a 'progress' like Henry's of 1541 – and loyal peers such as a Dudley, the zealously Protestant Earl of Huntingdon, or the experienced Earl of Sussex been installed as head of the 'Council of the North' to disarm troublemakers and promote Protestant clerics. Huntingdon, a remote royal cousin with a marginal claim to the throne which the more 'godly' nobles considered seriously during Elizabeth's illness in real-life 1562, would have been more congenial to Edward for his Protestant enthusiasm than he was to Elizabeth. He would have been imposing reformed clerics and the canon laws of 1552 on the Northern Church, and evicting more unofficially Catholic clergy for evasion or defiance than Elizabeth's officials did. If Edward had been married to Mary Stuart and/or the Reformation been imposed on Scotland c. 1560 the Northern Catholic lords could not have relied on official Scots support – the Protestant Earl of Moray was the likeliest head of a pro-Edwardian government in Edinburgh in the 1560s. Had ˙Edward been intervening in the French civil war in the mid-1560s to back the Huguenots, this would have provided a logical reason for the Guise faction to meddle with his own dissidents in retaliation and send support to Catholic rebels. The result may well have been the equivalent of the real-life 'Revolt of the Earls' of 1569–70, though if Mary Stuart had been married to Edward she would not have been available as their figurehead. They would have been crushed in any case, with Edward being as brutal as Henry VIII had been in 1536–7.

From 1560, England's French ally was distracted by growing religious turmoil over the rising power of the Huguenot congregations and their noble sympathizers. The sympathies of the Edwardian regime would have been with their fellow Protestants, and with Mary Tudor presumably now dead and Philip of Spain preoccupied at home England would not have needed French military aid against the Habsburgs. (If Edward had married Mary Stuart, it would have posed a dilemma in that the Catholic 'ultras' in France were led by her maternal Guise relatives.) As an adult male war-leader and a Protestant zealot, Edward VI is likely to have led his troops to France in 1562/3 – in the tradition of his father in 1513 and his grandfather in 1492 –

and given military assistance to the Huguenots in the North. As with Henry in 1544, Boulogne – handed back to France by Northumberland as too costly to maintain – would have been an obvious target as it could be besieged by land and sea, and Normandy liable to be invaded by sea from Southampton or Portsmouth. Edward may not have been as cautious over the cost of intervening in force as Elizabeth was, as he valued religion more highly, and thus a larger force than in real life was likely to end up attacking 'New Haven' (Le Havre) c. 1563.

England and France could also have been clashing over Scotland by this point. If England had secured Mary Stuart and a Union of Crowns in 1548 – or, less likely, by agreement with France in the 1550s – the French would have been baulked of their ambitions in Scotland in the 1550s and would not have been garrisoning troops there. Presumably England would have sponsored a reformation to crush the power of the Church in Scotland, aided by land-hungry Francophobe peers in the manner of the real-life 'Lords of the Congregation' that Elizabeth and Cecil backed in 1560. The union would not have prevented the discomfited Catholic peers, a vociferous minority looking for outside Catholic help as in the real-life 1560s to 1590s, seeking to expel English influence and Protestantism – and an Anglo–French rift would have enabled France to back them. The Empire and Spain would have been likelier allies for Highland Catholic peers in the 1550s, in order to distract England from aiding France; but after the Franco-Spanish peace of 1559 France had less reason to need English aid. Catholic zealots such as the Guises were likely to encourage Catholic revolt in Scotland even if Queen-Mother Catherine de Medici's government did not; if Mary Stuart was under Edward's control (as his wife) in London their likely agents would have been the next dynastic heirs, the powerful Lowland family of the Hamiltons under the pro–French Duke of Chatelherault.

If the union had not gone through in 1548 or the 1550s, Mary Stuart would have stayed in France until 1561 and then returned home as independent sovereign of Scotland. The English government of the 1550s could still have backed a Protestant peers' revolt against the pro–French, Catholic regency of Marie de Guise in Scotland in order to weaken Catholicism and French influence – while pretending to their ally Henri II that it was purely a Scottish matter. Any attempt by the Edwardian regime to aid a Protestant revolt to overthrow the Guise regency in the 1550s or to coerce an adult Mary thereafter would have annoyed the French government, adding to tension. At the latest, if Marie de Guise had kept control of Scotland for her daughter and her Church as she did in real life the weakening of French power from 1560 would have enabled England to aid a Protestant revolt and further the Reformation then, as in real life.

Government by a pro-English faction of nobles, possibly led by Mary's half-brother the Earl of Moray, and a Kirk led by the pro-English Knox would have faced Mary on her return home. Edward, like Elizabeth, would have been keen to marry off Mary to a reliable husband to produce Protestant heirs; as in real life, his cousin Margaret Douglas could have pushed the claims of her son Lord Darnley.

It is uncertain if Edward would have intervened in the French civil war in 1562/3 in person in the manner of Henry V, taking advantage of the turmoil at court to assist his co-religionists in Normandy. But he is likely to have put more resources into the campaign than the dubious Elizabeth did, believing in it as a 'godly' cause and being able to utilize the still-English foothold at Calais. Thus the English army could have secured Le Havre and aided Huguenot nobles in Normandy better than Ambrose Dudley did in real-life 1563, giving the Huguenots a better bargaining-position for resulting negotiations and a stronger military position in the uneasy truce of the later 1560s. Edward would have come out of the crisis as the champion of European Protestantism, and his possession of Calais enabled him to put military pressure on the French regency government to keep to whatever terms were agreed. If the Valois regime had still dared to risk another English invasion from an adult male ruler by massacring the Huguenots in 1572 – arguable if they felt their survival as a Catholic state was at threat – Edward VI is more likely than Elizabeth to have responded militarily to the atrocity, plunging England into a French civil war as in the 1410s. The main 'caveat' to this scenario for post-1572 is that Edward might already have been aiding the 'Sea Beggars' in their Dutch revolt against Philip II of Spain from 1568 with more enthusiasm than the cautious and parsimonious Elizabeth – meaning that he could not fight both Spain and France. In that case, like Elizabeth, his expressions of horror at the atrocities would not have led to active intervention provided that he received assurances about future conduct and French promises would have had to suffice.

If Edward was keenly acting as the chief ally of European Protestants in the 1570s and early 1580s – the course of action urged on Elizabeth by the more zealous of her advisers, such as Leicester (Robert Dudley) and Walsingham – English volunteers, and ultimately troops, could well have been active in Holland from 1572 and a larger-scale intervention have been underway before 1585. The cost would have been as large as that which put Elizabeth off intervening, though a more vigorously Protestant zealotry for new laws in Parliament would have encouraged the 'Puritan' MPs in the latter to fund such a foreign policy (at first, anyway) as in the 1620s. In retaliation, Spain would have been meddling in Ireland and Scotland to encourage Catholic revolt – if Mary Stuart was Edward's (Protestant)

Queen, quite possibly backing a Catholic pretender (a member of the Hamilton dynasty, the next heirs, or a Spanish princess promised to a Catholic noble?). If Mary Stuart had not been secured as Edward's wife for a Union of Crowns but had returned to Scotland from France in 1561, married Darnley and then Bothwell, and been overthrown as in real life, Edward VI's government would have been backing the Protestant regency for James VI – promising him one of Edward's daughters as a wife? If Edward had married Elizabeth of Valois c. 1557–9 as arranged by the 1551 treaty, any daughters of the marriage would have been around James VI's age (possibly a little older); in real life she married Philip of Spain and their daughter Isabella was born in 1566.

If exiled in England or back in France from 1568, Mary would have been the Spanish candidate to lead Scotland back to Catholicism and keep England busy at home. Edward was as capable as Elizabeth of keeping a potentially dangerous Mary Stuart prisoner for years if necessary, though as the marriage of Henry VIII and Jane Seymour was not regarded as illegal by Catholics (Catherine of Aragon had been dead by then) Mary and her papal sponsors could not claim that she was rightful Queen of England. At best Mary was Edward's heir, and then only if he had no children. On the legalistic grounds of Henry VIII's will, indeed, she was less likely to be regarded as eligible for the English throne by senior figures at court than were the children of Jane and Catherine Grey. The Dudley clan, probably Edward's closest advisers, would have backed the Greys due to Jane marrying Guildford Dudley; only marginalized Catholc peers could be expected to back Mary Stuart. The Pope could not have issued a bull denouncing Edward as a usurper as he did to Elizabeth in 1570, as his parents' marriage was legal in Catholc eyes. But Philip II would have been able to cite English Protestant persecution of Catholics (after a Northern revolt?) as a reason for deposing the Tudor 'heretic' once England and Spain moved into conflict.

An early Edwardian intervention in the Netherlands to assist the Dutch might have brought that conflict forward from the 1580s, Elizabeth in real life having done all she could to postpone it and not sent troops to Holland until after the assassination of William 'the Silent' in 1584. But a more belligerent, Edwardian England would have had an army with more recent large-scale military experience on the Continent than Elizabeth's and would have been less likely to make such a poor showing in Holland from 1585. The King's religious zeal would have won plaudits if not (once the price of war became apparent) money from religiously radical MPs, and the English army would have had experience of larger-scale campaigns in France after 1562 than in reality. Possessing Calais with its port, they could harass Spain at sea more widely than they did in the real-life 1570s, hindering Spain's seaborne aid to their troops in the Netherlands. Assuming Philip did not win over the French government to accept his aid in blockading Calais and taking it from the 'heretics', France is unlikely to have had the military power and unity in the 1570s to take Calais and its English squadron would have been a constant irritant to Spanish convoys. Indeed, it would be one reason for Philip to delay breaking diplomatic relations with England as long as possible whatever the provocations from pirate squadrons roaming the Caribbean and the Pacific. Once war broke out England could cut his links to his troops in the Netherlands, as well as sending its own troops by land into Flanders to mount a 'pincer' attack on Bruges, Brussels or Antwerp with the Dutch.

Drake and Hawkins would have been as important to Edward as to Elizabeth in waging war with Spain on the cheap at sea, and in London the ministerial proponents of an aggressive Protestant foreign policy in Europe – Leicester (Robert Dudley) in particular – would have been backed up more firmly by their sovereign. (The caveat to this is if the King had become as parsimonious as his grandfather Henry VII in his middle years and the cost of a full-scale war seemed excessive.) Edward would have recognized the talents of the resolutely Protestant spymaster Walsingham, ambassador in Paris at the time of the 1572 massacre, as readily as Elizabeth did, although finance and the need to avoid fighting both France (even in its divided state) and Spain would have argued in favour of a delay in outright hostility. Conversely, Philip could not support the Catholic cause in France as the Guises' paymaster, fight the rebels in the Netherlands, and tackle England all at once, and is unlikely to have declared war on England as long as he could fight a 'proxy' war by stirring up rebellion in Ireland. The outbreak of open war between England and Spain is unlikely until the 1580s due to the pivotal role of France, but once that country had broken down into outright civil war the English King would have been morally obliged to support the Huguenots again and the Catholic 'Holy League' would have been duly outraged and thus willing to aid Philip against Edward. The 'pay-off' for Philip could well have been Guise support for a siege of Calais, to break the English naval threat to his shipping in the Straits of Dover and enable his convoys to pass unharassed to deliver troops and supplies to his army in the Netherlands. Thus around 1585 the Anglo-Spanish war would have broken out as in reality, though with an initial focus on control of the Calais fortress and with English ships attempting to destroy an 'Armada' aimed at assisting the Spanish and French Catholics on shore in ending the English Continental empire.

Other possible political outcomes of the 1550s and after
The Tudors were never renowned for their fertility and many of them were
not robust. So:

*(i) Could a strength-sapping Continental campaign with a long siege of
Le Havre in 1563 have undermined Edward VI's health and precipitated
his death in his mid-twenties?*
The epidemics that afflicted sixteenth century warfare were well-known,
and some campaigns – including that of 1563, in real life centred around an
English attack on Le Havre to aid the Huguenots – resulted in returning
soldiers bringing disease back to England. (The commander, Ambrose
Dudley, was never physically robust after his wounds in the campaign.) The
King would have had the best accommodation available, with the sort of
sumptuous tents that Henry VIII had used at the 'Field of the Cloth of Gold'
and on the 1544 campaign. The English would also have been able to use
Calais as their headquarters, as in this scenario England and France would
have been allies through the 1550s and Henri II would have had no reason
to seize Calais as he did when England was a Habsburg ally in real-life 1558.
Edward would have been keen to 'prove himself' with a victory in the
manner of the young Henry VIII at the 'Battle of the Spurs' in Flanders in
1513. He could still have been exposed to bad weather on the march in
Picardy or Normandy to aid the Huguenots, or while encamped outside the
walls of a strategic town like Le Havre ('Newhaven') during a siege. It does
not seem to have taken much for tuberculosis to take hold on him in winter
1552–3, possibly assisted by his weakness after the measles in 1552;
genetically speaking, his uncles Arthur and Henry Fitzroy had succumbed
to lingering declines in their teens (fifteen and seventeen). The Lennox
brothers, Lord Darnley and Charles Stuart, descendants of his aunt
Margaret Tudor, were unhealthy – Darnley was a drunkard and may have
had syphilis, and Charles died at twenty-five in 1576. Margaret's son James
V died at thirty in December 1542 after a seemingly minor illness added to
depression after the military disaster of the Solway Moss debacle. Even if
Edward had escaped the threat of major illness in his teens he could have
been at risk from the strain of campaigning, and the events of summer 1563
in Northern France proved too much for him. So it is possible that he would
have died on campaign or soon after his return to England, aged twenty-five
or six.

Elizabeth would have then succeeded, assuming that Mary Tudor was
dead and that Edward did not think up some solution to the dispute over
Anne Boleyn's marriage like the real-life 'King's Device'. By then Jane Grey,
aged twenty-six and Guildford Dudley would have been likely to have

children, so if Edward had been keen on the same line of succession as in real-life 1553 Jane could have had an 'heir male' of around seven or eight to take the throne. There would have been no need to substitute Jane for her unborn heir as in real life. This would have entailed a long regency with Jane and/or Guildford as regent; little is known of Guildford's capacity (and speculation about him has usually been derogatory) but Jane was intelligent, high-principled, and devotedly Protestant so congenial to Edward. The Duke of Northumberland, if still alive, would have been around sixty and would have come in for as fierce criticism for masterminding a 'Dudley coup' as he did in real life in 1553 – but with the excluded Tudor princess the Protestant Elizabeth she would have been more acceptable to dubious councillors than the Catholic Mary.

The adult Elizabeth, if not married off abroad (in Sweden as queen to Eric?), would have been a wiser choice of heir for Edward in 1563 and could have been backed by the assorted ministers and courtiers offended by the pretensions of Jane's parents, the Duke and Duchess of Suffolk, and the Dudleys. If Elizabeth had not been married off abroad on account of her dubious legitimacy, the mysterious death of Amy Robsart at the foot of the stairs of Cumnor Place in 1560 could have assumed importance as in real life. The suspicious death of Robert Dudley's wife would have been a problem if Elizabeth, as in real life, sought to marry him – and as probable heiress but not yet queen the barrier it placed to the match would have been less. Elizabeth could have gone ahead in 1561 or 1562 and married Dudley secretly, as Catherine Grey married Edward Seymour (Earl of Hertford) in defiance of the sovereign. The Dudleys would then be accused of endeavouring to secure a grip on the Crown by marrying the two closest heiresses – Elizabeth Tudor and Jane Grey – and Edward would have been in the position of Henry VIII in 1514, his sister married in defiance of him to his close friend. Like Henry then, Edward would probably have accepted the match – and Robert could have had the earldom of Leicester, his compensatory title of real-life 1564, from him. If Elizabeth, only thirty in autumn 1563, and Robert Dudley had had a child by the time Edward VI died and Jane been childless (or she or Guildford had died), the Dudleys could then have backed Elizabeth as queen in an uneasy alliance with the Howard family – Elizabeth's cousins – against Catherine Grey and her son. Catherine as queen would mean the return to power of the Seymours, who Northumberland had removed from government in 1549, and if the Duke of Somerset had been executed (as in real-life 1552) Northumberland's sons would be very reluctant to have Somerset's son as 'King Consort' in 1563.

(ii) If Edward VI had only had daughters like Henry VIII in the early 1530s, would a daughter and heiress (born around 1560?) then have been engaged to the safely Protestant James VI of Scotland for a new Union of Crowns?

There was no clear rival male contender for the marriage among England's allies, except possibly the youngest son of Henri II of France, Hercule/Francis, born in 1553 – the would-be fiancé of Elizabeth Tudor in real-life 1581. Edward's daughter would have been born in the late 1550s at the earliest, though if he had married Elizabeth of France (as planned in 1551) the Princess would have been facing a marriage to her uncle, which the Church would hardly approve of. Such marriages were a matter of 'realpolitik' and acceptable among the Habsburgs, with Philip II marrying his Austrian niece in the 1570s, but not in England or France. As a result, a marriage to a younger brother of the eccentric King Eric of Sweden (John or Charles) would have been more likely, producing a Tudor-Vasa dynasty on Edward VI's death. The age of any participants would have meant that only an engagement could be agreed, not an actual marriage – and an Anglo-French marriage-agreement would have been a probable casualty of any Anglo-French dispute during the religious wars. This brings the possibility into play that the militantly Protestant Edward could have married his heiress to the young Huguenot leader Henri of Navarre (later Henri IV of France), born in 1553, before the latest failed Catholic/Protestant truce in France saw Queen-Mother Catherine de Medici betroth her daughter Marguerite to him as in real life. The Valois, Henri's dynasty, would thus end up on the English not the French throne – and an English- Navarrese alliance would be tempting for an aggressive Edward as promising a restoration of English influence in his ancestors' duchy of Aquitaine, next-door to Navarre.

It is conceivable that part of an Edwardian English move in support of the Scots lords who deposed Mary in 1567 would have been to insist on the union of Edward's heiress to Mary's infant son, excusing it as vital to protect Scottish Protestantism against the Catholic Mary and her Guise sponsors. As in real life, the shaky Protestant regency for James VI would have been in need of English support and Edward VI could have exploited this. Thus England would accept Mary's deposition if her son married the Tudor heiress, and Mary herself – as a Catholic, with no hope of Edward's hand if he was a widower – would have been held in 'protective custody' in England as safer than allowing her to go to France. Despite the religious wars, the French Crown – organized by her Guise relatives – could mount an expedition to restore her and Catholicism to power in Edinburgh if she arrived in Paris.

Thus the infant James VI would be engaged to a daughter of Edward VI and Elizabeth of France, probably his near-contemporary. The marriage would take place in the 1580s as England sought James' assistance in dealing with the Armada, and if Edward had lived to something like his father's age James would have succeeded to the English throne (albeit only as co-ruler) around 1593.

Chapter Six

What if Jane Grey had been successfully installed in power in July 1553?

The regime of the controversial sixteen–year–old Jane, the choice of the dying Edward VI as his Protestant successor to exclude his sisters, never achieved significant recognition outside London. Unlike other Tudor regimes, it failed to capitalize on possession of the sinews of power – the capital, the Tower arsenal, and the support of the senior ministers – and fell to a provincial revolt, launched by the gentry of East Anglia on Mary's behalf. The exclusion of Henry VIII's daughters, Mary as a Catholic and Elizabeth as of dubious legitimacy, ignored Henry's own will and passed the Crown onto the eldest grand-daughter of Henry's younger sister, Mary, Queen of France and Duchess of Suffolk (1495–1533), whose family were next heirs in Henry's will. The family of Henry's elder sister Margaret, Queen of Scotland (1489–1541), had been excluded as foreign-born; in any case her eldest grand-daughter, Mary Stuart, was already engaged to the Dauphin Francis, the heir of France.

The surprising choice of heir in June 1553 had some legal basis if it was accepted that the annulment of Henry's first two marriages was more important than his subsequent ignoring of this in his will, but the first draft of Edward's 'Device' on the succession had not chosen Jane at all. Instead, he had settled on 'the Lady Jane's heirs male', followed by the male heirs of her sisters Catherine and Mary, in order to provide a male heir.[1] Only having been married on 25 May, a few weeks before the initial draft of the 'Device', Jane and her husband, Guildford Dudley, were not going to produce this heir in less than eight to nine months at best – and as Edward was already gravely ill it is open to question if he seriously thought he could live until they did. Mary had been married at the same time as Jane, to Arthur Grey, but was only about thirteen; Catherine was still unmarried. The initial 'Device', in Edward's own hand, may have been put together without the advice of his Council or his doctors, and was in line with his precocious interest in policy and his devotion to the evangelical cause in which Jane had been tutored by her parents, the Duke and Duchess of Suffolk. It represented an attempt to preserve Henry's belief in a male ruler as well as the main reason of keeping the throne with a Protestant. Frances, Duchess of Suffolk, Jane's ambitious and boorish mother, born in 1517, was closer to the throne but not popular or – possibly the clinching factor for Edward – as zealously religious as Jane.

Some time before 25 June Edward informed his ministers of it, and the resulting discussions were dominated by the effective regent since 1549, the Lord President of the Council John Dudley, Duke of Northumberland, whose advice was presumably conclusive in the resulting change. As he was Guildford's father, it was subsequently assumed that the whole idea of giving the Crown to his daughter-in-law was his as yet another Dudley 'power-grab'. Certain councillors were apparently unhappy at excluding the legitimate heir even if it was to preserve the gains of the 'Edwardian Reformation' from Mary's inevitable religious alterations, although the extent of their worries at the time may have been less than they endeavoured to assert in retrospect once Mary had secured power. Even recently, with Edward clearly dying if possibly living for some months yet, grants of land to Mary by the Council may indicate that even Northumberland had not turned against her succession.[2] But the King's wishes and the need to save the Church won out, with the chance of putting his son-in-law on the throne as consort another reason for Northumberland to support the drastic and risky coup against Mary. It should, however, be noted that Northumberland had initially been trying to have Guildford married off into the Hastings family as part of a normal inter-magnate marital alliance, rather than to Jane; when the May 1553 marriages of the Dudley children were being arranged he was not chiefly considering a Guildford-Jane alliance to put the latter on the throne. If he had been looking for a Dudley on the throne, until Edward fell ill he had the opportunity to marry the King to his daughter Catherine, and if he had been aiming for Jane and Guildford as his candidates once Edward's health declined seriously (in February–March 1553) that marriage would have been considered then. A rushed Jane-Guildford marriage then could have been hoped to produce an heir before Edward died, with Northumberland as regent for the next twelve to fifteen years as more politically and militarily experienced than the child's father. But there is no sign of the Duke taking quick measures to assure his position at this stage, as could have been expected had he decided that he could not allow Mary to succeed. The fact that he did not back Elizabeth, who was nineteen, a daughter of Henry VIII so able to act as a focus of popular loyalty unlike the unknown Jane, and capable of being a strong Protestant ruler, does not mean that he cynically preferred a 'puppet' married to his son. More likely, Edward decided to exclude her on account of the doubts over her parents' marriage being legal – even though it had been performed by his godfather and Archbishop, Thomas Cranmer.

The ports were closed and a news 'blackout' imposed when Edward died on 6 July at Greenwich, and on the 9th the unaware Jane was summoned from Chelsea to a meeting of senior ministers with her parents at the Northumberland residence outside London, Syon House. Informed of her accession as the late King's desire, she showed no eagerness for usurping the throne of the expected successor, Mary, and had to be bullied into compliance by her parents and Northumberland. The following day she was escorted down-river to London to be proclaimed queen and be lodged in the Tower. Unfortunately Mary, summoned from her residence at Hunsdon (Essex) to Greenwich by Northumberland in the King's name on the 6th, was warned en route by her jeweller at Hoddesdon that Edward had died and she should flee – Sir Nicholas Throckmorton, a junior courtier (and a Protestant), later claimed he had sent the message out of alarm at the illegal usurpation. Fleeing into Cambridgeshire and staying the night at Sawston Hall, Mary evaded the pursuing Dudley henchmen sent after her under Northumberland's third son Robert who passed through Sawston and continued to Cambridge on the 7th while she had turned off onto the Newmarket road. Discovering their mistake, Robert turned back to search for Mary and set fire to Sawston Hall, but gave up on the pursuit and thus enabled her to reach sanctuary at Kenninghall, the South Norfolk stronghold of the conservative Howard clan.

As Robert returned to London empty-handed, the coup started to unravel. No enthusiasm for Jane had been shown in London during or after her proclamation, and Northumberland did not trust the nervous councillors enough to allow any of them out of the Tower lest they attempt to flee to protect themselves from prosecution if Mary won. Outbreaks in Mary's name occurred as widely apart as Devonshire, Oxfordshire, and Bedfordshire, led by the local gentry in the name of legitimacy, and as local gentry families and the Earl of Bath led levies to Kenninghall to assist Mary the latter stiffly wrote to the Council on the 10th demanding acceptance of her claim. With neither Mary nor the Council willing to back down, an armed clash was inevitable, but Northumberland could not trust most of the Council with the unwavering determination to carry out an expedition to Norfolk rather than go over to Mary if she looked as if she would prevail. He had the most military experience of the Council, but if he went the councillors left behind could not be trusted to resist the growing movement of rebellion in the shires. Deciding against his initial choice as commander of the Duke of Suffolk, Jane's father so with the most to lose if the coup was thwarted, he set out for Norfolk himself on the 14th. He sent his cousin Andrew Dudley to France to obtain troops from his ally Henri II with a tempting offer to hand over Calais and Ireland. But by now more levies were flocking to Mary, who had moved to stronger and safer Framlingham Castle near the Suffolk coast, and a force of loyalist ships sent to Great Yarmouth to attack her in the rear deserted to her.

Once desertions began they took on a momentum of their own, and in London the councillors persuaded Suffolk to let them leave the Tower to consult the French Ambassador. Instead, they held a private meeting at Baynard's Castle where it was agreed that the coup was failing and they had to save themselves from Mary's revenge. Only immediate surrender, recognition of her as lawful queen, and putting all the blame on Northumberland might save them. Conservatives such as the Earl of Arundel (later a pro-Catholic Marian stalwart) had clearly been unhappy from the start but unwilling to defy Northumberland. Even Suffolk, the likeliest apart from Northumberland to face execution as a leader of the plot, concurred with their decision and on the 19th they announced their recognition of Mary in the City to public rejoicing. On their return Jane, left alone in the Tower while her father-in-law and the other councillors abandoned their oaths of allegiance of nine days before, was abruptly told to abandon her royal state – which she did with relief. Northumberland, reaching Cambridge with his troops slipping away, Mary's levies clearly outnumbering him and growing every day, and no evidence of public support, gave in and proclaimed Mary queen himself. His belated pretended conversion to Mary's cause did not save him from the probably inevitable executioner's block, and his shameless abandonment of Protestantism before his execution did his reputation no favours, though it was probably aimed at reducing the Queen's retaliation against his family. To Mary's credit, only his closest followers, Gates and Palmer, shared the ultimate penalty and even Suffolk was reprieved until the failure of the Wyatt rising the following spring, as were Jane and Guildford Dudley.

The reprieved councillors were keen to blame the greed and ambition of Northumberland for the attempted coup, and in her initial desire for reconciliation Mary went along with that version of events.[3] Northumberland's father, Edmund Dudley, had already been an unpopular minister of Henry VII, sacrificed to his critics and beheaded by Henry VIII in 1510, and now Northumberland was portrayed as a power-crazed mastermind of intrigue who had led the move to evict the late King's uncle Somerset – the 'Good Duke' allegedly favourable to the poor – from the Lord Protectorship in 1549, had him 'framed' for plotting and executed in

1552. Guildford Dudley's execution in February 1554 represented the third generation of Dudley males executed for treason. The 'Black Legend' of the family remained an important strand of opinion throughout the Elizabethan period, with Robert Dudley, Earl of Leicester and royal 'favourite', not as powerful as his father under Elizabeth I but equally controversial and hated by many aristocratic rivals and critics of his support for Protestant evangelism at home and abroad. The family were portrayed as a brood of unscrupulous traitors, and in this version of events the marriage of Jane Grey and Guildford Dudley and the 'King's Device' of June 1553 were part of Northumberland's attempt to create a Tudor-Dudley dynasty and seat his grandchildren on the throne.[4]

But in reality, as examined in the latest biography of the Dudley family, the probability is against such a deep-seated plan and the succession-ploy had more to do with the desires of Edward himself.[5] Moreover, for a supposed mastermind of intrigue Northumberland showed little skill or ruthlessness in carrying out the plan to usurp the throne. Most noticeably, he failed to secure the two Princesses' persons in London or at Greenwich when Edward was dying and thus pre-empt a challenge. The timing of the King's death may have taken him by surprise, and Edward had rallied before as his condition declined. But Edward had clearly been unlikely to survive for more than a few months when he left Whitehall for Greenwich in April, and he had been near-critical for several weeks before 6 July. Even if the replacement of Mary was Edward's idea and did not become a serious option until the Council approved – and altered – the 'Device' around 25 June, from then on Mary (and to a lesser degree Elizabeth) were potential threats to the succession-coup and arrangements should have been made to send troops out to their suburban country houses, within a day's ride of London, to secure them at a moment's notice. Instead, Mary was not even summoned to London until Edward was either dead or within hours of death and when she received a warning and fled only a small force was sent after her. Northumberland had made no attempt to put the French ambassador Noailles on notice that Mary would be set aside; her cousin Emperor Charles V could be expected to back her claim even if there was no rising in England, and troops would be needed. Nor had Northumberland's own troops, mercenaries stationed on the Scots border, been summoned to London ahead of the King's death to be turned on any provincial rising with the appropriate brutality that Northumberland had used against rioters in East Anglia in 1549.

There had been several weeks to arrange all three of these crucial actions before Edward died, yet none were taken. If the Princesses had been secured, no rising in outer counties in Mary's name would have been able to use her as a figurehead and she would have been in the helpless position of Jane Grey and Elizabeth in February 1554 – liable to Council investigation of her links to the rebels once her 'liberators' had been repulsed, and at serious risk of the block. The risk of imperial wrath would have made her execution difficult, given that Charles V was not currently at war with any of his multitudinous enemies across Europe (e.g. the French, the Protestant German states and the Turks) and was thus able to send an expedition over from Flanders if he was prepared to risk war with England's ally France. Having secured a favourable treaty with Edward and the return of Boulogne and now in a dominant position in Scotland with his troops assisting Mary of Guise's regency, Henri II would not have wanted a Habsburg candidate on the throne of England. As a firm Catholic he had no doctrinal sympathy for the Edwardian Reformation, but the Habsburg-Valois rivalry across Europe was more important to France and in addition he had possession of his own candidate for the English throne if needed – Mary Stuart, grand-daughter of Margaret Tudor, excluded from Henry VIII's will but dynastically closer to the throne than Jane Grey and unlike Elizabeth of unchallenged legitimacy. Usefully, Mary was engaged to his eldest son and heir, Francis. Henri could be sure to intervene if Charles attempted to invade England, and as Mary Tudor would have been the focus of any unsuccessful anti-Jane rising in England she could be conveniently implicated in it and lodged securely in the Tower under threat of execution as Elizabeth was to be in 1554. At the most blatant, Charles could be informed that Mary would be executed if he attempted to invade on her behalf but would not be touched if he took no action. Naturally inclined to caution, he would probably have backed off invading and within a year or two would have been preoccupied with his next war with France as in reality. The only unfortunate result for England of this demarche would have been that Henri was likely to have required the return of Calais as the terms for aid, particularly if an imperial invasion-force was being mustered, and this would have been as unpopular in England as was Calais' fall in 1558.

What if the crisis had been delayed?

Northumberland seems to have suffered from unusual hesitation and lethargy in 1553, perhaps due to poor health and/or a genuine doubt about implementing a plan that was Edward's, not his, idea. He also seems to have expected Edward to live longer, given the haste and the fumbling with which he acted after 6 July. But given a few more weeks to act in July–August 1553, with the King rallying again, he should have had the time and nerve to secure Mary's person and require her to stay under guard close to or in London. (Edward's death took her by surprise too, as she had to be warned not to go on to London after setting out to answer the fake summons sent to her after his death.) Edward seems to have grasped the principle of *cuius principo, eius religio* – that the monarch's personal religion would determine the people's – better than Northumberland did. He presumably used the Continental example, where the religious identity of the states in the rival Protestant and Catholic 'blocs' in Germany in the later 1540s followed the local prince's beliefs.

Decisive action in securing the alternative heir, and bringing in his Border troops to tackle armed risings, should have given Northumberland the advantage over any revolt in the provinces by poorly armed gentry. The risings would have had better-armed and directed leadership than the conservative, lower-class-led religious Cornish revolt and the 'economic' lower-class Norfolk revolt of 1549, and so potentially been as dangerous as the gentry-led Wyatt revolt of 1554 if not quickly challenged. The gentry in charge would have been communicating with rebels in other counties to co-ordinate strategy, would have had horses and arms to make their movement militarily effective and mobile, and been marching on London. But they would not have been led by Mary in person, or (probably) by a senior member of the aristocracy with military experience and a force of armed tenants. Wriothesley, the senior court conservative of the mid-1540s as Henry VIII's last Lord Chancellor, was luckily dead (1550) and the ageing but ruthless Duke of Norfolk in the Tower; the conservative Earl of Arundel was in London acting – reluctantly – with the majority of the Council.

There would have been greater danger if a senior magnate had been available to lead the rebels, most logically from the faction that had backed Mary's rights in the 1530s. In that respect Northumberland was lucky that the son of Mary's eponymous aunt and outspoken backer the Duchess of Suffolk, Henry Brandon (born 1516), had died young; had he been alive he would have had the advantages of Tudor blood and his father's duchy and resources. As brother to Jane Grey's mother, Frances, he would have been ahead of Frances and Jane in the succession-stakes and so been named as residual heir in Henry VIII's will; Edward and Northumberland might still have set him aside if he was Catholic and anti-reformist like his parents but this would make Jane seem even more a usurper. The late Duke of Suffolk had married again after Princess Mary died in 1533, but his sons by this marriage had also died young in the 'sweating sickness' epidemic of 1551; if they had been alive they would have been in their late teens, young to command armies but still capable of objecting to the usurpation. Their mother, Catherine Willoughby, was a reformist (and went into exile under Mary Tudor in 1553–8), but Edward and Northumberland could not choose one of them as king rather than Jane as they were not half-Tudor by blood.

(Jane was the grand-daughter of Princess Mary and the Duke of Suffolk; the boys were Suffolk's sons by his second marriage, to Catherine.)

Nor would the rising have been close to London so its directors could strike quickly at an unprepared capital, as Wyatt was to do from Kent in February 1554. The crucial leaders of East Anglian support for Mary against Northumberland, their persecutor of 1549, the aged Duke of Norfolk and his grandson Thomas, were both safe in the Tower and most other Catholic magnates had lands well away from London. This would give the government time to raise troops or bring in the French before any revolt in the south-west, Midlands, or North assumed dangerous proportions and/or led to a march on London. Ultimately no Tudor revolt succeeded apart from Mary's in East Anglia – which was reasonably close to the capital, 'legitimist' as far as the majority of the 'political nation' was concerned, and led by their candidate for the throne in person. The Wyatt revolt came closest, by launching a speedy and fierce assault on the centre of government – even more than Mary's, it was centred close to London. (The Kentishmen had occupied London already in 1381 and 1450 and had to be fought off in 1471.) But it is likely that if Northumberland had had time to bring in troops and had secured a quick, decisive victory over the main force of leaderless rebels the example would have disheartened the remaining groups of armed resisters who were spread across several counties and not co-ordinated. His Border troops could take the Midlands rebels in the rear, and a rebel army from the south-west was containable as long as it was kept on the south side of the Thames as in 1497.

The Emperor was not in a position to send in troops from Flanders quickly to stiffen the East Anglian rebel army, Edward's imminent demise and the usurpation not being anticipated. The widespread extent of the revolt among all classes made it particularly serious, but numbers alone had not made the Northern rebels of 1536 or the East Anglian rebels of 1549 prevail and the Marian party could have been dispersed similarly. Northumberland would have had the advantage of time to strike a swift blow at the most dangerous rebels before they linked up with other forces in distant counties. The uncertainty of the loyalty of the councillors back in London would have been less if Mary – and Elizabeth – had physically been in Dudley hands, as in that case the rebels' cause would have seemed as hopeless as in 1536 or 1549. (Even in real life, Mary and the foreign ambassadors all had doubts about her victory.)

Both wavering or conservative councillors in London and the majority of magnates in the country could be expected to wait until the resolution of the immediate crisis before making a decision to stand up for Mary's rights, with Mary herself unable to lead the rebellion. Even the solidly

Catholic magnates and gentry in the North – who would not have heard of the usurpation for several days and would have been unclear as to what was happening elsewhere – would have been unlikely to act coherently in Mary's favour for some days and would have been wary due to memories of 1536–7.

A swift military victory over the main rebel force by Northumberland would have made it clear who would win and thus decided waverers' minds for them. Once the Duke had seen off the immediate challenge, the advantage would have lain with him as the leader of the regime in possession of London, the capital's resources, and military force. The discontented among the provincial leadership would have hesitated to be the first to challenge him, with no immediate prospect of imperial military aid to fend off royal troops and France aiding the English fleet to patrol the Channel. The government would have been wise to require some of the Border troops being brought south to halt at Newcastle, York, and Hull to overawe local gentry and deny the ports to the Emperor's ships. As with Henry VIII's equally controversial divorce from Catherine of Aragon and bastardization of Mary in the early 1530s, widespread anger and dislike for the usurpers across the country would not crystallize into armed resistance without adequate leadership. Henry could survive even a mass-movement against his policies in the North in 1536 with the aid of judicious temporization and blatant lies until his military forces were ready to act, and Northumberland had shown in Norfolk in 1549 that he was just as ready to use force mixed with judicious offers to rebel deserters.

What if Mary had fled abroad in 1550/1?
What if Mary had already left England for the Continent by 1553? Her insistence on the now–illegal Mass being heard in her household had been a source of strife with the government since 1549, and she had withstood lectures by Edward and intimidation from the Council or their representatives. She was of the same religious opinions as the anti-reform rebels in Cornwall in 1549, and if the government troops had been defeated and terms been reached abandoning the innovations she would have been a beneficiary. She seems to have been considered as a possible ally by Somerset's conservative opponents in 1549, with even a mention of her as nominal head of the new regency Council, but her revived political importance declined as the new government stabilized under the cautious leadership of John Dudley (Duke of Northumberland from 1551). The initial halt to evangelical reform was followed by new measures, with Dudley outmanoeuvring the conservative councillors whose support he had initially needed. In 1550 Mary regarded her situation as serious enough to consider

fleeing to imperial-held Flanders, and emissaries were sent to Charles to arrange it. Both she and the Emperor were aware that her position as Edward's heir would be endangered if she left the country, making it difficult for her to take over and aid her religion if the King died suddenly. Accordingly, though Charles went as far as to send ships to lie off Harwich ready for her departure she did not take up the offer and the Council became aware of it. In 1551, there was another series of clashes with the Council, this time her senior household officials being arrested for breaching the religious laws, but she was unrepentant. From then on she maintained an awkward position as effective figurehead of the religious resistance, not actually under house-arrest as the similarly placed but less obstructive Elizabeth was to be in 1554–5 and treated with respect by Edward but still an implicit threat.

Unlike Mary's own treatment of Elizabeth – admittedly in a worse legal position as arguably a bastard – there was no Council talk of execution, and no plot against the regime to justify it. But it is possible that Mary could still have fled the country, and if Edward had lived longer and the government not been paralysed in spring 1553 by his and Northumberland's poor health the Council would have returned to the issue of her illegal Masses. Similarly, until Edward married and had a child she was the next heir and her succession would mean the reversal of the Edwardian Reformation so committed clerical and lay leaders of the latter had much at stake in keeping her from the throne. At some point the government had to face up to that issue, and the uneasy 'stand-off' between them and Mary could have been broken by a determined effort to make her convert or face the consequences with the idealistic, dogmatic King believing that his sister was committing sin and imperilling her soul. Despite Edward's clear reluctance to punish her he had stood aside cold-bloodedly while his maternal uncle was executed for supposed treason in January 1552, though Somerset may have been less innocent than his historical partisans believed and genuinely been plotting to kill Northumberland. He was equally capable of abandoning Mary if she seemed to be defying the law, and if faced with arrest by a more vigorous Edward in 1553/4 she could have decided to flee to Flanders after all. If that happened, any subsequent decline in the King's health would have left her unable to lead a revolt on her exclusion from the throne.

The Emperor's widower son Philip was available as a husband, and the Marian-Habsburg alliance could have been cemented by her marriage to Philip in Brussels or Antwerp after her arrival with Charles proclaiming her Queen of England as soon as Edward died. Seeming a Habsburg puppet as much as the French-backed claimant of 1558, Mary Stuart, seemed a Valois puppet, she would have been less likely to touch off spontaneous revolt in England than in real-life 1553. Her cause would probably have become subsumed in the Habsburg-Valois war of 1555–9, and reliant on a successful invasion of England to link up with a provincial revolt. The latter was not impossible, given that Northumberland would have been as unpopular as Mary was in 1558 over the return of Calais to France and his government was short of money after the 1552–3 currency crisis. There were no more Church lands to plunder as Henry and Somerset had done to remedy their poor financial positions and buy support from the nobility and gentry, and any attacks on pro-Marian Catholic peers (to fine them or sell off their property) would have been a provocation capable of touching off a 1569-style Northern revolt. But if the Emperor had been primarily interested in the long struggle to secure the Franco-imperial border towns of Flanders and Lorraine the imperial fleet may never have been readied for an invasion, and the absence of serious revolt in England discouraged him from attacking as much as the united Anglo-French fleet and the French threat to his possessions. Once Mary died in 1558 – assuming that she was childless – the opposition to Jane would have lost its figurehead and her husband Philip would have been more concerned with peace with France (and England) to enable him to concentrate on his new kingdoms.

The aftermath of success for the new regime: the mid- to late 1550s
Whether Mary Tudor was in Northumberland's hands on Edward's death or exiled in Flanders, the defeat of her unco-ordinated partisans on Edward's death would have given the new regime time to consolidate itself. It would have been weaker than a continuing Edwardian government in the years after 1553, given the widespread feeling that Mary was the legitimate heir and had been illegally set aside, but the crucial element for its survival – the local gentry and peers – would have been unlikely to mount a successful rising that took the regime by surprise. The Council would have been unlikely to challenge the 'status quo'. Some were committed Protestant Dudley partisans keen to see the survival of the Reformation (e.g. Cecil and Gates); some were practical men willing to support any incumbent regime (e.g. Paget and Paulet); and the peers who had the resources and prestige to lead a plot were either linked to the Dudleys by marital alliance (Pembroke) or unwilling to run risks by revolting (Arundel). Northumberland and his close supporter Suffolk would have been unchallenged, though the lack of public enthusiasm for their protégé in London (e.g. at her coronation) would have given them reason to proceed cautiously and not stir up excuses for rebellion. The 1552 Prayer-Book is likely to have been the last religious innovation for a time, and the lack of observance of the religious laws in the Catholic North been allowed to go unchallenged as in the equally insecure early Elizabethan years. Unlike Mary, the government would not have been

keen to secure its religious legislation by making examples of its opponents. Ironically, given that many of the pre-1553 Council and their administrative reforms survived under Mary the civil legislation of the government would have been similar to Mary's. (The extra councillors who Mary was to bring in in 1553/4 were mostly loyal gentry and her own Household officials; they seem to have had little political influence or initiative.) The major difference apart from religion would have been in foreign policy, with France an ally and the Empire the main enemy (at least until Mary died).

The main danger to a long-lived Grey/Dudley regime would have been the mortality of its leadership. Jane, the focus of the government, was a zealous and learned Protestant and would in due course have accepted that her elevation to the throne might have been irregular but it enabled her to promote her faith and continue Edward's godly work. Her health had been weak, however, with a possibility of what has recently been suggested as anorexia in her mid-teens (a thesis backed up by her frail appearance in a newly identified portrait). She had shown no enthusiasm for her marriage or her husband, had been on good personal terms with Mary despite increasingly deploring her religion, and did not get on well with her own bullying parents. It is probable that her main exemplar as a godly female in high politics was the late Queen Catherine Parr, in whose household she had resided at Chelsea Palace in 1547 with evident relief to be away from her uncongenial parents. She had the temperament and the determination to become a conscientious sovereign with her own ideas for government, and Northumberland had been careful to bring the precocious Edward into the business of government and could have done the same for her. By 1553 he was in poor health, and seems to have been showing weariness of rather than lust for power, unlike the legend of his vaunting ambition would suggest.

However, unlike Edward she was a woman, and her rule would have been as unprecedented as was Mary's in 1553. Any interest in government on her part would thus have been as uncongenial or as surprising as Mary's and Elizabeth's involvement was to some councillors. Unlike Elizabeth who was twenty-five in November 1558, she would have been relatively inexperienced in the 'bear-pit' of Tudor court politics, having been brought up in the country (probably at Bradgate Priory) by her boorish, hunting-obsessed parents, Henry and Frances Grey, who allegedly scorned her love of learning. (In 1547 she had been living at Chelsea in the household of Queen-Dowager Catherine Parr, but not at court.) Unlike Elizabeth, she would have faced a government under the control of one dominant figure – in 1558 Elizabeth could play off contending nobles against each other and dangle her hand as a prize to rivals without ever deciding for one or the other.

A woman was expected to defer to her husband – hence the real-life fear of Philip using his power over Mary to advance Spanish interests in 1554. Guildford Dudley – who did not share his wife's scholarly interests or religious enthusiasm – does not seem to have shown any concern for politics in his brief career, and been keen to see that he acquired the title of king and could show off his eminence. There is the possibility that this immature youth could have been as vain, temperamental, and incompetent a co-ruler as was Lord Darnley in Scotland in the 1560s, rather than the support to his wife that the experienced administrator Philip was to Mary. The Suffolks showed scant concern for their daughter except as a political tool, and are reputed to have been capable of violence. They were unlikely to have been of any political or personal use to her, and to have continued to see her as a political tool for their aggrandizement. As a rare female ruler struggling to make a personal impact, Jane would have been more likely to rely on sympathetic members of the Council for support and in this regard William Cecil, a rising Dudley protégé but not yet a senior political figure, might well have developed the same sort of relationship with the Queen as he did with Elizabeth – acting as a mentor in business and with Northumberland able to trust him to act in Dudley interests. He was already secretary, so had a crucial role in private advice to and contact with his sovereign. Northumberland, aided by his sons, Suffolk, Palmer, Gates, and Cecil, would have had to continue as the leading figure in the government for the duration of the crucial Habsburg-Valois war, particularly if the Emperor had been recognizing Mary as rightful sovereign and in danger of invading, as he was the 'lynch-pin' of the government and likely to be executed as a scapegoat if it fell. He could not rely on his colleagues to prosecute Jane's interests with the same determination. (If the Emperor or Philip landed and a revolt broke out, other councillors could desert to Mary and put the blame for the 1553 coup on the Dudleys and Greys.) But by the peace of 1559 he would have been keen to retire from the business of ruling the country, whether or not he had trained Cecil to take on his role as mentor to the Queen in alliance with his sons. There is a chance that if the royal marital relationship had not produced an heir and/or had broken down the Queen would have been confident enough to seek a divorce from some acquiescent clerics. Cranmer was used to doing whatever his sovereign demanded from the 1530s, and had he been dead by this point – c. 1560? – his successor as archbishop might have been willing to back the Queen against the Dudleys had the latter's Council rivals taken the opportunity to support her. As the 1560s showed, Robert and Ambrose Dudley (and had he lived, the equally arrogant Guildford) had plenty of enemies among the older nobility.

The personal capacity and political and military interests of Northumberland's eldest son, John, who would have succeeded to his titles and lands in due course, are unclear as he died in real life in 1554; the younger sons, Ambrose and Robert, were, however, adequate soldiers and were prominent Elizabethan Protestant figures. Assuming that Guildford had not matured satisfactorily or proved an amiable but tolerable nonentity, and Jane decided to be rid of him, his brothers could have survived as stalwarts of the Grey regime even if he had been set aside and a useful foreign Protestant prince (John, second son of Gustavus of Sweden? A German Lutheran?) been sought as consort. The more confident Queen could also have been rid of her parents' influence as she built up a body of support among the court nobility, Frances dying in real life in 1559, and her (politically inept) sister Catherine's real-life marriage to the son of the late Protector Somerset would have been a valuable rapprochement with the Seymour family. Arundel, who in real life had hopes of marrying the young Queen Elizabeth after 1559, had the social standing, ambition, and Council experience to manoeuvre himself into a senior position – though his conservative religious views would not have attracted Jane.

It should, however, be noted that the survival with full resources of the Dudley sons through the 1550s and into the 1560s would have meant that the eldest kept the title of Duke of Northumberland and the accompanying Northern lands taken from the local Percies, who would thus have been alienated from the Grey regime and a focus for potential revolt. The Emperor's agents may have sought to use them – or the Catholic Nevilles, Earls of Westmorland – as the leaders of an armed rebellion to distract England from sending troops to France once war broke out c. 1555.

Jane's heirs?

There remains the possibility that Jane would die in childbirth or in one of the periodic epidemics, given her poor health and the state of sixteenth century medicine. If Jane's death occurred without her providing a son, the 'King's Device' of 1553 provided for the sons of her sister Catherine as next heirs. Assuming that Catherine (born 1539) had been able as the Queen's sister to contract a marriage earlier than she did in the real-life 1550s as the sister of an executed usurper, she could have provided this heir before Jane died. Indeed, her real-life choice of husband, Edward Seymour (junior), had much to commend him in ending the Dudley-Seymour feud that had seen Northumberland lead Edward's father Somerset's deposition as regent in 1549 and later have him executed. Their infant son – born in 1561 in reality – could thus have succeeded Jane, or she could have designated Catherine as her successor to avoid a long regency. Even if Jane had survived through the

1560s and 1570s, with or without Guildford as her consort, she might not have had a child and the succession may still have been a problem. The French King could hardly have defied his English allies in 1558 by recognizing Mary Stuart as queen once Mary Tudor was dead as he did in real life, having been supporting the regime of Queen Jane since 1553, though if Jane had died he would have had to choose between his own daughter-in-law Mary and whoever Jane designated as her heir. From the time of Henri's death in a tournament in July 1559, however, the inadequacy of a series of young Valois rulers and the drift to religious civil war mean that France's possible meddling on behalf of Mary Stuart was less important.

There remains the possibility of a claim to the throne on Jane's death by Elizabeth, adult, Protestant, and resident in the country. The 'legitimist' arguments were not as strong in Elizabeth's favour as they were in Mary's, given the dubious nature of Henry VIII's marriage to Anne Boleyn. Catholic opinion in England would have been in Mary Stuart's favour, as in real life, once (1561) she would have been back in Scotland as resident sovereign rather than a resident of France as future, current, or past queen. A remote case could also be made out for Mary's aunt Lady Margaret Douglas, as daughter of Henry VIII's sister Margaret Tudor by her second marriage – in real life Mary Tudor considered her as heir in the mid-1550s as a Catholic. But Elizabeth had her supporters as a Protestant, and if the Suffolks had been making the most of their access to power and patronage in the 1550s they could well have built up a mood of resentment among discomfited court rivals and holders of older peerages as 'arrivistes'. The Howards, Elizabeth's maternal relatives, were a crucial factor here (see below).

These people would not wish to see another Grey girl, or a Grey-controlled regency for Catherine's infant/under-age son, take over the country on Jane's death. The councillors who in real life rushed to desert Jane for Mary and blame the Dudleys and Suffolks in 1553 could have staged their own coup on Jane's death, assuming that by this date (1558? the 1560s?) Northumberland was dead or in retirement and his sons as unpopular as they were in the real-life 1560s. Arundel, a conservative magnate who in real life had hopes of marrying the unmarried Elizabeth at this point, could have seen himself as Elizabeth's consort and been the prime mover in getting rid of the Dudleys and Suffolks. Alternatively, an attempt to increase reconciliation among the nobility in the mid- or late 1550s would naturally focus on the rehabilitation of the Howards, destroyed by the dying Henry VIII in 1547 and a useful focus of loyalty in trouble-prone East Anglia. Thus the late Duke of Norfolk's (d. 1554) grandson Thomas, born in 1536, could have had his lands and some titles restored before Jane died and – as in real life – turned into the leading noble foe of the 'parvenu' Dudleys. He was married (thrice) so not available for Elizabeth's hand except at limited periods, but as her cousin was a natural focus for a move to put her on the throne. If Jane's unpopular family and 'in-laws' had still been dominating her regime at the time, her death could have seen a second coup to alter the succession and the enthronement of Elizabeth I. But the latter's friendship with Robert Dudley would have ensured that the Dudleys, as in real life, were able to stage their third 'come-back' from political disgrace.

Chapter Seven

Late Tudor 'what ifs'

(i) Elizabeth I: a marriage? The missed – or sabotaged? – opportunity with Robert Dudley

E lizabeth has become defined as 'The Virgin Queen', the sovereign who never married and told her Parliament that she was married to her realm, not to a person. Her reasons for her choice seem to have been partly personal, partly political, and acres of academic study, psychological analysis, and historical fiction have been expended on them. She did not want to become eclipsed by her husband and tied to their country or political faction as her sister had been, her sister's and father's marriages had been a succession of traumatic disasters, and if she chose one candidate in the 'marriage stakes' it would upset the delicate political balance of her realm and foreign policy by alienating their rivals. As of her accession in November 1558 it was assumed that she undoubtedly would marry, as had been the case with Mary, and an unmarried woman exercising authority as Queen Regnant without a husband was unnatural by the standards of universal custom. Conversely, as women were subject to men – husbands then fathers – in law and by biblical authority her husband would have a right to exercise authority over her, though Mary had specifically limited her husband's legal rights in England by statute and this could be repeated. Elizabeth's choice of husband was also bound to be contentious if not, as some pessimists assumed, inevitably ruinous. A foreign prince or king, of equal rank to the queen as was socially seemly, would subject England's interests to his own state's – and the mere threat of Philip doing this to England had touched off a bloody revolt in 1554. A domestic husband of high social standing from the nobility would arouse jealousy from his rivals – by one estimate half the kingdom's great men would oppose any noble who was so chosen, presumably in arms.[1] If Elizabeth chose someone of lower social rank who did not have these enemies, the 'insult' to the nobility of their having to defer to a man of lower rank would allegedly cause them to rise as one and murder both Elizabeth and her husband.[2] This panic was probably exacerbated by fresh memories of the two unpopular and contentious consorts of 1553–8 – Guildford Dudley, an inexperienced teenager chosen for Jane Grey by her and his power-hungry parents, and the foreign Catholic Philip. It did not reflect any knowledge of the new Queen's cautious and canny personality, or of the effects of the trauma of her investigation for alleged dalliance with Thomas Seymour in 1548 and imprisonment and near-execution in 1554–5.[3] As was to be the case throughout her life, Elizabeth chose the wisest course of never alienating one powerful party or faction – domestic or foreign – by throwing her lot in with their rivals unless absolutely driven to it. This was visible even in her first months in power, as she did not hurry to restore Protestantism or to evict the resented persecuting Marian bishops, or even to prosecute particular abuses of authority in the recent religious persecutions.[4] Even the loathed Bishop Bonner of London initially kept his see, though Elizabeth refused to let him kiss her hand as she arrived in London to assume power.[5] Her caution was thus present even in winter 1558–9, not learnt with experience on the throne – and choosing one candidate for her hand would risk an unnecessary crisis. At this point, even her closest ally Cecil (no fan of a marriage to a Catholic prince, or to Dudley) was assuming that she would marry and provide an heir.

But was her decision not to marry inevitable, and seen as such by her from the start of her reign? Would personal feelings ever have caused her to throw caution to the minds, or a desire for one particular alliance abroad with a strong 'Power' have caused her to risk alienating their enemies by marrying their candidate? She certainly seems to have considered marrying her long-time admirer, friend, and contemporary Robert Dudley in 1560 despite the bad reputation and many senior aristocratic enemies that the 'parvenu' Dudleys had acquired during the 1550s. Their indiscreet conduct gave despair to the prudent William Cecil who feared the Queen would disregard his pleas and such a marriage would cause rebellion.[6] Her closest female confidante and 'mother-figure', Kat Ashley, who had been in charge of her domestic attendants since her early years, was driven to beg her on her knees not to marry Dudley and thus cause civil war, citing the fact that she would have to answer to God for ruining the country if that happened.[7] Mistress Ashley was not, however, known for her political acumen; she had been arrested by the Somerset regency in 1548 for encouraging Thomas Seymour's near-treasonable flirting with the Princess. Elizabeth was able to operate on a separate personal and political 'level' and to enjoy flirting and showing off her new power without closing her eyes to the consequences of acting on her emotions – unlike Mary Stuart. She showed her attentions to a number of handsome young(-ish) admirers in her first years as Queen, not just Dudley – and in spring 1559 rumours about an engagement also centred on the gallant and good-looking Protestant courtier Sir Wiliam Pickering, recently returned from exile, of gentry not noble blood, and in his mid-thirties.[8] She was to continue to 'play the field' and lap up admiration from admirers into late middle age, as was notorious, and her susceptibility to a handsome and accomplished flatterer was supposed to have been behind the rise to influence later of Sir Christopher Hatton and Sir Walter Raleigh. In the meantime she was already taking her lifetime 'line' that she considered herself married to her country, not to a man, and was content for this to remain so, as she addressed a Parliamentary delegation asking her to marry in January 1559.[9]

But as far as the Spanish diplomats in London and their masters at home were concerned, the domestic candidate to watch out for was Dudley. He was evidently seen as an acceptable compromise if the match that Philip proposed for his ex-sister-in-law with the Archduke Charles did not succeed – and neither Philip II nor the Archduke's father Emperor Ferdinand thought fit in 1559–61 to nudge the Archduke into paying suit to Elizabeth in person to speed up matters. Indeed, at one Thames river-party on a barge in 1561 Bishop de Quadra, the Spanish ambassador, is said to have offered to marry Elizabeth and Dudley on the spot[10] – which would have given Elizabeth the diplomatic bonus of tying the military might and Catholic zeal of Spain to supporting her choice of husband. Would this have conceivably given Elizabeth the reassurance that she could get away with marrying Dudley, with Spanish troops in the Netherlands at hand to aid her if her husband's domestic enemies revolted? Or was the memory of the indignant reaction to the last unpopular royal marriage (Mary and Philip) in 1554, the Wyatt revolt in Kent, too vivid?

As with the proposal by Henry VIII to marry Anne Boleyn in Calais in 1532 with Francis of France as witness and supporter, there were advantages for a cautious and politically isolated Tudor ruler in having a major international ally visibly associated with their controversial marriage. Certainly the Queen had shown no willingness to consider other, more appropriately 'old nobility' suitors such as her own cousin Thomas Howard, (Catholic) widower Duke of Norfolk (born 1536), and the older and more conservative Council veteran Henry Fitzalan, Earl of Arundel. Her personal approval lay with her contemporary and fellow-ex-prisoner of 1554, Dudley, despite the dislike of most of the Council for him and his ambition and arrogance. There were also hereditary fears of or distaste for the 'low-born' Dudleys as 'arrivistes' by great nobles of ancient birth, in particular those with partial royal descent such as the Howards (descended from Thomas of Brotherton, younger son of Edward I) and the Fitzalans. In addition to the aristocratic disdain that Norfolk's grandfather had shown for Wolsey and a variety of nobles forced to pay up extortionate bonds for good behaviour had shown to Robert Dudley's grasping ministerial grandfather Edmund Dudley in the 1500s, there was the matter of feuds left over from Edward VI's minority and the 1553 coup. Conservative Arundel, more comfortable with Mary Tudor's Catholic regime than with the radical Protestant tone of Edward VI's government (which Robert Dudley's father Northumberland had led), had backed Northumberland against the Duke of Somerset in 1549–53 but then abandoned him – literally – as Northumberland left Arundel in charge at the Tower and tried to attack Mary Tudor in Norfolk in July 1553. This gave rise to fears on Arundel's part that Robert might seek revenge for this betrayal, which had ended with Northumberland being arrested and executed by Mary – and other councillors who had abandoned the Dudleys in 1553 were still in office too, led by Lord Treasurer Winchester.

There was thus a danger of Council alarm at Robert's power and capacity for revenge, which would have worsened significantly had he married Elizabeth and so become 'Consort' as well as a personal intimate of the Queen's. The shrewd Elizabeth was unlikely to have given Robert, son and grandson of executed 'traitors', the 'Crown Matrimonial' and thus legal authority, which her cousin Mary Stuart was to give to her immature and greedy young husband Darnley in Scotland in 1565. Robert's perceived arrogance would have increased with a semi-royal rank, but his actual power would probably have been limited – and he was not yet a proponent of a vigorous anti-Catholic foreign policy as he was to be in the 1570s. Indeed, his relations with the Spanish ambassadors were cordial as he sought their approval for him marrying Elizabeth. Thus his marriage would not have alarmed Philip II, though it would have ended his hopes of marrying off Elizabeth to the Archduke Charles. Nor did the potentially alarmed nobles have a rival candidate lined up to replace an Elizabeth/Dudley alliance in an armed revolt. The heir under Henry VIII's will, Lady Catherine Grey (born 1539), was young, impulsive and malleable – and Protestant – but had recently caused a scandal and been imprisoned for secretly marrying the son of the Duke of Somerset, a man who Arundel and his allies had also abandoned (in 1549). It would have made no sense to overthrow a 'Dudley puppet' Elizabeth in favour of the wife of another heir of an executed rival of theirs who could seek revenge.

The likelihood is that even if Elizabeth had married Robert Dudley the resulting criticism would have not turned into a widespread revolt as long as Elizabeth kept her policies and her access to court and other lucrative offices unchanged. Unlike in 1554–8 when France backed the enemies of Mary Tudor, as of 1560–4 Elizabeth had not irrevocably alienated either France (ravaged by civil war from 1562) or Spain to the point of them invading to assist a rebellion – and the majority Catholic population of the North had not been persecuted for defying the ban on the Mass either. However, this does not rule out the chance of an affronted noble infuriated by Dudley arrogance taking his offended sense of honour as far as launching a 'revolt' – or at least an armed protest that was not supported by enough armed men to be a serious threat – based on his own obedient tenantry. Elizabethan nobles did not necessarily consider their own self-protection above all else if they had been personally slighted, and a futile armed protest is likeliest to have come from Norfolk, Dudley's principal personal rival in the 1560s, given his real-life sulking on his estates and refusal to attend the Queen over her ban on his marrying Mary Stuart in 1569. Norfolk notoriously threatened Dudley with violence with his tennis-racquet at a match in front of the Queen after the 'favourite' borrowed his sovereign's handkerchief to mop his brow in real life, and it is highly plausible that he would have refused to do obeisance to a 'jumped-up' new consort and withdrawn from court under threat of arrest for insolence.

Mary Stuart, Mary Tudor, and Elizabeth: the post-1553 stage of the tripartite rivalry of Tudor, Habsburg, and Valois. Policy and chance turn out differently?
In the latest act of the long-running hostility of Valois for Habsburg, Mary Stuart had been recognized as rightful Queen of England by France in November 1558 – she was the lineally senior descendant of Henry VIII's elder sister Margaret, though Henry himself had excluded this 'foreign-born' line of claimants. The chances of military action by Henri II to enforce Mary's claim against Habsburg ally England were considerable as of November 1558, with England still at war with France in an enmity stretching back to the accession of Mary Tudor in July 1553. The accession of Mary Tudor had resumed the old question that Henry VIII had faced in the period from 1516–27, namely whether his heiress was to be married to a Habsburg or Valois candidate – and given her advanced age for childbirth (thirty-seven) and need of a Catholic heir in 1553 it was even more urgent. Had Jane Grey prevailed in the July 1553 crisis, her and the Duke of Northumberland's strong Protestant orientation plus the recent (1551) French alliance would have impelled England into the Valois orbit and caused Habsburg alarm, as explored above. The choice by Mary Tudor to marry Charles' son Philip not the native-born English candidate Edward Courtenay was opposed by a strong faction in both the Council (led by Bishop Gardiner, now Chancellor) and the 1554 Parliament;[11] the arguments against England being swallowed up by its Queen's powerful new marital ally

anticipated those made against Elizabeth's marriage to the Duc d'Alençon in the late 1570s. Elizabeth was to be as firm in her reaction to domestic criticism as Mary was; the xenophobic 'Puritan' pamphleteer John Stubbs wrote a fulminating pamphlet about England being swallowed up by France due to the marriage ('The Gaping Gulf') and she had his hand chopped off for seditious libel. Unlike Mary, however, she listened to the criticism – and Stubbs protested his devotion to her even as the sentence was being carried out.[12]

Eventually England, provoked by French support for the 1556 Dudley conspiracy, joined the latest Habsburg-Valois war in 1557. As a result, the multiple ironies that occurred saw Mary's enthusiastic reunion with the papacy – an unexpected bonus for the latter's influence in North-West Europe – fall victim to the political exigencies of the Habsburg-Valois conflict. The Henrician legislation separating the English Church from Rome was all cancelled as soon as practicable in 1553–4 and the exiled Cardinal Reginald Pole, a scholarly Catholic descendant of the Duke of Clarence and arch-critic of the late King who had executed his brother in 1539 and mother in 1541, returned to England in triumph after over twenty years in exile in Italy. Having been considered for the papacy and missed election by one vote in 1550,[13] he now ended up as Archbishop of Canterbury and supervising the reunion with Rome and rebuilding of the English Catholic Church. Had Pole been elected as pope, he would have been an invaluable prop to Mary and her Spanish husband in terms of firm international Catholic backing for the re-conversion and would probably have sent priests from Rome to help his cousin; there would have been far greater interest in the project than in Rome in 1555–8 in real life. The new pope of 1555–9, Paul IV (Gianpetro Caraffa), was an opponent of Spain and broke off relations with Philip so Mary was ironically at odds with the papacy thereafter. While the Pope's forces made futile war on Philip and were totally defeated in 1557, Mary's realm was placed under papal displeasure with a rupture of diplomatic relations at the time when she needed strong papal support (and restraint on the religious executions?). Possibly a more cautious and less intolerant pope would have had the desire as well as the theological power to urge Mary to greater caution, or have sent a picked group of Jesuits to assist the re-conversions; Paul IV preferred to fume at Mary's alliance with his foe Philip. What if Paul's zealously 'reformist' and anti-corruption predecessor Marcellus II had not died suddenly in May 1555? Would the cultural patron Marcellus – who began the preparations for the later reformist Council of Trent – have urged Mary to prioritize preaching, not executions, and would she have listened to him to the improvement of her reputation? In another irony, the later leader of the anti-Catholic party at Elizabeth's court, Robert Dudley, and his brothers proved their loyalty to the regime that had executed their father but pardoned them by fighting valiantly for Philip against France at the battle of St Quentin in 1557; one brother, Henry, was killed. This loyalty was arguably one reason for Philip and de Quadra's support of Robert in 1560–1. Nearly thirty years later Robert was to command the anti-Spanish English army in the Netherlands, with his subordinates including his equally militantly anti-Catholic nephew Sir Philip Sidney, King Philip's godson. As a result of the Anglo-French war of 1557 England finally lost Calais to a surprise attack by the French under the Duc de Guise in 1558, widely perceived then and later as a national humiliation summing up the disasters of Mary's reign.

Also arising from the Anglo-French war, when Mary died on 17 November 1558 Henri II refused to recognize Elizabeth as queen. At the time the issue for this determinedly anti-Protestant ruler was not the threat to the Catholic Church from her religion – she had converted back to Catholicism under Mary, however much her sincerity might be suspected. Nor had Mary ever gone as far as to declare her a bastard and remove her from the succession, despite encouragement from assorted courtiers – Gardiner had even wanted the Princess executed in 1554 on the excuse of her suspicious conduct during the Wyatt revolt.[14] Did Gardiner's death in late 1555 aid Elizabeth's partial rehabilitation, and diminish the chances of Mary selecting the safely Catholic Lady Margaret Douglas as her heir once her own pregnancy was proved false? But Elizabeth's position remained ambiguous. The illegality under Catholic law of Henry VIII's marriage to Anne Boleyn was used in Paris in 1558 to argue that Elizabeth was illegitimate, being born while Henry's first wife was still alive, and had no right to the English throne. Henri thus proclaimed his daughter-in-law Mary Stuart as Queen of England, as the lineal closest heir and grand-daughter Henry VIII's elder sister Margaret Tudor,[15] and as a vigorous forty-one-year-old war-leader at war with England was in a position to press the claim. This, in turn, caused his foes Elizabeth and Philip to continue the Anglo-Spanish rapprochement for the moment, with each needing the other for political reasons. There was no move to restore Protestantism in England until the end of the Franco-Spanish war at the Treaty of Cateau-Cambresis in March 1559 brought Anglo-French peace and ended the threat of invasion. Elizabeth even considered dissolving her first parliament as it inopportunely pressed her to cancel Mary's religious legislation too soon. Arguably the Marian bishops over-played their hand, by snubbing her (e.g. in the funeral sermon for her late sister) and all but one refusing to crown her as a bastard. Did this help to push her to restore Protestantism? And would the Elizabethan Church have been more like Henry's 'Anglo-Catholic' one but for Elizabeth having to sack them? Indeed, the bizarre possibility of Philip marrying Elizabeth was initially raised by the widowed Spanish King, and political need of his support meant that it was officially tolerated during winter 1558–9.[16] It ended with his engagement to Henri's daughter Elizabeth of Valois (Edward VI's ex-fiancée) as a result of Cateau-Cambresis, but instead Philip proposed the candidacy of his cousin the Archduke Charles (a younger son of Emperor Ferdinand so not in line for the imperial throne). Charles was seven years Elizabeth's junior, and Elizabeth was to keep dangling the possibility of her acceptance of him into the mid-1560s to ensure Spanish goodwill – though this did not stop agile Spanish ambassadors considering favourably the alternative (more palatable personally to Elizabeth) of her marrying Robert Dudley.

As of spring 1559 England seemed militarily encircled by the Valois and in need of Spanish military support, the kingdom's treasury being empty and military forces enfeebled as the new Secretary of State William Cecil warned Elizabeth.[17] Henri's troops had been in Scotland to back up the regency regime for Mary Stuart ever since they were invited in 1548 to evict the Duke of Somerset's English army, and Mary's mother Marie de Guise (former putative fiancée of Henry VIII in 1538–40) was regent there. Firmly Catholic, Marie was also the sister of the conqueror of Calais, the Duc de Guise – France's foremost Catholic military commander and head of an immensely rich and ambitious dynasty descended from the Dukes of Lorraine. The Guise dynasty, as 'de facto' rulers of Scotland and maternal relatives of Henri's heir's fiancée, seemed the likeliest threat to newly Protestant England and to Elizabeth Tudor as of spring–summer 1559, and were so feared by contemporaries.[18] There had been a French military contingent in Scotland since it aided the regency to evict Protector Somerset's English garrison from Haddington in Lothian in 1548, although this was largely a defensive rather than offensive measure given the weakness of the Scots regency. The regents, first the Earl of Arran (the Hamilton claimant to the Scots throne, who held a French dukedom) and after him Marie de Guise, lacked a standing army and could not rely on the Scots nobles for military support, given their reputation for factionalism and treachery; thus the French troops preserved domestic stability as well as keeping English attacks at bay.

The threat of Henri attacking England ended with his unexpected death in a tournament-accident in July 1559, as a splinter went through his visor as he took part in combat himself.[19] Mary Stuart was now queen of both France (by marriage to Henri's son Francis II) and Scotland. Her feeble and ailing young husband Francis II was to die in December 1560, but military action to put her on the English might still be taken by her maternal Guise relatives. This ended with the French religious civil wars that broke out in 1562, which Henri's repression of the rapidly spreading Huguenot sects had made more likely but which immediately resulted from the willingness of senior Huguenot nobles (led by the Prince de Conde and Admiral Coligny) to take up arms against the French State. The latter arose directly from their perception that the government – now a regency for Francis' next brother, Charles IX – was hopelessly under the control of the Guise dynasty and their allies. Arguably the replacement of the older but ailing and vulnerable Francis, sixteen at his death in December 1560, by the nine-year-old Charles could well have ended the Guises' power, given that they were no longer the King's 'in-laws' and could not control Charles through Mary as they had done Francis; while Francis was still alive the Huguenot nobles had been reduced to a Scots-style plot to abduct the King at Amboise to seize power.[20] But the existence of a need for long-term regency for the new King meant that faction-struggles intensified and combined with the 'grass-roots' sporadic provincial violence between Catholics and Protestants to overwhelm the governance of the Queen-Mother, Catherine de Medici, in civil war from spring 1562. The latter was reckoned politically and religiously untrustworthy by the Guises and their ally Philip II, and indeed the subterranean political manoeuvres of 1561 led to the Guises seeking to betroth the widowed Mary Stuart to their Spanish ally's sixteen-year-old son Don Carlos.[21] Had this been carried out Mary would have been heading for Spain rather than back home to Scotland in 1561, and as she would be wife of Philip's heir the main threat to England would have been a Spanish-Scots union; Philip could not have been expected to tolerate the recent (1560) takeover of Scotland by rebellious Protestant nobles and enforced 'Reformation'. Nor would Elizabeth's government, which had encouraged and militarily aided the 1560 rebels in order to destroy the pro-French Guise regency government in Edinburgh, have accepted Spanish troops and clerics restoring Catholicism across the border. The chances would have been that Elizabeth, prodded by the more militantly Protestant Cecil, would have sponsored a Scots noble revolt against Mary, with the latter's Protestant half-brother the Earl of Moray as the likeliest leader. The clique of ruthless nobles led by the Earl of Morton and Lord Ruthven, who took part in the real-life 1566 plot to rid Scotland of Mary's Catholic Italian secretary Rizzio (and perhaps Mary too) by violence, were probable English allies in this. The Queen's Hamilton kinsmen and her violent Borders lord admirer Bothwell would also have been likely to line up against a Catholic-Spanish alliance, pitting them against the Catholic chiefs of the north-east and the Highlands led by the Earl of Huntly (who in real life died during a bungled rebellion to coerce the Protestant-dominated Queen in 1562).

The timing of the Scottish revolt against the Francophile regency in 1559 to Elizabeth's benefit was coincidental. The outbreak of a Protestant rebellion in Scotland was due as much to growing 'grass-roots' anger among the Lowlands laity, lairds and peasantry alike, at perceived 'Popish idolatry' (stirred up by preachers such as John Knox) as to the desire of greedy nobles to seize the estates of the Church and the monastic orders. Hatred of the Church and its wealth and power had been spreading in major towns such as St Andrews, Dundee, Perth and Edinburgh since the 1540s, when a mob of urban zealots had assisted the self-appointed task force of 'godly' conspirators who murdered the Francophile chief minister Cardinal Beaton (in bed with his mistress) at St Andrews and held out in its castle for months.[22] This combined in the 1550s with dislike of the French domination of the regency and its foreign policy (and large demands for money), though in fact Marie de Guise's government was one of the less partisan or self-seeking of recent decades. Excluded nobles resenting French control of power and appointments plus spreading Protestant preaching, which these men were promoting, meant that anger was 'coming to the boil' for domestic reasons in the late 1550s, independently of any support from England (which was Catholic anyway until 1559). What aid came from England for this was strictly unofficial and unconnected to the government. This then exploded into action after the death of Mary Tudor, as large-scale petitioning of the Marie de Guise regency in favour of religious reform led to urban disturbances and iconoclastic vandalism. The anti-French nobles raised their tenants to join the rising, and a civil war followed with the regent 'holed up' in Edinburgh Castle and her Scots/French forces struggling to hold onto the vital port of Leith. The replacement of Mary Tudor by Elizabeth and the first moves to reform in England in spring 1559 gave the petitioners and the land-hungry nobles more confidence to act, but the turbulence of Scots politics was such that some sort of armed rising against the regency was probable as soon as French attention and military commitment wavered – which would have been likely once Henri II died, even if Mary Tudor was still Queen of England. The fall of the regency regime was a mixture of armed aristocratic coup (normal for Scotland), populist Protestant revolution led by radical preachers, and later English armed intervention to drive out the regency's French troops. When the English army arrived – after initial hesitation from Elizabeth and greater enthusiasm from Cecil[23] – the French were blockaded into evacuating Leith and returning home. Marie de Guise opportunely died of dropsy (some said aided by English poison), and a Protestant noble junta, the 'Lords of the Congregation', took control and imposed the secularization of monastic property in the Reformation. Mary Stuart had to recognize this 'fait accompli' on her return home in 1561.[24] But it was lucky for the Protestant rebels of 1559–60 that Mary Tudor had died and Elizabeth was willing to help them with troops in order to bring an end to French influence north of the Border – and that Henri II died and his sons' government had other priorities. The previous unpopular Francophile regency of Scotland after 1514 (for James V), led by the Duke of Albany who had been in exile in France for decades and called in French troops, had been able to hold onto power thanks to French troops despite Henry VIII's ill-will and noble conspiracies. This regency failed to do so, though the religious revolt added to the challenge it faced. As a result, Mary Stuart returned home to be constitutionally and religiously constrained in a manner foreign to her ancestors, and was unable to act in the interests of the Guises against England even had she wished to; her Protestant half-brother Moray and other great nobles on her Council were aligned to England as guarantor of their new Protestant faith. The political and personal isolation of the Catholic Queen, brought up since she was five at a genteel court in France not in the rough-and-ready world of Scotland, was shown by her experiences as a new sovereign in fiercely Protestant Edinburgh. She politely attended the popular and charismatic Knox's sermons at first to win support, only to have him uncompromisingly denounce her religion and her foreign entourage. The first time her priest celebrated Mass privately in the Chapel Royal at Holyrood, as he was legally entitled to do, an indignant mob gathered outside and tried to storm in and lynch him; the Earl of Moray had to bar the door to them.

Luckily for Mary Stuart, she was not to be married off to the mentally defective, emotionally unstable, under-sized sadist Don Carlos (later to die in bizarre circumstances in 1568 and receive an unlikely posthumous heroification in opera). Catherine de Medici managed to halt the plan, and another one to marry Mary off to the Guises' putative ally Anthony of Bourbon.[25]

The strange death of Amy Robsart: 'cui bono'? Elizabeth's embarrassing position in 1560 foreshadows Mary's in 1567

As of 1559–60 the political odds in England were that Elizabeth would marry Robert Dudley, who was showered with gifts and was constantly in her company. The Spanish ambassador, Count Feria, wrote that he was in Elizabeth's apartments at night and people said that when his wife Amy, already ill (probably terminally), died they would marry.[26] In April 1559 Feria reckoned that Elizabeth was in love with Robert;[27] and marrying him would end the loudly proclaimed expectations of the main English Catholic conservative claimant, the arrogant Earl of Arundel (a councillor and leading defector from the Grey coup in 1553). Moreover, at this point Robert, the future anti-Spanish leader of the 1580s, was friendly to the interests of Spain as in January 1561 new ambassador Bishop de Quadra reported that Robert had sent his brother-in-law Sir Henry Sidney to propose that if Spain backed the Dudley/Elizabeth marriage Robert would help their interests.[28] He might even favour a return to Catholicism according to rumour.[29] Robert also suggested that he could be sent to the reforming Church Council of Trent as the English ambassador – an observer rather than a participant as England was now Protestant again, but still a sign of his goodwill.[30] The fervently anti-Catholic English ambassador to France, Sir Nicholas Throckmorton, was writing to his employer Secretary Cecil speaking of Robert as a threat to England's Protestant alignment and calling for him to be stopped.[31] Also, as of 1560–1 the traditional enmity between the Dudleys and the older nobility was more important at court than the later 'religious' alignment that saw Robert allied to other Protestant nobles in opposition to the pro-Catholic Howards; the Earls of Arundel and Pembroke were hostile to him due to his potential for seeking revenge on them over their abandonment of his father, Northumberland, in July 1553.[32] The potential thus existed for an alliance of the precariously powerful Robert Dudley with the Spanish ambassadors against other great nobles, with Cecil allied to the latter due to his fears of Catholic influence. However, this was not going to translate into action – in a royal marriage or in foreign policy – without the Queen's approval and Elizabeth significantly refused to send any 'observers' to the Council of Trent in 1561–2.[33]

In this context, not only Cecil but traditional aristocratic foes of the 'jumped-up' Dudleys had something to gain if Robert was disgraced and expelled from court – or at least 'smeared' enough to make the Queen wary of marrying him. In this context, Robert's wife's death can bear different interpretations. Did Robert rid himself of her out of impatience with her survival, or did his foes kill her to ruin his eligibility as a royal consort? Or did the latter exploit a genuine accident? Amy was kept from court, whether by her own ill-health or by Robert's wishes is unclear, and when Arundel was staging elaborate pageants for the Queen at Nonsuch Palace in Surrey in June 1559 to woo her Robert deserted his wife to accompany the Queen there.[34] Elizabeth's totally loyal ex-governess Kat Ashley, who had been with her since her girlhood and had been the principal target of an angry Council interrogation in 1548 about her charge flirting with Thomas Seymour, unsuccessfully begged the Queen on bended knee to abandon Robert and find a suitable husband elsewhere. Late in 1559 the favourite's aristocratic arch-enemy Thomas Howard, Duke of Norfolk and Elizabeth's cousin, nearly came to blows with him and was reported as saying that Robert would not die in his bed.[35] Whether or not he was intending to see that that was the case, Elizabeth sent Norfolk off to Northern England as its commander-in-chief in what amounted to exile from court.

But any chance of Elizabeth gambling on a *fait accompli* and marrying Robert was reduced when Amy was found dead at the bottom of a staircase at Cumnor Place on 8 September 1560. She did not own the house; the move had been arranged by Robert, whose steward leased it, which some found sinister due to what happened later. Despite the stories of her ill-health, her private accounts show that she was perfectly capable of and vigorous in transacting household business so she was not medically incapacitated; a natural fall was possible. She had sent her servants out to Abingdon Fair, as shown at the inquest, and insisted on one who wanted to stay behind going; but there was no indication that she had got rid of them to facilitate a suicide-attempt. One servant said that she had prayed for release from her suffering (her illness or Robert's philandering?), but there was no suggestion that she was prepared to commit the capital sin of killing herself. Oddly, that same day Elizabeth told the new Spanish ambassador, Bishop de Quadra, that Amy was 'dead or nearly so';[36] this seemed suspicious in retrospect but may have related to Robert's latest account of his wife's condition. She cannot be acquitted of having a sense of anticipation about what Amy's (natural) death would mean for her, but proving anything more against either her or Robert is impossible. In any case, the scandal of Amy dying violently was to the detriment of the presumed lovers' future; it was a simple matter to wait for her to die naturally.

The coroner's jury returned a verdict of accidental death, and it was probable that the sick Amy had accidentally over-balanced – or, less likely, committed suicide in despair at the open nature of her husband's flirtation with the Queen. But it was suspiciously convenient for Robert for those who did not know Amy was seriously ill, and coincided with rumours that he would get a divorce. Also, the jury was carefully vetted to include men loyal to Robert who would not dream of accusing him of murder. No question was raised about one of his closest henchmen, Sir Richard Verney, who Robert had charged with supervising his wife's household, having been the only person known to be in Cumnor Place at the time of the accident. (In the early 1580s Robert's detractors were to claim in the libellous 'Leicester's Commonwealth' that Robert had asked Verney to poison Amy.[37]) In the immediate aftermath, Elizabeth prudently sent Robert away from court to Kew to wait for the coroner's verdict; de Quadra could not be certain that she would marry or if the scandal would cause her to be deposed. If she was removed, his guess for the new king was Henry Hastings, Earl of

Huntingdon, the nearest male Protestant descendant of the Clarence line.[38] Henry was also to be considered a 'front-runner' for the throne by the Protestant Council of State when Elizabeth was seriously ill with smallpox in October 1562[39] – an occasion when she could easily have died and so been seen by posterity as a very minor, short-lived ruler subject to unstable passions for Dudley rather than as a great queen. But the crisis of Amy's sudden 'accident' brought an end to the possibility that the worried Cecil, hopeless about his eclipse by the Dudleys and in despair at his capricious mistress' behaviour, would resign.[40] It raises the possibility that Cecil's faction may have had Amy pushed down the stairs to cause a scandal and make it impossible for Elizabeth to marry Robert Dudley; though this can only be guesswork and must rely on Cecil's apparent foreknowledge of the accident (which could be coincidence). Some historians have argued that Cecil, a protégé of Dudley's father, Northumberland, but a personal rival of Robert, was a ruthless enough operator to be capable of this.[41]

The Queen's rival Mary Stuart gave voice to stories abroad in commenting maliciously that Elizabeth would marry her 'horse-keeper' (Dudley was Master of the Horse) who had murdered his wife to make way for her.[42] In 1567 Mary's next husband-to-be, Bothwell, was commonly believed to be the mastermind behind her husband Darnley's death, but she married him anyway – and was deposed by outraged lords within months. Elizabeth saw sense and did not proceed with marriage to her 'Robin', but had she taken the risk of doing so and a revolt resulted the obvious Protestant beneficiary was Catherine Grey or Huntingdon. If the marriage had gone ahead, Robert's aristocratic enemies might have believed his position to be invulnerable and their own position under threat if they did not rebel. The Howards under his personal foe Norfolk, ironically Elizabeth's cousin, were one potential source of trouble, the disappointed royal suitor Arundel another. Both had been enemies of Dudley's father, Northumberland, in 1553. But Elizabeth, unlike Mary Stuart (or her own mother in 1536), kept her feelings in check and chose the path of discretion by balancing the court factions against one another.

It should, however, be pointed out that the scandal did not immediately end attempts by Robert and his allies to create a 'ground-swell' of elite opinion to pressure the Queen to marry him, as his ally the Earl of Sussex attempted (unsuccessfully) to organize a petition for this at the annual Garter ceremonies at Windsor Castle in April 1561.[43] At the following year's Garter ceremonies feeling against Robert had abated, and for once his enemy Norfolk was prepared to back the proposal; in this case a majority of those Garter knights present agreed but Arundel and his ally the Earl of Northampton (Queen Catherine Parr's brother) walked out in disgust.[44] There is also the murky business of the claims of Amy's half–brother John Appleyard, who spent several years trying to prove that the 1560 inquest was a 'cover-up' and when arrested said that an anonymous Thames boatman had approached him with an offer of £1,000 from certain great lords to help his enquiries. These men were supposed to include Norfolk and Sussex, who if this was true were keen to see the Dudley marriage prevented. But nothing could be proved, and Appleyard was thrown in the Fleet Prison, interrogated by the Council, and probably 'lent on' with a threat of severe punishment; he grovellingly 'confessed' that he had wickedly made up his story to slander the totally innocent Dudley and other lords.[45] At the least, the interest that people took in Appleyard's campaign and the State's desire to shut him up as late as 1567 showed that the issue was still a dangerous one to investigate.

The need to balance England's international position between the Habsburgs and the Valois – at peace since the Treaty of Cateau-Cambrensis in 1559 but still mistrustful – also meant that any final choice of a foreign suitor from one 'Power' would alarm the other. Thus Elizabeth deciding to marry the Archduke Charles would cause French enmity, and deciding to marry a younger brother of Charles IX – Henri until he assumed the French throne in 1574, and thence Francis/Hercule – would alienate Philip II of Spain. This diplomatic tangle, like the need not to totally alienate either France or the Empire in the 1520s, held up any decision on the Queen's marriage quite irrespective of her personal distaste for it and her habit of procrastination. After 1568 relations with Spain were deteriorating, largely due to the use of English ports by refugee Dutch privateers at war with their country's Spanish occupier, and Spanish persecution of Protestantism in the Netherlands encouraged militant Protestant ministers and courtiers in London (e.g. both Cecil and Dudley) to oppose alliance with Philip and seek to undermine his rule; resisting the Habsburgs took on a more religious dimension than it had had earlier.[46]

(ii) Rising Anglo-Spanish confrontation, a plot to remove Cecil parallel to that against Cromwell in 1540, and the added factor of Mary Stuart

Cecil vs Norfolk: the coup that failed?
Contrary to retrospective patriotic Protestant myth, the Queen was far from an assured backer of the anti-Catholic faction in her Council and a split between their personally antagonistic leaders, Cecil and Leicester, led in 1569 to an unlikely temporary alignment of the latter with the leading Council conservative, the fourth Duke of Norfolk. The seizure of Genoese

funds on Spanish ships that put into Plymouth late in 1568, en route for the Spanish army in the Netherlands, brought confrontation. The commercially crippling Spanish Netherlands embargo on English trade which followed – eased once alternative buyers could be found – brought embarrassment to the chief mover in the seizure, Cecil, in spring 1569 and a Council plot to have him arrested. Like Thomas Cromwell in 1540, he was condemned by nobles like Norfolk (the equally arrogant grandson of Cromwell's arch-enemy, the third Duke) as a low-born 'usurper' of the nobility's rightful role in Council and a religious fanatic. Norfolk was the Queen's closest male relative and was generally trusted at this point, though his occasional physical clashes with his rival Leicester – son of a major foe of the Howards from the 1540s – were politically dangerous to him. Leicester, a dangerous foe to Cecil as the Queen's favourite, joined in Norfolk's campaign and even suggested that the realm was not safe until Cecil was beheaded.[47] Did he resent Cecil, a protégé of his father, Northumberland, who had risen to unexpected power, out of mere jealousy or out of knowledge that Cecil had ruined his chances of marrying the Queen in 1560?

Had Elizabeth given the 'go-ahead' as her father had done in 1540, Council foes were more than ready to have Cecil kidnapped or arrested at the Council and dragged off to the Tower – and once an enquiry into a fallen minister was underway they had their own momentum. Fortunately Elizabeth continued to give Cecil her unswerving backing,[48] and he survived the crisis. But had he been arrested in spring 1569 the uneasy alliance of Leicester (normally a militant Protestant but temporarily favourable to Spain) and Norfolk would have been likely to see a more pro-Spanish policy in the 1570s, with the replacement of the determined, methodical, well-organized, and ruthless Cecil's unwavering pro-Protestant 'line' in foreign policy by a more uncertain one. Cecil, a superb administrator and effective chief minister to Elizabeth for forty years (as Secretary of State to 1572 and Lord Treasurer 1572–98), was a force for stability and consistency; neither the hot-tempered, extravagant, 'showy' Leicester nor the arrogant and politically naïve Norfolk were likely to prove as competent in determining international policies had they had Cecil's influence removed. Nor was there any guarantee that their alliance would continue for long, as quite apart from their sporadic personal tensions their religious interests were at odds (Leicester was a patron of 'reformist' Protestants and Norfolk was only nominally Protestant).

The chief result of Cecil's fall would have been that Norfolk was safe from the political ruin that befell him in 1570–2 in the aftermath of the reign's first Catholic revolt, the rising of the 'Northern Earls', to which his attitude was alleged by his enemies to be equivocal. Even had Norfolk been a vital

Council ally of the dominant Leicester after Cecil's arrest, it does not mean that Leicester would have been able to persuade the Queen to allow Norfolk to marry Mary Stuart (which course he apparently backed in 1569, to the Queen's anger[49]). Elizabeth's fear of Mary ran too deep to allow that aggrandisement of her potential successor in any circumstances. In the event, the failure of the 1569 plot to unseat Cecil had the crucial result that the latter now took the offensive against his Council foes, and seems to have been the prime mover behind Norfolk's disgrace and execution over the 'Ridolfi Plot'. Norfolk was clearly naïve if not worse, and talked too enthusiastically of his hopes to marry Mary at a time when it was anathema to a suspicious Elizabeth. Crucially, he failed to inform Elizabeth of his plans on two occasions in 1569 when she gave him a chance in conversation – which could be interpreted in a sinister fashion. His alleged treasonable conversation with the plot's 'leader' Ridolfi before the latter left England to seek foreign aid rests on the circumstantial evidence of later second-hand summaries, filtered through the prism of Cecil's agents. (Ridolfi himself never testified, and remained safe in Italy.) But his crucial retirement to his Norfolk home at Kenninghall and failure to turn up quickly at court when summoned as the Northern revolt broke out in 1569 politically ruined him with his royal cousin. As with Elizabeth's similar failure to attend quickly on her half-sister Mary during the Wyatt revolt, it seemed that he was waiting for the rebels to succeed so he could join them. It is far from certain in this murky episode that the 'evidence' of Norfolk's involvement with the supposed conspirators, especially incriminating documents conveniently found at his London residence, were not 'planted' by Cecil's agents to incriminate him.[50] After he had tried to have Cecil arrested the latter had every excuse to regard him as a mortal foe and destroy him – and to contemporaries, including Cecil, the parallel would have been the third Duke of Norfolk's part in destroying the 'low-born' and radical Protestant ally Cromwell in 1540.

Anglo-Spanish tension: inevitable or did it get out of hand?

The Council power struggle that came to a head in 1569 coincided with the escalation of the Dutch crisis. Resistance to Philip had now passed from the hands of the nobles, who he had suppressed, to more humbly born – and religiously antagonistic – Protestant subjects. The refugee Dutch Protestant privateers/pirates, the 'Sea Beggars', who took refuge in English harbours in the late 1560s and harassed the Spanish supply-routes from Spain to the Netherlands were assisting the cause of Protestantism as well as keeping Spain weak by their action. They thus aided England, by distracting the powerful army sent to the Netherlands under the Duke of Alva in 1567 from completing their task of repression and being free to threaten England. They were thus backed by Elizabeth's more militant privy councillors, led by the Earls of Leicester (Robert Dudley) and Huntingdon and by Cecil; Elizabeth tolerated such a course but did not commit herself openly.[51] The Queen could not sit on the fence and assert her ignorance of what was going on to Philip (or avoid doing anything about his complaints) forever, and the Spanish King was under his own pressure from Alva and anti-English zealot ministers at his court such as Cardinal Granvelle. They believed that the flow of unofficial English support for the Netherlands rebels was such that the revolt would never be put down without tackling England too, and the nomination of one of their party, Guerau de Spés, as the new Spanish ambassador to England in 1568 was a sign of Philip's movement towards their views. Unlike his predecessors, de Spés was a Catholic zealot keen for the triumph of his faith in England by all means possible, including contacts with plotters among the 'opposition' and staging a coup – and the fortuitous arrival in England of the refugee Mary Stuart on 16 May 1568 provided them all with the next Catholic heir to England as a pretender ready to hand.

Elizabeth's dominant financial concerns (amounting to parsimony as with Henry VII) added to her irritation with Spain in the first major Anglo-Spanish crisis in November 1568. She ordered the confiscation of the contents of four Spanish treasure-ships driven into Plymouth by the 'Sea Beggars', an £85,000 loan from Genoese bankers to Alva to fund his armies in the Netherlands. Technically the money was Genoese not Spanish and the Genoese were at liberty to cancel their arrangement; they were induced to transfer the loan to the English government.[52] But the politico-military intention was to hamper Alva's campaign, and presumably Leicester, Cecil, and the other anti-Spanish councillors hoped to provoke a reply, ruin good Anglo-Spanish relations and Elizabeth's accompanying laxity on English Catholics, and force the Queen into a more vigorous defence of the Protestant cause. At this point Cecil at least did not envisage open war with Spain but merely 'proxy' conflict in the Netherlands, as seen by his correspondence with the Dutch rebels and the French Huguenot leader Coligny; he accurately thought Philip was too preoccupied for open war.[53] The inevitable retaliation came in the form of an embargo on English trade-goods and seizure of those currently in the Netherlands by the angry Alva, as advised by de Spés. This heightened feeling against Spain in England, and strengthened the case for open anti-Spanish action made by the 'hawks' in the Council. (The contrary policy, of backing down and blaming and arresting Cecil, was also a possibility in spring 1569, as discussed above.) The English could divert their trade from the Netherlands, though Alva endeavoured to disrupt it at sea, and the balance of commercial loss ran against 'over-extended' Spain; accordingly the latter had to make efforts to end the breach with England. Had Mary Stuart not had her international reputation damaged by the circumstances of her involvement with Bothwell at the time of Darnley's murder (and publicly exposed in the 'Casket Letters' investigations), the alternative course of replacing Elizabeth with Mary would have seemed more attractive to Philip – and it was not until 1570 that Pope Pius definitively absolved English Catholics from their allegiance to a 'heretic usurper'.[54] Even so, the scandal did not affect the enthusiasm of de Spés for meddling in plots to remove Elizabeth in Mary's favour.

Elizabeth responded to Philip, and in spring 1572 she finally expelled the 'Sea Beggars' as a goodwill gesture to Philip; they proceeded to take over the Dutch ports of Flushing and Brill in open revolt against Spain. In the coming years several thousand English volunteers, including Drake's half-brother Sir Humphrey Gilbert, joined their struggle for independence; most of them were recalled by the Queen in 1573–4 as the immediate crisis with Spain eased. In association with this policy of weakening Spain by proxy, a naval campaign began to stop the flow of South American silver to Spain to fund their warfare and Drake was despatched to raid shipping and ports on the 'Spanish Main' (the Caribbean coasts of Colombia and Venezuela).[55] The concomitant English effort to patch up relations with France and use the latter against Spain seemed viable as the 1560s religious conflicts there were temporarily in abeyance and Catherine de Medici's government had patched up an uneasy truce, and in spring 1572 an alliance was agreed at Blois. This assured the support of either signatory to the other if the latter was attacked by a third party (i.e. Spain).[56]

The danger of Philip backing the Catholic 'ultras' in France, led by the Guises, against the French government as too tolerant of the Huguenots seemed to impel the Queen-Mother's faction into alliance with the latter, hence the projected marriage of Catherine's daughter Marguerite to the Huguenot leader Henri of Navarre and the despatch of the Protestant zealot, future spymaster Sir Francis Walsingham, to Paris as ambassador to organize pan-European Protestant alliances between England, the French regime, the Huguenots, and the Dutch; but the 'Massacre of St Bartholomew' in August 1572 ended that prospect in a spectacular manner.[57] The notion that the French government would put religious fanaticism above the usual imperative of the traditional Valois/Habsburg antagonism was thus unsuspected by and unwelcome to Elizabeth. Had Catherine de Medici and her weak-willed, impulsive son Charles IX not listened to their more fanatical advisors and decided to destroy the Huguenot 'threat', by eliminating their leadership when the latter were in Paris for the Henri/Marguerite wedding, a return to the Anglo-French alliance of the early 1550s would have been expected. The involvement of the rebel Dutch in it would have given it a new ideological slant alien to earlier alliances, however, and the fervent Protestant Walsingham clearly favoured a new-style, ideological rather than a traditional dynastic alliance. This would have been profoundly uncomfortable to the devout Catholic Catherine, who could be worked on by pro-Spanish clerics concerning the 'sin' of allying herself to rebel heretics and to a queen whom the Pope had declared a bastard. She would also have been uneasy at the prominence given to Henri of Navarre in the alliance's plans for war against Spain, as his independently led Huguenot troops posed a threat to the supremacy of her son's government within France. Would this have soon wrecked the Anglo-French alliance?

Once the initial revulsion at the massacre was over, however, Elizabeth showed that she was more interested in 'realpolitik' than in religious solidarity with the Huguenots. She remained willing to use France against the increasingly hostile Spain, at least in the form of its army securing the independence of the Netherlands from Philip's army – as long as that did not entail the equally horrendous prospect of a French conquest of the Channel Ports. As in international crises of the seventeenth century to 1940, the crucial English concern was to keep the line of ports from Dunkirk to Flushing out of the hands of a hostile 'Great Power'. As of the 1570s, that Catholic power could be either France or Spain, and English support for the French expeditions into the Netherlands was reduced when the latter's success seemed to presage a French conquest; the more expensive (and provocative) option of direct English military intervention was avoided for as long as possible. Only the assassination of the Dutch leader, William 'the Silent', in 1584 and the impending collapse of the Dutch resistance forced the Queen to send a – small – expeditionary force under her trusted Leicester, and even then she was furious when he became too deeply involved in Dutch politics and seemed ready to assume political control of the state.[58]

Elizabeth's own preference of the late 1570s and early 1580s was in line with traditional diplomacy, for a combination of a dynastic alliance with France and hiring 'proxy' armies to restrain Philip rather than a 'godly' ideological war to aid the Dutch rebels (who had evicted their lawful sovereign Philip, albeit due to tyranny and persecution, which offended her sense of monarchic solidarity). Hence her decision to lure France, Philip's arch-rivals, into a military alliance whereby they would bear the brunt of the cost of fighting him in the Netherlands, and her enthusiasm for the suggestion that she should cement this alliance by marrying King Henri III's next brother Francis, Duke of Alençon and Anjou. Alençon was the proposed commander of a French expedition to the Netherlands, and

Elizabeth made much of the 'running' in the marriage-talks and seems at one point to have seriously thought of marrying him as she announced it openly – a rare instance of diplomatic boldness by her.[59] Perhaps she was for once not in control of her emotions, and was genuinely anxious for a partner and fond of the short, squat, admiring, and personally non-threatening Duke? Or was this just an attempt to reassure his elder brother and sovereign, the determinedly Catholic Henri III (an unlikely ally for the Protestant Dutch), that Elizabeth was serious and was not just seeking to lure him into fighting Spain in the Netherlands for her own cynical reasons of parsimony and strategic safety? The complex feints of Anglo-Franco-Spanish bluff and counter-bluff, a traditional three-way confrontation of Tudor, Valois, and Habsburg as seen in the 1510s to 1550s, were now given a further layer by religion, and the 'Guise party' of ultramontane conservative Catholics at the French court were pressurizing Henri to ally to Spain not Elizabeth so she had to be accommodating to his envoys and his brother (who was his heir at that point). She seems to have been genuinely fond of Alençon, who she nicknamed her 'Frog' for his appearance, and her Council feared that she would accept and marry him and so drew up detailed arguments to persuade her not to do so.[60] But the matter was given an element of bizarreness by the fact that Alençon was twenty-one years younger than Elizabeth, and she was more of an age to be his mother than his wife as ageing Henrician councillor Sir Ralph Sadler pointed out.[61] Had her need of tying France to a major commitment to the Netherlands campaign ever driven her to go through with this marriage in the 1579–81 talks, producing an heir from it was unlikely though her doctors assured her that it was feasible.[62]

(iii) Mary Stuart, 'Daughter of Debate': in Scotland to 1568 and in England. Was her political triumph in either realm a serious possibility?

Mary in Scotland, 1561–5: the search for an Anglophile husband to control her

The arrival of Mary Stuart in England in May 1568 provided an extra danger for the English government in the form of an 'on-the-spot' Catholic pretender for use by disaffected Catholic plotters or a foreign power (probably Spain, given de Spés' aggressive attitude). The prospects for co-operation between the cousins had always been limited, although the overthrow of the Catholic Church (and the French military alliance) by English-backed Protestant nobles in 1560 meant that the Catholic Mary had returned in 1561 to a firmly Protestant realm linked to an English alliance.

Her Catholicism and her Guise family connections were thus less of a political threat than they would have been had the Reformation not been imposed on Scotland before her return. The political neutralization of Mary's religion did not prevent her from insisting on practising it in private rather than following her people into Protestantism, despite the fulminations of John Knox, and in an era of *cuius principo eius religio* there was danger of her assisting her Catholic nobles in restoring Catholic rule. The Gordons (Marquises of Huntly) in the north-east and the Hamiltons (next heirs to the Scots throne) in the south-west were the most dangerous of these; and it was lucky for the English government and their Scots allies that active, aggressive foreign Catholic assistance for their co-religionists had not yet developed. The French ultras, the Guises, were too concerned to thwart the Huguenots in France and from 1562 were in sporadic armed conflict with them; Philip was also concentrating on France and from the mid-1560s faced escalating armed defiance from autonomist nobles in the Netherlands (e.g. Egmont and Horn); and the papacy – restrained by Philip – had not yet definitively broken with Elizabeth. By the time Jesuits and Spanish agents were on the scene in the 1570s and seeking to use Scotland to undermine Elizabeth's regime, the Scots Catholic nobles had lost the advantage of a co-religionist on the throne and the regency for James VI was determinedly Protestant.

Attempts were made, unsuccessfully, in 1561–5 to politically 'control' Mary as a safe ally – either directly or via a reliable husband. Elizabeth offered her the services of Robert Dudley, now raised to the earldom of Leicester to make his rank closer to that of the Scots Queen, as a safe Protestant husband to defeat the risk of Mary marrying a pro-Catholic Hamilton, Don Carlos of Spain, or the Archduke Charles. This ingenious idea was never likely to succeed, as quite apart from Mary considering Elizabeth's 'cast-off' lover beneath her Leicester preferred to keep his power in England to an uncertain future in Scotland. He went along with his mistress' orders in wooing Mary, but without enthusiasm or success.[63] During the English efforts to find Mary a suitable husband, Elizabeth sought to tie Mary down to her own priorities by inducing her to formally renounce her claim to the English throne for Elizabeth's lifetime in return for unofficial hints about the succession; but the Scots Queen's envoys insisted on a public promise, which Elizabeth would never give anyone for forty-four years.[64]

Cecil failed to make headway with his warnings that the more a formal promise of the succession was demanded, the less likely Mary was to receive it but if she was patient and undemanding there was a greater chance of it.[65] Mary's proposed personal meeting with Elizabeth to resolve their differences in August–September 1562 at York never took place, though it was apparently acceptable to the latter and only the eruption of civil war in France in July halted it. It was unlikely to have ended their mutual suspicions, and was cancelled again in 1563. Crucially, Mary's ambassador to England in spring 1563, her secretary William Maitland, explained to the Spanish ambassador that Mary would never marry either a Protestant (though he had tried to change her mind on this) or a nominee of Elizabeth's. If Mary had done either it would have eased her position with Elizabeth and her potential as a successor, whether or not in the circumstances of exile in England after 1568; though an equally obdurate Elizabeth told Maitland that she would never name her successor as it would put her in the humiliatingly abandoned position that Mary Tudor had been in November 1558. Them that had 'most right' would succeed her when the time came[66] – and genealogically that meant Mary and in due course the latter's son, provided that Henry VIII's ban on foreign-born heirs was ignored.

Given that Mary would not marry Elisabeth's nominee Leicester, one solution might have been her cousin, James Hamilton, Earl of Arran – lineal next heir to Scotland behind his father, as senior descendant of James III's sister Mary. (This was assuming that his parents' marriage was counted as legal, about which there was some doubt.) His father, who held the French dukedom of Chatelherault, was Catholic and pro-French and as such was suspected by the English government; but unlike Mary's chosen husband he had no claim on the English throne. His marriage to Mary would bring the hope – and the danger – of one major Scots noble faction, the Hamilton dynasty, being incontrovertibly linked to and thus protecting her security. Unfortunately Arran was mercurial and increasingly mentally unstable, and was soon to be placed under restraint by his father. At one point Mary expressed interest in marrying Philip of Spain's son and heir Don Carlos, who was not yet publicly known to be mentally unstable – but her French Guise relatives opposed this and tried to interest her in a less dangerous Habsburg, Elizabeth's ex-suitor Archduke Charles.[67] The Don Carlos idea does not say much for Mary's political wisdom, as it would have led to a Spanish-Scottish union and alarmed England as much as the Franco-Scottish union did in 1558–60; possibly she was hoping to leave cold, bleak, and Protestant Scotland for sunny Spain?[68] But Spain had already dangled Don Carlos in front of Elizabeth's alternative heir Lady Catherine Grey in 1559–60,[69] and was clearly using him as a means of 'controlling' whoever was likeliest to succeed Elizabeth.

Mary's eventual choice of husband in 1565, Margaret Tudor's grandson Lord Darnley (three years her junior), was denounced by Elizabeth in advance once the engagement was known, and was clearly not an official

English choice. At best, Leicester and Cecil had encouraged Darnley (living with his mother in Yorkshire but educated in France like Mary) to go to Scotland in 1564 as a way of stopping Elizabeth's plan to marry Mary to Leicester and the Spanish marriage idea.[70] Indeed, Elizabeth had granted him permission to go there even if she later regretted it. Elizabeth threw his mother, Margaret Douglas (her own possible rival as heir to Mary Tudor in 1554–8, and a Catholic), in the Tower of London for suspected collusion,[71] and the fact that Margaret was lineal next heir to England after herself and Darnley next after his mother added to the Queen's sensitivity about implications for the English succession. Possibly Margaret and her ambitious, naïve son had hopes of two crowns rather than one in due course.

Yet Elizabeth had allowed Darnley's father, the pro-English Scots Earl of Lennox, to go to Scotland to canvass for the match earlier and had (jokingly?) referred to Darnley as not only one of her two choices for Mary but as a better candidate than Leicester.[72] The possibility remains that Elizabeth intended to play the two off against each other and keep Mary unwed for as long as possible, her usual policy in case of uncertainty in a crisis being delay. If she had not allowed Darnley to go to Scotland he would not have married Mary, at least in 1565. The alternative to controlling Mary via a pro-English husband was physical coercion by a coup within the heavily armed Scots nobility, always a possibility in the turbulent world of Scots politics but especially with a female or under-age ruler. This seems to have been attempted by unofficial support for Mary's rebellious half-brother, the reliably Protestant Earl of Moray, in 1565, but he was defeated and driven into exile in England.[73] If his armed faction had succeeded in seizing Mary and turning her into their puppet he was quite capable of keeping her unwed so as to improve his own chances as her successor; luckily for Mary, Darnley's growing unpopularity for his arrogant petulance had not yet alienated most of the nobles as it did in 1566–7. Moray's rashness in staging a revolt at this stage undermined his chances of future influence at Mary's court, and by splitting brother from sister arguably produced disastrous results for the Queen's future by throwing her into the unstable hands of alternative male advisers – firstly Darnley and then Bothwell. Had Moray bided his time and been more conciliatory to his sister, could he have provided her with stable assistance to curtail Darnley's blunders (e.g. assisting the Riccio murder plot) in 1566–7 and so saved her throne? Or would Mary have always listened to a husband rather than a brother, and so allowed a jealous Darnley to talk her into exiling Moray?

Nor was Darnley's titular Catholicism a problem; he attended Protestant services without protest and was more interested in alcohol than in religion. Moray's timing was wrong; could he have succeeded in a coup and expelled

Darnley from the country had he waited a year or so? That would have left Moray as the Protestant 'strongman' at the head of a council of nobles using Mary as their puppet, with the Queen probably less alienated from her Protestant nobles than she was to be in real life after a clique of them murdered her secretary Riccio in her presence. But it is still possible that Mary, resenting Moray's control, would not have acquiesced with his rule for long and would have turned to his rivals – the Hamiltons? – for military help. Once she had had a son, the Moray faction could contemplate deposing her for obduracy and installing James VI as their new protégé for a lucratively long regency.

Mary and Darnley, 1565–7. Murder and deposition

The disaster of Mary's second marriage and its breakdown produced a crisis in which Mary's hitherto blameless reputation was to be fatally affected. This did not prevent her steadfast attitude to her religion continuing her appeal as a puppet Queen of England to Elizabeth's hard-headed 'Counter-Reformationary' European foes in the 1570s and 1580s, but it damaged her as potential heir in more fastidious people's opinions. Indeed, at one point it seemed possible that Mary would be eliminated from the equation altogether, without a child – the sordid violence in her private chamber at Edinburgh Castle when her secretary David Riccio was killed on 9 March 1566 could easily have caused her to miscarry the future James VI. The conspirators who deliberately set about to kill her favourite servant in her presence, power-hungry 'ultra' Protestants including Lord Ruthven and the future regent Morton, were allies of Mary's exiled half-brother Moray and their 'bond' of alliance was formally aimed at forcing his (Protestant) exile faction's restoration, coupled with the grant of the full royal powers ('crown matrimonial') to Mary's reliably Protestant husband Darnley. But the nature of the open murder of Riccio in front of the pregnant Queen, which was chosen instead of an equally effective private stabbing or kidnapping, suggests that it was hoped it would cause the death of the pregnant Catholic Queen who was not allowed any medical attention afterwards – and thus give the full Crown to the weak and malleable Darnley. The English ambassador Thomas Randolph informed Leicester on 13 February that there were rumours of this intention.[74] It cannot be thought likely that if Mary had died of a miscarriage the new 'King Henry', a weak and petulant character open to bad advice and no doubt seeking refuge in drink, would have lasted long as king in the hands of the circle of predatory nobles around him. He would have been the puppet of his installers, led by Ruthven and the Earl of Morton, and would have faced the wrath of Moray (a son of James V so a potential rival) and the Hamiltons and probably of Mary's French relatives too.

Mary and Darnley were already at odds, but his agreement to his allies' insistence that he take part in the effective coup – they apparently left his dagger in Riccio's body to point out his guilt – inevitably caused their relations to deteriorate further once Mary had quick-wittedly charmed her unstable husband into helping her to escape from the plotters on 10 March and reassert her power.[75] Anyone with more sense than the vain, petulant, and not too intelligent Darnley would never have allowed themselves to become involved in this situation, whether jealous of the suave Italian secretary Riccio or not. Once the breach with Mary had occurred, and husband and wife started to live apart, any senior Scots peer with a minimal degree of self-preservation who was in Darnley's position as consort would not have run the risk of returning to Edinburgh with a supposedly repentant wife without an omnipresent armed guard. It might be beyond normal probability that his wife would kill him, but he had other enemies (including members of the Riccio murder plot) who in winter 1566–7 were intent on removing him from the political scene. Given the usual parameters of Scots politics, this meant a murder plot was quite possible and in addition the existence of a rival monarch in the person of Mary's son James VI (born June 1566) meant that ambitious nobles who could not trust either Mary or Darnley to act as their puppets could remove both of them, crown Prince James, and have the luxury of a long regency to govern the country.

As of December 1566 Darnley was relatively safe in his family stronghold of Glasgow, near his father's earldom of Lennox, and surrounded by family retainers, and was plausibly rumoured to be – sporadically? – plotting against his wife again, presenting himself as a potential Catholic champion to the Pope and Philip II.[76] This may imply that he had hopes of replacing his wife with his son as sovereign, with himself as regent backed by international Catholic troops – though his immaturity and lack of political skills make it implausible that he could ever have run a coup effectively. (Could his father and Huntly have acted for him in staging a revolt?) Yet he consented to come to Edinburgh to complete his convalescence after a bout of measles (his enemies said syphilis), and did so without armed protection – which would imply that he trusted Mary with his security. Not to accept her request, or to travel with armed retainers, would have been expected of someone less naïve however 'insulting' either measure would be to his wife. If either had happened, the chances of his enemies smuggling a large quantity of gunpowder into his residence and exploding it undetected would have been small. There were no Lennox retainers around at night at the house at which he chose to stay on the outskirts of Edinburgh, which was a serious mistake on his part. It was left to his manservant to spot men acting suspiciously in the garden and alert him; apparently a pile of gunpowder had been dumped in a room on the ground floor without anyone noticing it. Had he had bodyguards, even the boldest plotter might have hesitated about removing him so dramatically. This is not to say that the Mary-Darnley marriage would have lasted beyond 1567, however; the chances are that Mary was considering divorce, which may explain the apparent overtures to Archbishop Hamilton that midwinter.

The nature of Mary's collusion with the plotting of Darnley's enemies at Craigmillar Castle at the end of November 1566 has been hopelessly muddied by the partisan accounts of all the 'witnesses', Mary's account being intended to acquit her of complicity in murder and the murderers' being to incriminate her. Once she was deposed as queen the following summer, the accusation of murder served as an important part of the indictment and so all partisans of the new government had a reason to avoid exonerating her. All parties, it is agreed, wanted her to be rid of Darnley as consort. But it seems likely that she was mainly concerned with a divorce or, failing that, some other means that would be ratifiable by Parliament; she requested their help in this and Secretary William Maitland promised that if she left it to them the method used would be duly ratified.[77] She did not enquire further, and granted the plotters' request to pardon Morton and other exiles from the Riccio murder plot. Her part was to bring Darnley to Edinburgh, which would prevent him from either plotting revolt or fleeing abroad quite apart from making him available for murder; her supporters were able to argue that her intention was the former, not the latter. Quite apart from assessments of Mary's character, it made no sense to act against Darnley (murder or exile?) unless a divorce plan had been blocked by his family or the Church.

The events surrounding the choice of Darnley's destination make it clear that she did not lure him to his death at Kirk o' Field, a small and isolated house on the outskirts of the capital suitable either for convalescence from an infectious disease or for murder. Her choice for his residence was Craigmillar Castle, which he refused, and once he was at Edinburgh the choice of the provost's lodging at Kirk o' Field was his. The mysterious events of the night of 9–10 February have been explored exhaustively ever since, and rival theories about the responsibility for the explosion have even suggested that Darnley intended to murder one of his rivals (Moray?) and was detected and punished by Bothwell. Mary's innocence of the means used to remove her husband seems reasonably certain, given the famous incident a few hours before the murder during a party for leading protagonists (and the victim) at the house. She publicly scolded one of the plotters (her page Paris), who had begrimed himself carrying gunpowder into the house, for his appearance – hardly the act of someone who knew what was going on downstairs. This is more significant than her refusal to sleep in the house that night, and the whole plan to blow up the house bears signs of quick improvisation to get rid of Darnley before he ended his convalescence and moved out to safer Holyrood Palace. As it was, he and his attendant apparently became suspicious and escaped through an upper window in the middle of the night, minutes before the explosion, without having time to dress; they were found strangled in the garden afterwards. The culprits were presumed to be an armed posse of Douglases who were guarding that part of the escape route, who witnesses heard Darnley pleading with for mercy. The latter probably saw them or Bothwell's men outside the house and assumed they were about to storm in to kill him more conventionally.[78] There was not much of a chance that Darnley would have got away safely from the scene and returned to Glasgow to seek help, in his nightshirt and without a horse, but if he had had time to find a hideout with Lennox family allies in Edinburgh he and his father could have been expected to launch a rebellion against Mary within weeks. That would then have pitted the Lennox tenantry against a loyalist Marian army, probably led by her stalwart Borders supporter Bothwell.

The fatal part of the Kirk o' Field crisis for Mary was her hasty decision to marry the chief suspect, Bothwell. He was generally being accused of it in Edinburgh within days – in public, despite the threats he made to kill any accusers – and had apparently been seen at the scene on the night of the explosion. One of his attendants there, his employee John Hepburn, apparently confessed their role in laying and lighting the gunpowder on his deathbed in prison later to his cell-mate, who gave evidence at the French tribunal for nullifying the Mary-Bothwell marriage in 1575. However, the 'official' version of events put out after Mary's deposition and Bothwell's flight – from its nature, bound to damn them both – confused the issue, as a 'culprit' alleged that he and Bothwell's other men carried the gunpowder through the streets openly in two barrels on horseback from apartments at Holyrood to Kirk o' Field.[79] This would have been risky (what of the city watchmen or any passing Lennox partisans?), and it is more likely that the detail was invented to emphasize Bothwell's role and distract the public from that of his co-plotter Sir James Balfour, brother of the landlord of Kirk o' Field. Did Balfour bring the gunpowder, which Cecil was told he had purchased, to store it at his brother's house next-door? Balfour was given the governorship of Edinburgh Castle by Mary and Bothwell's regime a few months later – depriving the Earl of Mar, guardian of Prince James, who joined the 'opposition' – but treacherously defected when rebel lords revolted after Mary's marriage to Bothwell. He was duly pardoned for all past offences, which quite possibly included a large role in the Kirk o' Field explosion.[80] If he had not defected, would he have joined Bothwell in being named as a murderer in a rather more plausible scenario?

Bothwell was accused of murder by Darnley's father, Lennox, but the latter then failed to turn up at the official enquiry in March 1567 to give evidence – ironically, thanks to his scruples in obeying the law by not bringing a large entourage to protect him. Bothwell had 4,000 armed tenants at large in Edinburgh at the time – and Mary did not order him to send them home.[81] However, if Lennox had brought enough men to protect him and given evidence, it was not likely to have led to Bothwell's conviction – he had plenty of noble allies, e.g. the later regent Morton, willing to supply alibis. Also, Mary's principal non-noble adviser and confidante, Secretary Maitland, had loathed Darnley and was involved in the murder plot so he was not willing to ask the Queen to be more even-handed. But even if Mary was determined to support Bothwell, and could not 'target' anyone else (e.g. Balfour) without the fear that they would reveal embarrassing details, the failure to convict any 'scapegoat' (even a minor henchman) added to international disquiet.

Bothwell's formal acquittal at the official enquiry was a farce given his provocative armed stance there. His behaviour was outrageously bold, even for a notoriously arrogant hothead used to intimidation, and if Mary had had any sense of self-preservation she would have steered clear of him for a few months. Her only close (though now alienated) adult male relative, her potential ally Moray, had left for England and she had no aristocratic adviser – with armed tenants at hand – willing to stand up to Bothwell. There was logic in her choosing a new husband in the hiatus of spring 1567, and even some in selecting one of the more quick-acting, ruthless and intelligent of the Protestant Border lords. Indeed, despite the rumours about Bothwell's part in the murder he managed to persuade (or threaten?) a gathering of earls, barons and bishops at Ainslie's Tavern in Edinburgh a few weeks after his acquittal into signing a 'bond' supporting his candidature as a husband – though he also had to divorce his current wife first.[82] Possibly hard-nosed lords such as Morton, Argyll, Rothes and Huntly thought that at least he would provide stability. But the speed with which Bothwell and Mary acted was disastrous. Instead of keeping her distance from him for a few months, Mary chose to run off with him – officially 'abducted' against her will to the castle of Dunbar while returning from visiting her son James at Stirling, but possibly by collusion. She did not seem too outraged when Bothwell intercepted her entourage and demanded that he accompany her – and some of his allies knew his intentions beforehand.[83] Her hysteria and apparent threats of suicide followed her marriage and return to Edinburgh by some weeks.[84]

It is unclear whether or not the impatient Bothwell forced the issue to make Mary carry out an earlier proposal to marry him, by making it appear that he had raped her and she had no choice but to marry him to save her honour. By Borders brigands' standards this was a logical solution to her hesitation. But her decision to put herself totally in his hands cost her her political credibility and her subsequent tearful depression and threats of suicide imply that she soon had second thoughts. Worse, some of her leading supporters fled from the newly-weds – Secretary Maitland claiming that Bothwell had tried to murder him.[85] A revolt by his aristocratic enemies followed, which had clear popular support within the capital, and thanks to Mar being deprived of Edinburgh Castle they had Prince James as their figurehead so they could depose Mary and acclaim a new sovereign. The future (and life) of the current Scots ruler was always in trouble if rebels had possession of their heir, as James III had found in 1488; the deposed sovereign was likely to meet with a violent end. Lennox ostentatiously used an emotive banner portraying the infant Prince praying by his murdered father's body under the words 'Judge and avenge my cause, O Lord', showing that he had won the battle of 'spin'. When the rebels advanced on the small royal army most of the latter deserted – but Mary's capture, the decisive move, was her own fault and not inevitable. Firstly she allowed herself to be caught unawares by the rebel advance at isolated Borthwick Castle (where were her husband's scouts?) and had to parley while Bothwell slipped away to raise more men.[86] Then they accepted an offer from the double-dealing Balfour (who had not officially defected yet) to advance from Bothwell's 'safe' Borders region towards Edinburgh to join him at the Castle – which was a trap to lure them within reach of the advancing rebels.[87] Finally, caught outnumbered by the rebels, Mary parleyed for hours with the superior rebel army while Bothwell swaggered around offering to have 'single combat' with any rebel lord, and as her men started to desert she accepted an invitation to surrender. Her husband, who had more sense of reality, fled and ended up fleeing to Denmark to be imprisoned for life by the embarrassed authorities. Rumour had it that this was the revenge of the relatives of a Danish mistress who he had discarded.[88]

Mary had good reason – and time – to slip away too, as she was to do after the defeat at Langside a year later, and would have been deposed but then could have argued that she was still legally queen. Her logical destination would have been England, as a year later, given that the border was near. Possibly her surrender was because she hoped to gain time for Bothwell to raise an army in Moray (his first destination) and rescue her. Instead, she was treated with ignominy by her ex-father-in-law and his allies and exposed to her subjects' anger. Having been greeted with public vilification and on her arrival been booed as a whore in the streets of Edinburgh, Mary was locked in the provost's house overnight within earshot of the baying crowd (presumably to unnerve her). Moved to Lochleven Castle in Fife, she was deposed by her Council in favour of her infant son, James VI, under the legal fiction that she had willingly abdicated.[89] The crucial mistake for her survival had been to put herself in Bothwell's hands so soon after the murder and so excuse a revolt by the latter's many enemies, in alliance with Darnley's family (the Lennoxes), which both factions could now aim at her personally. The Lennox faction were unlikely to accept her innocence of the murder of Darnley and so would plan a coup to install Prince James as king at some point, but Mary joining up with Bothwell gave them extra momentum; Bothwell's other enemies had not until now been antagonistic to Mary. She thus worsened her position at a time when her alternative strong, Protestant male 'protector', Moray, was at odds with her (as he had been since the 1565 revolt). She needed a capable and ruthless political 'operator' to rely on in spring 1567 and so chose Bothwell (who had a private army of tenants to hand), but Moray would have been a less controversial choice – and also a potential threat as a man of semi-royal blood and so a possible regent if he decided to depose her later. Moray was absent in England excusing his recent actions to Elizabeth for crucial weeks, but Mary could have recalled him. In choosing Bothwell, she probably put sexual preference above politics unlike the wiser Elizabeth; but Bothwell may have forced her hand in the matter of a quick marriage. What if she had not gone to visit James without a strong bodyguard and so not been abducted and had had time to change her mind?

The deposition followed her bold refusal to divorce Bothwell, which her captors initially demanded, and it is possible that the new ruling clique had not originally intended to proceed to such extremities but merely to force her to act as their puppet. Did she refuse to co-operate as she was pregnant by Bothwell and did not want her baby (or twins?) bastardized, or was her deposition only a matter of time in any case? Apparently she was told she would be killed if she did not abdicate,[90] which would have infuriated Elizabeth but saved her the problem of a captive Mary in 1568–87.

The only Scots sovereign to have been deposed and staged a 'come-back', David Bruce (as a boy) in 1333, had been out of his enemies' grip and had been able to escape into exile while his loyal partisans fought on. Furthermore, his supplanter Edward Balliol had been installed by an English army and was seen as a puppet of King Edward III; within seven years David's supporters had won his throne back. Mary would have been advised to follow his precedent and flee, sailing with Bothwell to the Continent if she could not trust Elizabeth I. Instead, she was able to feature for the rest of her life as a romantic 'lady in distress' and persuade a succession of impressionable young men to attempt to restore her to the throne, starting with her captor's assistant George Douglas at Loch Leven Castle. The new, Protestant regency by a clique of pro-English nobles, led by Moray, was always going to be at risk from power-hungry rivals given the normal turbulent history of past Scots regencies, quite apart from the added 1560s elements of religion, foreign intervention, and the sort of romantic support that Mary was already attracting. Elizabeth was initially so angry at the idea of a crowned queen's deposition that she threatened invasion to restore Mary,[91] which would have been likely to lead to the implacable Moray faction executing their captive to prevent her rescue. It was always difficult to decide what to do with deposed sovereigns, and the only Scottish one to be overthrown in their son's name before (James III in 1488) had been murdered within hours as he fled the battlefield. Would Mary go the same way?

Elizabeth's suggestions of joint government by Mary and (nominally) her infant son James, with the new regent Moray guaranteed the continuation of his regime,[92] but was unlikely to have been acceptable to Moray's faction and would have had to been forced by an English army allied to the pro-Marian faction, led by the Hamiltons. Mary's unexpected escape from her captivity at Loch Leven to head a revolt did not attract major backing apart from the Hamiltons, and owed much to luck and the slackness of her captor, Moray's half-brother; a kinsman besotted with Mary managed to smuggle her out of the castle in a rowing-boat during May Day celebrations and steal the bungs in the bottoms of all the other boats.[93] The rebels included an impressive nine earls and had a larger army (c. 6000) than did Moray, but were intercepted en route to Marian-held Dumbarton and defeated at Langside near Glasgow in May 1568. The regent's army had a more coherent force, with more modern weapons, led by a better general (Kirkcaldy of Grange), but their victory was by no means assured and they might easily have failed to catch Mary's army on the march and had to blockade her in impregnable Dumbarton instead. One of the Marian commanders, Lord Herries, failed to rout the regent's disciplined pikemen with his Galloway cavalry, and the Earl of Argyll put the matter beyond doubt by failing to act decisively on the battlefield and withdrawing from the fight (alleging that he had been taken ill).[94] Coincidentally or not, he was Moray's brother-in-law.

Fleeing to the coast of the Solway Firth, Mary now made the decision to go to England and seek Elizabeth's aid – though at the time she could easily have decided to go to France instead with the proviso that she did not have a large ship to hand and it would have been risky to try to sail all the way in a fishing-boat.[95] A compromise would have been to head for the Isle of Man (owned by the Stanley family as Elizabeth's vassals) or Dublin and utilize the sympathies of local Catholics to protect her while she wrote to both Elizabeth and Charles IX. She was assured of a comfortable material existence in France as a dowager queen, if not much military backing from the embattled Guises whose priorities were the continuing religious struggle (halted by at a truce in 1568). Her scandalous third marriage and rumoured part in Darnley's murder would cost her much Catholic support, and Catherine de Medici was unlikely to welcome her re-emergence in French public life as a Guise ally. Seeking an immediate divorce from Bothwell would have been politically necessary, if not publicly repenting her 'sins' at a suitable convent. The embarrassment of giving her sanctuary, if not the requested aid, thus fell to Elizabeth; and the Queen's fellow-feeling for another crowned monarch was unlikely to prevail over Mary's threat to the established orders of both England and Scotland. The Moray regime was Elizabeth's ally, and had no desire to risk Mary's return home given her recent revolt against it and her international Catholic backing.

Mary as refugee in England, from May 1568. Did she make her chances of help worse, or were these hopeless?
Elizabeth was thus faced with Mary as an unwelcome guest and the question of restoring her – the English Queen's initial idea on her deposition,[96] before Moray had published Mary's damning letters to Bothwell – refusing aid but allowing her to seek it abroad, or holding her in custody. Delaying a decision until the 'truth' had been established about the Darnley/Bothwell scandal suited Elizabeth's normal policy of obfuscation in a dilemma, and her letters to Mary in 1567 show that she had been puzzled and annoyed at the latter's foolishness in marrying not punishing the presumed murderer Bothwell.[97] The alternative of allowing the embarrassing royal guest to proceed on to France would risk the possibility of Mary securing a Guise-led Catholic expeditionary force that might in due course attack Protestant England too. Allowing Mary to come to court in the south, as was rumoured would happen, would make her a focus for English Catholic loyalty – and as she was the lineal heir to England it might result in them flocking to her in the way that embattled Protestants had flocked to Elizabeth herself in Mary Tudor's last days. She had never renounced her right to the throne as had been proposed in 1561–4, although even if she had done this under oath she might go back on her word (or be absolved by a priest). Keeping her under restraint in Northern England, officially an 'honoured guest' but kept away from her potential allies and under constant watch, was thus the logical option to the problem. So Elizabeth alleged that her honour meant that she could not receive Mary, accused of murder, until that matter had been dealt with.[98]

It was lucky, but not decisive, that Mary's reputation was so morally equivocal after the episodes of the murder of Darnley, her open support of and marriage to the suspected murderer Bothwell, and her deposition from the Scots throne. But all precedent favoured granting restoring or at least granting asylum to a crowned sovereign who had been illegally deposed by a faction and not even tried – indeed, was it legal at all to depose or try a monarch? No Scots monarch had been tried before, and the English Queen's instincts for 'collective solidarity' among sovereigns thus acted in Mary's favour. Even Cecil, Mary's arch-foe, was reduced to reckoning that the alleged collusion with murder (i.e. immorality) was the only ground for keeping Mary from her throne when he drew up his list of the 'pros' and cons' of granting her request for aid on her arrival.[99] Elizabeth herself wrote in her letter to Moray on 20 September that Mary was not going to be restored by her if the coming enquiry failed to clear the Scots Queen of guilt for the Darnley murder;[100] and it was up to Elizabeth to determine the outcome of that investigation. The two groups of Scots commissioners, Mary's and Moray's, were bound to back up their patrons – with the 'caveat' that Mary's representatives, Lord Herries and the Bishop of Ross, were not among her unswerving supporters (those who had stayed loyal during the Bothwell marriage), one of Moray's commissioners (Maitland) wanted Mary to rule jointly with James VI, and Mary herself supposed that the enquiry was only a necessity to ensure Elizabeth's support for her restoration.[101] Thus it was very unlikely that the Scots commissioners would all agree, and Elizabeth would have to give the deciding 'vote' via her representatives. The best that can be said for a degree of impartiality given to the English commissioners is that although Sussex and Sir Ralph Sadler were firmly Protestant foes of Mary's restoration (and thus acquittal) the third, the Duke of Norfolk, was a potential ally and would soon consider marrying her himself.

The written 'evidence' of adulterous relations with Bothwell made it easier for the 1568 English enquiry to come to the politically desirable verdict that Mary was morally unfit to be returned to her throne and thus Elizabeth 'regrettably' could not accede to her requests for aid. The most determinedly Protestant and anti-Marian of the three commissioners who carried out the investigation (initially at York, later moved to London), Sussex, expected this to be the desirable outcome with Mary to be denied the advantage of a personal appearance to justify herself.[102] There is a major question over the accuracy of at least some of the 'Casket Letters', the alleged evidence of Mary's adultery and collusion in the Darnley murder with Bothwell, which Moray sent to England and was produced at the investigation. For one thing, the number of letters sent to London was seemingly larger than those initially found in the 'casket' in Edinburgh in June 1567; Moray had initially only referred to one damning letter, and his propagandist George Buchanan's Latin phraseology (in the first publication on the issue) could refer to one or several.[103] The allegedly damning discovery had not been used against Mary at the time by Moray's regency despite their urgent reasons to blacken her name. Nor was the alleged betrayer of their location, George Dalgleish, questioned in detail about the casket at the time; therefore it had not appeared that important when the anti-Marian regime's leadership came into custody of it and supposedly read the shocking contents. Had extra, more damning letters been composed later? Nor were the dates of the published letters definitive, as their writer 'Mary' had not dated them; it was the new regime's 'editorial hand' that linked the writing to specific, dated events in the Darnley murder-plot.[104] A good English lawyer (or a pro-Marian commissioner) could have torn the official Moray regency 'line' to shreds, but clearly Elizabeth did not wish this to happen and was colluding with Moray to keep Mary out of politics.

Mary was clearly emotionally involved with Bothwell before the murder and denounced her husband to her admirer; in this situation the worst interpretation could be put on the fact that she had married Bothwell who was widely assumed in Edinburgh in February 1567 to have done the killing. But it is likely that the letters were 'doctored' to suggest more collusion between the two than in fact occurred, although Mary may have been aware that Darnley was to be murdered (though not how).

The 'smearing' had been begun by Moray's regime, which had discovered the documents and published a first version – their aim was to ruin any chances of support that the deposed Mary retained in Scotland in 1567–8. As far as precedent went, no Scots sovereign since 1097 had been formally deposed by their own subjects apart from the withdrawal of allegiance to the under-age David Bruce by most of the nobility on Edward Balliol's invasion in 1333–4; Edward I had deposed John Balliol in 1296 for alleged treason to him, his overlord. The second investigation and publicization, by the English government in autumn 1568, was carried out to decrease Mary's chances of acceptability to discontented English Catholics as Queen of England as well as excusing the failure to put her back on her throne in Scotland; there was currently a proposal to marry Mary off to a leading English conservative noble, the Duke of Norfolk (Elizabeth's cousin), which Elizabeth vetoed in 1569.[105] A meeting of the Scots peers to consider the matter saw a majority body of opinion against it.[106]

Had they voted in favour, this would have undermined Moray's assurances that the Scots did not want Mary back on the throne – and it would have helped had Mary already been prepared to send an envoy to the Pope to ask for a divorce from Bothwell (which she only did several years later). Due to Norfolk's part in the attempted coup against Cecil in spring 1569, his marriage to Mary was implacably opposed by that leading minister – but not by Leicester. As some English supporters of the Mary–Norfolk marriage saw it, it would supposedly make Mary a more satisfactory potential heir to Elizabeth and keep her under political control in England as the ward of her allegedly loyal husband. But Elizabeth would have none of it, as usual totally averse to any idea of planning for the succession, which might lead ambitious courtiers to desert her for the future sovereign – as they had notably abandoned her half-sister Mary to rally to her in November 1558.

(iv) After the 'Casket Letters' trial: still not Mary's final chance?
Elizabeth had been prepared to abandon her childhood religion to save her position as probable heiress (and her life?) to a suspicious Queen in 1554–5; Mary was not so astute or was more principled. But her religion was not as important an issue in Elizabethan elite politics in 1568–70 as her refusal to abandon her claim to be Elizabeth's heir, which the latter's ministers sought of her in writing in vain.[107] Had she been prepared to sign up before the 'Casket Letters' investigation, would this have led to a more charitable verdict that explicitly absolved her of involvement in Darnley's murder? Given the way that the tribunal was filled with the English Queen's senior ministers and transferred to York then to London, it is clear that Elizabeth not the judges had the final word on any verdict. None of the judges would have dared to defy the Queen's requirements and take an independent line, except perhaps the arrogant and sporadically rash Duke of Norfolk who loathed Cecil (and at times Leicester) and had hopes of Mary's hand. At this stage, however, he was hoping for Elizabeth's co-operation in the matter and so would not have been so rash. It was the Queen's attitude to her cousin, not the evidence sent from (or even invented in) Scotland, that counted in reaching a verdict. Crucially, Elizabeth refused throughout the process to bring Mary to London or to meet her – the Scots Queen's famous charm was not to be allowed to assist her. But even a documentary renunciation of Mary's claim handed obligingly to Elizabeth before the trial would have been inadequate to end Elizabeth's fears, as this could be withdrawn at a later date.

   Also, Moray was determined to keep Mary off the Scottish throne, although he made favourable noises about the idea of a Mary/Norfolk marriage (presumably to avoid seeming obstructive in case Elizabeth backed it). Until his murder (early 1570) he would have been blocking any attempt by Elizabeth to negotiate Mary's restoration, assuming that the tribunal had been more explicit in finding nothing to Mary's detriment. It is unlikely that Elizabeth would have pushed matters to the extent of sending troops to install a compliant Mary in Edinburgh if this would face strong resistance. But could a more favourable verdict for Mary that acquitted her formally have meant that once Moray and his successor, Darnley's father Lennox, were dead the 1571–2 Marian revival (see below) would have had extra impetus in affecting Elizabeth to negotiate with Mary? A crucial question is whether Mary would have been allowed to marry a 'safe' English peer who could be seen as 'controlling' her once she was restored to Scotland. That role was not ideal for the sole duke in England, Norfolk, as he had proved his enmity towards Cecil. But what if another, 'tamer' great peer had been available as a loyal, Protestant widower of high rank? It should be noted here that Elizabeth was as parsimonious about creating peers as her grandfather had been – Norfolk was the only duke in England as of 1568.

The failure to marry off Mary to Norfolk helped to push the more irreconcilable great nobles of the north-east, the Earls of Westmorland and Northumberland, over the brink into revolt in late 1569. They already felt that their religion and semi-feudal autonomy were under threat from the tightening grip of the government and its Council of the North, led by the harsh Protestant Earl of Sussex, and so were being 'cornered' into drastic action. As of the early-mid 1560s the celebration of illegal Masses in this still mostly Catholic area had been tolerated by the Queen, but Sussex's intrusive governance was ending this – a revolt was thus already plausible before Mary arrived in England to provide a Catholic figurehead for the Catholics. The failure of the 'Casket Letters' tribunal to exonerate Mary and pave the way for her restoration was thus a sign of English State ill-will to them, and the impatient cabal encouraged Norfolk to react to Elizabeth's opposition to the marriage in September 1569 by throwing his lot in with them in armed defiance. Instead, Norfolk wavered and had the worst of both worlds – he disobeyed orders to leave court and sulked at Framlingham in Norfolk, arousing fears of his revolt but did not join the 'Northern Earls'. Instead, he eventually obeyed a summons to court and was thrown into the Tower.[108] His prolonged defiance of his queen would have added to her fears that she could not trust him with Mary – but it did not create these. It is, however, debateable if Mary's or Norfolk's position with Elizabeth would have been easier if the primary Protestant heiress to England, Lady Catherine Grey, had not died in 1568. Queen Mary had a stronger genealogical position as a result of this, as Catherine had been the next heir under Henry VIII's will of 1544, which barred the Scots line from the English throne. Her death improved Mary Stuart's chances of assuming the English throne if Elizabeth died. But Catherine had left a sister, another Mary, to keep the Grey claim alive – and Elizabeth was notoriously fearful of all potential heirs. The diminutive Mary Grey was also to end up in custody facing the Queen's wrath for a secret marriage – to a minor royal official much her social inferior and much taller than her.[109] Neither of the younger Grey girls had much political sense, to their cause's detriment.

Marrying Mary Stuart to the conservative (though technically Protestant) Norfolk in 1569 would have reassured the 'Northern Earls' of Elizabeth's goodwill towards their religion and the hopeful chance of a Catholic heir succeeding her. Would this have headed off revolt for long – or would the sight of enthusiastic Northern 'papists' buzzing around Mary's court like bees round a honey pot have induced apoplectic rage and a desire to arrest all parties concerned by Elizabeth's hard-line ministers Cecil and Walsingham after the international 'scene' turned into 'Catholic vs Protestant' confrontation with the Massacre of St Bartholomew's Day in 1572? (It was suggested by Elizabeth's 'hard-line' Protestant cousin and close aide Sir Francis Knollys that Mary should be married off to a safe junior Protestant courtier, his own son Sir George Carey – but Mary was unlikely to have accepted this.)

It should be pointed out that the traditional 'narrative' of Mary's role in Anglo-Scottish affairs after 1568 has her totally marginalized as a result of the 'Casket Letters' trial and reduced to being a powerless pawn of events, held captive in England at Elizabeth's mercy and abandoned by her people. The latter was not actually true, and this version is somewhat 'determinist', judging her role in the 1570s as if it was all part of the long road to the execution-block at Fotheringay Castle in February 1587. In fact, the regency for James VI in Scotland was in a precarious position in the early 1570s, its 'strong-man' Moray having been fatally shot by one of the Hamiltons in an ambush in the street in Linlithgow on 10 January 1570.[110] Its leadership changed several times thereafter, with Darnley's father the Earl of Lennox (as implacable towards Mary as Moray had been) being appointed regent – as was his right as the King's nearest male kin – after the divided Scots Protestant nobles had been lobbied strongly for this solution by Elizabeth. Her success in this blow to Mary's fortunes owed much to the nobles' need of her military help against the 'Marians', including the Earl of Huntly and Lord Herries, who despite the disaster at Langside still held Dumbarton and were to add Edinburgh Castle. Unfortunately Lennox was then murdered too, in August 1571 in a botched 'Marian' attempt to kidnap him and other Council members during a meeting of the regency leadership at Stirling. The ambushers had the element of surprise as they rode into the town (where were the regency nobles' armed tenantry?), but their targets were rescued by loyal troops and Lennox was shot in the melee. What if the attackers had made a 'clean sweep' and decapitated the anti-Marian faction and seized control of King James' person and his residence at Stirling Castle? Could they have held onto their fortresses until the French sent ships to assist them, or would the retreating anti-Marian lords (e.g. the Earls of Mar and Morton) have summoned English help first? Mar then died, leaving Morton as the fourth head of the regency council in four years. Again, when the shaky regency held a Parliament in Edinburgh city centre in 1572, their Marian foes were now holding the Castle above the streets (Kirkcaldy of Grange having defected to them) and were able to fire their cannons down at the meeting, disrupting proceedings. Marian lords then marched into Edinburgh and held a rival Parliament of their own under the protection of the Castle guns, before being driven out later.[111]

The stalemate in Edinburgh showed that the two sides were militarily evenly matched. The regency had to call on Elizabeth to send in troops with long-range artillery, which duly battered the Castle into submission. Kirkcaldy was forced to surrender and executed, and Mary's ex-secretary Maitland killed himself before the Castle fell to avoid execution.[112] This was a final blow to the armed Marian cause in Scotland, but events could easily have gone the other way if either France or Spain – the latter at odds with Elizabeth over the English help to Dutch rebels in 1569–72 – had sent ships in time to assist the Marians in Edinburgh in 1571–2. But at this time Philip was not ready to intervene openly in British affairs, while Mary herself refused an offer of help to escape in 1570 because she was still hoping that either Charles IX or Philip would put diplomatic pressure on Elizabeth to release her.[113] Indeed, the crucial English 'hard-line' Protestant minister Cecil took part in a formal mission from his Queen to visit Mary at Sheffield Castle and discuss a treaty with her in October 1570 despite the effective blackening of her reputation by the rigged 'Casket Letters' investigation. The proposed terms would have involved Mary's restoration to Scotland in return for her formally renouncing her claim to England and allowing Elizabeth to choose any future husband of hers, plus James VI taking her place as a hostage in England.[114] These three concessions would place Scots policy as affecting England under Elizabeth's veto, and counter the papal declaration that the Queen was a bastard who should be removed in Mary's favour – and James would be available to be placed on the Scots throne as an English puppet if Mary reneged on the deal (or had a priest absolve her from any promises). In effect, Mary would be a puppet of her Council – all or mostly strong Protestants, allied to England. At this point James VI was only four, the regency was distinctly shaky, and Marian loyalists still held Dumbarton where French or Spanish troops could land to aid Mary. If Mary had given way and signed up to this, would Elizabeth have agreed to her restoration in 1571? In retrospect, this was probably Mary's best chance of returning to rule Scotland, albeit as a puppet of Elizabeth who would have to come to terms with Mar and Morton and kept Spanish or French offers of help at bay.

Chapter Eight

1588: a close-run thing? The Spanish Armada – could it have landed successfully, and what then?

Elizabeth and 1588: myth and reality

The clash between Elizabethan England, bastion of Protestantism, and the current Catholic 'super-power' Spain in 1588 came to define Elizabeth's reign and role in popular memory for centuries. It was as much the defining moment of sixteenth-century English history as 1940 was of the twentieth century, as England stood alone against a brutal and malign tyranny intent on the conquest of Europe. Elizabeth I was portrayed in the national myth, recycled in the literary and artistic media and in school textbooks, as the ultimate symbol of sturdy and defiant English patriotism. Her famous speech to her troops at Tilbury as they awaited the Armada – 'I may have the body of a weak and feeble woman but I have the heart and stomach of a king, and a king of England too'[1] – came to assume the iconic status later accorded to Winston Churchill and his most famous Parliamentary speech in June 1940 – 'we shall fight them on the beaches'. The successful defeat of the might of the European Catholic 'super-power' and its massive fleet was enshrined as the culmination of a heroic and inevitable struggle between the Protestant 'Gloriana' and her doughty 'sea-dogs', such as Sir Francis Drake, on the one hand and the repressive and implicitly (or explicitly) Satanic Catholic would-be invaders on the other. Victory against this menace – a power as notorious for its authoritarianism and atrocities as the Nazis – was England's just reward, due on moral grounds as much as military.

The religious element of the confrontation helped to build a determinist picture of the crisis in the accounts of it presented by writers in the following decades, a picture broadly being recycled as late as the Victorian and Edwardian eras. The tone of the coverage of the war by 'progressive' nineteenth-century 'Whig Historians' and of anti-Catholic patriotic novelists such as Charles Kingsley (in *Westward Ho!)* (and for boys G. A.

Henty) was still broadly in line with that of the Protestant propagandists of late Elizabethan and Jacobean England. In both it was seen as the culmination of decades of advancing Catholic power, which had at least received a decisive check at the hands of plucky English seamen, with a long list of Catholic oppression and brutality from the time of the Marian persecutions punctuated by the assorted plots to remove Elizabeth in favour of her cousin Mary Stuart. The list of unspeakable and treacherous Spanish-led Catholic 'crimes' and would-be crimes against England were duly laid out in lurid detail, as in a famous early Jacobean pamphlet of 'papist' plots throughout the period of 1560–1605 (ending in the Gunpowder Plot) with illustrations of the episodes and the villains' fates and accompanying rhymes. The emphasis of this storyline was that the struggle was an existential one between 'good', i.e. Protestantism, and 'evil', i.e. Catholicism, and that England and its queen had triumphed due to Divine approval and protection.[2] It cast England in the role of the 'New Israel' and Spain in that of the Philistines or Egyptians in the Bible, the centrepiece of Elizabethan weekly Church services so familiar to the entire nation. Spain assumed the role of the imperialistic and aggressively Catholic enemy of England and Protestantism, in which role it was already emerging due to the atrocities of its army in the reconquest of the rebel Netherlands (e.g. the sack of Antwerp in 1576). The 'Black Legend' of villainous Spanish cruelty and the need for England to take the lead in fighting it was born, and was still visible in the national psychology in the reactions of some governmental leaders (e.g. Oliver Cromwell), MPs, and literary figures to Spain in the second third of the seventeenth century. The seeming ease and cheapness of a naval war against Spain, its use in cutting off the financial supplies that kept the Spain 'war-machine' operating on the Continent, and its 'inevitable' string of successes in terms of captured treasure-ships were important in the Protectorate's decision to attack Spain in 1654–5.[3] This nostalgia for the Elizabethan naval triumphs of the 1580s, especially of 1588 in the Channel, played a role in building up a major political faction in Parliament and the country in the eighteenth century that preferred a 'blue-water' approach to British foreign policy – fighting a 'cheap' naval war and avoiding costly European land-wars that lost more lives and money and only benefited our perfidious European allies. (This was mainly seen in the emerging 'Tory' party, and came to prominence during the War of Spanish Succession in 1702–13.) Drake and his 'forward policy' of attacking Spain at sea was being evoked nostalgically as late as the 1730s, during agitation for another war with Spain due to its brutal treatment of English traders (hence the so-called 'War of Jenkins' Ear' in 1739).[4] The rightful role of English admirals was to sack ports on the 'Spanish Main' and seize Spanish treasure-ships, as Drake had done – with Cromwell and his propagandist poet Edmund Waller having evoked Drake's memory in the Protectoral attacks on Spanish shipping in the mid-1650s.[5] These clamours for a 'cheap' naval war (and exciting seizures of treasure-laden galleons) of course owed more to patriotic simplifications of what had actually happened. They forgot the many occasions when things had gone wrong on Elizabethan naval expeditions, from the failure of the post-Armada invasion of Portugal to install an Anglophile pretender (Dom Antonio) in 1589 to the useless 'Isles Voyage' of 1597 when the English fleet failed to intercept the Spanish 'Plate Fleet' of American treasure-vessels in the Azores.

Elizabeth's 'game-plan' for the early-mid 1580s – and how the Armada expedition could have been avoided

In the same nostalgic vein, Elizabeth the warrior-queen was shown as the modern equivalent of the Old Testament Israelite female war-leader Deborah, or in British terms the first-century anti-Roman war-leader Queen Boudicca (aka Boadicea).[6] In this guise she entered the pantheon of British heroes, and was still being used as the template for any portrayal of a female war-leader (particularly one fighting those of Spanish origin) in cartoons of Mrs Thatcher during the Falklands War of 1982. There was of course an irony in this simplistic and inaccurate view of a heroically belligerent Elizabeth – she had not wanted the war with Spain, had spent thirty years endeavouring to keep out of conflict in Europe, and had only sent an expeditionary force to help the beleaguered Dutch rebels in 1585 when they were on the point of collapse and it seemed likely that the vital ports of the provinces of Holland and Zeeland would fall into the hands of a hostile Spain. It was the balance of power in Europe and the safety of England from invasion that mattered to Elizabeth, not the international Protestant cause – and the Dutch had embarrassingly revolted against their legal hereditary sovereign, Philip (descended via his great-grandmother Duchess Mary, d. 1482, from the Dukes of Burgundy). Her original plan for preserving Protestant Dutch (and hopefully 'moderate' Catholic Flemish) independence from Philip's aggressive Counter-Reformationary Spain in the late 1570s had been to use the Spaniards' hereditary foes, the – Catholic – French. Hence her project of marrying King Henri III's brother Hercule Francois, Duc d'Alençon/Anjou, planned leader of the French expedition to the Netherlands, who was meant to act as the English-funded 'proxy' in the Netherlands and tie his Catholic country into war with not alliance to Spain. This was not entirely cynical – as a Catholic the Duc would be more acceptable to the Catholic inhabitants of the southern Netherlands (now Belgium) than was the northern, Dutch Protestant leader William ('the

Silent') of Nassau, Prince of Orange. But his expedition proved a military failure against the better-trained, disciplined, experienced, and armed Spanish infantry phalanxes (the 'tercios') and he then died.

The Spanish gradually assumed the upper hand due to weight of resources plus disciplined competence, led by the highly competent Duke Alexander of Parma. This army was the one that Philip hoped to use to invade England in 1588, and unlike the much smaller English army (which mostly consisted of short-term levies called up via local landowners for a specific time-limit) it was a 'professional' body of men used to fighting together with modern muskets and pikes and plenty of experience. With no French troops in the Netherlands to hold the Spanish advance up Philip's troops could secure the vital mouth of the Scheldt estuary with Sluys (site of a previous English naval defeat of a potential invasion fleet in 1340) in 1587. But it should be remembered that Philip's resources of men, money and shipping were substantially improved from 1580 when he assumed the Crown of Portugal and united the two kingdoms. His vain and incompetent nephew King Sebastian had been killed without children in a glory-seeking 'crusading' invasion of Moslem Morocco in 1578, where his army was destroyed (thus inhibiting military resistance to Philip), and when his elderly uncle Cardinal Henry died in 1580 the male line of the House of Avis was extinct and their distant cousin Philip claimed the throne. The last time Spain/Castile had attempted to incorporate Portugal in such a union in 1383 a nationalist revolt, aided by England, had driven them out. This time the conquest succeeded though a pretender (Dom Antonio) fled to England where his being allowed to stay added to Anglo-Spanish tension. Portugal also provided much of Philip's shipping for 1588, with officers experienced at sailing in Atlantic waters from their voyages to the colonies in Brazil and treasure from there to fund preparations. It was also important for Spanish freedom of action in 1587–8 that Philip's Mediterranean fleet did not have the distraction of war with the Ottoman Turks, whose main fleet had been destroyed by Philip's at Lepanto (Naupactus) in the Gulf of Corinth in Greece in 1571. This major victory for Christian Europe halted the Otttoman naval threat for good, freeing Spanish resources for Atlantic and North Seas conflict (though most of the actual ships used in the Mediterranean were oared galleys and so were little use in the choppy Northern seas). It also provided reinforcement for the Spanish 'self-image' of themselves as the Divinely-blessed warriors of Christendom and helped to reinforce Philip's self-confidence in his militancy towards the enemies of the Faith. The Lepanto campaign had assumed the status of a 'crusade' (literally, with papal approval) and this religious element was also to be used for the Armada campaign. The 'heretics' and the Jews had been dealt with in Spain; the English, Philip's late second wife's subjects, were next.

When the Dutch leader William 'the Silent', Prince of Orange, was assassinated by a Catholic agent in 1584 Elizabeth reluctantly sent Leicester, 'cheerleader' of the international Protestant cause at her court, with a moderately-sized army (6,000 infantry, 3,000 cavalry) to assist the Dutch – but tried to keep the costs down and continued negotiating with Spain. The war was thus an embarrassment to her, not a glorious Protestant cause as it was for Leicester's militant nephew Sir Philip Sidney (who was fatally wounded in a skirmish at Zutphen and received a State funeral on the Thames in London as befitted his iconic national status). She was insistent on Leicester remaining her controllable subordinate, not assuming any independent powers as the Dutchmen's new ruler.[7] She did her best to nudge the suspicious Dutch into joining negotiations with the Spanish commander-in-chief Parma, and was indeed still negotiating with him for a truce despite considerable evidence of Spanish insincerity as the Armada (which he had denied had hostile intent) was entering the Channel.[8]

Keeping costs down and avoiding provocation came first, and aggressive Protestant ideology was absent from her motives; such swashbuckling but expensive attitudes to foreign policy were left to Leicester and his nephew Sir Philip Sidney. She was quite prepared to marry a Catholic French Valois prince (1579) only seven years after his mother and brother had been involved in the St Bartholemew's Day Massacre in order to cement an Anglo-French alliance, to the despair of anti-Catholics such as the pamphleteer John Stubbs. His indignant literary reply, the 'Gaping Gulf', implied that she was willing to risk abandoning the national interest for her would-be suitors – and he was promptly mutilated with the full rigours of the law for libel. Unlike her spymaster Sir Francis Walsingham (a witness of the atrocity), she did not let the events of 1572 in Paris turn her into a foe of the Catholic government of France; 'realpolitik' and cost trumped ideology. Even when her potential French husband for whom she felt a degree of affection, Alençon/Anjou, died (1584) she was prepared to assist his more explicitly Catholic brother Henri III, a devious and mercurial bisexual who could not be trusted to oppose Spain, to rule most of the Netherlands to avoid a costly English intervention.[9] This would have put the one-time national enemy France, ruled by a Catholic dynasty responsible for the 1572 massacre and teetering on the brink of another religious civil war, in charge of ports that could be used to attack England. But it would have tied France down to a firm English alliance and given Philip, his ancestral lands handed to a rival 'power', two foes not one for the mid-late 1580s. Had this plan worked, would a French expeditionary force in the Dutch lands have been such an affront to Philip that he had no time or resources to plan an attack on England in 1588? Logically, he would have had to commit the Duke of

Parma's army to fight Henri in the Netherlands and would probably have stirred up his new 'ultra' Catholic allies in France, the militant Catholic League led by the Duc de Guise, to take on Henri in France in another civil war. These campaigns would have left no men or money for the option of attacking England – instead the real-life war of French 'ultra' Catholics/Spain vs the French monarchy/the Huguenots of 1589–94 would have occurred half a decade earlier.

In a similar vein, Elizabeth's attitude towards war at sea was no more belligerent than that concerning war on land, although 'long-distance' colonial attacks far from England might usefully employ hotheads, earn treasure, and avoid a conflict closer at hand in Europe. Naval encounters could be excused as accidents or replies to provocation if both parties to an incident were so minded; and even the seizure of some Spanish ships in English ports in 1568 had not led to war. Drake's famous privateering expedition to the Spanish colonies in 1577–80 had been marked by a desire to avoid open confrontation with Philip. Her role in financing Drake was kept secret and she was clearly ready to deny any involvement with him were he captured or killed; it was not clear on Drake's return whether he would be rewarded or arrested. Throughout the early-mid 1580s Elizabeth avoided retaliating for Spanish armed interference in Ireland, where Philip landed troops to aid Catholic Gaelic rebels against her colonial authorities with the technical excuse that these men were private citizens who had volunteered to fight for an expedition paid for and authorized by the Pope.[10] (In effect, this was a 'tit for tat' to Elizabeth for allowing thousands of English volunteers to fight for the Dutch rebels.) She was prepared to let this Spanish-backed attempt to keep Ireland Catholic and expel her subjects, and the Dutch 'proxy wars', continue without escalation to keep England itself out of conflict. Philip was at this point wary of open embroilment with the private initiatives of enthusiastic English Catholic militants to overthrow Elizabeth in Mary Stuart's name, counselling caution on his ambassador Mendoza in London;[11] by 1583, however, his embassy was embroiled in a complex Marian/Guise/Spanish/papal project for both Spain and the Guises to land troops in England to liberate Mary. (This is generally known as the 'Throckmorton Plot' from the identity of the main English Catholic 'go-between' and eventual victim, Francis Throckmorton.[12]) Mendoza ended up expelled and the role of the Spanish embassy as a honey pot for disaffected English Catholics (and 'double agents' sent by Walsingham) came to an end. But Elizabeth's reaction to all this was more limited than that of her Parliament, the forum of public opinion among the landed classes, which made it a capital offence to convert to Catholicism in 1581 and now linked the religion explicitly with treason. This equated peaceful and loyal

Catholics of ancient hereditary allegiance to both Crown and Catholic Church, people who would not dream of rebelling and who were embarrassed by the papal declaration deposing Elizabeth, with fanatical young converted zealots. These had been reclaimed for Catholicism in the 1570s–80s by a new Jesuit missionary campaign masterminded from Rome. This campaign of conversion was in Philip's strategic interests (as was Elizabeth's murder), and had the potential to save Philip from a costly frontal attack on a united England by creating 'home-grown terrorists' (in modern terminology) who would obligingly murder Elizabeth and thus cause chaos in England, hopefully rescuing Mary Stuart too. The ambitious regicidal schemes of Catholic zealots were assisted by the Spanish embassy in London from Ridolfi (1571) to Throckmorton (1583), but were not initiated by it. The English State reaction arguably drove more Catholics than before to take up involvement in plots out of resentment at the persecution of their faith. The rising English Protestant paranoia about Catholicism *per se* and alarm at the treasonable potential of all its adherents resembles the manner of post-'9/11' Westerners equating all Moslems with 'Al Qaeda', and as with modern Britain there was always a danger that a plot by men not on the English secret service's 'radar' would escape detection and carry out an atrocity. If Elizabeth had been murdered as William of Orange had been in Holland, from 1584 a formal plan existed in legislation (the 'Association') for the assumption of full power over the leaderless country by her Privy Council.

It was Walsingham that had to push Elizabeth into trying and then executing Mary Stuart, the act that at least provided an excuse for if not directly causing Philip's decision to invade. Walsingham's agents in Mary's household provided the incontrovertible 'proof' that Mary had actively encouraged her hot-headed ultra-Catholic admirers to murder Elizabeth so she could take her throne; she had been aware of the 'Throckmorton plot' plans but not definitively involved. The English Queen seems to have been very reluctant to move against someone who was not only her cousin but a fellow-monarch, even a deposed one. But it should be remembered that the destruction of Mary in 1586–7 could have been avoided if her own plan for her titular restoration as co-ruler of Scotland, the 'Association', had been acted upon in the early 1580s. Once her son, James VI, was a teenager able to act politically without his anti-Marian regents (and once Mary's arch-foe Morton was executed in 1581) Mary had conceived the hope that he would help her return home, as his co-ruler but without impinging on his authority. This plan was to be promoted by her representatives in Paris, using her family link to the Guises so the latter could insist on her freedom as part of any of the current Anglo-French negotiations. France would then stand guarantor that she would not become involved in politics again. The French had been supporting her claim that her detention was illegal and pressing for her release, but their government did not make it a *sine qua non* of a treaty with England. Nor did her son, James, who appears to have preferred to leave her in captivity rather than risk alienating Elizabeth and jeopardizing his chances of the English succession. The exile of his pro-French cousin, confidante, and chief adviser Esme Stuart, Duke of Lennox (a Catholic), after a coup by jealous Scots Protestant nobles in 1582 weakened Mary's chances; had he stayed in power, would this Guise confidante have talked James round? Crucially, Mary's choice of envoy to James to persuade him to press Elizabeth for her restoration, the French-educated and ultra-devious young 'Master of Gray', promptly abandoned allegiance to her and took up James' lukewarm views on the project instead. At this point Elizabeth was reliably said to be so fed up with Mary's presence in England that she would release her if France and James would agree to guarantee her goodwill and political marginalization.[13] The Machiavellian betrayal of Mary by Patrick Gray and the lack of insistence on her release by the Guises finally ended the plan's chances of winning Elizabeth's consent. But had James, persuaded by a more loyal Gray, and the Guises both insisted on Mary's release could she have been returned to Scotland as nominal co-ruler in an Anglo-French treaty in 1584 or 1585 and so been safe from implication in any more English Catholic plots? Would Philip have found another excuse to invade anyway – or would his envoys have persuaded Mary, back in Scotland, to offer herself as his puppet-queen in 1588? In lieu of Mary or her unreliable son, James, Philip's choice of sovereign for a conquered England was to be his own daughter Isabella, a far more remote claimant to England – he was descended from Edward III's son John 'of Gaunt' via the latter's daughter Queen Catharine of Castile.

The vital written evidence of Mary's approval for a murder plan by the next group of English conspirators was apparently acquired by Walsingham's secret agents, who controlled and read all letters passing to and from Mary in custody, deliberately letting a letter containing an adherent's provocative request for this approval get through to her (in a beer-cask). The 'middle-man' in the transmission of the message, Mary's supposed loyalist George Gifford, was actually an agent of Walsingham's – which raises the possibility that he may have forged her handwriting to incriminate her. Mary (probably) fell into the trap, and her apparent permission for Elizabeth's murder could be used as proof that she was planning regicide and was thus guilty of treason. (Walsingham's agent Thomas Phelippes, superintending the transit of the vital letter in the beer-cask, notoriously drew a 'doodle' of a gallows on the incriminating document before he sent it on to Walsingham.[14] Mary was supposed to have given written approval for the Ridolfi plot to murder her cousin in 1571 but the document (forged or not) has not survived; this one was more damning as the political situation was more dangerous. A pre-prepared plan to remove Mary could go according to the script, with lurid details of her wickedness released to inflame Parliament and put pressure on Elizabeth to act. Mary was put on trial, with conviction a certainty in the inflamed atmosphere of rising inter-religious and international confrontation. But Elizabeth had been reluctant to put a queen on trial due to the precedent, and notably did not sign the death warrant until repeatedly reminded to do so – and then she claimed that she had not meant it to be sent out and acted upon and 'scapegoated' the unfortunate official (William Davison) who had done so.[15] Philip's fury at the execution then probably pushed him into the final decision to invade England himself, at a time when Elizabeth was endeavouring to wind down her involvement in the Netherlands, negotiate a truce with Spain keeping English troops in vital ports, and withdraw her troops after Leicester's failure to make any impact on the war there (partly due to her niggardliness with money). Elizabeth was even prepared to sign up to a treaty if Philip would guarantee to tolerate Protestantism in the Dutch provinces for two years, turning a blind eye to what he would probably do after that.[16] Her decision to put naval preparations for a war with Spain underway and allow Drake to make a pre-emptive raid on the Spanish naval headquarters at Cadiz in 1587 only followed incontrovertible evidence that Philip had played her false and was preparing an invasion.

In fact, Parma – a crucial figure as the probable commander of the invasion and Philip's most experienced general – was against an immediate invasion of England despite his desire to deal with the 'heretic' Queen. His zeal for the cause and willingness to achieve it by brutal means were undeniable and he had committed as many massacres of civilians in fallen towns (e.g. Ypres) as the Duke of Alva had, but his strategy was different from Philip's. His preference was to overrun the Dutch provinces and their ports one by one, thus securing the coast, and only move – from Holland – once he had complete control of the invasion ports.[17] As of spring 1588 the English still held Flushing – the nearest Southern Dutch port to East Anglia, on the island of Walcheren with a wide estuary for his invasion-barges to use – and Brill, and the Dutch rebels held the coastal province of Holland. The English were also holding Ostend, one of the nearest Flemish ports to their coast. Thus, the real-life 1588 attack had to involve sending invasion-barges down the Scheldt from Sluys (taken in 1587) along the Flanders coast past Ostend to Spanish-held Dunkirk to embark Parma's troops there. Had Philip waited until Parma had taken the Dutch coastal ports, his task would have been easier – but would this have meant a delay until the renewed civil war in France in 1589 distracted Philip again? Only a full-scale onslaught by Parma on Ostend or the Dutch coast in 1587–8, meeting with success, would have 'cleared' the obstacles to an easier Spanish embarkation in August 1588. The remaining English troops in Holland and Ostend stood in the way of this, proving the wisdom of Elizabeth's commitment of this force to this 'front' in 1585.

The myth of Elizabeth the dauntless and heroic warrior-queen masterminding the successful Protestant English resistance of 1588 is thus far from reality. As seen above, her desires were for containment, as cheaply as possible, not confrontation with Spain. She was forced into an unwelcome Continental role in the Netherlands in 1585 by the failure of the French alliance and death of her chosen agent, the Duc d'Alençon, and then the assassination of William of Orange; and by late 1587 she was winding down her Dutch involvement and Leicester was leaving Holland. As of July 1588 she was still negotiating with Parma for a truce in the Netherlands that would preserve English interests, which in the parallels with 1940 would make her an 'appeaser' not a Churchillian confrontationist. The calculating analyses of Spain's rising hostility and probable hostile intent in the early 1580s were done by William Cecil, Lord Burghley, who had been seeking to halt Philip's Dutch warfare by financial pressure as early as 1568–9; the unstinting vigilance to guard against Spanish spy-networks and their English collaborators (and cynical entrapment of Mary Stuart) was done by Walsingham. These two and Leicester were the government's ideological backers for a 'Protestant' foreign policy, based on support for England's co-religionists abroad and hostility *per se* to Catholic powers. But ultimately policy was decided by the sovereign, not by their ministers; and the confrontation of 1588 was not Elizabeth's choice. Nor was there a consistent and irreversible collapse in Anglo-Spanish relations that 'inevitably' led to the despatch of the Armada; as we have seen, if Elizabeth had succeeded in embroiling France in her Netherlands policy Philip would have faced two foes not one in 1588 and probably been too committed in Europe to attack England. If the 'Association' had succeeded and Mary Stuart been released in 1582–4 she would not have been in England in 1586 to be implicated in plots and executed, though Philip could have found another excuse for invading – Pope Pius V had declared Elizabeth deposed in 1570. In this case, however, Mary could have been available to act as Philip's nominee for the throne in 1588 and had the advantage over the 'Infanta' Isabella of being the lineal next heir to England by genealogical descent. Given the enthusiasm of Northern English Catholic gentry plus assorted hot-headed young plotters for her since 1568, this would have been crucial had any Spanish troops landed in England.

The increasing of pressure on England by means of international alliances with the Catholic 'ultras' in France, interference in Ireland, and constant involvement with and patronage of domestic conspiracy in 1578–87 was directly down to Spanish policy – which ultimately meant the personal choice of Philip II. Notably he was already planning an invasion of England while Mary Stuart was still alive, as his ambassador Mendoza planned to organize this with the aid of the Guises in France and Catholic nobles in Scotland in 1582–3. Similarly, his then governor/general in the Netherlands, his half-brother Don John of Austria (successful commander at Lepanto in 1571 but rather too optimistic of Northern success), had proposed in the late 1570s to launch a sudden cross-Channel attack by a small but well-trained force to rescue Mary Stuart and aid an English Catholic rebellion. This had been seriously considered and vetoed as too implausible. Philip's decision to attack in 1587 was not due to sudden virtuous indignation at the 'martyrdom' of a Catholic sovereign by 'heretics' – Mary's execution was no more than a propaganda bonus. As of 1570 any Catholic aggressor had the excuse that the Pope had deposed Elizabeth so an invasion was carrying out God's lieutenant's will. The only difference was that pre-1587, like Elizabeth, Philip was intent on achieving his goals by cheap means, namely hiring a French army provided by the 'ultra' Catholic faction in France, led by Mary's Guise kinsmen, and asking the Pope to pay for it.[18] Only after this plan failed and Parma had achieved major success in the Netherlands (e.g. the fall of Sluys in 1587), which opened access to some local ports, did he resort to the plan of providing his own fleet to transport his army in the Netherlands to England.

But the question must be asked – if Mary had refused to incriminate herself in writing and so open herself to a treason-charge would Walsingham and Cecil have ever managed to talk Elizabeth into executing her? And if Mary had not been 'martyred' – providing a religious impetus for the attack and European sympathy for her cause – would Philip have continued to hesitate about an invasion until he could gain military support from the Guises and money from the Pope, or until Parma had overrun Holland? Would this ever have come? The Guise faction was bogged-down in the French succession-dispute once the death of Elizabeth's ex-suitor Alençon/Anjou in 1584 meant Henri III would be succeeded by his Protestant cousin Henri of Navarre, which was unacceptable to them. Indeed, the lynchpin of their cause, the militant Duc Henri de Guise, was to be assassinated by his resentful sovereign Henri III (who was later murdered in turn) in October 1588 so the 'window of opportunity' for a Philip-Guise invasion of England was small. The best chance was the few months in summer 1588 when Henri III temporarily agreed to the demands of the Guises' 'Catholic League' that he adhere to strictly Catholic policies and disinherit his Protestant heir, his distant cousin Henri of Navarre. But once Guise was dead at Henri III's hands, stabbed in a royal ante-chamber at Blois palace by the King's minions, France was bound to fall back into civil war and Philip would need to back up the Catholic faction or face Navarre, enemy of the League, taking the throne. As events turned out Henri III was soon murdered too, and Philip's armies were to be tied down in fighting the new, Protestant King of France, Henri IV (Navarre), the head of the House of Bourbon, as Philip sought to install a safely Catholic king as his own puppet. The chances of a full-scale Armada attack on England after summer 1589 were small, as France was a higher priority for Philip. Thus, had Philip not acted in summer 1588 – whether Mary Stuart was alive or not – he would have had no freedom to invade again until the French civil war ended with Henri IV's conversion to Catholicism in 1594, and by that time had aged considerably and lost substantial amounts of resources.

The Armada campaign 1588: was England extremely lucky that Parma did not land? Did the invaders have a chance of success?

The two sides – and how military competence could have been improved
As the Spanish Armada sailed up the English Channel in July 1588 to embark Parma's troops it proved worryingly immune to the 'pin-pricks' inflicted on it by the English navy. Much has been written about the weaknesses of the fleet, commanded by a less experienced, ultra-religious, and cautious Castilian grandee of ancient family (the Marquis of Medina Sidonia) not by the original intended admiral, the Marquis of Santa Cruz, who had died inopportunely in February 1588. The latter had the necessary military and naval experience for this complex campaign, having commanded the Spanish fleet that defeated Portuguese pretender Don Antonio (and some English captains, who fled the battle) in 1582 and then landed troops on the Azores to recapture the town of Terceira from him by armed assault in 1583.[19] He was also a military realist, who had ignored the impatient Philip's orders to sail at once for Flanders to pick up Parma's troops and invade despite the danger of bad weather in late 1587. Philip came close to sacking him for this impertinence, and showed his own military ignorance by requiring Santa Cruz to position his fleet off Margate and 'cover' the movement of Parma's barges across the Straits of Dover in mid-winter (at night)without thinking of the weather or what the English fleet would do if it was not defeated first. He declared that God would give

them good weather, and in an act of risk-taking encouraged Parma to set sail with his barges for England without waiting for the Armada to arrive if the chance of an easy crossing presented itself.[20]

When Santa Cruz, senior commander at Lepanto and a 'fighting admiral' able and willing to command in close combat at sea, died he was replaced by the immensely wealthy administrator Medina Sidonia. The new commander was a capable and loyal official who had organized the successful protection of Cadiz (close to his vast estates) in 1587 but had only limited naval experience and never been in overall command. His role was clearly to obey his king's instructions and assist Parma,[21] not show any initiative in a crisis at sea – though the prickly Parma would not have taken easily to working with a social inferior, Santa Cruz, and Medina Sidonia had the high rank to ensure that all the noble regimental commanders and captains deferred to him. At this point (February 1588) the Armada assembling at Lisbon only had thirteen galleons instead of the fifty that Santa Cruz had said he needed, four 'galleases' not six, and around seventy other ships not three hundred. Many of those were in poor condition or were impounded private merchant naval vessels, and the crews were afflicted by disease and desertion.[22] Even with more vessels constructed or seized the fleet was clearly not going to be large and well-armed enough to achieve that total superiority over the English navy that Medina Sidonia reckoned necessary to give it the only real chance of success.[23] He advised Philip to call off the campaign, but his letter was never handed to Philip by the King's close advisers (due to their commitment to the plan or to fear of the King's wrath rebounding on them?). He was refused an audience with Philip so he could not appeal to him in person, and was told that if he backed out he would be called a coward so he agreed to carry on with the campaign. But it is unlikely that Philip, whose grasp on the reality of conditions in the likely 'war zone' was limited and who was convinced of his religious mission, would have listened to any 'defeatist' talk anyway. The supreme bureaucrat of the fortress-like Escorial Palace, his giant and forbidding-looking residence outside Madrid, was as detached from the problems of his forces' battle-readiness and co-ordinating a successful campaign as Hitler was to be in the latter stages of the Second World War. At least Philip was assured of full papal backing (with a much-needed one million ducats for his cause) for the forced conversion of England by invasion despite continuing reservations in Rome about Spanish imperial ambitions. The ex-Inquisitor Pope Sixtus V indeed rebuked Philip for having negotiated with a heretic queen for so long first. However, the 'leaky' nature of politics at the Curia meant that as soon as a papal/Spanish treaty for the financial gift had been signed (July 1587) word got out, as Philip had been warned, and the Dutch soon captured a cardinal's talkative nephew and sent the details to Walsingham in London. They were delayed en route by the Hispanophile English ambassador in Paris, Sir Edward Stafford, but the Queen had details of the Armada's planned size and schedule well in advance.

Heroic efforts were made by Medina Sidonia to provide more ships and secure all the men, cannons, and ammunition available, while the Church played up the nature of the war as a holy cause to redeem England from heresy. Eventually a total of 134 ships were gathered in Lisbon, with twenty galleons, four 'galleases', four giant 'galleases' from Naples, and four oared Mediterranean-style galleys, divided into a first line of three squadrons of fighting-ships and a second line of four squadrons. There were thirty-four fast pinnaces for transporting messages and shallow-water fighting, and twenty-three huge but unwieldy 'hulks' carrying the troops, supplies, and siege-train that would be needed in England. The ships were built in a mixture of styles from all over Spanish-ruled or allied Europe, and had not been designed for service in the stormy English Channel against a fleet of fast, smaller ships but had been commandeered from the shipping of different countries built for different purposes. The huge Spanish and Portuguese 'galleons' that led the fleet were all crowned with high superstructures, built as 'firing-platforms' but making the ships unwieldy. Those built or adapted especially for this campaign had a premium placed on defence, with sides four to five feet thick, not speed or manoeuvrability. As has been exhaustively analysed, they were impressive to look at and resembled floating fortresses but were not fast or manoeuvrable in the changeable winds that they were to meet. The ships had a complex system of signals so they could keep in touch in daylight or dark and manoeuvre as ordered, and the captains actually had charts of the English waters (an innovation). But they were only effective for speed with the wind behind them, and due to the need to keep the squadrons together they could only sail at the speed of the largest and slowest hulks (about four knots). The soldiers and crewmen were of equally disparate origin (and languages) and had similar problems of not being used to fighting together; there were around 10,000 trained Spanish, Portuguese, and hired Italian soldiers but many of the rest were untrained impressed peasants. Overall the methodical Medina Sidonia reckoned that he had 130 ships carrying over 30,000 men (19,295 soldiers) with 8,450 seamen, 2,088 galley-slaves and 3,000 noblemen, gentlemen volunteers, priests, physicians, and officials, many with their own servants (hundreds per man for the most important nobles).[24] The result was intended to strike fear into the enemy and if possible paralyse the will to resist, combined with an intensely religious atmosphere on board to keep up morale and ensure Divine blessing.[25] As in a Crusade, the first armed clash with the English on 31 July was to be preceded by a religious service, with the Sacred Host and holy banner of Christ raised to the masthead of the flagship. In terms of 'spin' the 'Invincible Armada' certainly achieved an impressive effect as the greatest fleet that ever put to sea, though this was to make its defeat seem equally heroic and Divinely assisted. The scale, Catholicity, and hubris of the expedition duly played into the hands of English Protestant literature, with sensationalist writers claiming that the Spanish Inquisition was on board ready to launch a persecution as soon as it landed and had brought along a choice selection of whips ready to use on its victims.[26]

Greater preparedness: was this possible, and was the absence of it Elizabeth's fault?

The readiness and strength of English defence forces were such as to make it difficult to take on the Armada at sea in a frontal attack, let alone tackle Parma's army once it had landed. The weight of resources in both land and sea forces lay in Spain's favour, as Philip ruled not only Spain but Portugal and parts of Italy (e.g. Milan and Naples) and also had a colonial empire in South and Central America to produce ships, men, and treasure plus allies across Catholic Europe. Parma's troops had a fearsome reputation and had had a string of successes, and Elizabeth did not even have a 'standing' permanent army apart from the garrison of Berwick-upon-Tweed and the Yeomen of the Guard, her bodyguards. As in medieval England, troops were levied as and when needed by commissions to prominent local figures across England, and were thus bound to be inexperienced and of dubious quality. Those men with military experience by 1588 were the volunteers who had gone to fight for England in the Netherlands since the 1572 rebellion broke out, with 4,000 of Leicester's original notional army of 6,000 (reduced by illness and desertion) recalled to fight at home. However, their competence in action had been patchy, many were Catholics and/or Irish, and some had surrendered to Parma sooner than fighting. Leicester, now appointed commander-in-chief in England, was in his mid-fifties and had a poor record in his 1584–7 campaigns, with accusations of sluggishness, incompetence, avoiding confrontation, and arrogance; he was already ill and was to die weeks after the Armada was defeated. In 1573 the growing threat from the Continent had led to the creation of a volunteer force of 'Trained Bands' in each county, which met regularly for training (some under experienced captains) and so were technically capable of fighting experienced soldiers. However, the full potential of this force had not been used properly, as shown by the first muster in 1575 – 182,929 men were then registered for action but only 2,835 cavalry and 11,881 infantry received training, weapons and equipment and a further 62,462 received equipment only. The extent of available arms and ammunition provided by 1588 on paper did not necessarily reflect reality, with officials anxious to reassure their masters that all was ready when it was not (and to cover up graft, incompetence and laziness on their own part). Provision of materials and adequate training depended on the effectiveness of the local, self-governing county military system – the lords lieutenant, their deputies, and muster-masters and captains appointed by them. The usual mixture of muddle, slackness, and outright incompetence plus evasion of responsibilities marked this force, a 1580s equivalent of 'Dad's Army' of 1940, and only parts of the Bands were probably 'battle-ready'. None had seen action.[27]

Nor were their supplies of firearms and ammunition adequate and contemporary muskets were primitively constructed, often difficult to fire or badly made. The troops in the Bands and the Netherlands expeditions in the 1570s and 1580s were gradually converting from the use of longbows to using mainly muskets, but still in 1588 some 300 men out of 1,800 mustered in Surrey only had bows as did around 600 out of 1,700 men in Kent. Only 400 of the 1,000 troops from London had any weapons, and the poorer counties were even worse off; Cornwall, the first county within reach of the Armada, armed its levies with 1,500 bows and 2,000 halberds or billhooks (poles with axes on the end).[28] Some counties even got round the legal requirements to have a certain amount of weapons ready for official inspection by staging their musters on different dates and lending neighbouring counties some of their weapons for inspection, thus fooling the authorities into thinking that they were better-armed than in reality.[29] Some of the extant stockpiles that the Trained Bands used had been sent to the Netherlands and not replaced, and other suffered from embezzlement, inaccurate accounting, or being sold off in money-making 'scams' by crooked officials. Even if the weapons and gunpowder existed there were not enough carts and horses or oxen available to carry them to the muster-points and then the rendezvous for the 1588 campaign, let alone any plans for a 'rehearsal' to check that the plans for a muster in the event of attack would work in practice and that everyone would arrive as and when required and know where to go. Many of the experienced or properly trained soldiers, officers and men – those who had served overseas, or those properly equipped by capable and generous landlords who took the crisis seriously – had another problem. They would be needed in any campaign to act as a 'leaven' on the rest, but were connected by service or social ties to important local landowners. Many of them were called off from their counties in summer 1588 as their employers/landlords were summoned to bring their tenants and servants to form the Queen's personal army of around 10,000 troops, which was set up around London to protect her, depriving the county militias of their services.

Thus the actual situation in terms of military capability was far inferior to the one that existed on paper. Technically, the Queen's army was ready to defend London as the Armada approached, and some 2,500 cavalry and 27,000 infantry were stationed ready to protect the south coast, a further 12,500 were stationed at Tilbury in Essex to protect East Anglia and the northern side of the Thames estuary (though we shall see that this army did not form up until mid-crisis), and smaller forces were positioned to protect the Humber and north-east which were less likely to be attacked.[30] But the military capability of these forces was substantially lower, particularly for a pitched battle against a large and experienced army (which not even Leicester had fought since 1557). The situation was symbolized by the fact that the giant chain placed across the Thames to stop the Armada sailing up it had been broken by the strong tides and not replaced.[31] Nor were the assorted fortresses and walled towns that dotted the south coast in good enough repair – or provided with enough competent gunners and stockpiles of ammunition – to have held up a large army with a siege-train for long. Compared to 1804 or 1940 there was no systematic chain of blockhouses or 'in-depth' fortresses, though the poor roads would hamper an invader as much as the defenders. The best hope for England had the invaders landed was in geography rather than in the quality of its military preparations, with Kent – where Philip's instructions show he intended a landing – only having one large, well-walled, relatively well-stocked fortress (Dover) that could hold the invaders up.

Elizabeth's niggardliness with money and refusal to prepare for an attack until evidence of Spanish ill-well was overwhelming made matters worse than they need have been, although she had a point in protesting that a fully staffed fleet held in readiness cost £12,000 per month in pay and provisions and her peacetime revenue was only £240,000 a year. (Thus half of her annual revenue would go on a fleet held in year-long readiness.[32]) Drake insisted that a strong fleet held in readiness was essential, but did not have to pay for it; there was thus practical sense in Elizabeth's keeping the fleet at only 'half-strength' until summer 1588 despite the evidence of massive preparations in Lisbon and Cadiz (which Drake disrupted in a daring and morale-boosting attack on the latter in April 1587). Cecil grumbled that it would be best for England if the King of Spain attacked quickly, but would he oblige? But there is a doubt over whether Elizabeth took the threat seriously enough, given her readiness to carry on negotiating with Parma in the Netherlands. She lacked Walsingham's belief in a long-term and existential Spanish/Catholic threat, for example, and arguably failed to see that in modern parlance the 'rules of the game' had changed. The watchful 'spymaster' had been willing to believe in the potential for Counter-Reformationary aggression aimed at England ever since the French massacre of 1572, and had as Secretary (post-1572) created a network of spies to watch and alert the government to all possible plots. He had also been prepared and eager to remove the Queen's potential Catholic replacement by judicial murder. Elizabeth did not think in these ideological terms, preferring to maintain the traditional foreign policy of a 'Habsburg vs Valois' balance in Europe and evidently hoping that Philip's religious bluster would not overrule his political need of an English ally against his long-term French rivals. Similar to her father in her strategic approach to European politics and disparaging of ideological factors in diplomacy, she never got over her distaste at the Dutch for expelling their legitimate sovereign (Philip) and was still negotiating with Parma as the invasion loomed. Nor did she commence serious naval preparations to resist attack until 1587, although the first vague Spanish invasion-plans for England (admittedly from men like Netherlands governor Don John and ambassador Mendoza, not Philip) were being mooted five to eight years earlier. Her father, Henry VIII, had launched a massive project of creating new dockyards in the late 1530s and early 1540s to combat overseas threats to his rule, whereas Elizabeth had let Portsmouth become virtually moribund. The impetus in naval construction in the 1570s had come from Sir John Hawkins, not his sovereign – though Henry VIII had been better able to pay for grandiose schemes due to the financial boost of closing down the monasteries. As seen from a strictly military viewpoint and hindsight, Elizabeth 'should' have relied on a more experienced and competent supreme commander than her personal favourite Leicester whose failings had been shown up in Holland. More of the experienced officers in Holland could have been directed to come back to England in 1587 to train troops and badger the officials in London and the counties into a proper preparation of arsenals of weapons and ammunition.

Elizabeth was also hampered by a lack of widespread martial traditions among the nobility (the potential 'officer class') and financially useful colonies and European vassal-states to pay for creating arsenals, as Philip possessed. Lacking many dedicated proto-'factories' of skilled craftsmen to manufacture cannons and gunpowder due to a lack of military tradition or bureaucracy in 'decentralized' England, she would also have needed to provide the cash if such a scheme had been contemplated for preparing England as the Spanish threat became apparent. The 'time-line' of Spanish ambassadorial involvement in London in planning her overthrow, an obvious sign of this being directed from Madrid, suggests that if she had been as convinced as Cecil or Walsingham at this danger the date would have been around 1583–4. What if she had been convinced of the threat and that Philip would go to the lengths of invasion? She would have needed to rally Parliament (with stirring speeches about the papist threat?) into a rare willingness to vote massive taxes to hire Continental mercenary troops and buy ammunition, for which the *quid pro quo* would no doubt have been executing Mary Stuart. An equivalent of her famous 'Tilbury speech' of August 1588 would have been essential – but as of 1584–8 Elizabeth was still hoping for peace and in spring 1588 she was still prepared to sacrifice the Dutch to gain this.

Would her conversion to Walsingham's (or Drake's) sense of urgency after an event such as the Throckmorton plot (or the Babington plot in 1586) have worked in providing more troops and arsenals in time? The combination of nationalist religious fervour against the 'Catholic menace' and paranoia about Spanish plots and 'fifth columnists' was evident in Parliament in 1586–7, as shown by the loud calls to execute Mary Stuart. The alleged danger from Catholic subversives was in fact exaggerated; most of the Old Faith's adherents were firm in their loyalty although a few hundred exiles did sail in the Armada in 1588. There was no rising in the North (scene of one in 1569) as the Armada sailed up the Channel. But the country's social elite had a habit of being less willing to pay for a war than to declare one – as was to be shown by the attitudes of an equally 'interventionist' Parliament at a time of international Catholic threat in paying for the European war planned in 1621–4. Nor was it easy for any late sixteenth-century ruler to rely on the so-called 'professional' commanders to direct their military strategy if these were men of low rank; the more competent commanders in the Netherlands were mostly gentry (e.g. Sir Roger Williams) not nobles and the usefully high-ranking English general who had ruthlessly suppressed the 'Northern Rebellion' of 1569–70, the Earl of Sussex, had died in 1583. Relying on Leicester was perhaps inevitable, with so few English nobles having experience of serious (that is, Continental) warfare rather than tackling half-armed Irish 'kerns'. The navy was of course also affected by this tradition of social precedence, as the Lord Admiral and overall commander in 1588 was the Queen's cousin, the inexperienced Lord Howard of Effingham – who luckily listened to the 'professionals' like Drake and Grenville. The Spanish King also relied on his great nobles, most notably Medina Sidonia and the various lordly commanders of the Armada warships and their army regiments, but due to Spain's European position and dominions and aggressive history many of these men had military experience that the English nobility lacked. Alexander Farnese, Duke of Parma, indeed, was not a 'native-born' Spanish subject but the hereditary ruler of a Spanish-allied Italian principality (part of the papal states) and grandson of a former pope; he was married to a princess of Portugal and had been considered for its throne when King Henry died in 1580. He was to some extent a potential 'loose cannon' for Philip, who distrusted his ambitions and independence enough to forbid him to leave Spanish military service and return home to Italy. Philip was thus as reliant on socially august but not necessarily competent noble commanders as Elizabeth was; the difference was that due to Spanish imperial ambitions some of his lieutenants had vastly more experience of 'real' war.

In 1588 there was no efficient centralized governance or system of national military command in the creaky, antiquated English state (let alone a predatory tax-system capable of raising adequate funds from the wealthiest citizens to pay for military preparations). Compared to the cumbersome and slow but well-resourced bureaucracy of Spain, England was a minor power ill-fitted to dealing with a major emergency and adequate preparations would have needed a long-term overhaul of the system of government for which the social elite was no more inclined than was Elizabeth. The Queen was thus at a disadvantage quite apart from her combination of her grandfather's parsimony and a lack of ideological beliefs or urgency in her attitude to the invasion threat. Observers were convinced, probably correctly, that if Parma did land he would make mincemeat of the unprepared English army.[33] England in 1588 was reliant on a combination of naval genius and the geographical advantages of weather and tides in the Straits of Dover. Luckily the navy was in a more useful state than the army, thanks to a long naval tradition dating back to medieval times, considerable governmental financial 'input' to modern methods of shipbuilding on a regular basis since Henry VIII's reign, and a solid base of well-trained officers and men, many of whom had regularly sailed in Atlantic waters. The civilian seamen of West Country villages and ports were used to naval service in war conditions, and their captains were used to raising and equipping crews and ships from their own resources and to taking on independent initiatives as both merchants and pirates. Local Devon heroes Drake and Sir John Hawkins, of course, were the most notable of these – with legends already established to win them recruits in a crisis. The ferocious reputation of the swashbuckling plunderer Drake, *El Draque* ('the Dragon'), for aggressive brutality against the enemy mirrored that of Parma on the Spanish side; and he was a similar master of war with a flair for the unexpected. By the 1580s the English commanders and men had a tradition of hostility to Spain from decades of clashes and a rising myth of Spanish 'treachery', dating back to the surprise attack by the Spanish American authorities on visiting (illegal) trader Hawkins' ships at San Juan de Ulua in 1568. On a more practical level, Elizabeth had been building a substantial fleet for years ahead of 1588, and although her thirty-four galleons could not match the Spanish numbers they were far more suitable for action in the Channel. Hawkins had been superintending a project to build new ships on revolutionary lines that gave them far greater speed and manoeuvrability, and the new ships were lower in the water than the tall Spanish galleons but could sail closer to the wind (a vital asset in seas where the winds constantly shifted). The extensive 'boom' in mercantile ventures in recent decades could provide both 'back-up' private ships (135 of over 100 tons and 656 of smaller size according to 1588 estimates) and capable officers and men.[34] Crucially, the English ships had far better armament, and English cannons were now superior to Spanish in 'reach', accuracy and fire-power so they could do far worse damage – to ships that were larger and slow-moving and so were 'sitting ducks'.[35] English gunpowder was also superior in quality due to the acquisition of saltpetre.[36] As of the 1588 campaign the English ships were also commanded by experienced, usually non-noble captains who did not have to defer to the orders of the nobles or gentlemen commanding the troops on board, as the Spanish captains did – only five of the thirty-four commanders of top fighting-ships in the English fleet were nobles and of these five one, the Earl of Cumberland, was himself an experienced privateer captain (a 'trade' that a Spanish noble would have thought beneath his dignity).[37]

The campaign: a victory for luck or skill?

The balance of probability thus stood in favour of the Spanish land-forces and of the English navy, with two counter-balancing factors. In the first place, Parma had to march his troops to a Flemish port (probably Dunkirk) in co-ordination with the Armada arriving off shore and have a collection of flat-bottomed barges ready for embarkation, then get his men across the Straits of Dover with the tide and hopefully the wind in his favour and the Armada keeping the English fleet at bay in the meantime. Only then could he bring his military superiority into play, and he would still be operating at risk of having his supply-route behind him cut off if the English navy was undefeated. If he could not clear the seas, was it any use defeating the English army or even taking London? (Julius Caesar, also with overwhelming technological and probably numerical superiority, had defeated the defenders of Kent and the Thames valley in 54 BC but had had to retreat as his control of the coast and the Channel was not secure long-term.) But Spain's fleet was so immense that the English technological and logistic superiority at sea might not be sufficient to damage their ships in time to wreck the invasion-plan. A few galleons and more smaller ships might be 'picked off' one by one in isolation and the rest raked with cannonfire, but as long as the majority of the Armada was seaworthy when it arrived at the Straits of Dover it should still be able to protect the invasion-barges. Would the immense damage caused by the English artillery be enough to disable or sink the huge 'floating castles' on which Spain relied? The English ships were manoeuvrable enough to avoid serious damage from the Spanish cannons unless they sailed in close for a concentrated barrage, and could fire at will into the enemy in clashes and cause serious damage – but actually sinking an Armada galleon was another matter. Taking them by storm and then burning them was almost impossible given the large numbers of experienced Spanish soldiers on board each one – the attackers were likely to be overwhelmed and their own ships sunk by Spanish cannons as they were alongside. Indeed, the Spanish were largely reliant on the tactic of grappling with an enemy ship and then sending soldiers aboard to overwhelm the defenders – the 'land battle at sea' tactic, which was normal for a 'Great Power' more comfortable fighting on land since the time of the Romans' victories over Carthage in the First Punic War (264–241 BC). This had worked against the Ottomans at Lepanto and was the classical tactic of Spanish Mediterranean warfare, which Lepanto victor Admiral Santa Cruz would also have used had he still been alive and in command in July. But the English kept their distance as the battles raged during the Spanish advance up-Channel, and denied Spain the opportunity of boarding their ships. The arena of combat at sea seemed destined for a stalemate – the Spanish musketeers on their high decks and most of the cannons below were unable to fire at targets within reach, the Spanish grappling-hooks had no enemy ships to entangle, and the superior and faster-reloading English artillery would need a sustained barrage to penetrate a Spanish hull four or five feet thick.

The way for the Spanish to deal with the superior English firepower and manoeuvrability was to minimize casualties by keeping their fleet in formation and preventing isolated ships being surrounded and overwhelmed by a 'pack' of smaller English ships (like larger African wildlife being pulled down by a pack of smaller lions). This was duly adopted, and the Armada kept its distinct 'crescent' formation during the battles in the Channel – as seen in the remarkable series of charts of the battles produced subsequently by the English.[38] Indeed, when the Armada was first sighted on 30 July Admiral Howard of Effingham only had fifty-four ships available in his squadron at Plymouth as many others were still loading on supplies at ports further up the Channel and Elizabeth had ordered a squadron to the Flemish coast to watch Parma's barges. The English had to be cautious and avoid a major clash until they had more ships available – and thus gave the Armada time to land troops in Cornwall (the Fal estuary?) or Devon

(Torbay) if this had been allowed in Medina Sidonia's orders (which was not the case). Did this inflexibility on King Philip's part lose his fleet a vital chance to secure a foothold in England and tie down English forces to meet it?

A running battle at 'long range' now proceeded as the Armada moved up the Channel. The English did not take the risk of attacking one of the greatest galleons, the *San Juan de Portugal* under vice-admiral Martin de Recalde, when it was separated (accidentally or not) from the main body of the Armada on the first day's battle despite the potential to overpower it. This showed that they were too cautious to risk being trapped and blown to pieces by a force of Spanish rescuers, whether or not the incident was a trap.[39] When the *Rosario* was severely damaged by a squall Medina Sidonia left her to her fate rather than try to use her as bait to draw English ships into a close-quarters confrontation or detaching ships to escort her to safety up–Channel, showing that he was cautious too. Drake, unable to resist the prospect of loot, hastened to secure it.[40] Next day (1 August), the *San Salvador*, crippled by an accidental explosion in the hold and unable to keep up with the fleet, was taken too.[41] The ammunition looted from these two ships was equivalent to a third of the English fleet's current stock, and so may have given them vital resources to avoid running out in the crucial clash off Calais later.[42]

The English held the 'weather-gauge' in the Westerly winds and hung onto the Armada's flanks and rear, attacking and then withdrawing at will, and there was no sudden calm that could have enabled the Spanish to send oared galleys in to attack them before they could detach sailors in longboats to row the ships out of range. But the serious damage inflicted on two of the most powerful Spanish galleons, the *San Juan* and *San Mateo*, on which Howard of Effingham's ships concentrated off Portland Bill, was not adequate to sink or cripple either of them[43] – an ominous sign that superior firepower and tactics were not enough against the sheer weight of the enemy force. The battles of the first few days were thus not decisive, and the English – struggling to force the enemy to move on beyond the potential havens of first Plymouth, then Torbay, and then the Solent – were unaware that Medina Sidonia had no latitude to drop anchor or land and was supposed to head straight for Calais. The English defence were in fear of the vast enemy fleet taking up a position in a bay or channel secure from adverse weather and then presumably landing troops, as they lacked the forces on land or sea to disrupt this. Seen from a strategic point of view, the Spanish would have been in a strong position had they done this as they had the concentrated firepower to keep an English assault at bay and could not be overwhelmed. Dropping anchor off the Isle of Wight in the lee of the island, off Portsmouth, on 3 or 4 August and then landing troops on the island would have been impossible to stop – and on the island there was only one serious fortification to storm, Carisbrooke Castle, with commander Sir Henry Carey (the Queen's cousin) and around 3,000 troops positioned on the cliffs and beaches and over 9,000 more waiting in Southampton to reinforce them. The French had landed on the island successfully in 1545 during the naval clash off Portsmouth when the *Mary Rose* sank, so this had a historical precedent within living memory. Moreover Philip himself knew the locale from personal experience – in 1554 he had landed at Portsmouth en route to marry Elizabeth's sister Mary Tudor at Winchester. The English were half-expecting a landing on 4 August, the name-day of Medina Sidonia's ancestor St Dominic so possibly an auspicious day for him to fight, and for some hours in the morning the incoming tide was running in the right direction for the Armada to sail into St Helen's Roads off Brading Harbour and drop anchor. A landing on the island by troops ferried there by longboat would have been problematic, but the defenders would have been shelled by the Armada's artillery and Spaniards could have landed at dozens of points at once and overwhelmed the untried defenders. The English duly launched a frantic attack to force them to sail on up-Channel, taking risks at close quarters.[44]

But the chance of a Spanish landing – the best real possibility of securing a base on English soil? – was not realistic unless the Spanish admiral had defied his king's orders, not likely from the loyal bureaucrat Medina Sidonia. On Philip's orders the Armada moved on with the westerly wind behind it to the dangerous waters of the Straits of Dover, and the main clash was to take place there. On 5–6 August, as he approached Calais Roads, messengers were sent to Parma urging him to have his men ready to march to Dunkirk (twenty-seven miles from Calais) and embark.[45] The Armada was more or less intact as planned, but the westerly wind made any attempt to venture back down-Channel impractical and the tides in the Straits added to the difficulty of manoeuvring. They also made it inadvisable to risk moving the Armada right up to Dunkirk itself, where the currents could sweep it along the coast past hostile Holland into the North Sea, and Medina Sidonia accepted pilots' advice to halt off Calais in deeper water. Shallow water and the menace of the waiting Dutch fleet (like the English, smaller in size but lethal in firepower and speed) made it impractical to take the Armada right up the Flemish coast to the Scheldt estuary.[46]

Thanks to the limited nature of Parma's 1587 and spring 1588 campaigns and local resistance – an unnoticed reason for England's survival? – the Spaniards did not have possession of Ostend in Flanders or Flushing in Holland. Instead he had to rely on the small and shallow harbour of

Dunkirk, which the Armada could not enter. Medina Sidonia, with some of his captains already advising calling the expedition off, which testifies to the effect of prolonged battering by English cannons, sent frantic messages to Parma asking him to send forty or fifty shallow-draughted 'flyboats' along the Flemish coast to Calais to help him tackle the fast and nimble English ships.[47] Parma did not have many of this sort of vessels – sixteen hired and around thirty impounded ones or possibly a few more. The Dutch had around 400, all ready to sink Parma's barges if they ventured out of port to take his troops to the Armada.[48] But the Armada could have beaten off the Dutch shallow-water craft if it had been adequately provided with Mediterranean galleys, which could be rowed into shallow water irrespective of the wind; those few available could not be spared. The fault was Philip's, as he had ignored Santa Cruz's and Medina Sidonia's requests to spare many more of his galleys for the expedition.[49] The barges that Parma had ready in Dunkirk were cumbersome, leaky, and without cannons, masts or sails, as reckoned by English deputy commander Lord Henry Seymour.[50] Parma had warned Philip in June that if he ventured to sea in these boats without a protective screen of warships they would be cut to pieces and they could not withstand large waves either.[51] Philip was aware of this need to secure naval supremacy before the barges ventured out.[52] But the messenger that Parma sent to the Armada to warn that he could not send the barges out without the arrival of naval support did not reach his destination in time.[53] Ironically the presence of the Dutch 'flyboats' close offshore, which helped to panic Parma into refusing to move his barges, was not their original plan – their commander Justin of Nassau had originally intended to wait out at sea to lure the barges out then attack but had to change plans after his English allies (under Seymour) arrived to hover 'inshore' within sight of land.[54] Without that enemy visibility, however, it is still unlikely that Parma would have risked sailing out to head for Calais in a squadron of unwieldy and unprotected barges. Medina Sidonia waited off Calais and Parma waited in Bruges with no sign of haste by the latter. The Armada's earlier envoy Don Rodrigo Tello arrived back on Medina Sidonia's flagship off Calais on 6 August to report that Parma had told him he expected to have everything ready for embarkation at Dunkirk in around six days, but this had been shown to be inaccurate as no such preparations had been underway in Dunkirk when Tello passed through.[55] Parma did then arrive at Nieuwpoort (a minor port East of Dunkirk) on the 8th and wrote to Philip that he had embarked 16,000 of his troops there and then, going on to Dunkirk for a similar procedure. But another source indicates that when the troops arrived at Dunkirk hardly any cannon or provisions were ready let alone loaded. Even if Parma did load up some of his troops on the 8th or 9th, with or without supplies, this does not mean that he intended to set sail – merely that he was covering his rear by carrying out the King's orders to embark. In any case, a gale made sailing impractical.[56] While the embarkation failed to materialize, the English moved in to attack the Armada according to a plan formulated at Howard's council-of-war on the morning of the 8th. They had no idea of Parma's caution, and were apparently worried that despite all their expenditure on ammunition (now running low) the Armada was still in one piece, in a coherent formation that had the firepower to repulse attack and presumably with plenty of ammunition and food-supplies. Accordingly it was decided to send in fireships at night to panic the Spanish into breaking up their close formation and scattering across a wide area. Once their ships were reduced to individuals or small groups they were easier to attack, and would be demoralized by the fire-attack and operating in unfamiliar waters with the prevailing south-westerly wind blowing them away from the English coast.[57]

The risk of an attack by fireships on the Armada was realized on board the fleet, with the 'high command' aware of the possibilities and nervous of the presence in English service of the Italian engineer Federico Giambelli who in April 1585 had used two ships converted into 'floating bombs' to explode against and wreck the boom that Parma had been constructing to block the Scheldt downstream from Antwerp. The blast on that occasion had blown Parma off his feet and killed hundreds. The arrival of more ships at the blockading English fleet that day was thought by Spanish observers to indicate the presence of probable fireships ready to be sent against them, and Medina Sidonia made arrangements for his captains to be prepared to slip their cables and sail off to safety if they saw burning English vessels heading in their direction while volunteers moved in to tow the unmanned attackers away from Spanish shipping.[58] The attack was thus not a surprise, but the sight that night of eight burning ships heading straight for the Armada was still traumatic and the Spanish response was predictably muddled as each captain acted for himself. As a mixture of luck and good Spanish seamanship had it, no fireships set light to their targets; but the chaos did its work and most of the fleet was caught in the tide and wind and blown north-eastwards away from Calais into the North Sea. A number of vessels crashed into each other, with the great galleon *San Lorenzo* crippled and drifting ashore off Calais, and only five of the main galleons managed to manoeuvre back into position once the danger had passed. Around twenty-five were close to the Admiral and so responsive to orders.[59] Next morning the English fleet moved in to take advantage of the chaos and could fight on much more equal terms than previously, though Howard and his men wasted valuable time closing in on, boarding, and looting the impressive but militarily neutered

San Lorenzo. Drake and Sir Martin Frobisher tackled the flagship *San Martin* at close quarters, risky but with a good chance of success if they maintained momentum as the Spanish could not reload their cannons to blast the English ships quickly. The nine-hour battle saw the Armada raked with gunshot at close quarters, too disorganised to co-ordinate its defence and hindered by a strong north-westerly wind that was blowing it away from the seas off Calais towards the shallow shoals off Zeeland. The hand-to-hand fighting and constant cannonades showed the English superiority on both counts – though they had the wind, familiarity with the local waters, and a tradition of individual initiative in combat under charismatic commanders aiding them. By Howard's reckoning, the Armada lost sixteen or seventeen ships in the battle – though numerically speaking this was not a serious loss and the overall damage to the sails, rigging and crews of the remaining ships was more vital.

The onset of fierce squalls eventually assisted the Armada in breaking off combat and sailing off into the North Sea, but no longer as a coherent force capable of landing anywhere in England. Having cut their anchors as they fled from the fireships, they could not halt in shallow water off the Dutch coast to collect as a coherent formation but had to press on at the mercy of the wind, with losses of sailors and sails making steering difficult; some ships lost all control and drifted onto the Dutch shoals to be wrecked. Among the 'prestige' ships, named after the Apostles, the *San Mateo* and *San Felipe* were both lost in this way; Medina Sidonia escaped disaster in the *San Martin*. Steering in cohesion was now impossible for many ships, so no more fighting as a unit was possible whereas the damaged English ships could put into port to refit. The horrendous damage and loss of life was not enough to sink most of the ships, which only started to fall victim to the weather and lack of knowledge of local waters off Scotland and Ireland after a week or two more at sea. But morale was shattered. By the Spaniards' own reckoning, out of 123 ships that had been present in the expedition when anchored off Calais only 86 could now be accounted for. Their casualties were reckoned at 600 dead and possibly 800 seriously wounded, probably an underestimate.[60] The English had light casualties but were virtually out of ammunition, so attacking the fleeing Spaniards and overwhelming more ships was not an option. Only a change in the wind saved Medina Sidonia and most of the remaining Armada from an even more humiliating fate, that of being blown onto the shoals off Zeeland in full view of the English.[61] Medina Sidonia sought to save his own reputation and put a good 'spin' on the fleet's morale in his official diary, claiming that his council-of-war was willing to return to the fight for the honour of Spain but that they had to wait for the wind to shift out of the south-west to enable this to happen; as it did not after four days they gave up. His deputy Recalde more realistically wrote that all but the Admiral voted to abandon the campaign and head back round the north of Scotland to safety and Medina Sidonia had to give in.[62] The Admiral took refuge in grudge-driven court-martials of captains who had failed to obey orders to return quickly to their original position and prepare to fight on the night of the 8th–9th after the fireships had passed by.[63] In fact, lack of supplies forced the pursuing Howard to order his ships back to port on 12 August, so technically if the wind had shifted the remaining Armada ships might have been able to turn and head back to Dutch waters to look for Parma's vessels before the English could re-equip.[64] But shattered morale made this impractical after the mauling that they had received off Calais. Instead they faced the horrors of the mountainous seas and unfamiliar coasts off Scotland and Ireland and in many cases death by starvation, epidemic, shipwreck, or murder onshore.

The myth of English readiness at the crucial moment

The famous appearance by the 'Virgin Queen' at her subjects' camp at Tilbury on 18–19 August was really a public relations exercise rather than a case of a valiant warrior-queen seeking to rally her troops against an imminent threat and to live and die with her soldiers. The real threat of invasion was over after the battle off Calais on 8 August, news of which reached the Queen while hunting in Epping Forest the next day, and by the date of her appearance at Tilbury the enemy were known to be severely damaged and in headlong retreat across the North Sea. (This did not preclude a landing in northern England or Scotland, both of which were put on alert.) Thus, the Queen's heroic speech to her waiting troops on the 9th was really a piece of 'spin' to reinforce her reputation and pour scorn on her challengers, and the royal procession down the Thames by barge a victory pageant. Indeed, the contents of the actual speech were only recorded, in a limited account, by one witness; the well-known 'heart and stomach of a king' verbiage appears in the later, 'official' printed version and may or may not have been used.[65] At the time, Elizabeth's main reaction to the battle was anger that more Spanish ships had not been sunk and more treasure not taken.[66] For that matter, the Tilbury camp itself had serious shortcomings and was not a sign of a competent English government and its local commanders ready to meet the enemy. The counties' Lords Lieutenant had been ordered to prepare for invasion on 8 July, but were not ordered to summon their troops until three days after the Armada was sighted[67] – by which time it could have landed in Cornwall (probably around the sheltered Fal estuary) or sent troops ashore to besiege Plymouth. The volunteers raised in London, the presumed principal target of invasion, from March were mostly armed with bows until more advanced weapons were provided by stripping these from the militias of neighbouring counties. For that matter, the seamen in port had been on the brink of mutiny over serious backlogs in their wages as the enemy approached despite frantic pleas for money to London by Hawkins.

The work fortifying the great camp at Tilbury did not commence until 3 August, and the local levies did not arrive for five more days after being sent to Brentwood instead. By the time the Armada was off Calais only around 4,000 infantry and a few cavalry, plus 1,000 Londoners, had arrived at Tilbury; provisions were in short supply and an order had to be issued for no more troops to turn up at the camp unless they had these. In Kent meanwhile, parts of a force of 4,000 men positioned near Dover, a prime target for the invaders, started to desert. The disaster that wrecked Giambella's planned chain across the Thames has already been mentioned. Nor were the defending commanders agreed over what strategy to pursue, with experienced Sir John Norris arguing for a concentration of the main army at Canterbury (centrally placed to reach any invaded part of Kent) but local Sir Thomas Scott preferring a 'show of force' on the Downs above Dover (where Parma could see what strength he faced from his ships) and placing smaller contingents at each possible landing-point.[68] If that had happened the defenders would have been overwhelmed before they could concentrate a large enough army to meet the militarily superior force that landed. In the end, the local forces were concentrated at inland mustering-points from each of which they could easily reach several threatened positions on the coast. But the overall size of the English forces has been reckoned at around 22,000, less than a third of that which Henry VIII had mustered to meet the French attack in 1545. If the enemy did reach London its walls and ditches were in poor condition to meet a sustained attack, though defensive lines and chains had been set up.[69] For that matter, did it really make sense to have the principal concentration of troops at Tilbury, on the north bank of the Thames? This was intended to meet an invasion of East Anglia, but the Spanish sources make it clear that Parma intended to land in Kent and Philip specifically named the Armada/Parma rendezvous position as 'the Cape of Margate' (i.e. the North Foreland).[70] As of the crucial weekend of 6–7 August when the Armada was positioned off Calais, the ramshackle and inadequate main English army was on the wrong side of the Thames to deal swiftly with a landing in Kent. The reality of the English readiness to fight invaders adequately was thus as much a myth as that the Tilbury speech was a reaction to an imminent invasion.

And if Parma had managed to land…?

The exploration of 'what ifs' of the Armada landing have included modern novels focussing on a complete Spanish victory and the reconversion of England, such as Harry Turtledove's *Ruled Britannia* (where William Shakespeare is reduced to providing pro-Spanish propaganda plays under the new regime).[71] By these accounts London has been taken and the Archduchess Isabella installed as the new queen, and Elizabeth has either surrendered or been assassinated. This is all very imaginative, but such a victory is unlikely to have occurred. The logistics of the international situation in 1588–94 point the other way; those writers who assume that Parma and his experienced army had the capacity to occupy all of England neglect the fact that Philip had many priorities and these included France as well as England. It is certainly arguable that had Philip provided an adequate force of galleys for the Armada, these could have rowed up the coast from Calais to Dunkirk on or around 8–10 August 1588, brushing aside the Dutch 'fly-boats' and having the firepower to keep the English warships at bay. A protective 'screen' of galleons could assist if the wind was right. They could then have embarked Parma's troops – perhaps 15,000 men at most, given the current strength of his force. As we have seen, the English attack on the moored Armada off Calais by fire-ships caused chaos but failed to sink any ships, and perhaps twenty-five of the great Spanish galleons were able to move back into position after the raid. Had the Spanish commanders shown more coherence in re-grouping and more ships then fought in formation on 8 August, there was a chance of the stalemate of 31 July – 6 August repeating itself as the English were forced to keep their distance to avoid being boarded. The damage they did to the Spanish ships would then have been serious but not as fatal as in reality – at least if the wind had not blown the Spanish away from Calais up the Flemish coast towards the Zeeland shoals. In addition, the English might have run out of ammunition sooner had they not been able to seize Spanish supplies from the two captured galleons in the Channel.

Had the main Armada force managed to fight off the English attack on 8 August and stayed in position around Calais with a favourable (or no) wind, and Philip provided galleys that could load up Parma's men, a crossing to Kent was still feasible – if there was then an easterly wind. A 'Catholic wind' in 1588 could have been as decisive as a 'Protestant wind' was in 1688, unlikely though this was in terms of the prevailing weather conditions. Once Parma had landed his men, he could have had time to defeat the Kent levies before the main army arrived from Essex (which it would have had to do by marching via London, particularly if the Armada could move into the mouth of the Thames to threaten Tilbury). Military victory against an uninspiring and possibly dying Leicester and his inexperienced troops could then be followed by the capture of London, which did not have adequate defences to sustain a prolonged attack. Given all the wooden houses and lack of adequate fire-precautions,[72] a prolonged bombardment during attack could have been expected to start a major fire in the City whether or not the ruthless Parma favoured starting one deliberately to cause chaos and smoke out the 'heretics'. A 'Great Fire of London', a bonus for Catholic 'terror tactics' then and for Protestant propaganda thereafter, would have led to an exodus of refugees to add to the problems of the retreating English army, and Parma would have had the time to mount a systematic siege of the Tower of London and later of the only other major local strongpoint, Windsor Castle. Their fall would have completed his effective conquest of the south-east of England, though it is unlikely that after her experiences of the Tower of London and near-execution in 1554–5 Elizabeth would have surrendered meekly to await Philip's decision as to her fate. She is more likely to have made a stand at Windsor and then moved back westwards, possibly to Oxford, while the occupation-force installed a 'puppet government' in the name of the Archduchess Isabella and kept a military 'corridor' open to the coast. Part of the Spanish army would have had to remain at strongpoints such as Dover castle, and would presumably have occupied Chatham so the Armada could use the Medway safely. Assuming that the demoralized English fleet was unable to launch another attack without reinforcements of ammunition, it would have had to retreat to a safer base away from the Thames estuary, possibly the Solent (unless Philip or Parma ordered the Spanish fleet to use an Easterly wind to occupy Portsmouth next) or even Portland Harbour (then not fortified but a natural harbour protected from the west by Chesil Beach).

But the Spaniards' problems would only have started with victory, not least as there was no ready-made force of pro-Catholic 'quislings' ready to assist them in London despite English propaganda about 'papist' conspiracies. In France in 1588 the local 'Catholic League' under the Guise family assisted Philip's agents in blackmailing King Henri III into disinheriting his Protestant cousin and heir Henri of Navarre in favour of Henri's uncle Cardinal Charles of Bourbon. When the King played them false and murdered Guise (October 1588) and was then assassinated in turn (August 1589) Henri's accession was met with a Spanish-sponsored civil war, with the League aiding Philips' troops in a five-year effort to install a Catholic King under Spanish control. This alliance indeed held Paris until Henri IV deftly mollified moderate Catholic opinion by converting to Catholicism himself in 1594. But there was no equivalent body of Catholic social leadership and popular support in 1580s England, and the remaining strength of local Catholicism was in the North, which was far from London and did not include many major landed gentry or nobles. Hardly any of them had expressed pro–Spanish opinions before or during the crisis. Parma would have had to rely on isolated ambitious 'time-servers' with nothing to lose by backing him, some already Catholic such as the devious and 'marginalized' court noble Henry Howard (brother of the executed Duke of Norfolk and uncle of the imprisoned 'prisoner of conscience' Philip, Earl of Arundel). Possibly Arundel, as the most socially prestigious current victim of Walsingham's purge of suspect Catholics and in 1588 held in the Tower, would have been persuaded to assist his co-religionists by his ambitious uncle by going into Spanish service. (Henry was to become a leading Catholic courtier under James I as Earl of Northampton.) But other prominent defectors would have been few and far between as long as the Elizabethan leadership held together with a viable army in 'exile', probably in western England, and it would have been a risky task for Parma to march hundreds of miles from London to seek out battle with extended communications plus a lack of reinforcements. Possibly 15–19,000 soldiers on board the Armada plus 20,000 brought from Flanders by Parma would have been adequate to hold down south-east England, and possibly to secure major strategic positions such as Portsmouth, Oxford, and Norwich, but not to hold the entire country. Provided that battle was avoided, the Protestant cause would have had the advantage of time.

The assassinations of Guise and then Henri III plunged France into a new civil war, a major distraction for Philip II that had not been foreseen in July 1588. This was far more strategically important for him than England, and the departure of Parma and most of his men from the Netherlands would have led to the Dutch being able to retake much of the territory that they had lost. Their fleet would have been undefeated and able to intercept Spanish ships carrying supplies and men from Calais and Dunkirk to England, whatever state the exhausted English navy had been in with some major arsenals lost. The Armada could not have stayed in English waters (presumably the Thames and/or Chatham) indefinitely, with hired vessels' commanders from across Europe wanting to return home at the end of their contracts and bad weather and English attacks on individual ships probably causing casualties. The likelihood is that the winter storms would have led to Parma having to act on the defensive in London, even if he could 'live off the land' and obtain supplies by pillaging, and the French crisis would have caused Philip major problems of finance and military tactics in 1589. Losses of his own hereditary lands to 'heretic' reconquest by the Dutch Protestants while Parma was in England would cause his priorities to be reassessed, no doubt with urgent appeals for aid from the crumbling government in the

Spanish Netherlands and from the Catholic League in France. If his army in England had not achieved a decisive result over Elizabeth's forces in autumn 1588 it is probable that he would have had to negotiate with her after all, and offer to withdraw Parma in return for a treaty of non-belligerence. That would mean no English military aid to the French King and his Huguenots as in real-life 1589–94, and possibly defeat for Henri IV in the French civil war. Nor would the damage that had been inflicted on London and the South-East in the invasion have done Elizabeth's long-term reputation as a capable ruler any good. But the balance of resources and the international situation in 1588–9 make this more plausible than a complete Spanish victory. And if this had been the result of the Armada it would have been a partial success – and a religious one if Elizabeth had been forced to sack Cecil and Walsingham, admit Catholic peers like Arundel to her Council, and allow freedom of religion for her Catholic subjects in the peace treaty. This would have been necessary to save Philip's 'face' and portray the war as a success. Indeed, it can be said that Philip could possibly have achieved the military neutralization of England in 1588 far easier if he had concentrated on landing a large, well-supplied, and competently led army direct from Spain in Cornwall or around Portsmouth at the beginning of August. As we have seen, the 'window of opportunity' for this existed – and in 1595 another Spanish expedition was able to land unopposed in western Cornwall and sack Penzance. English military unpreparedness was its 'Achilles heel'; inflexibility was Philip's.

Notes

Chapter One: What if the early Tudors had not had such dynastic bad luck?

1. Arthur's frailty has no solid evidence, apart from his slightness recorded at his appearance for his wedding: see J. Leland, *De Rebus Britannica Collectanea*, ed. Thomas Herane (London 1724) vol 4 pp. 204–7. It is often presumed from his early death, and from the amount of attention Henry VII gave to providing him with first-class physicians.
2. See Leland, vol 5, pp. 373–81 on Arthur's death.
3. *The Collected Works of Erasmus*, tr. and edited by R. A. B. Mynors and D. F. S. Thomson (Buffalo and Toronto 1974–8), vol I p. 118.
4. See J. Scarisbrick, *Henry VIII* (Methuen 1968) p. 25.
5. See Thomas Penn, *Winter King: the Dawn of Tudor England* (Penguin 2012) pp. 270–4, 315–17, 337.
6. Ibid, pp. 314–15, also pp. 262–3 and 279–80 on Edmund Dudley; also David Starkey, 'Court and Government' in Starkey and C. Coleman, editors, *Revolution Reassessed: Revision in the History of Tudor Government and Administration* (Oxford 1986) pp. 51–2.
7. *The Receyt of the Ladie Kateryne*, ed. Gordon Kipling (Early English Texts Society, old series, no. 296, Oxford 1990) pp. 6–8.
8. Scarisbrick, p. 23.
9. At the time of the wedding of Arthur and Catherine, Arthur had certainly claimed to have consummated the marriage (telling his attendant Lord Willoughby de Broke 'Bring me some ale as I have been in Spain'). But this does not rule out that he did not do so fully.
10. Scarisbrick, p. 25.
11. Penn, pp. 316–18.
12. Penn, pp. 204–6; Nicholas Orme, *From Childhood to Chivalry: the Education of the English Kings and Aristocracy, 1066–1530* (London and New York 1984) pp. 36–8.
13. Penn, pp. 300–01.
14. Garrett Mattingley, *Catherine of Aragon* (London 1942) pp. 76–7; *Calendar of State Papers Spanish*, (CSP Spanish), ed. G. Bergenroth (London 1962) vol I, nos. 511, 525.
15. *CSP Spanish*, no. 603; Penn, p. 337.
16. *CSP Spanish*, nos. 549, 550. 552; *Calendar of State Papers Spanish: Supplement*, ed. G Mattingley (London 1868) no. 23.

17. 'The "Spousells" of the Princess Mary, daughter of Henry VII, to Charles, Prince of Castile, 1508', ed. James Gairdner (Camden Society, new series, vol, 53) in *Camden Miscellany* vol 9 (London 1895) pp. 32–3.
18. *Correspondencia de Gutierre Gomez de Fuensalida, ambassador en Alemannia, Flandes e Ingleterra (1496–1509)* (Madrid 1907) pp. 516–20.
19. Penn, p. 357; and *Letters and Papers of Henry VIII*, eds. J. S. Brewer, J. Gairdner, and R. H. Brodie, 21 vols (London 1862–1932), vol I nos. 39, 84, 119.
20. See Scarisbrick, pp. 218–62, especially pp. 249–50.
21. *Letters and Papers of Henry VIII*, vol I, no. 5 (ii), and *Calendar of State Papers: Venetian*, ed. Rawdon Brown (London 1864) vol 2, p. 11.
22. Scarisbrick, p. 634.
23. Alison Plowden, *Lady Jane Grey and the House of Suffolk* (Sidgwick and Jackson 1985) pp. 18–24.
24. *CSP Spanish*, nos. 419, 436, 439.
25. Penn, pp. 197, 207.
26. *Letters and State Papers Illustrative of the Reigns of Richard III and Henry VII*, ed. J Gairdner, 2 vols (Rolls Series, London 1862–4) vol ii, nos. 133 and 143.

Chapter Two: Early Tudor dynastic bad luck
1. For Arthur Plantagenet, Lord Lisle, see the Introduction to volume 1 of the *Lisle Papers*, ed. M. St Clare Byrne. For Edward I, see Michael Prestwich, *Edward I* (Methuen 1981) pp. 131–2; for Edward III, see Ian Mortimer, *The Perfect King* (Pimlico 2007) p. 435.
2. For Norfolk's role in the destruction of Cromwell, see G. Elton, 'Thomas Cromwell's Decline and Fall' in *Cambridge History Journal* vol x (1951) p. 155 ff; for Norfolk and the fall of Catherine Howard see L. B. Smith, *A Tudor Tragedy: the Life and Times of Catherine Howard* (London 1961) p. 115 ff and Jessie Childs, *Henry VIII's Last Victim: the Life and Times of Henry Howard, Earl of Surrey* (Vintage 2008) pp. 158– 60.
3. Childs, pp. 160–3, 260–1, 334–5, 345–6; on Surrey and Fitzroy, see Childs pp. 55–60, 122–6, 235–6. Also see M. L. Bush, 'The Rise to Power of Edward Seymour, Protector Somerset, 1500–1547', unpub. Cambridge PhD thesis (1961) pp. 113–14 and 191–3.
4. See *New Dictionary of National Biography*, vol 49, p. 862: article on Hertford (Edward Seymour) by Barrett Beer.
5. John Foxe, *Acts and Monuments*, ed. Pratt, 8 vols (London 1874) vol v p. 553 ff.
6. Childs, pp. 72–3 and 190–7.
7. Ibid, pp. 287–91.
8. Ibid, pp. 253–5, 265–6, 276–7.
9. Ibid, pp. 270–3.
10. National Archives: S.P. 1/227, f. 105.
11. Childs, pp. 129, 261–2, 275.
12. Ibid, pp. 306–7; also Lord Herbert of Cherbury, *The Life and Raigne of King Henry the Eighth* (Bodleian Library Oxford, Mss. 624) pp. 563–4.
13. National Archives: S.P. 1/223, f. 36.
14. *Letters and Papers of Henry VIII*, vol xxi, no. 1537.

15. Childs, pp. 311–13.
16. Foxe, *Acts and Monuments*, vol vi, p. 163.
17. Linda Porter, *Mary Tudor: the First Queen* (Piatkus 2007) pp. 267–8.
18. As Chapter 1, n. 23. Alison Plowden, *Lady Jane Grey and the House of Suffolk* (Sidgwick and Jackson 1985) pp. 18–24.
19. Porter, pp. 271–3.
20. See Christopher Skidmore, *Death and the Virgin* (Weidenfeld and Nicolson 2010) pp. 105–24.
21. Skidmore, *Death and the Virgin*, pp. 246 ff, which makes it clear that both Elizabeth herself and Dudley kept up the possibility of a marriage well into 1561 despite the scandal caused by Amy's death; and Cecil's fears of this outcome did not abate quickly either.
22. Porter, pp. 20–4.
23. *Calendar of State Papers: Venetian*, vol iii, pp. 68–9, 95, 108, 119.
24. Thomas Rymer, *Foedera, Conventiones, Litterae etc.* (London 1704–35) vol xiii p. 632 ff.
25. *Calendar of State Papers: Venetian*, vol iii p. 119.
26. Scarisbrick, pp. 105–6.
27. *Letters and Papers of Henry VIII*, vol iii no. 125.
28. Scarisbrick, pp. 116–22.
29. *CSP Spanish*, vol iii pp. 285, 288; *Calendar of State Papers: Venetian*, p. 98.
30. William Roper, *The Life of Sir Thomas Moore, Knight* (Early English Texts Society, 1935) p. 21.
31. Scarisbrick, p. 209.
32. *Letters and Papers of Henry VIII*, vol iv no. 3686.
33. Ibid, nos. 3751, 3756.
34. Ibid, no. 4120; and Scarisbrick, p. 274.
35. *Foedera*, vol xiv, p. 237 ff.
36. N. Pocock, *Records of the Reformation, the Divorce 1527–32*, 2 vols (Oxford 1870), vol I p. 141.
37. Scarisbrick, pp. 282–3.
38. Pocock, vol ii p. 431.
39. *Letters and Papers of Henry VIII*, vol iv no. 4897.
40. Ibid, nos. 4721, 4736–7, 4857.
41. Scarisbrick, p. 287.
42. National Archives: S.P. 1/54, ff. 362v–363.
43. *Letters and Papers of Henry VIII*, vol iv, nos. 5375, 5423, 5471.
44. Ibid, nos. 5441–3.
45. *CSP Spanish*, vol iii, pp. 652, 676–7.
46. Scarisbrick, p. 294.
47. *Letters and Papers of Henry VIII*, vol iv no. 5780.
48. Scarisbrick, p. 148.
49. *Letters and Papers of Henry VIII*, vol iii no. 3372.
50. *CSP Spanish*, vol iii, part ii, p. 842.
51. Quoted in Alison Weir, *Henry VIII: King and Court* (Jonathan Cape 2001) p. 218.

52. See S. J. Smart, 'John Foxe and the Story of Richard Hun, Martyr' in *Journal of Ecclesiastical History*, vol 37 (1982) pp. 205–24.

53. Michael Jones and Malcolm Underwood, *The King's Mother: Lady Margaret Beaufort, Countess of Richmond and Derby* (Cambridge UP 1992) pp. 153, 183–8. Lady Margaret was a notable patron of religious education, e.g. as founder of St John's College Cambridge and ally of Bishop Fisher; but her reputation for piety may have been exaggerated due to her vow of chastity as a widow (not that unusual) and her nun–like appearance in her surviving portrait.

54. C. Allemand, *Henry V* (Yale UP 1992) pp. 273–8.

55. *CSP Spanish*, vol iv, p. 349 ff.

56. John Strype, *Ecclesiastical Memorials*, 3 vols (Oxford 1820–40) vol I, part i, p. 172.

57. Scarisbrick, pp. 327–8.

58. Robert Hutchinson, *Thomas Cromwell* (Weidenfeld and Nicolson 2007) pp. 159–60, 168–70, 226–31.

59. For Henry's additions to the proposed Six Articles, all of a conservative nature: *British Library Manuscripts Cleopatra*, E V, ff. 327, 330. For discussion, see Scarisbrick pp. 521, 528–31, 543– 4, and pp. 521–42 generally on Henry's conservative theology and horror of 'heresy'.

60. Scarisbrick, p. 543.

61. Foxe, vol x, pp. 430–6.

62. Margaret Aston, *The King's Bedpost: Reformation and Iconography in a Tudor Group Portrait* (Cambridge UP 1993) pp. 26–53 on Henry and Edwardian Iconography.

63. *Letters and Papers of Henry VIII*, vol xiv, part I, no. 920.

64. Scarisbrick, p. 480.

65. *Letters and Papers of Henry VIII*, vol xv, nos. 822–3 and 850; on the threat to Cromwell, ibid no. 861 (2).

66. *Letters and Papers of Henry VIII*, vol xvi, pp. 589–90.

Chapter Three: What if Henry VIII had been killed in the near-fatal tiltyard accident of January 1536?

1. Mary's elite support is implied by the fact that Imperial ambassador Chapuys planned to 'rescue' her from Greenwich Palace and carry her off as figurehead for a rebellion in 1534/5. The chosen instrument of this was to be Catherine of Aragon's ally Lord Darcy, who in 1536 was to join the Pilgrimage of Grace. The 'Pilgrims' also made much of restoring Mary to her rightful rank in the succession in their list of demands at Pontefract: see Geoffrey Moorhouse, *The Pilgrimage of Grace* (Phoenix 2003) p. 205. On Henry's accident: *Letters and Papers of Henry VIII*, vol x, nos. 200 and 427; *CSP Spanish 1536–8*, p. 67.

2. Eric Ives, *Anne Boleyn* (Blackwell 1986) pp. 308–11.

3. Porter, pp. 112–13, 118–19.

Chapter Four: Other possibilities to be considered for Henry VIII's reign – three queens survive for longer, or a different queen in 1538/40

1. Ives, *Anne Boleyn* p. 230

2. Ives, pp. 210–12; Nicholas Harpsfield, *A Treatise on the Pretended Divorce Between Henry VIII and Catherine of Aragon*, ed N. Pocock (Camden Society, second series, vol 21, London 1878) pp. 234–5 for a Catholic view. On Warham, see Scarisbrick p. 429, Ives p. 191.

3. *CSP Spanish 1531–3*, p. 699.

4. Ives, p. 207.

5. *Letters and Papers of Henry VIII*, vol v, no. 216; also Ives, pp. 172 and 175–6 on instances of Anne's arrogance and bad temper after 1533, which may have seemed more significant in retrospect than at the time. Some accounts are from her enemy Chapuys, hopeful of the King tiring of her.

6. Ives, pp. 199–201; *CSP Spanish 1531–3*, pp. 609, 625.

7. Nicholas Sander, *The Rise and Growth of the Anglican Schism*, ed. D. Lewis (1877) pp. 93–4 for a later Catholic view.

8. Ives, p. 230; Scarisbrick, pp. 421–2.

9. See *CSP Spanish 1531–3*, p. 788 for Chapuys' reaction.

10. *CSP Spanish 1534–5*, pp. 67 and 234; *Letters and Papers of Henry VIII*, vol vii, nos. 556, 958, 1193.

11. *CSP Spanish 1531–3*, p. 760; and for the story of Henry fancying another woman at court in 1534, see *Letters and Papers of Henry VIII*, vol vi no. 1534. Analysis in Ives, pp. 240–3.

12. *CSP Spanish 1531–3*, p. 788 for a September 1534 report by Chapuys, which he admitted was over–hopeful.

13. Chapuys' first mention of Jane Seymour, *CSP Spanish 1536–8*, pp. 39–40; see ibid pp. 81, 84–5, 106–7 on her and the King in spring 1536. For 'back-dating' the King's disillusionment once Anne had been executed, ibid p. 127.

14. After Anne's arrest, Henry claimed that she had poisoned Catherine and tried to poison Mary: *CSP Spanish 1536–8*, p. 121.

15. See Moorhouse, *The Pilgrimage of Grace*, pp. 26–7.

16. *CSP Spanish 1536–8*, p. 28.

17. Ives, pp. 39–40.

18. Ibid, pp. 349–50.

19. Alexander Ales' letter to Queen Elizabeth, 1559: National Archives S.P. 70/7, ff.1–11. For Anne's exchange with Norris, see *The Life of Cardinal Wolsey* by George Cavendish, ed. S. W. Singer (London 1827) p. 452.

20. See Ives, pp. 370–4 on how the coup unfolded and how Cromwell barred access to the King.

21. See Julia Fox, *Jane Boleyn: the True Story of the Infamous Lady Rochford*. Also Ives, pp. 376–7 and Herbert, *The Life and Raigne of Henry the Eighth* (Bodleian Library Mss. Folio 624) p. 384.

22. Ives, p. 350.

23. *CSP Spanish 1536–8*, pp. 54, 89, 91, 93.

24. Porter, *Mary Tudor* pp. 94–5.

25. Ives, pp. 302–7; contemporary quotes on Anne's religiosity include Foxe (*Acts and Monuments*, vol v p. 175) and Alexander Ales (National Archives S.P. 70/7 ff. 1–11).

26. *CSP Spanish 1536–8*, p. 31.
27. Ives, pp. 305–6, 391–2.
28. *Letters and Papers of Henry VIII*, vol xi, p. 860.
29. Foxe, vol v, p. 553 ff.
30. Derek Wilson, *The Uncrowned Kings of England: The Black Legend of the Dudleys* (Robison 2005) pp. 189–91, 201–4; D. McCulloch, *Thomas Cranmer* (Yale UP 1996) p. 496.
31. *Letters and Papers of Henry VIII*, vol xvi, no. 1339.
32. Ibid, no. 1426.
33. Ibid.
34. Ives, pp. 375–80 and 391–7. The theory that Cromwell invented the charge of incest so that Anne could not claim she was pregnant and so postpone an execution is logical but only a guess. Most serious historians do not believe that Anne committed incest, though it is taken up in fictionalizations such as Philippa Gregory's novel *The Other Boleyn Girl*.
35. Ives, pp. 375–6. The main source of the 'incest' story is Bishop Gilbert Burnet's *History of the Reformation*, ed. Nicholas Pocock (Oxford 1865) p. 316, written 150 years later.
36. *Letters and Papers of Henry VIII*, vol xx, part ii, no. 787.
37. Ibid, vol xii, part ii, no. 1004.
38. Ibid, vol xiii, part i, nos. 56 and 203.
39. Ibid, nos. 1347, 1451; vol xiv, part i, no. 62; also Scarisbrick pp. 464–9 on the negotiations between Henry and Charles V.
40. *Letters and Papers of Henry VIII*, vol xiii, part 1, no. 1198; Scarisbrick, pp. 474–91 on Henry's negotiations with the German princes.

Chapter Five: What if Edward VI had not died at fifteen in 1553, and the 'Edwardian Reformation' was not halted by Mary I?

1. D. McCulloch, *Tudor Church Militant: Edward VI and the Protestant Reformation* (Penguin 1999) pp. 22–3; and pp. 62–3 and 104–5 on Edward as 'Josiah'.
2. Scarisbrick, pp. 30–1.
3. Wilson, pp. 215–21.
4. See authorial comments in W. K. Jordan, *Edward VI: the Threshold of Power* (Allen and Unwin 1970).
5. McCulloch, pp. 26–30.
6. Ibid, pp. 37–8; BL Harleian Mss. 353, ff. 130–138v.
7. P. S. Crowson, *Tudor Foreign Policy* (A and C Black 1973) p. 35.
8. Wilson, pp. 214–19; Plowden, pp. 85–7.

Chapter Six: What if Jane Grey had been successfully installed in power in July 1553?

1. Wilson, pp. 215–21.
2. Ibid, p. 220.
3. Robert Wingfield, *Vita Mariae Angliae Reginae*, ed. and tr. D. McCulloch in Camden Miscellany, fourth series, vol 29 (1984) pp. 250–6; *A Chronicle of Queen Jane and the*

First Two Years of Queen Mary, ed. J Nichols (Camden Society vol 48, 1850) pp. 5–26. Also Wilson, pp. 214–20; Plowden pp. 90–104; on the blaming of Northumberland alone, see Porter pp. 105–6; Plowden pp. 221–2.

4. Wilson, p. x.

5. Jehan Dubois' report on the incident in *CSP Spanish*, vol x, pp. 124–50 and also pp. 80– 117. Also Porter, pp. 169–81.

Chapter Seven: Late Tudor 'what ifs'

1. Victor Klarwill, *Queen Elizabeth and Some Foreigners* (London 1928) p. 93.

2. Ibid.

3. For the Thomas Seymour incident, see Frank Maumby, *The Girlhood of Queen Elizabeth* (London 1909) pp. 40–57. For Elizabeth's imprisonment in 1554, see Mary M. Luke, *A Crown For Elizabeth* (Michael Joseph 1971) pp. 386–99.

4. Jasper Ridley, *Bloody Mary's Martyrs: the Story of England's Terror* (Constable 2001) pp. 215–17.

5. Ibid, p. 212.

6. *CSP Spanish: the Reign of Elizabeth*, vol I pp. 174–5.

7. Mary M. Luke, *Gloriana: the Years of Elizabeth I* (Gollancz 1974) p. 87.

8. Christopher Skidmore, *Death and the Virgin* pp. 137–8.

9. Wilson, p. 259.

10. Alison Weir, *Elizabeth the Queen* (Vintage 2003) p. 120.

11. Porter, pp. 271–2.

12. William Camden, *Annals of Queen Elizabeth* (London 1675) p. 270. Discussion in Wallace MacCaffrey, *Queen Elizabeth and the Making of Policy 1572–88*(Princeton UP 1968), pp. 256–61. J. N. D. Kelly, *The Oxford Dictionary of Popes* (OUP 1986) p. 262.

13. Luke, *A Crown For Elizabeth* pp. 397–8.

14. Linda Porter, *Mary Tudor*, p. 312.

15. *CSP: Venetian*, vol vi, part iii, p. 1571; Antonia Fraser, *Mary Queen of Scots* (Granada 1970) pp. 114–15.

16. J. A. Froude, *History of England* (London 1870) vol vii pp. 29–36. Philip's ally the Duke of Savoy was also mentioned as a Spanish candidate to marry Elizabeth; he was of reigning royal rank (and Catholic) and a Union of Crowns would be less politically difficult than uniting England and Spain again, which Philip's diplomats noted was unpopular.

17. Conyers Read, *Mr Secretary Cecil and Queen Elizabeth* (London 1955), p. 124.

18. Luke, p. 182.

19. *CSP Foreign: Elizabeth I*, ed. J. Stevenson (London 1863) vol I, pp. 256 and 347.

20. Fraser, pp. 124–5.

21. *CSP: Venetian* vol vii, p. 290.

22. Fraser, p. 48.

23. Gordon Donaldson, *Scotland, James V to James VII: the Making of the Kingdom* (Edinburgh: Mercat Press 1965) pp. 95–8.

24. Donaldson, *Scotland: the Making of the Kingdom, James V to James VII*, pp. 99–103, 108–12.

25. Leonie Frieda, *Catherine de Medici* (Phoenix 2003) p. 186. This was a Spanish/Guise Catholic 'ultra' scheme to tie Anthony down to their cause against the Huguenots in 1562–3.
26. *CSP Spanish: Elizabeth I*, vol I (1558–67), p. 27.
27. Ibid, p. 57.
28. British Library: Harleian Manuscripts, 48023, f. 455r (rumours); Skidmore, p. 255 ff.
29. Skidmore, ibid.
30. *CSP Spanish* pp. 182, 197.
31. National Archives: S.P. 70/21, f. 177v.
32. Skidmore, p. 255 ff.
33. Ibid, pp. 266–7.
34. Wilson, p. 263.
35. *CSP Spanish: Elizabeth*, vol I, p. 113–14.
36. Ibid, p. 175.
37. Skidmore pp. 338–9.
38. *CSP Spanish: Elizabeth*, vol I, p. 175.
39. BL Harleian Mss. 787, f. 16. This may be behind Elizabeth's subsequent failure to give Huntingdon or his ambitious wife any preferment at court.
40. Wilson, pp. 273–5.
41. Ibid.
42. BL Additional Manuscripts 35841, ff. 121–3.
43. Simancas Archive, Spain: Mss. AGS, E 815 ff. 76–7.
44. BL Additional Mss. 48023, f. 363.
45. Hatfield House: Cecil Papers, ms. 153, d.168v; *Historical Manuscripts Commission Reports: Hatfield Papers*, vol I, nos. 1136–7 and 1151; *Historical Manuscripts Commission Reports: Pepys Papers*, vol I, nos. 111–12.
46. Wilson, pp. 299–300.
47. Luke, *Gloriana* pp. 343–7; Wilson pp. 303–4.
48. Luke, ibid.
49. J. Martin Robinson, *The Dukes of Norfolk: a Quincentennial History* (Oxford UP 1982) pp. 61–2.
50. Ibid, pp. 62–4.
51. MacCaffrey, *Queen Elizabeth and the Making of Polciy 1572–88*, pp. 224–6; on the blaming of Cecil for the inflammatory Protestant tone of the government's foreign policy to France and Spain at this point see Froude, *History of England*, vol ix, p. 377 (reports of French ambassador Fenelon and Spanish ambassador de Spés).
52. Luke, pp. 342–3.
53. However, Cecil did believe that Philip II was only temporarily quiescent and intended to attack England when he had the resources and time available, i.e. after he had enrolled France as an ally. See his 'Short Memorial of the State of the Nation' submitted to Elizabeth's Council in 1569.
54. Alice Hogge, *God's Secret Agents: Queen Elizabeth's Forbidden Priests and the Hatching of the Gunpowder Plot* (Harper Perennial 2005) pp. 46–7.
55. John Sugden, *Sir Francis Drake* (Barrie and Jenkins 1990) pp. 96–8.

56. Frieda, *Catherine de Medici* pp. 276–7.
57. Ibid, pp. 288–318 and (reactions to massacre) 318–21; MacCaffrey pp. 171–2.
58. MacCaffrey, pp. 351–2, 357–9, 364–6, 384–5.
59. Mary M. Luke, *Gloriana*, pp. 448–50, 452–4; MacCaffrey pp. 249–66.
60. *Historical Manuscript Commission Hatfield Manuscripts*, vol ii, pp. 238, 239, 249, 253, 267, 271–2; MacCaffrey pp. 263–4. On Elizabeth telling Alençon that public opposition to their marriage was too strong, see *CSP Spanish: Elizabeth*, vol ii pp. 704–6 and *HMC Hatfield Mss.* pp. 273, 275, 293, 298.
61. Froude, vol xi, pp. 471–2.
62. J. E. Neale, *Queen Elizabeth* (London 1934) p. 237.
63. Antonia Fraser, *Mary Queen of Scots* pp. 258–9, 263–4.
64. Luke, *Gloriana*, pp. 199–203.
65. Conyers Read, *Mr Secretary Cecil and Queen Elizabeth*, p. 237; J. E. Neale, *Queen Elizabeth*, p. 114.
66. Fraser, pp. 257–8.
67. Conyers Read, *Mr Secretary Cecil and Queen Elizabeth*, p. 229.
68. Fraser, pp. 253–8.
69. Plowden, *Lady Jane Grey and the House of Suffolk*, p. 147.
70. Fraser, pp. 266–7.
71. Ibid, pp. 274–5.
72. Ibid, pp. 266–7.
73. Ibid, pp. 282–6.
74. Ibid, pp. 301–10.
75. Ibid, and pp. 311–13 on Mary's deteriorating relations with Darnley.
76. Ibid, pp. 339–41.
77. Ibid, pp. 334–5 and 340.
78. Ibid, pp. 356–65 on the Kirk o' Field explosion and its 'time–line'.
79. Ibid, pp. 357–8.
80. Ibid, pp. 369, 372–3, 393.
81. Ibid, pp. 374–5.
82. Ibid, pp. 375–6.
83. Mary's account of her abduction by Bothwell is in A. Lobanov-Rostovsky, *Lettres et Memoires de Marie, Reine d'Ecosse*, 7 vols (Paris 1844) vol ii p. 20.
84. Sir James Melville, *Memoirs*, ed. Francis Stewart and T. Thomson (Bannatyne Club, Edinburgh 1827) p. 154; R. Keith, *History of the Affairs of Church and State in Scotland*, ed. JP Lawson, 3 vols (Spottiswoode Society, Edinburgh 1844) vol ii p. 588.
85. *Calendar of State Papers Scotland*, vol ii p. 336.
86. Keith, vol ii, p. 628; John Herries, *Historical Memoirs of the Reign of Mary Queen of Scots* (Edinburgh 1836) p. 93.
87. Fraser, p. 393.
88. Ibid, pp. 403, 418–19.
89. Ibid, pp. 412–13.
90. Ibid, p. 412. Mary' s secretary Claude Nau wrote later that Elizabeth's ambassador Throckmorton sent a message assuring Mary that her abdication could be cancelled

later as done under duress: *Nau, Memorials of Mary Stewart*, ed. J. Stevenson (Edinburgh 1883) p. 62. For the rumour that the Hamiltons, next heirs after Mary and James, would have preferred it if Mary had been killed, see *CSP Scotland*, vol ii, p. 373.

91. F. A. Mumby, *The Fall of Mary Stuart* (Constable 1921) pp. 297–8.
92. Donaldson, pp. 159–60.
93. Nau, p. 84 ff; Fraser pp. 433–9; *CSP: Venetian*, vol vii p. 414.
94. Labanof, vol ii, pp. 76, 117.
95. Ibid, vol ii, p. 117; vol vi p. 472.
96. See n. 91.
97. Luke, pp. 270–4; and for Elizabeth's letter to Mary on hearing of Darnley's murder, Froude vol ix, pp. 109–10.
98. Fraser, pp. 440–2.
99. Conyers Read, p. 402.
100. *CSP Scotland*, vol ii, pp. 509–10.
101. Fraser, pp. 456–62.
102. Ibid, p. 458.
103. Ibid, p. 447.
104. Ibid, pp. 420 and 465–80; on Maitland as possible forger, pp. 481–2.
105. Fraser, pp. 458, 463, 493–5.
106. *Register of the Privy Council of Scotland*, vol ii pp. 8–9.
107. Luke, pp. 318–22, 326–8, and 331–2 on Mary's unco–operative attitude.
108. Luke, pp. 352–3.
109. Plowden, pp. 168–9.
110. Fraser, pp. 458–9 and 497–8.
111. Donaldson, pp. 165–6.
112. Fraser, pp. 499–501.
113. Ibid, p. 511.
114. Ibid, pp. 502–3.

Chapter Eight: 1588: a close-run thing? The Spanish Armada – could it have landed successfully, and what then?

1. Neil Hanson, *The Confident Hope of a Miracle: The True Story of the Spanish Armada* (Corgi 2003) pp. 520–2.
2. Reproduced in *The Horizon Book of the Elizabethan World* (Paul Hamlyn 1967) pp. 332–3.
3. Worcester College Oxford: *Clarke Papers*, vol iii pp. 203–6, 207–8 (Council of State debates).
4. E.g. in *The Craftsman* newspaper on 18 March 1738, as quoted by Edward Pearce, *The Great Man: Sir Robert Walpole, Scoundrel, Genius and Britain's First Prime Minister* (Jonathan Cape 2007) p. 395
5. Quoted in Antonia Fraser, *Cromwell Our Chief Of Men* (Weidenfled and Nicolson 1973) p. 589.
6. E.g. in a sermon of Richard Curteys, Bishop of Chichester, given at court in 1575: P. McCullough, *Sermons at Court: Politics and Religion in Elizabethan and Jacobean Preaching* (Cambridge UP 1998) p. 84.

7. MacCaffrey, pp. 357–9.
8. Ibid, pp. 393–9.
9. Ibid, pp. 274–6.
10. Hanson, p. 57; MacCaffrey, pp. 293–4 and 318.
11. MacCaffrey, p. 315 (Philip counsels caution) and pp. 323–5 (advice followed by his ambassador in 1580–1).
12. Ibid, pp. 326–8; R. Holinshed, *Chronicles*, 6 vols (1807–8 edition), vol iv, pp. 536–48.
13. Donaldson, pp. 179–70; Fraser, pp. 541–5. The devious Master of Gray became the anti-hero of a trilogy of late twentieth novels by Scots author Nigel Tranter.
14. Fraser, pp. 555–6, 566–70, 572–7; for Elizabeth's fury at Mary's involvement with Babington in 1586 see J. Morris, *Letter-Books of Sir Amias Paluet* (1874) p. 267.
15. Luke, pp. 533–41 and 551–3 on the Queen's decision to execute Mary and hesitation in carrying it out.
16. MacCaffrey, pp. 395–8.
17. Hanson, pp. 219–20.
18. *CSP Spain: Elizabeth*, vol iii, pp. 121–5, 202–3, 400–01, 412–13, 463–4, 475–6.
19. Hanson, pp. 58–60.
20. Ibid, pp. 147–8.
21. Ibid, pp. 150–2.
22. Ibid, p. 149.
23. Ibid, p. 153.
24. Hanson, pp. 63–7 (Philip and the Papacy) and 156–3, 167 (Armada preparations).
25. Hanson, pp. 166–8.
26. *Thomas Deloney's Works*, ed. F. O. Mann (Oxford 1912) p. 67.
27. Hanson, pp. 233–8.
28. C. G. Cruikshank, *Elizabeth's Army* (Oxford UP 1966) pp. 17–40; Hanson, p. 236; also A. L. Rowse, *Tudor Cornwall: Portrait of a Society* (1941) p. 387.
29. Hanson, pp. 236, 240.
30. Hanson, pp. 240–1 and 513–17.
31. Hanson, p. 513.
32. Quoted in *The Horizon Book of the Elizabethan World*, pp. 280–1.
33. See Hanson, pp. 169, 416–22. It should be remarked that few commentators note the real importance of current French provincial politics in summer 1588, due to which the Norman ports and Boulogne were in the anti-Spanish Huguenots' hands and the Armada could not use them.
34. Henry E. Huntingdon Library: *Ellesmere Manuscripts*, no. 62068, ff. 14–15, 18–19.
35. Hanson, pp. 255–8.
36. Ibid, pp. 259–60.
37. *New Dictionary of National Biography*, vol 12, pp. 87–8: article on Cumberland (George Clifford) by Peter Holmes.
38. Augustin Ryther, *Expeditionis Hispanorum in Angliam vera descriptione Anno Domine MDLXXXVIII* (Brussels 1590), reproduced in Hanson, colour plate section 2, and in *The Hamlyn Book of the Elizabethan World* pp. 284–5.
39. Hanson, pp. 339–40.

40. National Archive: State Papers CCXV f. 67, CCXIII f. 42; BL Mss: Cotton Julius, F X ff. 111–17; Hanson pp. 353–4, 360–3.

41. State Papers CCXIII f. 59; CCXIV f. 42; CCXV f. 36 and (inventory of the 'San Salvador) f. 49; CCXVIII f. 24; Hanson pp. 352–3, 368–9.

42. Hanson, p. 369.

43. Sir John Knox Laughton, ed., *State Papers Relating to the Defeat of the Spanish Armada*, 2 vols (Temple Smith/Navy Records Society, Aldershot 1987), vol 2: 'Relation of Medina Sidonia', pp. 354–70; National Archive: S.P. CCXIV, f. 42; B.L. Mss: Cotton Julius F. X ff. 111–17; Hanson, pp. 377–9.

44. SP CC XIII ff. 40, 71; CCXIV f. 7; Hanson, pp. 389–98.

45. Hanson, p. 406.

46. Ibid, p. 405.

47. Ibid, pp. 406, 408–9; H. P. O'Donnell, 'The Requirements of the Duke of Parma for the Invasion of England' in P. Gallagher and D. W. Cruikshank, eds, *God's Obvious Design: Papers for the Spanish Armada Symposium*, (Tamesis 1990) p. 197.

48. Hanson, p. 409.

49. Ibid.

50. National Archive: S.P. CCXII, f. 69.

51. Hanson, p. 411.

52. *Calendar of State Papers Spanish: Elizabeth*, vol iv p. 319; Hanson p. 348.

53. Hanson, pp. 41–12.

54. Ibid, p. 413.

55. Laughton, vol ii, pp. 354–70.

56. *Calendar of State Papers Spanish: Elizabeth*, vol iv pp. 384, 390; Hanson p. 417.

57. National Archive: S P CCXIV ff. 7, 43; *Calendar of State Papers Spanish: Elizabeth*, vol iv, pp. 439, 470.

58. Hanson, pp. 424–5.

59. S P CCXIV ff. 43, 67; *Calendar of State Papers Spanish: Elizabeth*, vol iv, p. 385v; Hanson, pp. 427–30.

60. Laughton, pp. 354–70; National Archive: S.P. CCXIII ff. 63–4, 67; CCXIV f. 2; *Calendar of State Papers Spanish: Elizabeth*, vol iv, pp. 385, 402, 439.

61. Laughton, pp. 354–70; National Archive: S.P. CCXIV 42v.

62. Laughton, ibid; *Calendar of State Papers: Elizabeth*, vol iv p. 439; Colin Martin and Geoffrey Parker, *The Spanish Armada* (Mandolin 1999) pp. 209–10.

63. BL Mss: Cotton Julius F. X 111–17.

64. National Archive: S.P. CCXIV, ff. 27, 42, 50; BL Mss: Cotton Julius F. X 111–17.

65. James Aske, *Elizabetha Triumphans* (London 1588); Hanson pp. 519–22.

66. National Archive: S.P. CCXII f. 69; CCXV 24, 34, 59.

67. Hanson, p. 514.

68. National archive: S.P. CCXIII ff. 27, 38, 71; Hanson pp. 514–16.

69. Hanson, pp. 516–17.

70. *Calendar of State Papers Spanish: Elizabeth*, vol iv p. 141.

71. Harry Turtledove, *Ruled Britannia* (Roc Books 2002).

72. Hanson, p. 217.

Bibliography

Primary sources

Bernard André, Annales Henrici: in *Memorials of King Henry the Seventh*, ed., J. Gairdner, Rolls Series (London 1858).

James Aske, *Elizabetha Triumphans* (London 1588).

British Library, Additional Mss. 35841, 48023.

—— *Cotton Mss. Julius*, F X.

—— *Harleian Mss. 787*.

Calendar of State Papers Domestic: Edward VI, Mary, Elizabeth, ed. R. Lemon and R. Green (HMSO 1856–72).

Calendar of State Papers Foreign: Elizabeth I, ed. J. Stevenson (HMSO 1863).

Calendar of State Papers relating to Scotland 1509–89, ed. M. Thorpe (HMSO 1858).

Calendar of State Papers Spanish, ed. G. Bergenroth (HMSO 1862–6).

Calendar of State Papers Spanish: Supplement, ed. G. Mattingley (HMSO 1868).

Calendar of State Papers: Venetian, ed. Rawdon Brown (HMSO 1864–98).

William Camden, *Annals of Queen Elizabeth* (London 1675).

A Chronicle of Queen Jane and the First Two Years of Queen Mary, ed. J. Nichols, Camden Society, vol 48 (London 1850).

Correspondencia de Gutierre Gomez de Fuensalida, ambassador en Alemania, Flandes e Ingleterra (1496–1509) (Madrid 1907).

Thomas Deloney's Works, ed. F. O. Mann (Oxford 1912).

Literary Remains of Edward VI, ed. J. G. Nichols (London 1857).

Erasmus, The Collected Works, ed. and tr. R. A. B. Mynors and D. F. S. Thomson, 8 vols (Toronto 1974–8).

John Foxe, *Acts and Monuments*, ed. J. Pratt, 8 vols (London 1874).

Edward Hall, *Chronicle* (London 1806 edition).

Nicholas Harpsfield, *A Treatise on the Pretended Divorce Between Henry VIII and Catherine of Aragon*, ed. N. Pocock, Camden Society, second series, vol 21 (London 1878).

Hatfield House: *Cecil Papers*.

John Hayward, *The Life and Raigne of King Edward the Sixth*, ed. B. de Beer, Kent, Ohio 1993.

Lord Herbert of Cherbury, *The Life and Raigne of King Henry the Eighth* (Bodleian Library Oxford, Mss. 624).

John Herries, *Historical Memoirs of the Reign of Mary Queen of Scots* (Edinburgh 1836).

Historical Manuscript Commission Reports: Hatfield House; Pepys Papers, Magdalene College Cambridge, HMC Report on the Pepys Manuscripts preserved at Magdalene College Cambridge (HMSO 1911).

Raphael Holinshed, *Chronicles*, 6 vols (London 1807–8 edition).

R. Keith, *History of the Affairs of Church and State in Scotland*, ed. J. P. Lawson, Spottiswoode Society (Edinburgh 1844).

Sir John Knox Laughton, ed., *State Papers Relating to the Defeat of the Spanish Armada*, 2 vols (Temple Smith/Navy Records Society, Aldershot 1987).

John Leland, *De Rebus Britannica Collectanea*, ed. Thomas Hearne (London 1774).

—— *Antiquarian Repertory*, ed. F. Grose and Thomas Astle, 4 vols (London 1807–9).

Letters and Papers Illustrative of the Reigns of Richard III and Henry VII, ed. J. Gairdner, 2 vols, Rolls Series (London 1862–4).

Letters and Papers of Henry VIII, eds. J. S. Brewer, J. Gairdner and R. H. Brodie, 21 vols (London 1861–1932).

J. Lilly, ed., *Black-Letter Ballads and Broadsides Printed in the Reign of Queen Elizabeth Between the Years 1558 and 1597* (London 1870).

The Lisle Papers, vol 1, ed. Mary St Clare Byrne (6 vols) (University of Chicago Press 1981).

A. Lobanov-Rostovsky, *Lettres et Memoires de Marie, Reine d'Ecosse*, 7 vols (Paris 1844).

Sir James Melville, *Memoirs*, ed. Francis Stewart and T. Thomson, Bannatyne Club (Edinburgh 1827).

J. Morris, *Letter-Books of Sir Amias Paulet* (London 1874).

National Archive: *State Papers CCXII, CCXIII, CCXIV, CCXV, CCXVIII* (unpublished 1588).

Claude Nau, *Memorials of Mary Stewart*, ed. J. Stevenson (Edinburgh 1883).

Nicholas Pocock, *Records of the Reformation: the Divorce, 1527—32*, 2 vols (Oxford 1870).

The Receyt of the Ladie Kateryne, ed. Gordon Kipling (Early English Texts Society, old series vol 296, Oxford 1990).

Register of the Privy Council of Scotland, vol 2, eds. J. H. Burton and D. Masson (Scottish Record Office, Edinburgh 1880).

William Roper, *The Life of Sir Thomas Moore, Knight*, ed. Hitchcock (EETS 1935).

Thomas Rymer, *Foedera, Conventiones, Litterae etc.*, 20 vols (London 1704–35).

Nicholas Sander, *The Rise and Growth of the Anglican Schism*, ed. D. Lewis (Oxford 1877).

'The "Spousells" of the Princess Mary, daughter of Henry VII, to Charles, Prince of Castile, 1508', ed. J. Gairdner, Camden Society, new series, vol 53 in *Camden Miscellany* vol 9 (London 1895).

The State Papers of Henry VIII, 11 vols (HMSO 1830–52).

John Strype, *Ecclesiastical Memorials*, 3 vols (Oxford 1820–30).

The Life of Cardinal Wolsey by George Cavendish, ed. S. W. Singer (London 1827).

Robert Wingfield, 'Vita Mariae Angliae Reginae', ed. and tr. D. McCulloch in *Camden Miscellany*, fourth series, vol 29 (London 1984).

Charles Wriothesley, *A Chronicle of England under the Tudors From AD 1485 to 1559*, ed. W. Hamilton, Camden Society (London 1877).

Secondary sources

Alford, S. *The Early Elizabethan Polity: William Cecil and the British Succession Crisis, 1558–69* (Cambridge UP 1998).

—— *Kingship and Politics in the Reign of Edward VI* (Cambridge UP 2002).

Allemand, C. *Henry V* (Yale UP 1992).

Aston, Margaret *The King's Bedpost: Reformation and Iconography in a Tudor Group Portrait* (Cambridge UP 1993).

Beer, B. L. *Northumberland: the Political Career of John Dudley, Earl of Warwick and Duke of Northumberland* (Kent State University Press, Ohio 1973).

Bentley, S. in his *Excerpta Historica*, (London 1831).

Bernard, G. W. *The Tudor Nobility* (Manchester University Press 1992).

Boynton, L. *The Elizabethan Militia 1558–1638* (Routledge 1967).

Burnet, Gilbert *History of the Reformation of the Church of England*, ed. N. Pocock, 7 vols (Oxford 1865).

Bush, M. L. 'The Rise to Power of Edward Seymour, Lord Protector Somerset, 1500–1547', Cambridge University PhD thesis 1961.

—— *The Government Policy of Protector Somerset* (Edward Arnold, London, 1975).

Childs, Jessie *Henry VIII's Last Victim: the Life and Times of Henry Howards, Earl of Surrey* (Vintage 2008).

Coleman, C. and Starkey, D. *Revolution Reassessed: Revision in the History of Tudor Government and Administration* (Oxford 1986).

Cross, Claire *The Puritan Earl: Henry Hastings, third Earl of Huntingdon 1536–1595* (Macmillan, 1966).

Crowson, P. S. *Tudor Foreign Policy* (A and C Black 1973).

Cruikshank, C. G. *Elizabeth's Army* (Oxford UP 1966).

Dickens, A. G. *Later Monasticism and the Reformation* (Hambledon Press 1994).

Donaldson, Gordon *The Scottish Reformation* (Cambridge UP 1962).

—— *Scotland James V to James VII: the Making of the Kingdom* (Mercat Press, Edinburgh, 1965).

Elton, G. *Reform and Renewal: Thomas Cromwell and the Common Weal* (Cambridge UP 1973).

—— *The Parliament of England 1559 to 1581* (Cambridge UP 1986).

Erickson, Carolly *Bloody Mary* (Macmillan 1978).

Fletcher, Anthony *Tudor Rebellions* (Longmans 1983).

Fox, Julia *Jane Boleyn: the True Story of the Infamous Lady Rochford* (Random House 2007).

Fraser, Lady Antonia *Mary Queen of Scots* (Granada 1970).

—— *Cromwell Our Chief of Men* (Weidenfeld and Nicolson 1973).

Frieda, Leonie *Catherine de Medici* (Phoenix 2003).

Froude, J. A. *History of England* (London 1870).

Gallagher, P. and Cruikshank, D., eds, *God's Obvious Design: Papers for the Spanish Armada Symposium,* (Tamesis 1990).

Gwyn, Peter *The King's Cardinal: the Rise and Fall of Thomas Wolsey* (Barrie and Jenkins 1990).

Haigh, Christopher ed., *The Reign of Elizabeth I* (Athens, Georgia 1987).

Hanson, Neil *The Confident Hope of a Miracle: the True Story of the Spanish Armada* (Corgi 2003).

Harbison, E. H. *Rival Ambassadors at the Court of Queen Mary* (Princeton University Press 1940).

Hoak, D. E. *The King's Council in the Reign of Edward VI* (Cambridge UP 1976).

Hogge, Alice *God's Secret Agents: Queen Elizabeth's Forbidden Priests and the Hatching of the Gunpowder Plot* (Harper Perennial 2005).

The Horizon Book of the Elizabethan World (Paul Hamlyn 1967).

Hoyle, R. W. *The Pilgrimage of Grace and the Politics of the 1530s* (Oxford UP 2001).

Hutchinson, Robert *Thomas Cromwell: the Rise and Fall of Henry VIII's Most Notorious Minister* (Weidenfeld and Nicolson 2007).

Ives, Eric *Anne Boleyn* (Blackwell 1986).

Johnson, Paul *Elizabeth I: A Study in Power and Intellect* (1974).

Jones, Michael and Underwood, Malcolm *The King's Mother: Lady Margaret Beaufort, Countess of Richmond and Derby* (Cambridge UP 1992).

Jordan, W. K. *Edward VI: the Young King* (Allen and Unwin 1968).

—— *Edward VI: the Threshold of Power* (Allen and Unwin 1970).

Kelly, J. N. D. *The Oxford Dictionary of Popes* (Oxford UP 1986).

Klarwill, Victor *Queen Elizabeth and Some Foreigners* (London 1928).

Knecht, R. J. *Francis I* (Cambridge University Press 1983).

Levive, Mortimer *The Early Elizabethan Succession Question 1558–1568* (Stanford UP 1966).

Loach, Jennifer *Edward VI* (Yale UP 1999).

Loach, Jennifer and Tittler, T. R. eds, *The Mid-Tudor Polity* (London 1980).

Loades, D. M. *Two Tudor Conspiracies* (Cambridge UP 1965).

—— *The Reign of Mary Tudor: Government and Religion in England 1553–1558* (St. Martin's Press, 1979).

—— *Mary Tudor: a Life* (Basil Blackwell 1989).

—— *John Dudley, Duke of Northumberland 1504–1553* (Clarendon Press 1996).

Luke, Mary M. *A Crown For Elizabeth* (Michael Joseph, 1971).

—— *Gloriana: the Years of Elizabeth I* (Gollancz 1974).

MacCaffrey, Wallace *The Shaping of the Elizabethan Regime* (Princeton UP 1968).

—— *Queen Elizabeth and the Making of Policy 1572–88* (Princeton UP 1981).

McCulloch, Diarmaid *Thomas Cranmer* (Yale UP 1995).

—— *The Reign of Henry VIII: Politics and Piety* (Macmillan 1995).

—— *Tudor Church Militant: Edward VI and the Protestant Reformation* (Penguin 1999).

McCullough, P. *Sermons at Court: Politics and Religion in Elizabethan and Jacobean Preaching* (Cambridge UP 1998).

Maumby, Frank *The Girlhood of Queen Elizabeth* (London 1909).

Mathew, Colin *New Dictionary of National Biography* (Oxford University Press 2001)

Martienssen, A. *Queen Katherine Parr* (McGraw-Hill 1973).

Martin, Colin and Parker, Geoffrey *The Spanish Armada* (Mandolin 1999).

Mattingley, Garrett *Catherine of Aragon* (London 1942).

—— *The Defeat of the Spanish Armada* (Pimlico 2000 edition).

Moorhouse, Geoffrey *The Pilgrimage of Grace* (Phoenix 2003).

Morey, Adrian *The Catholic Subjects of Elizabeth I* (Allen and Unwin 1978).

Mortimer, Ian *The Perfect King: the Life of Edward III, Father of the English Nation* (Pimlico 2007).

Muller, J. A. *Stephen Gardiner and the Tudor Reaction* (New York 1926).

Mumby, F. A. *The Fall of Mary Stuart* (Constable 1921).

Murphy, Beverley *Bastard Prince: Henry VIII's Lost Son* (Sutton 2001).

Neale, J. E. *Queen Elizabeth* (Harcourt, New York/London 1934).

Orme, N. *From Childhood to Chivalry: The Education of the English Kings and Aristocracy 1066–1530* (London and New York 1984).

Parker, Geoffrey *The Dutch Revolt* (Penguin 1977).

Parmiter, Geoffrey de C. *The King's Great Matter: a Study of Anglo–Papal Relations 1527–34* (Longmans 1959).

Pearce, Edward *The Great Man: Sir Robert Walpole, Scoundrel, Genius and Britain's First Prime Minister* (Jonathan Cape 2007).

Penn, Thomas *Winter King: the Dawn of Tudor England* (Penguin 2012).

Plowden, Alison *Lady Jane Grey and the House of Suffolk* (Sidgwick and Jackson 1985).

Porter, Linda *Mary Tudor: the First Queen* (Piatkus 2007).

Prestwich, Michael *Edward I* (Methuen 1988).

Read, Conyers *Mr Secretary Cecil and Queen Elizabeth* (London 1955).

Ridley, Jasper *Bloody Mary's Martyrs: the Story of England's Terror* (Constable 2001).

Robinson, J. Martin *The Dukes of Norfolk: a Quincentennial History* (Oxford UP 1982).

Rodriguez–Salgado, M. J. and Adams, S. *England, Spain and the Gran Armada* (Savage, Maryland 1991).

Rowse, A. L. *Tudor Cornwall: Portrait of a Society* (Jonathan Cape 1941).

Scarisbrick, J. *Henry VIII* (Methuen 1968).

Skidmore, Christopher *Edward VI: the Lost King of England* (Weidenfeld and Nicolson 2002).

—— *Death and the Virgin: the Mysterious Fate of Amy Robsart* (Weidenfeld and Nicolson, 2010).

Smith, L. B. *A Tudor Tragedy: the Life and Times of Catherine Howard* (London 1961).

Somerset, Anne *Elizabeth I* (Doubleday 1991).

Starkey, David ed., *The English Court from the Wars of the Roses to the Civil War* (Longman 1987).

Sugden, John *Sir Francis Drake* (Barrie and Jenkins 1990).

Turtledove, Harry *Ruled Britannia* (Roc Books 2002).

Weir, Alison *Henry VIII: King and Court* (Jonathan Cape 2001).

—— *Elizabeth the Queen* (Vintage 2003).

Whiting, R. *The Enterprise of England* (Sutton Books 1988).

Wilson, Charles *Queen Elizabeth and the Revolt of the Netherlands* (Macmillan 1970).

Wilson, Derek *The Uncrowned Kings of England: the Black Legend of the Dudleys* (Robinson 2005).

Articles

Adams, S. L. 'The accession of Queen Elizabeth' in *History Today* (May 1953).

Aird, I. 'The death of Amy Robsart' in *English Historical Review*, vol lxxi.

Andrews, K. R. 'The aims of Drake's expedition of 1577–80' in *American Historical Review*, vol lxxiii, no. 3 (February 1978), pp. 724–41.

Beer, B. L. 'Northumberland: the myth of the wicked duke and the historical John Dudley' in *Albion*, vol xi (1979).

Bernard, G. W. 'The fall of Anne Boleyn' in *English Historical Review*, vol cvi (1990).

—— 'Anne Boleyn's religion' in *Historical Journal*, vol xxxvi (1993)

Bindoff, S. T. 'A kingdom at stake, 1553' in *History Today*, vol iii (1953) pp. 642–8.

Chambers, D. S. 'Cardinal Wolsey and the papal tiara' in *Bulletin of the Institute of Historical Research*, vol xxviii (1965).

Christy, M. 'Queen Elizabeth's visit to Tilbury 1588' in *EHR*, vol xxxiv (1919).

Collinson, Patrick 'The politics of religion and the religion of politics' in *BIHR*, vol 82 (2009).

Cooper, J. P. 'Henry VII's last years reconsidered' in *Historical Journal*, vol ii (1959).

Dawson, Jane 'Sir William Cecil and the British dimensions of Elizabethan foreign policy' in *History*, vol lxxiv (1989).

Dowling, M. 'Anne Boleyn and reform' in *Journal of Ecclesiastical History*, vol xxv, part 1 (1984) pp. 30–46.

Elton, G. 'Thomas Cromwell's decline and fall', *Cambridge History Journal* vol x (1951).

—— 'The political creed of Thomas Cromwell' in *Transactions of the Royal Historical Society*, fifth series, vol vi (1956).

Gairdner, J. 'Mary and Anne Boleyn' in *EHR*, vol viii (1893) pp. 53–60.

Glasgow, T. 'The shape of the ships that defeated the Spanish Armada' in *Mariners' Mirror*, vol li (1964) pp. 177–87.

—— 'The Royal Navy at the start of the reign of Elizabeth I' in *Mariners' Mirror*, vol lii (1965) pp. 73–6.

Haugaard, W. J. 'Katherine Parr: the religious convictions of a Renaissance queen' in *Renaissance Quarterly*, vol xxii (1969) pp. 346–59.

James, H. 'The Aftermath of the 1549 Coup and the Earl of Warwick's intentions' in *BIHR*, vol lvii (1989).

Jensen, J. de Lamar 'The Spanish Armada: the worst–kept secret in Europe' in *The Sixteenth Century Journal*, vol xix (1988).

Koerner, R. 'The imperial crown of this realm: Henry VIII, Constantine and Polydore Vergil' in *BIHR*, vol xxvi (1953).

Loomie, A. J. 'The Armadas and the Catholics of England' in *Catholic Historical Review*, vol Lxix (1973) pp. 385–463.

MacGurk, J. 'Armada preparations and arrangements made after the defeat' in *Archaeologia Cantiana*, vol lxxxv (1970).

Mears, Nathalie 'Counsel, public debate and queenship: John Stubbes' The Discoverie of a Gaping Gulf' in *Historical Journal* (2009).

Nolan, J. 'The muster of 1588' in *Albion*, vol xxiii (1991) pp. 387–407.

Parker, G. 'The dreadnought revolution of Tudor England' in *Mariners' Mirror*, vol lxxxii (1996) pp. 269–300.

—— 'The Place of Tudor England in the messianic vision of Philip II' in *TRHS*, sixth series, vol xii (2002) pp. 167–221.

Reid, R. B. 'The rebellion of the earls, 1569' in *TRHS*, second series, vol xx (1906) pp. 171–203.

Smart, S. J. 'John Foxe and the story of Richard Hun, martyr' in *Journal of Ecclesiastical History*, vol 37 (1982) pp. 205–34.

Smith, L. Baldwin 'The last will and testament of Henry VIII: a question of perspective' in *Journal of British Studies*, vol ii (1962).

Warnicke, Retha 'The fall of Anne Boleyn: a reassessment' in *History*, vol lxx (1985) pp. 1–15.

Index